Silent Service

An MC McCall Novel of Suspense
Book Two

By

Judy M. Kerr

Launch Point Press
Portland, Oregon

A Launch Point Press Trade Paperback Original

ISBN: 978-1-63304-037-3
E-Book: 978-1-63304-269-8

FIRST EDITION: First Printing: 2022

Editing: Kay Grey, Sue Hardesty
Formatting: Patty Schramm
Cover: Lorelei

Published by:
Launch Point Press
www.LaunchPointPress.com

Author's Note

Dear Reader: No law enforcement agency can provide all its investigative techniques and secrets to outsiders. I've taken liberties with duties and protocols of all the law enforcement agencies mentioned in this book. The agencies mentioned are real, but the circumstances, characters, procedures, and some locations are fictitious. While I did research, please know that any mistakes are my own. Fiction writers make stuff up and at the same time work to ensure believability—it's what we do in the name of entertainment. I hope you are all entertained.

To Mom, for all your love and support, and for always asking, "When's your book coming out?" I love you and I'm so glad you're my mom.

Special additional dedication:
To my dear friend, Joan (Geary) Eineke.
I'm heartbroken that you're gone from this world. How is that possible? I'm so lucky to have shared many decades of friendship, laughter (so much laughter!), and love with you. And while I know that I'm no Loni Anderson, I was beyond thrilled to see you reading a copy of *my* book. Your star will forever shine brightly, my friend.
I'll miss you every day.

Chapter One

US Postal Inspector MC McCall was ready and jacked for action, if only she could concentrate her thoughts on the present and not the cesspool of the past. Come on, she told herself. Focus.

For a brief moment she wished for a stiff infusion of Grey Goose to light a fire in her belly on this bitter cold late Thursday night.

Suck it up, McCall. She shut out the dastardly thoughts of booze and yanked a navy knit cap over her ears to ward off the chill. MC planted her feet firmly on the slick ground and steeled herself to take on the unknown, despite the less-than-optimal weather.

She understood she'd been all over the map in the reliability department over the past couple months. Tonight, she was determined to alleviate any doubts her work partner, Cam, might still have.

Laser focused.

Dependable.

Effective.

Present.

Now here they all were, poised for action in the frigid late-night air. The full moon colored the night a cold dark blue. MC studied the age-battered house and the warped screen door. They had no idea of the number of occupants.

Weak, watery light from the rear of the house pushed against the pitch black in the front.

MC's thoughts meandered. The average human had no clue how cops breached structures. The TV shows had it all wrong. Law enforcement didn't kick doors in with barely a nick or splinter. They didn't glamorously enter with guns blazing looking all fresh-faced and pressed.

Nope.

The work was gritty, nerve-sizzling. Locate and isolate the threat in a quick, calm, and methodical manner. Safety of officers and anyone else on scene was imperative. The number one concern.

She swiped her sleeve under her nose, leaving a glimmering iridescent streak on the blue nylon fabric. Snow and muck stuck to her boots. Her eyes watered from the freezing temps. Not a pretty sight.

Cam's voice sounded low and clear in her earpiece.

He assigned positions to the crew, including to two fellow inspectors, Ullrich and Andersen. Deputy Sheriffs Don Harmon and Noah Xiang would cover the garage behind the single-story house. St. Paul officers Sean Young, Molly Wells, and Ursula Ellis would take the back door, and he, MC, and the two DEA agents, Greg Tolliver and Jill Brownwirth, would make entry through the front door.

Cam said, "Ullrich and Andersen go around the corner post up at the end of the alley. Everyone set?"

Each responded, "Affirmative."

Cam said, "Go!"

MC's heart raced as they scattered to their respective locations. She was with Cam and DEA agents Tolliver and Brownwirth, heading straight for the front door. She slowed her breathing, concentrating on the task at hand.

Before they made it onto the porch, a gunshot somewhere toward the rear of the house shattered the night.

Cam's voice came tight and fast in her ear. "Shots fired! Go! Go!" He twisted the doorknob. Unlocked.

No need for the battering ram. With hand signals, Cam motioned everyone into place, MC slightly behind and to Cam's right, Brownwirth and Tolliver after MC.

He yelled, "Law enforcement!" and they went in.

Brownwirth and Tolliver peeled off to clear the hallway and any rooms to the right between the living room and dining room. MC followed Cam's broad-shouldered figure, his head nearly brushing the top of the door frame when they strode through the living room and a dining room the size of a phone booth, moving toward the back of the house.

Her nerves were stretched taut. Memories flooded through her of a bleak morning several months earlier when she should have been at another house when gunshots erupted there.

Not just another house. Her house. Her home. But that was a different time, a different story.

She forced the images from her mind, focused on the heft of the SIG Sauer and scanned the house's interior.

MC and Cam arrived in the kitchen.

Pots, pans, scales, and other paraphernalia were scattered across a rickety wooden table and on open countertops. Two of four chairs were upended.

She swept her gun left to right across half the room while Cam mirrored her on the other.

"Clear," Cam shouted.

From other rooms, MC heard Brownwirth and Tolliver shout, "Clear."

MC surveyed the room. A shiny splat of reddish orange on the dingy cabinet doors below the sink looked like someone had loaded a paintball gun and used the space for target practice.

Under the table, MC noticed a pile of blackish fur. Dog? Cat?

She skirted the table and bent. "Raccoon."

No movement. The blood-soaked fur glistened, and viscera was splattered across the linoleum. The poor thing was deader than a doornail.

A pyramid of clear plastic bags of white powder sat on the table next to several stacks of cash secured with rubber bands.

Obviously, some type of lab or distribution operation had been set up in the kitchen.

New IS protocols dictated that inspectors collect all suspicious powders and forward the samples to the Inspection Service's world-class National Forensic Lab in Dulles, Virginia, for testing.

Voices sounded in her earpiece, Deputy Harmon saying, "Garage is clear. Nothing but a busted-up lawnmower and a few Mason jars full of nails and crap."

His comical partner, Xiang said, "Don't forget to tell them how the big bad mouse scared the shit outta you!"

"Screw you, asshole."

Officer Sean Young from SPPD said, "Side and back yard are clear. You need backup on that mouse sighting, Harmon?"

Laughter echoed from Young's two teammates.

Harmon said, "Fuck all y'all."

Cam said, "The property is clear then."

A pan lay on its side on the floor in front of the stove in a puddle of viscous red goo. A spoon sat on the spattered stovetop.

The back door opened, and the threesome from SPPD filed in, followed by the Abbott and Costello comedy duo from Ramsey County.

"Nothing outside," Officer Ellis said. She scanned the room.

"Nothing inside either." Brownwirth entered from the dining room, Tolliver behind her.

Cam said, "No idea how many were here tonight."

MC said, "Looks like one." She pointed to a single dinner plate heaped with pasta on the far side of the stove. "Dinner for one."

Cam walked to the sink. "Pot full of cloudy water. Spaghetti sauce in the pan." He pointed at the metal pot on the floor. "Probably what's splashed on the cabinets. So, the guy's working. Gets hungry. Makes some pasta and sauce. Raccoon gets inside and freaks him out. He shoots the critter dead. Hears us outside and bolts?"

MC said. "That shithead got out of here fast."

Cam holstered his gun and pushed a clump of sandy hair off his forehead. No winter cap for him. "No basement. No attic. Not a lot of options. Probably heard us coming and escaped down the alley." He activated his radio. "Ullrich? Andersen? Any activity in the alley?"

Ullrich responded, "Negatory. Not a soul in sight. Want us to hang out?"

Officer Wells said, "Yard is hard-packed snow trampled from here to eternity. We won't get any usable footprints."

Cam said to Ullrich, "You guys c'mon back to the residence."

"Ten-four."

"Brilliant. Dammit." MC jammed her SIG in the holster on her hip. She kicked at a chair and missed, instead connecting with a table leg. The topmost plastic bag tumbled off the tier, momentum carrying it over the edge of the table.

Everyone froze. All sound faded as if her entire head had been submerged in water in slow motion.

Fuck me, MC thought.

The bag hit the scuffed linoleum floor. Powder puffed through a hole on the side. Time screeched to a halt.

Cam looked at her, blue eyes blazing. He waved a hand toward the mess. "Everybody, vacate now! We don't know if we're looking at fentanyl or cocaine or heroin or powdered sugar."

The clomping of many booted feet retreating echoed in her ears.

"MC?" he said.

For a split second she didn't give a rat's ass if she huffed fentanyl. She welcomed the idea of darkening death's doorstep. She'd be out of her misery.

"MC?" Cam's voice penetrated her befuddlement. He gripped her arm and dragged her out of the house.

"Sorry."

He leaned in so only she could hear him. "You're *sorry*? What the hell? We don't know what that shit is. You've endangered the entire team."

Cam had never in all their years working together sounded so angry. He was correct. She'd majorly screwed the pooch on this one.

"Cam, I don't know. I—I got pissed." Hard words to utter because she was a senior inspector and normally led by example.

He let go of her arm. "We'll talk later."

MC stalked back to the car and yanked the comm from her ear. She leaned against the passenger-side of the jet-black SUV and struggled to force air in and out of her lungs.

As she thumped her head on the smoke-colored window, the white, coiled wire attached to the earbud swung across her chest like a metronome. What the hell was wrong with her? This wasn't who she was. Or was it? Did she have a death wish? She wouldn't blame Cam one bit for reporting this clusterfuck to their supervisor, Team Leader, Jamie Sanchez. Sanchez headed up both teams in their domicile at the moment because her boss—or nemesis—Roland Chrapkowski was still on medical leave. He'd survived a heart attack in December.

Her damn luck sucked assballs.

Cam included her along with Eli Andersen and Roger Ullrich on the list of inspectors for tonight's raid. MC knew her inclusion was proof of Cam's loyalty to her, as a colleague and a friend.

Tonight's op was the first of several planned in coming weeks. Jamie Sanchez appointed Cam to lead the interagency team for this raid, and he definitely deserved the nod. He'd received a credible lead from the DEA's Heroin/Fentanyl Task Force, which was created a year earlier in 2014, to combat drugs entering the US via International Mail from labs in Mexico, China, and other foreign countries. The task force sent leads to respective Inspection Service field divisions, and the IS pursued the interception of packages. The end result, if all went according to the plan, was the imminent arrest of the mail recipients.

Not the outcome they'd had tonight.

MC yanked the hat off her head and glanced at the side mirror. She scraped a hand through her spiky salt-and-pepper hair. Was she getting too old for this shit?

She turned around and leaned her ass on the door, passively watching the action around the house like a TV viewer watching an episode of *Blue Bloods*.

Part of her, a tiny part, wished to go back in time to the moment before she let loose and kicked the table. Have a redo. Cam's warning prior to their hitting the street earlier echoed in her head. He'd said, "Remember, fentanyl is indiscernible from cocaine or heroin, or even white flour for that matter. Do. Not. Take. Chances."

The DEA had warned agencies not to conduct field testing if they even suspected the presence of fentanyl. Instead, a HAZMAT incident response team needed to take over. Fentanyl potency was mind-boggling—a mere three milligrams, a dose the size of a pinhead, could kill an elephant. And they'd seen a lot more than a pinhead's worth of product inside the house.

Suddenly she was hard-pressed to envisage anything other than a glassful of Grey Goose. Thursday had bled into Friday. Thankfully, a three-day weekend beckoned. Or loomed, depending on her state of mind.

Above all, vodka's seductive whisper tugged at her very being, the one tool she believed would erase her foul up.

Chapter Two

MC was ecstatic to be with Barb again . . . excited about being reunited. She'd missed her partner and best friend—the love of her life.

Where had Barb been since November?

Focus, McCall, she chided herself. Can't have a reunion until you reach her.

The goal: find Barb in the stark white maze before her. MC knew on a cellular level she needed to prevent anything bad from happening.

Why might anything bad happen? MC puzzled aloud.

"MC?" Barb called, her voice shaky.

"I'm on my way, Barb. Don't move. I'll come to you." MC's fear was visceral. Her muscles quivered, her mouth dry as a beach at low tide.

Blazing white light.

MC blinked, concentrated on gaining her bearings.

The light burned her retinas. She held an arm up like a shield to block the intensity. Her grip on the gun in her right hand was rock solid, but her nerves made it a challenge to keep her finger from slipping into the trigger guard.

"Barb, where are you?" MC's voice remained steady and strong, but her heart hammered, a battering ram inside her chest.

Muffled voices ahead.

Unrecognizable.

Indecipherable.

"Talk to me, hon."

"MC, help me. Please. Please, before they—"

"Keep talking," MC shouted. Her sense of direction had gone haywire. Where the hell was she? Definitely not their house. This place was a maze of fluorescent-lit, sterile, white-tiled hallways.

A hospital?

Some type of lab building?

She must be trapped in some bad B-movie insane asylum, except she'd not seen any doors leading off the hallways she traversed.

"MC, they're nervous. *I'm* nervous." Barb's voice sounded far away.

MC detected a slight tremor in the words, which jolted her system like a cattle prod. "Hang in there. Keep talking." MC angled left, the only option. A long corridor loomed. She again moved forward, leading with her gun.

"You're too late, bitch."

A thunderous boom was followed by a second blast.

"Barb?" MC screamed. "Answer me!"

Silence.

MC broke into a run, no longer caring what might be lying in wait. She had to reach Barb.

A sound like pinging radar shattered her concentration.

She whipped around. Something wrapped around her from behind, hampering her progress. The beeping increased in volume, ripping MC from the grips of another nightmare.

She'd failed to save Barb. Again.

Yet again.

MC extricated her arms from the mess of covers and snatched her phone off the nightstand. She swiped a thumb across the screen to silence the maddening alarm, knocking over an empty lowball glass onto a green leather-bound Moleskine notebook.

Last evening's vodka-induced muddle had morphed into another bout of night terrors, of failures to rescue the love of her life. She knew it'd been a dream, but the knowing didn't prevent the heavy dark cloak of guilt from descending upon her like the final curtain drop at the end of a play.

MC gripped the iPhone. The charging cable was still attached like some techno umbilical cord. She knuckled the sleep from her eyes and checked the screen.

A red dot on the Facebook app stared her down, an unread notification. She didn't remember having the app set to display notifications. She opened it.

Front and center was a "Facebook Memory From One Year Ago," a photo of MC and Barb surrounded by a heart-shaped frame. Barb had commented: "Happy Valentine's Day! I'll love you forever."

MC dropped the device on the bed as if it were a live grenade. She kicked loose from the tangle of sheets and blanket and leaped from the bed. Hands pressed hard on either side of her head to prevent it from exploding, she stared at her tormentor.

How was this possible? She couldn't remember the last time she'd accessed her Facebook account, much less toggled notification alerts.

Another realization dawned—if today was Valentine's Day, that meant it was Saturday. Why on God's green earth would she have set her alarm to go off at five in the morning? Five was her normal waking time during the workweek. On weekends, though, she followed a strict no-alarms policy.

Didn't remember setting the damn alarm. Didn't remember much of anything from the last twelve hours. She assumed the answers lay in the bottom of an empty bottle of Grey Goose, waiting to be tossed out with the recycling.

Nearly three months had passed since Barb was shot and killed in the kitchen of their home. MC had sold the house the moment it was cleared as a crime scene.

She now inhabited a one-bedroom apartment, basically four walls and a roof, a place to store her crap and sleep. Situated near Grand and Dale streets in St. Paul, the place was located a handful of blocks from Flannel, Dara and Meg's coffee shop. The duo were her best friends, maybe the only friends she had left.

MC approached her bed cautiously. The phone screen had timed out. With much trepidation she nudged it with a finger, and it blazed back to life. The image stared at her, confirmation she hadn't completely lost her mind. Anxiety, grief, and loss crushed her like Wile E. Coyote under the ACME anvil.

Barb was gone. Gone forever.

MC was absolutely guilt-ridden that she was alive while her wonderful vibrant partner was dead.

During the drug raid Thursday night, she'd tempted fate, kicking the table, not evacuating immediately when the white powder danger presented itself. She recalled a fleeting thought of dropping into the darkness, of joining Barb. She thrust the memory away knowing she'd have to deal with it on Tuesday at work.

Time plodded onward in this new life without Barb, dragging her in its wake. To keep herself afloat, she grasped at the life-preservers of work and of investigating Barb's death. She wasn't doing a great job. In fact, she was doing a downright abysmal job of it.

The morning's cloud of numbness slowly dissipated, leaving razor sharp edges of fury embedded painfully under her skin, like a file folder that accidentally slipped under a fingernail, piercing the quick. No fairy tale existence for her. Not even close.

MC barely made it through shitty day after shitty day. Today wasn't just a shitty day, it was a shitty Valentine's Day. Chocolates. Red hearts. Cupids with arrows full of love and hope. Crappy capitalism wringing money from people who didn't have enough to pay the rent, much less buy commercialized holiday junk. The knowledge didn't stop the masses, not the lovesick gobsmacked masses.

She left the phone on the bed, snagged the empty glass, and beat a path to the kitchen. The best way to launch a three-day-weekend, since Monday was President's Day and she was off work, was to ingest a clarifying glass of vodka and forget Valentine's Day existed.

The Goose anesthetized the anguish, deep-sixed the mental suffering.

Sweat-soaked and freezing, Quentin Laird awoke in the bottom bunk of the dilapidated wood-sided cabin he shared with his cohort, Nick Wooler. Nick was already awake and working.

Quentin rose, cursing the damn nightmare. On top of the punishing bad dream, Quentin suffered waking flashbacks, like a silent movie playing on repeat inside his head.

He took a quick shower, ignoring the black gunk around the bottom of the shower stall. Then he gathered all the packages ready to be mailed and made two trips to the car to load them.

"Later," Quentin said to Nick's back.

Nick ignored him, hunched over a desktop computer, pounding the keyboard like it was public enemy number one. He did all the online crap for his cousin Dirk's drug distribution business. Both Quentin and Nick prepped and packed orders, then Quentin did pack mule duty, hauling the outgoing items to the post office.

Over the past month, though, Quentin had been consumed by a sense of unease. Outright terror was a better descriptor. The nightmares about what they'd done—the reason they'd had to split from the Cities—gave him a nonstop case of heartburn.

He wasn't eating much, mostly pizza and beer, which didn't help his indigestion.

During the day he constantly checked social media on his phone. He kept tabs on the news in St. Paul, hoping not to see his or Nick's name associated with any crime stories. He'd created a page on Facebook, "Q

Gamer," to keep in touch with a handful of online friends. No one had a clue about his location, other than he'd moved away from the Cities.

One friend had a sister who worked in the kitchen at the nursing home where Quentin's mom lived. She kept an eye on Q's mom, had agreed to let her brother know if anything changed about his mother. Fortunately, nothing had happened since his move. Still, that knowledge didn't quell Quentin's apprehension. Guilt engulfed him. He'd abandoned his mom. He'd followed Nick, pretty much akin to the devil, and now he couldn't figure out how to extricate himself from this hell he was in.

Nick was oblivious to the unrest seething through Quentin. He was a wizard on the Dark Web, which pleased Dirk. But Nick also sampled the product and skimmed money, two activities that might shorten both their lifespans. In addition to the drugs to customers, Dirk also had them ship cash each week to his supplier. Quentin packed the stacks of cash in a box, to be shipped via the post office, just like their product.

The big problem was Nick often slipped several bills off a few stacks before Q boxed it, even though Quentin told him it was a terrible idea.

No way could Dirk be blind to Nick's thieving.

Quentin constantly sweated the certain-to-come repercussions. A deep tar pit resided where Dirk's heart should be, and he wouldn't be forgiving of their sins. Nick's messing with Dirk's business was a deadly proposition. And Dirk knew their secret.

The more pills Nick popped, the more erratic his behavior. An erratic Nick filled Quentin with unending apprehension.

What to do?

Quentin wondered about disappearing, ditching the North Shore and heading back to the Cities, or should he turn himself in, take his punishment? Problem number one was he knew Nick, if not Dirk, would be hot on his trail. They all had a lot to lose. The opioid business was thriving beyond Dirk's wildest expectations. Money flowed like Gooseberry Falls during a rainy summer. No way was he escaping that.

Quentin usually utilized the Two Harbors Post Office, but he needed some time away, so he drove farther along the North Shore to the Grand Marais PO. There, he'd discovered a haven to be alone with his thoughts and try to come to terms with what his life had become.

He dropped off the outgoing packages just before closing. Saturday hours were shortened, and because he'd awakened late, he barely had time to make the ninety-minute drive north before the post office shut down for the day.

After he completed the drop, he crossed the highway on foot and jogged a couple blocks to Lake Superior and the picturesque harbor. Grand Marais—Artist's Point specifically—was Quentin's secret. From Nick. The idea of having a private place gave him a sliver of peace.

He trekked west along the concrete wall toward the Grand Marais Lighthouse, careful to grasp the cable rail along the way. He didn't want to slip into the icy waters churning three feet below his boots. Despite the fresh air and having the seawall all to himself, Quentin's restlessness hadn't abated.

Dirk made Quentin's skin crawl. The guy evoked more fear in him than the Grim Reaper-ish character, Michael Myers, in the *Halloween* movies. Dirk embodied a darkness that oozed from his pores. Quentin did his best to melt into the woodwork whenever Dirk visited the boxy shack a bit north of Two Harbors. Dirk knew the guy who owned the house and had arranged for Nick and Quentin to live and work from the place.

A rent-free situation had sounded enticing, especially when they'd arrived with hardly any cash or possessions. After the nightmare in the Cities, they needed to ditch their ride and lay low. If only Nick hadn't lost his shit in St. Paul, they wouldn't both be paying the price.

One pig-headed decision had changed Q's life forever.

Initially, Quentin had appreciated Nick bringing him into the fold to work for Len Klein, the security guy for Stennard Global Enterprises. Klein hired them as armed bouncers and drug suppliers for Stennard's epic private parties. And they'd made loads of cash in the process.

But the law lowered the boom on Klein and on Stennard. All Stennard's businesses shuttered. The lucrative party gigs dried up faster than water in the desert.

Nick and Quentin were without income, with no job prospects, no nothing.

So Nick concocted a brilliant idea, but his drug-fueled attempt at revenge went off the rails and they'd had to flee the city. Nick had told Quentin not to worry, his cousin Dirk in Duluth would be able to help them.

They'd hotfooted it north on Interstate 35, and Nick spilled the beans about their plight to Dirk, who hadn't hesitated to help. He'd made a series of murmured phone calls and gave Nick directions to a location near the town of Two Harbors. Alfie Gunderson, the proprietor of Gunderson's Salvage Yard and Gun Range, owned a shabby cabin in the woods behind the salvage yard. At least the dump had electricity, running water, and a bathroom, along with warp speed Internet connectivity, no doubt thanks to Dirk.

Alfie also took care of their vehicle—whatever that meant. Quentin figured it best that he never saw that ride again.

Old Alfie was creepy and oddly resembled Big Foot with a limp and a missing front tooth. He drank Bud Light from sunrise to past sunset, and for all Quentin knew, ran an IV of the stuff throughout the night.

Now they were back on their feet and cash was coming in. Dirk provided them each with transportation, a Kia Sportage SUV in nondescript silver, so Quentin could deliver the goods to the post office and be allowed some freedom. And a black Ford pickup truck for Nick to rev around in.

Quentin had splurged on a Nintendo Wii U gaming system and big-screen TV with his first pay. His next goal was to stash cash for a payment to the nursing home where his mom lived . . . if "lived" meant being hooked up to a billion machines and having air and food pumped into you and hoses draining shit out of you. Literally. But she was alive. His mom was the only family he had. He'd removed his meth-head father from the equation years ago. That blob of inhumanity had been sentenced to a maximum-security prison, hopefully for life.

A breeze slapped him in the face and brought him full circle to the present. He stood on the icy, wet, over three-hundred-foot-long concrete seawall. A dangerous place to daydream.

Quentin's burner phone buzzed. Nick.

Where u at?

No way was Quentin going to tell Nick his location. Some things were best left undisclosed. *Unloaded the stuff. b there soon.*

The phone vibrated again.

haul ass. i got a hot date w/some fine pussy in D. V Day. gonna get turnt.

He understood D meant the city of Duluth. V Day? What the hell? Ah, Valentine's Day. He hadn't paid attention because he didn't have a girl. He imagined surprising his mom with a giant heart-shaped box of the best chocolates. She'd love that. For a brief moment he smiled.

Then the emotion faded like the paint on the west-facing side of a house. Even if he bought her candy, the treats would go uneaten. She was a vegetable. But Quentin was convinced she heard every word he spoke in her presence—believed that somewhere deep inside her soul she understood her circumstances.

He didn't acknowledge Nick's mention of a hot date. Or the fact he intended to get high, probably on some of Dirk's opioids.

On my way.

Chapter Three

Zero dark thirty. Zero degrees. Typical February day in lovely Minnesnowta, the land of ten thousand snowstorms.

MC fired up the Subaru, her breath rising like smoke signals in arctic air. Recalibration after the three-day weekend was in order. The best way to jumpstart her system and the work week was a cup of strong dark roast from Flannel. She'd overslept and had no time to brew a pot at home.

She gritted her teeth, willing the drumbeat in her head to cease, and drove the six blocks to the coffee shop. Her bleak outlook grew bleaker at the prospect of dealing with Dara. Her friend's joviality-laced concern tended to have the opposite effect on MC. Which is probably why she'd begun avoiding Dara and Meg.

That and the memories of Barb. The monstrous vacancy in all their lives. The gaping black hole in their universe.

Today, though, she desperately needed a caffeinated boost. She still possessed enough sensibility and loyalty to give her business to her friends rather than one of the conglomerate coffee houses in the area. She parked on the street a dozen feet from the door. Once inside the café, she paused to savor the hint of smoky, nutty flavors permeating the air.

"Shiver me timbers," Dara's voice boomed from behind the counter. "Look what the cat drug in."

Heads swiveled toward MC, and then away, probably deeming MC an uninteresting human who'd wandered in from the early morning snowscape.

"Nice to see you, Dara." MC barely managed to keep the sarcasm from her voice.

"How you doing?" Dara's brow furrowed, her jocular tone replaced with care and concern.

MC placed her gloves on the counter and squinted at the chalkboard menu hanging above and behind Dara's head.

"I'm fine," MC said. "The usual, please."

"All business this morning, eh? No travel mug?"

"It's at home. Tough weekend."

"Perhaps a meeting—"

"Dara!" She held up a hand. "No AA meeting." MC counted to ten as she put her hands in her coat pockets. She reminded herself Dara's heart was in the right place, though the merest reference to AA rubbed her very last nerve raw.

Dara snared a twenty-ounce paper cup and dispensed coffee from one of the three ginormous silver coffee towers. Tawny-colored liquid streamed from the spigot. Dara's gaze ping-ponged between the flow and MC.

"Meg texted you Saturday, see if you wanted some company."

"Tell Meg I'm sorry."

"And Sunday."

"I didn't have my phone on this weekend. Valentine's Day was rough." A whopper of an understatement.

"Which is exactly the reason we tried to reach out."

"I needed to be—alone." Not exactly solo—the Goose rode shotgun.

"Understandable, but you don't have to ride the waves on your own. We're a phone call or text message away. Meg worries."

"*Meg* worries?" MC arched an eyebrow at her friend.

"Okay, we both worry." Dara wiped a splash of coffee from the counter. "You're family. Maybe we do dinner one night this week? Reinitiate the old routine?"

The old routine. What a joke. MC was stunned that Dara thought their lives might return to times past. Did she believe Barb's death was a mere blip on the radar? Out of sight, out of mind?

Dara slid a cardboard sleeve, emblazoned with "Flannel" in Black Watch plaid lettering, over the cup and handed it to MC.

MC swallowed her annoyance. "Let me think about it, okay?" She doctored the coffee, ready to escape the tentacles of Dara's worry. The hamster wheel in her brain spun, trying to concoct an excuse to bow out of dinner.

"We hired a new barista."

"That's great." MC barely processed the news.

"Zane. His first shift is tomorrow. The evening shift. If you come for dinner, we'll do takeout here, and Meg and I will be able to hang around to help acclimate him."

"Wait. What happened to Kate?"

"She's carrying a heavier load at school this semester, so she had to cut back on hours. She recommended Zane. He's studying at Macalester. We believe he'll fit in perfectly."

"Sounds good." MC snapped a plastic lid on her cup and slipped on her gloves. "I better hit the road. Can't be late for work again."

"Don't forget about dinner."

"I'll get back to you."

Meg wandered out from the backroom after MC left the cafe.

Dara wiped the already-clean counter and tossed the towel over her shoulder. "I didn't say a word to her."

"You did good."

"I sure don't feel good."

Meg hugged Dara. "I understand. We agreed not to divulge any details to her until we know more."

"I know, dammit. But she needs to know you may be sick. You . . . we . . . may have a fight ahead of us. She's family, Meg."

"She is family. She's still reeling from the loss of Barb. And the demons chasing her."

"Demons easily squashed if she'd stop being pig-headed and try an AA meeting with me."

Meg clucked her tongue. "In her own time. You understand how addiction and help works. Need I remind you?"

"I don't need reminding. I remember like it was yesterday. You gave me the ultimatum—booze or you. Within a nanosecond I chose you."

"Granted, you acted quickly. Be honest, though. Claiming you took only a nanosecond is a bit of a stretch."

"I took all of one night to decide you—our life together—along with this business, meant I needed to make a change. My butt was in a chair at a meeting the following day."

"You've been strong and consistent over the past twenty years. You knew what we had was the best thing that happened to either of us. I love you for choosing us over whiskey." She patted Dara's cheek and planted a quick kiss on her lips.

"Doctor Doogie is supposed to call today?"

Meg gave her a stern look. "His name is Houser. Douglas Houser. Keep goofing around and you'll actually call him Doogie sometime, embarrassing yourself. And me."

"I'm sure he's heard the joke a million times. Who doesn't know about the TV show, *Doogie Howser, M.D.*?"

"Anyone born after the show stopped airing in nineteen ninety-three. Although, with the Internet and streaming apps, it's possible our Doctor Houser has watched an episode or two."

"So, Doctor Houser is supposed to call today with the results?"

"Yes." Meg shifted away and straightened the already perfectly symmetrical stack of napkins on the counter. Then she lined up the assorted pastries inside the glass case.

Dara watched, her heart shredding at the thought of the possible diagnosis Meg faced.

Breast cancer.

Would they be traveling a bumpy road ahead?

Could they depend on MC to be part of their support system? Or would Dara be on her own trying to keep everyone afloat?

Meg's voice cut through the barrage of questions firing through Dara's head. "Stop."

"What?"

"I can tell you're off to the races thinking the worst. We agreed to stay positive until we hear otherwise. That's what I intend to do. You better, too."

"Yes, dear."

"That's what I like to hear. Now I'm going to mop the kitchen. You okay to handle the counter?"

"Yep." Dara did her best to tuck away her angst.

"Good. Holler if you need help."

MC situated herself behind the desk in her cubby of an office. She booted up the ancient desktop and reviewed her Outlook calendar.

She scowled. A required two-hour-long online sexual harassment training session was scheduled for the morning. The same course was regurgitated year after year, which she was less than thrilled about. Why didn't HR allocate budget funding toward updating the course?

Jamie Sanchez, the supervisor of the Twin Cities Domicile's mail fraud, money laundering, and narcotics team, had also scheduled an hour-long team meeting at eleven to review everyone's workload. Great. One meeting after another.

MC was assigned to the Miscellaneous team where she mainly worked mail theft cases. Her boss, Team Leader, Roland Chrapkowski, was currently out on medical leave. Chrapkowski, whose name was pronounced "Trap-kow-ski," was not-so-affectionately nicknamed

Crapper by all his direct reports. The man had been nothing but a thorn in her side since Day One, and though she knew her thoughts were harsh, she was grateful to the Heart Attack Gods for rescuing her from his relentless recriminations.

Jamie Sanchez had been running both groups during Chrap-kowski's absence, and MC was fine with the setup. The Inspection Service's Twin Cities Domicile, made up of these two separate teams, operated with all inspectors expected to be flexible and capable of developing a case in all functional areas, especially when larger investigative operations occurred.

She jotted some notes to share at the meeting. Best to be prepared. Hopefully, the misstep she'd made at the latest op wouldn't be fodder for discussion. She felt horrible about her lack of professionalism and considered apologizing to Cam again.

MC removed a green notebook from her messenger bag, a five-by-eight-inch record of her "Life after Barb." Her daily ritual was to riffle through the notes and tidbits she'd extracted from Sergeant Sharpe, the homicide detective with St. Paul PD assigned to Barb's case. Each day's review felt like pulling an impacted wisdom tooth without Novocain. All she had to show for the tears and begging was a minimal framework of a case. She'd obtained more detail by interviewing her former neighbors than Sharpe had been willing to share.

All in all, MC thought the mess was a whole lot of nothing. She reread the pages, some tear-stained from late-night booze-fueled sessions at home.

A knock on the door broke her concentration.

Cam poked his head around the door, sandy hair flopping over his eyes. "Busy?" His tone was flat, very unlike Cam.

"Hi. Just assessing some material." She stashed the green notebook under a stack of manila file folders. "Come. Sit. How are you? How's the family? Tell me everything."

He shut the door and leaned his over six-foot-tall frame against it. His bright blue eyes and pearly-white grin always lifted her mood. MC glanced at him, and an odd twinge zinged along her nerves.

No pearly whites.

Blue eyes frosty as a frozen Minnesota lake.

"What's up?" She swallowed her pride and thought she'd beat him to the punch. "Cam, I'm sorry about the other night."

Without preamble he launched into her. "I can't continue to cover for you. No more. I'm done. I wanted to tell you out of earshot of anyone else, especially Jamie."

MC was confused—stunned, actually. "What do you mean?" A soft voice in her head, Barb's voice, said, "You had to know he couldn't cover for you forever."

She dropped her head into her hands and squeezed it for five seconds, trying to recenter herself.

Cam continued, "You're my colleague. Hell, you're my friend. And I'm advocating for you in both capacities. I'm worried about you. And I'm very concerned about your capability in the field."

A tide of fear and shame washed through her. She let her hands fall in her lap. "Cam, I had a momentary lapse in judgment. I kicked that table by accident. No harm, no foul."

"No harm, no foul. That's the best you can do? This isn't you, MC." He stuck his hands into his pants pockets, bending a little at the waist as if in pain. "What are we—you—going to do to rectify the situation?"

"I'm going through a rough patch. I apologize. Silver lining, no one was hurt. Have you received results from the lab on the powder?" Fingers crossed it wasn't fentanyl.

"MC, it's more than the other night." He straightened and locked gazes with her. "You missed the meeting Saturday morning. The recap of the op. Jamie asked about you. I got jammed up, told him you probably forgot. Where were you?"

Shit.

The alarm at five Saturday morning. She'd been hungover and hadn't recalled she had purposely set the alarm. It hadn't been some unexplained fluke.

Unlike the Facebook notification.

"Shit. The meeting. Slipped my mind. Saturday was one of the worst of my bad days."

"I recommend you concoct a more substantial excuse for Jamie." Cam stepped toward the door, hand on the doorknob. "MC, please get the help you need."

"It's called therapy, Cam. I have weekly appointments." He and Jamie knew about her sessions with Dr. Zaulk. After Barb died Jamie required her to attend two mandatory sessions in order to return to the job. She'd continued with the counseling, somewhat reluctantly, at Dr. Zaulk's urging.

"Therapy isn't cutting the ice, partner. You should consider dependency treatment." He sucked in a deep breath and slowly let it out. "To deal with the drinking."

"Drinking?" Cam hit the nail on the head, but she couldn't force the words from her mouth to tell him he was correct. "Cam . . ." Another attempt to open up to him left her distraught. She clamped her lips tightly together, berating herself for not being able to let this guy she trusted implicitly know how dire a situation she was in.

"Don't play me for a fool. Remember, we're friends. Friends don't let friends work drunk. Or so hungover they can't do their jobs." He released a long slow sigh. "MC, when you're not one hundred percent present on the job, you put everyone at risk. You know that. At least you used to know that."

She refused to cry. Instead, she let her constantly simmering anger encapsulate, insulate her.

"How did you spend Valentine's Day?" he asked.

Me? she thought. I stayed home, alone, all weekend. Drank myself into oblivion. Woke on Monday grateful for the extra day off to recuperate from the hangover. She straightened the precisely placed pile of folders on her desk. How would he like that answer?

As if he'd read her thoughts, Cam said, "Hell MC, drinking isn't doing you any good, ya know?" He scraped the hunk of hair away from his eyes. "Booze isn't the answer. It won't bring Barb back."

"Correct, my friend. Believe me, at every weekly session, my therapist has pointed out the folly of self-medicating." True statement, even though MC refrained from sharing with Dr. Zaulk that her nightly sidekick was the Goose. Let Cam assume what he would. "Those spirits sure do a fabulous job of deadening—pardon the pun—the pain."

A grimace crept across Cam's face. "I'm not trying to go all judgmental on your ass."

"Yet here we are." She spread her hands wide. "You judging me."

"Not true. I'm stating facts. Trying to help you stay alive and stay on the job. The job I know you love."

MC's heart twinged. Of course she loved this job. "Continue being you. And when I'm a complete asshat, remember we're friends and I'm a damn good inspector. I'll work through this. I don't know how long it'll take, but trust me, I'll conquer the beast. I promise." She glanced at him. "Cam, the job means everything to me. It's my lifeline. Actively ensuring the safety of postal employees and protecting the sanctity of the mail, these things keep me going. Make me want to drag myself from bed to fight another day."

"I understand that, but there's a monumental risk going at it the way you are."

"Want to know what else helps me maintain any sense of sanity? My resolute intent on tracking the scumbag asshole—or assholes—who killed Barb. That shit revs my motor every day. I hang by a thread, try to focus on work, but she still pushes in, begs for my attention, and the thread unravels. But I'll do better. Promise."

Cam said," Sharpe at SPPD warned you from the beginning about going rogue or insinuating yourself in his investigation. Losing Barb has been hard, but I sure don't want to lose you, too. Which is why—"

"I swear to you, Cam, I have the situation under control." By the slimmest of margins, she thought. "Honestly, Sharpe hasn't given me any news. I call him. He tells me he's working the case, I should be patient, allow him space to investigate. It's frustrating." MC stood and paced the narrow space behind her desk.

She stopped with her back to Cam and gazed through the slats of the tan plastic-backed vertical blinds covering the window. The drab parking lot faded from her focus, and her mind traveled to another place. "If I uncovered one clue, one nugget, to mold into a full-blown lead, I'd gain momentum and speed up the wheels of justice."

"SPPD is top notch, MC. You gotta trust them. I believe the bad guys will be caught. But we digress."

She dropped into her chair and wheeled around to face him. "You're always more optimistic than me."

"Optimistic?" he scoffed. "Right. I'm the epitome of optimism. Can we steer back on track? I know you're going through hell. But I can't continue to cover for you at work. Outside of work—"

"Got it, partner. Thanks for the pep talk. I guess I should prep for my next visitor, which I'm sure will be Jamie."

Cam sighed. "I wish there were a way to help you understand. I'm running on empty." His shoulders drooped, like he was carrying the weight of the world, or maybe the weight of her world. "I'm sorry." He left, quietly closing the door behind him.

She didn't recognize this person she was morphing into.

Was this to be their new normal? Cam's well of goodwill toward her run dry. Unyielding, quietly disappointed, suppressing anger? He wasn't an asshole, which was the reason she struggled with the new dynamic.

What could she possibly do with what he'd laid on her plate? The idea that Cam couldn't keep excusing her and that no one would trust her to have their back were bitter pills to swallow.

He'd covered for her when she was late to work. Or if she'd neglected to scan field notes into DigiCase, he'd jump in and take care of the task. DigiCase was the daily diary of each inspector's work life: time worked, leave taken, and all case notes. It was a pain in the ass. Overall, she hadn't skipped out on anything major, but the negligible bits snowballed, and MC understood Cam's frustration.

Then there was the drinking. All of it weighed on her like the world on Atlas's shoulders. The morning meeting ought to be interesting. What she needed was a distraction. Some trifling bit to recalibrate her mind.

MC punched in the numbers on her desk phone without having to think about them. The line rang twice. She looked at the time in the bottom corner of her computer screen. 8:17 a.m. He'd be at his desk by now. The ringing segued into a voicemail greeting and the inevitable beep. "Good morning, Detective Sharpe. This is MC McCall. I'm checking to see if you've any news on Barb's case. Please call me. Thanks."

MC cradled the phone, suspicious that Sharpe screened incoming phone calls, especially hers. She was certain her daily "what's up with the case" calls were an annoyance to the homicide detective, but she didn't care. All bets were off until the animal or animals responsible for Barb's murder were brought to justice, with or without Sharpe's assistance.

MC hoisted the handset again, finger poised to punch in patrol officer Kiara Reece's phone number. She'd wait until she heard from Sharpe before trekking the road not yet traveled. In the meantime, she needed more coffee—a lot more coffee—to stay awake during the harassment prevention training.

At the team meeting, Jamie assigned MC a smattering of mail theft complaints. Most had come in via the toll-free number and one from a report someone filed with Minneapolis PD's Second Precinct.

Other inspectors gave their spiel on open cases. MC held her breath while Cam updated the teams on the search warrant from the previous week's late-night op. He made no mention of her irresponsible action. In fact, he didn't make eye contact with her. She peeked around at the other inspectors, especially those who had been on scene, to gauge if anyone perceived Cam's editing of events. If they were aware, they were keeping it under wraps.

Meeting over, MC gathered her notebook and pen and launched herself from her chair.

"MC?" Jamie Sanchez said. "Mind sticking around for a minute?"

She allowed the others to file past. Her colleagues' gazes burned holes into her. Or maybe she was paranoid due to her overactive imagination.

Jamie shut the door.

"Please. Sit." He indicated a chair.

She sat without meeting his gaze.

"I need to talk to you about a couple of matters."

MC's jaw locked. A *couple* of matters? Shit. Finally, she worked her mandible into action. "What's up?"

"First, how are you doing?"

A trap?

Maybe he intended to have her sent through a Fitness for Duty protocol.

Keep cool.

"I'm okay, considering."

He paged through some notes. "I've noticed minor issues: late coming into work; field notes not scanned into the case management system in a timely manner; and the field op last week. What happened there? Can you explain?"

"Jamie, it's like I told Cam. I didn't mean to kick the table. In my frustration I aimed for a chair and missed. I didn't think in a million years a bag would bust open like that. I'm sorry. It won't happen again. Thankfully no one was adversely affected."

To her own ears the reasoning sounded beyond insufficient. Fentanyl was almost fifty times more powerful than heroin, and everyone else had acted cautiously that night because no one knew what the powder was. She, on the other hand, acted in a way no one, least of all her, would ever expect. No way Jamie was going to buy her bullshit. She wouldn't buy it if the roles were reversed.

"Missing the meeting on Saturday morning?"

Shit. "To be honest, I blanked. Forgot. Plain and simple. Admittedly, there're personal issues outside of work I've overlooked lately, too. I'm setting reminders for myself." Brutal honesty, the best tactic. "I take full responsibility for my blunders. No excuses. I apologize."

Pride swallowed. Not everyone had the courage to do that—admit their mistakes to their boss and go on to learn from them. "I apologized to Cam. I put everyone in a bad spot the other night. And missing the meeting—completely unacceptable. I swear to you, I'm going to do better."

"I hope so. I want to believe you, MC. You're one of the best inspectors we have. I hate seeing this decline you're on. I'm shocked by it, truth be told. I want your commitment that you'll pull your act together. You can prove yourself with these mailbox theft complaints. Dig in. Do what you do best. If you can't handle the job, you need to be truthful and let me know. Not me, actually—"

"I can handle the job. I *will* focus. You can count on me. Wait. What do you mean, not you?" Dread crushed her in a vise-like grip.

"That's something else I needed to tell you. Next Monday, Roland is returning to work. I know it's not the news you'd hoped for."

Not the news she'd hoped for was the understatement of the century." Nothing I can do except do my job. Anything else?" Her regular supervisor's return to work meant a definite escalation of shit rolling downhill aiming to bury her.

"I'll meet with him on Monday to give him the scoop on everyone's assignments. My best advice is to keep your nose to the grindstone. Do the job, like you've always done. Better than you've done lately. Remember, even though you're not assigned to my team, my door is always open."

"Thanks, Jamie. I appreciate the advice and support."

With the morning in the rearview mirror and a light lunch consumed, MC settled behind her desk. She focused on completing mundane tasks she'd stacked on the back burner, making triple sure she dotted all the i's and crossed all the t's. Now that she was on management's radar, she needed to be extra vigilant.

She'd let things slide and dug herself a hole. This morning's moment of clarity illuminated the situation. Either she devised a way to climb out of her hole or she risked losing her job. If that happened, it might be the end of her. Her mind required work like her body needed air to breathe.

She sorted and prioritized the new mail theft complaints. Then she opened a case on DigiCase, their illustrious case management tool, to complete the first report of possible mail theft from a home in Northeast Minneapolis. This one was different from the others in her stack, which were instances of mailbox fishing, a method of stealing mail from the postal service's blue collection boxes. She'd study the rest of the pile later, see if a trend popped.

MC's bandwidth narrowed as she plowed through the entry tasks, barely registering what she was doing. Her final task was to enter her time into DigiCase.

She needed a change of scenery. A focus outside of these four drab walls.

MC packed up and informed Chelsea, their office administrative assistant, she'd be away from the office for the last hour of the day. She was covering her bases in case anyone asked.

Not sure of her destination, she drove off. Her car may have been on auto pilot because MC landed in her old Highland Park neighborhood in St. Paul. She slowly cruised the block on which her old house was located.

She made another loop around the block, eyes peeled for clues. Perhaps she'd catch sight of the killer or killers sauntering from an alley." Hey, Inspector Clouseau. Let us help you—we did it. Arrest us."

This was life though, not a cartoon.

She rolled to a stop in front of her old house facing the wrong way on the street. Hank, her favorite ex-neighbor, was leaning out the door to retrieve mail from the black metal box attached to his house.

MC lowered the car window." Hi, Hank," she called out and waved.

He came outside the house peering toward the street. "MC? Is that you?"

"Guilty as charged." She cringed at her clichéd response.

"I thought I recognized the car. Do you want to come in for a visit? A cup of coffee?"

Hank knew coffee was the way to her heart. "Thanks, not today. Another time?"

"Come visit soon. Don't be a stranger."

"Will do. You get in the house before you freeze!"

He waved, his fist full of mail, and disappeared inside.

MC continued down the street, scanning the area for security cameras. Today presented her with enough time and daylight hours to look for cameras.

A tour of a six-block radius revealed exactly zero cameras.

Damn.

She wasn't surprised. The nearest camera, a city-operated traffic cam, appeared to be on Ford Parkway and Cretin Avenue. Not worth trying to obtain footage at this point. Image files from three months earlier would be long gone.

SPPD would've viewed footage from at least the hour prior to and the hour following the shooting. They'd try and decipher license plate details to run DMV checks on any vehicles passing within range. The effort would be as effective as looking for a snowflake in a snow pile.

Quitting time.

She pointed the Subaru in the direction of her favorite liquor store, which happened to be on the way to her apartment. Opaque bottles of Grey Goose neatly aligned on metal shelving were a vision beckoning to her.

Another day without results, but tomorrow would dawn brand new.

Chapter Four

MC felt slightly more motivated after her discussion with Jamie two days earlier. Another call from Minneapolis PD's Second Precinct and Jamie's words ringing in her ears prompted MC to put a blitz in play and give the mail theft complaints one thousand percent of her attention.

Her first task was to find the MPD officer who'd responded to the call of mail theft at the Northeast Minneapolis residence. A copy of his incident report might help.

Once she reached him by phone, the scant information and his "I've got more important things to worry about" attitude left her bristling with frustration. What the hell was wrong with the guy? Seemed like no one outside the Inspection Service took mail theft seriously. The thought kicked her into high gear.

At least he emailed her the incident report right away. She opened it in her inbox to peruse. The cop had gone to the house where the suspected mail theft had occurred, knocked, and no one responded. He completed a circuit around the house and found no indication of an attempted break-in. He wedged a business card in the front door with a notation to phone the precinct.

The report gave bare bones data about an interview with Hester Michaulik, the neighbor who'd called the police.

Irritation propelled MC from behind her desk to the mean streets of Northeast Minneapolis to interview the woman in person.

As she drove, she popped a trio of ibuprofen with a water chaser to dispel the nagging remnants of the day's hangover. Some things were still not under control.

MC located the house on Pierce Avenue. She reviewed her notes: Hester Michaulik matched the name on the report Jamie had given her two days ago at the team meeting. MPD had received a call from her over the previous weekend. She reported a suspicious man removing mail at the house of her neighbor across the street. The woman had called again yesterday, Wednesday, to report she'd seen the same guy pulling mail from the same neighbor's box.

MC tucked the Moleskine notebook and pen into the pocket of her navy peacoat. Cam's voice echoed in her head, making fun of her expensive notebook and pen obsession. She wished they were working together. But she'd lost Cam's trust after the previous week's snafu in the field. She'd show him, and everyone else, that she was back by digging in and solving this case.

The sunshine brought her unpleasantly to the present. Thousands of Barbie-doll-sized needles stabbed her eyeballs. Hopefully the pain reliever would kick in. Soon.

She approached the front door on a slightly sloping walkway, noticing the snow had been cleared down to the pavement, a direct contrast to the three-foot-high walls of snow on either side.

Before MC could knock, the door swung open revealing a stubby woman of solid proportions with a helmet of iron-gray hair. Was the woman psychic? Or had she seen MC approaching?

"Good morning, I'm Inspector McCall with the US Postal Inspection Service." She unbuttoned her coat and revealed her badge.

"Postal inspector, huh? About time someone took me seriously." The woman stood with one hand propping the storm door open. "Come in, can't afford to heat the outside."

MC entered and slipped the notebook and pen from her pocket. "Mrs. Michaulik?" She focused on the squat woman.

"Call me Hester. I certainly hope you'll take care of this—this situation." She waved an arm toward the front door. "The lack of police response the first time I called was maddening. When I seen it again—"

"Missus . . . er, Hester, I understand your frustration. Can you tell me what happened? I need an accurate account of the events."

Hester huffed and stomped to her perch, a chair covered in threadbare country-blue cloth material, next to a half-moon table with a worn wood top and sturdy wrought iron legs snugged beneath the picture window. A pair of binoculars and a cup with wisps of steam wafting from the top adorned said table.

The open living room led to a dining room. MC assumed the kitchen lay beyond that. The wood floors bore the signs of old age but were spick-and-span. A rectangular area rug in forest green with vines and flowers of various shades from tan to cocoa splayed across the middle of the room. A chunky round wood coffee table sat dead center on the rug. Not a speck of dust showed on the top.

The remainder of the room was furnished with a mission style sofa, a squat, square end table hunkered in the corner, and a glider rocker with matching footstool. A floor-to-ceiling built-in bookshelf took up the entire remaining wall. MC noticed an array of Agatha Christie and Sherlock Holmes titles crammed onto the shelves. *People* and *Entertainment Weekly* magazines were strewn across the coffee table.

MC did an internal eye roll. Good ol' Hester probably thought herself an amateur sleuth of sorts.

"Hester, would it be all right if I sat?"

"Of course. Sit. Sit." She swept a hand toward the sofa from her throne at the front window.

MC propped her notebook on a knee. "Thank you. Can you explain the situation the way you remember it?"

"On Saturday, this past Saturday, I was minding my own business sitting in this very spot reading the latest *People* magazine."

MC thought it highly unlikely Hester *ever* minded her own business.

Hester's voice gathered steam. "I noticed a man across the street digging in Shirley's mailbox. I'd never seen him before. I knew Shirley was out of town. Another neighbor told me last week."

"Shirley lives alone?"

"Yes, she's a widow, like me. In fact, our husbands both worked at the old Cream of Wheat factory many moons ago. Now it's condos or some sort. They convert anything into living spaces these days. I suppose you're one of those hipster types who likes that kind of thing."

"I'm not familiar with the factory. Let's focus on what you witnessed?

"Sure. Sure. Go ahead. Ask away."

"Did you notice the time? When you saw the man?"

Hester rested a finger on her chin, eyes aimed at the ceiling. "I'd have to say early afternoon. Maybe one-ish."

"Can you give me a description? Height? Hair color? Clothing? Any details you recall will be helpful."

"I remember him being tallish. Not Jolly Green Giant height, but definitely a towering fella. From the ground, he was easily able to open and reach inside the mailbox attached to her house."

"That's useful. What else?"

More ceiling gazing. "He wore a dark-colored jacket. Maybe leather? I can't be sure. Looked like he was wearing blue jeans."

"Any distinguishing features? Beard? Mustache?"

"No. Nothing. Oh, wait! Maybe a beard, like he hadn't shaved for a week or so. Not a Grizzly Adams full beard."

"Mustache?"

"That's part of the not shaving for a while, isn't it?" Hester sniffed in indignation.

"Yes."

"Don't you want to know the color of his hair? You asked earlier but didn't give me a chance to answer. I'd think hair color's important."

God, please give me strength, MC thought. Thus far the details matched the cop's report. MC paged through her notes. Wait. No mention of a beard in the incident report, so that's new info. "Hair color?"

"Brown hair. Long brown hair."

MC jotted the details on her notepad. "Long? How long?"

"His hair definitely touched the collar of his coat."

"You saw him at about one o'clock Saturday afternoon. Did you attempt to make contact? Ask what he was doing or if he knew your neighbor?"

"You're not serious? Why on earth would I go by myself to confront a criminal stealing my neighbor's mail? Especially when he looked menacing. You're not very smart if you think that." She crossed her arms, her gaze dared MC to argue the point.

MC chose not to take the bait. "Have you seen him any other time?"

"Yes. I saw him on Wednesday. Yesterday. I called the police to report it again."

"Same guy?"

"Yes."

"You're certain?"

"I may be old, but my eyesight is still good, Inspector. So, yes, I'm certain. Same guy took mail from Shirley's mailbox yesterday."

"Have you seen him today?"

"The mail hasn't come yet." She looked at a digital clock on the bookshelf. "I expect the mail to arrive any time now. Usually during the week it's delivered between ten in the morning and noon."

MC diligently recorded Hester's narrative, anxious to end the interview. She had a one-thirty appointment with Dr. Zaulk, her therapist, and she wasn't sure how much traffic she'd have to navigate at midday driving from Northeast Minneapolis to the Grand and Dale area of St. Paul. Traffic on I-94 was certain to be a slog.

"Okay, Hester one final question. Do you remember seeing a vehicle? Did you see the guy's car? Or did someone drop him off?"

"Seems that's more than one question."

MC bit her lip to keep from giving Hester a pie-sized piece of her mind.

Hester cast her gaze toward the ceiling, as MC was learning she was wont to do. After several seconds MC glanced upward, wondering what was so enthralling.

Finally Hester said, "I didn't see a vehicle. Maybe he parked by the garage? He came from the back of the house." She jabbed her finger in the air as if to say, "by golly that's it!"

"Perfect. I think that's everything I need for now. Have you spoken with your neighbor about your concerns?"

"No. I wouldn't have called the police if I'd been able to ask Shirley about the incident." Her tone was clipped. MC sensed Hester might be losing patience.

"True. Do you have Shirley's phone number?"

"Yes, her home phone, but like I said, she's not home."

MC finagled the number from the woman. "Do you know where she is? How long she'll be away?"

Hester crossed her arms. "No. She didn't tell me she was leaving. Maybe the man has kidnapped her. Has that idea occurred to the police? Or you?"

MC sneaked a quick peek at the library of murder mysteries crammed into Hester's bookcase. "Um, no. What makes you think that's a possibility?" Was Hester conflating her neighbor's absence with a plotline she'd read in one of her tattered paperbacks—Moriarty kidnapping Sherlock Holmes, for instance? "Didn't you say another neighbor told you Shirley was out of town?"

Maybe Hester and Shirley weren't friends, which would explain why she didn't have details of Shirley's whereabouts. Not to mention her overactive mystery-reading-fueled imagination.

Hester said, "But maybe Shirley isn't out of town. Something altogether nefarious may have happened and the other neighbor is covering for someone."

Quite the plot twist Hester'd invented. Why would a neighbor lie to Hester about Shirley being out of town? MC was ready to call it quits before Hester completely spiraled down the rabbit hole.

"Thank you for being a concerned neighbor and for talking with me this morning. We'll look into the situation and hopefully resolve it quickly."

"I certainly hope so! What if this man tries stealing another neighbor's mail? Or worse, mine? Lordy, we'd all be sitting ducks." She reached for the binoculars, snatched her hand back a nanosecond before clutching them, maybe sensing how it'd look with MC still in the house. Instead, Hester grasped the mug of tea, or whiskey-laced coffee or God knows what.

MC angled for the door. "I'll leave my card. If the man reappears or you recall important information, call me. Both my office and cell number are on there."

Hester accepted the card and followed MC to the door. "You'll be the first to know if I see or hear anything."

I'm sure I will, MC cringed at the thought. "Have a good day." She amscrayed to her car. She'd driven five blocks, mentally plotting the trip to St. Paul, when her cellphone rang. She glanced at the phone in the cup holder. A number she didn't recognize flashed.

MC pulled to the curb. "Hello."

"Inspector McCall?"

"Speaking. Who's this?"

"Hello, it's Hester Michaulik. You need to come! Now!" The woman screeched, a sound reminiscent of the flock in the movie, *The Birds*. "He's there!"

"Hester, relax. I'll be there soon." MC disconnected the call, whipped a U-turn, and headed back to Hester's. She parked in more or less the same spot she'd just vacated. Hester's head popped out her front door.

"Do you see him?" Hester pointed across the road to the house in question.

"Hester. Go inside and stay there." MC waited until Hester complied before crossing the street.

MC locked eyes with a man clutching an inch-thick stack of mail, sauntering down Shirley's walk toward the street. He stared at her. Probably he'd witnessed the whole interaction with Hester. The guy gave no indication of executing a cut-and-run, which she appreciated because she wasn't in the mood for a foot chase on the snow and ice.

He wore a brown sheepskin coat and jeans. MC noticed dark hair touching the furry collar of the coat and a close-cropped beard. Indeed, he was "tallish" like Hester had reported. Long-legged with an abbreviated thick upper body. Weightlifter?

MC flashed her badge. "Excuse me. I'm Inspector McCall with the US Postal Inspection Service. Do you live here?"

"No. Is there a problem?" He jutted his chin toward Hester's house. "Lady seemed upset."

Is there a problem? Seriously? Why would I be here asking this guy questions if there wasn't a problem? "Yes. There's been a report of possible mail theft." MC eyed the mail clamped in his fist. "If you don't live here, why are you removing mail from the mailbox?"

"Hey, I don't want any trouble with the law. I'm doing a favor for my aunt while she's on vacation."

"What's your aunt's name?"

"Shirley Birkelund. My name is Wayne Birkelund. My dad's Shirley's brother."

"Have some ID?"

He moved his left hand, the one not full of mail, toward his back pocket.

MC stiffened. "Easy. How about we move up to the house and you set the mail on the steps and unbutton the coat."

"What? Why?"

"To keep us both safe."

He complied. When MC was satisfied he didn't have a weapon, she allowed him to retrieve his wallet. Indeed, he was Wayne Birkelund. He shared with her that Shirley was on a bus trip to Branson, Missouri, along with his dad and some friends. They were due to return on Sunday.

No mail theft here, folks. Nothing to see. Move along. After letting Wayne get on with his day, she stopped by Hester's to clarify the situation for her.

Case solved. Elementary, my dear Watson. She mentally tipped an imaginary deerstalker cap in salute, satisfied with her sleuthing. Her brain had somehow melded those Sherlock Holmes books on Hester's shelf with her own investigating.

Back to the real world. She once again climbed into her vehicle and set off to keep her therapist appointment. She was in enough hot water with work, and the appointment was the thinnest thread keeping her tethered to life, professionally and personally.

Later, in the office, she'd share her solid investigatory diligence with Cam. Prove her veracity and hopefully make him feel a little better about her.

The positivity from her earlier encounter wore off during the drive to St. Paul. Drained by her meeting with Hester Michaulik and Shirley's nephew, MC climbed the stairs to Dr. Emily Zaulk's building. She wished she'd been able to sneak a quick shot of Goose at a nearby bar to re-energize herself.

How quickly the mighty fall.

Stop, she chided herself.

How could she even consider day drinking? She'd get busted and Crapper would fire her ass for sure.

MC had barely hung her coat before Dr. Zaulk entered the waiting area. The good doc was nicely dressed and wore Rachel Maddow glasses. Doc Z's eyes bore into the depths of MC's soul.

"MC, good afternoon." Dr. Zaulk stood aside and allowed MC to precede her to the session room.

MC appreciated the airy, inviting first floor office facing Grand Avenue. Giant windows were covered by sheers heavy enough to allow soft light to filter through, but not allow passersby to see inside. MC migrated to one of the two ivory-colored wingback chairs, her perch of choice on the "island," which is how she perceived the eight-by-ten-foot area rug. The remaining seating choices: a mission-style wood rocker; an armchair with golden corduroy cushions and wide sturdy arms; and a green beanbag hunkered along the edges of the area. Silent witnesses. MC had grown accustomed, though not exactly fond, of the weekly fifty-minute sessions. Sometimes the session seemed to last fifty years, other times fifty seconds.

Dr. Zaulk sat in the other wingback chair, notebook balanced on her lap, ready to delve into MC's psyche.

"How's the journaling? Are you finding it cathartic?"

MC mulled over the questions. Did she find release in writing? Possibly. The journal served two purposes: a story of love and loss, which drove her to drown her sorrows in the depths of a vodka bottle; and a crime diary, laying out facts and puzzle pieces. The goal: to flesh out clues that led to the assailant or assailants.

"I think I'm a different person lately. Judgmental. Impatient. Unfocused. Distant. Maybe numb is a better word. No one understands me.

This is not the type of person I am. I don't recognize myself. Maybe I'm lost? How do I find myself?"

Her questions caught her by surprise. Wow! Where'd all that come from? After months of weekly visits where she'd kept responses to a bare minimum, today she'd erupted, words like lava flowing from deep inside her. She gripped the arms of her chair to stay anchored, afraid she might float away on the sea of colors swirling beneath her feet. Maybe that wouldn't be so bad.

"Bereft," Dr. Zaulk said.

"Huh?" MC navigated her attention back to the therapist.

"You're bereft. Barb's death has left you feeling lonely—abandoned. And grief-stricken."

MC froze under Doc Z's scrutiny. The words drilled into her soul.

"What am I supposed to do with that?"

"You accept it. And we work on how to move past the trauma."

Multiple traumas. Doc Z knew about Barb. However, MC's parents and her older sister Cindy had been other deep losses she'd experienced, but hadn't revealed in a session—not yet. Cindy, a clear memory still after more than forty-five years. Her idol. That brilliant, scorching July Fourth at Minnehaha Falls was seared in her brain forever. Cindy skipping off with a group of kids—MC, at age four, too young to tag along. She'd sat pouting on the edge of a picnic bench. Soon the sound of traumatized kids screaming filled the stuffy air. Parents panicked. Next thing MC knew she'd been whisked away by a neighbor without explanation. She'd never seen her big sister again, and her parents, after the funeral, wouldn't talk about what happened.

MC hadn't learned the full story until almost six years later at age ten. A classmate, Teddy, whose older brother had been part of the big kids with Cindy and had witnessed her death, told MC that Cindy's head had busted open like a watermelon on the rocks beneath the falls. MC marched home and confronted her parents, who sat with her and narrated the story: Cindy had taken a dare from a boy to climb on the rail of the footbridge at the top of the falls. She'd lost her balance and fallen onto the rocks below. An accident. "Nothing to do but move on," her dad had said. And they never spoke of the incident again.

Some twenty years later, her parents were killed in a tragic car accident. Her entire family was gone.

Dr. Zaulk's voice broke into her reverie. "I think you need to abandon your avoidance and detachment tactics."

"What tactics do you mean?"

"For starters think about how you've pushed Meg and Dara away. You don't respond to calls or texts. Work is your excuse to be unavailable."

MC pondered the doc's words. All true.

Should she share the story of losing her family? She could cleanse her palate of loss by offloading how her sister Cindy had died. And how her parents had been killed. Or confirm the Grey Goose self-medicating? Not now. No way could she deal with all that. She ushered the memories into their respective compartments and flipped the deadbolt.

MC scuffed her foot against the carpet. "What I'm hearing you say is I should spend time with Dara and Meg instead of finding excuses to say no?"

"That's a good first step."

Thoughts hit her like a blitzkrieg, blasting MC's mind. Her friends were a constant reminder of the black hole in her life.

Her beloved Barb, her lifeblood, was dead.

She couldn't think about the actuality of Barb's physical death, so her mind went to solutions. Sharpe, the not-so-sharp cop in her opinion, refused to share any leads though. Her fixation on investigating Barb's case on her own fed an inner demon. Too much dark and dismal. Her ability to concentrate was blown to smithereens. She didn't even want to consider how she'd become unfocused, bordering on careless, at work.

"I had the dream, the nightmare, this past weekend." MC snapped out the words. Her vulnerability came out sideways. "The icing on the cake was my phone pinging with a Facebook notification."

"About what?"

She didn't want to talk about that. "I know for a fact I hadn't allowed notifications on the app."

Dr. Zaulk's normally placid expression changed to the tiniest of frowns. "Is it possible you forgot that you'd allowed notifications? Maybe you did it before Barb's death?"

What the hell? Was the good doc deaf? "No. I'm positive. The real punch to the ol' breadbasket was when I opened the app. A photo Barb posted last year, on Valentine's Day, stared at me. Frozen in time."

"A happy memory."

"Or someone is messing with me. Seriously, why can't you help me find a way to stop it from recurring—the dream, I mean?" She clamped her hands tightly together in her lap. "Hypnotize me. Electric shock.

Something. You've no idea how bone-crushingly painful it is reliving over and over how I couldn't save her. The dream is like a macabre mashup of *Friday the 13th* and *Groundhog Day.*"

"MC, I can't make the dream not happen. You didn't physically witness the event, but the depth of your trauma is bound to trigger nightmares and flashbacks. Your mind is trying to process and find a path toward healing."

"That doesn't help."

"I'd like for you to try meditation before going to sleep. Cut back on caffeine and alcohol. They can remain in your system for twelve hours or more and disrupt your sleep or ability to fall asleep. Yoga could also be helpful. Relaxation. Let's see if you see a difference in the frequency of the dream after employing these changes."

"I guess that makes sense." Not. Avoid alcohol and caffeine, which she pretty much mainlined daily? But what's the point in arguing with the doc? "What if the nightmare continues? Or happens more frequently?"

"If you have the dream more often, we can take a few weeks and focus on something called Imagery Rehearsal Treatment. Re-envision that nightmare into a dream with a positive outcome. Something for you to think about."

Great. More woo-woo work, MC thought.

"And I want you to focus on connecting more with Dara and Meg instead of avoiding them. Your survivor's guilt causes you to push them away when you need each other most. You've been coming to me for ten weeks, and I think it's time we dig deeper. Would you be ready for that?"

MC squirmed. "I guess."

"I know it isn't easy. You'll be operating outside your wheelhouse but trust me, evading Dara and Meg is costly to you and them. They've already lost Barb—" she lifted a hand, palm forward, to halt MC's rebuttal, "—hear me out. You've all lost Barb. Cutting them out means they lose you, too. And you lose them."

MC bit her tongue on the sarcastic diatribe about to spew forth and sucked in a cleansing breath. "Avoidance. Detachment. Classic symptoms of post-traumatic stress." MC parroted the doctor's words from an earlier session.

"I'm glad you remembered. That's progress." The corners of her mouth lifted in a slight smile. "What about eating? Getting to sleep? How's that going?"

The Goose helped her fall asleep. Vodka is made from wheat, that's a food, and fancy French spring water, which must be healthy.

"Sometimes I sleep. At times it's fits and starts—the damn dream interfering. In line with the old saying, some good days, some bad. Eating? If I remember, I eat, but I don't always have an appetite."

Dr. Zaulk sat quietly for a moment, then made some notes. She finished and looked up. "As I've said in the past, I think you'd benefit from attending a grief support group. Hearing others' experiences and what works for them might be the nudge you need if you'd just give it a try."

MC's internal eyeroll would've made the average human dizzy. Listen to strangers' stories of trauma? No way. Her own trauma filled her cup to overflowing. "Maybe I'll see if Dara and Meg want to do dinner." Nice, effective employ of the avoidance tactic on the communal therapy recommendation.

"I think that's a great idea. But I encourage you to consider the support group, too."

Not as effectively avoided as she thought. Damn. Was she going insane? Was it Einstein who said the definition of insanity was doing the same thing over and over and expecting the results to be different? Maybe it was some twelve-step program, Dara's favorite AA? Whatever. The truth was she was doing exactly that.

Dr. Zaulk glanced at her watch. "We're out of time. Think about what I said, and I'll see you next week."

On the drive to the office, MC considered the recommendation of a grief support group for roughly two blocks before she shelved it. Huddled masses sharing personal stories were so not her thing.

She focused her thoughts on what she'd write in her Investigative Memo, neatly shortened to IM by the forces in charge, for the mail theft case. With the first of the many cases cleared off her docket, maybe she could win some much-needed points with Jamie.

And then she'd find Cam and he'd resume his role of confidant, partner, and good buddy. They'd share a joke or two over Hester and her books. More importantly he'd see her making an effort to be her old reliable, engaged self, instead of asking him to cover her backside for some infraction or stupid oversight. She missed their friendship, but she missed their work relationship more.

Her phone chimed with an incoming text. When she braked for a red light, she checked her cell to find a message from Meg. *Dinner at the shop? 6ish? We miss u!*

An avalanche of guilt dropped on MC for not replying to Dara earlier. Doc Z's words rolled around in her head. She reluctantly dove in with both feet. *Sounds good! See you at 6!*

Fortified by two ounces of Grey Goose followed by a mouthwash rinse, MC decided it was time to traverse the half-mile from her apartment to Flannel. No sense in tempting the DUI gods.

She bundled into a new parka. The synthetic innards were supposed to keep her warm in temps down to thirty below zero. The current temp sat at a whopping goose egg but zero was better than that negative shit.

MC pushed through Flannel's door into a wall of warmth. The honey-colored wood floor and blond-bricked walls were like a welcome hug—like coming home. If she could only allow herself to feel it.

Dara's voice rumbled across the shop, "As I live and breathe! If it isn't the esteemed MC McCall."

"Hi, Dara." She shucked her coat.

Meg barged headlong out of the back. "Hi, hon."

MC bent to give Meg a squeeze. The stout woman gripped her so tight the breath whooshed out of her lungs. "Did you join a gym, Meg?"

"What?"

"That hug felt like someone ready to participate in a weightlifting competition. Or maybe you didn't want to let go for fear I'd run off."

Meg's gaze slid past MC and her face bleached of color.

Weird. MC was taken aback by Meg's change in demeanor. Before she uttered a word, Dara joined them.

"Group hug." She draped her arms around MC and Meg. "Yo, buddy, those rosy cheeks from the cold air?"

With Meg's paleness and sudden silence overridden, MC threw a scowl Dara's way. "I walked here. So, yeah."

Dara waved both hands. "Just asking."

The threesome stood huddled for several seconds before a baritone voice interrupted. "Anyone want a beverage?"

"Oh! MC, come meet Zane." Meg's face pinked and she dragged MC by the hand to the counter. "Zane, this is our dear friend, MC McCall."

Dara joined Zane behind the counter. “She has a super important job. Postal inspector. You don’t want to mess with the US Mail. That’s some serious shit. Before you know it, Inspector McCall has you in a closet with a bare bulb hanging from the ceiling, sweating the answers outta you.”

Zane stood rooted to the spot, mouth agape, eyes wide behind a pair of Buddy Holly-esque eyeglasses and diamond or zirconia stud earrings glittering in each earlobe.

MC reached over to shake his hand. “Funny, Dara. Please, don’t listen to a word she says, Zane. The only person I’d haul into an interrogation room and grill under hot lights would be her. Nice to meet you.”

He gripped MC’s hand firmly. “Ah, okay. Good to meet you.”

Dara slid a mug of coffee across the counter toward MC. “Our newest barista’s first solo brew.”

MC eyed Zane across the top of the cup before sipping. His sandy brown skin was smooth with the faintest dusting of dark stubble on his chin matching the color of his short afro. He was wide-hipped and about half a foot taller than Meg’s five-foot-three-inch height. A neat white t-shirt under a pale blue Oxford button down, untucked, over faded jeans indicated a basic, clean-cut, midwestern college student.

MC took a cautious sip. “Excellent job on the brew. How do you like working at Flannel?”

“Thanks. This is only my second night, but I love the vibe. The customers have been patient with me while I learn the ropes.”

“He’s a godsend.” Meg gave him a thump on the shoulder. “Kate recommended him and we’re so pleased.”

Zane gave a wide smile revealing a perfectly aligned set of pearly whites. “Aw, go on. You’re too nice.”

The door opened and a guy clomped in toting a red insulated food delivery container. “Pizza for . . .” he scanned a strip of paper in his gloved hand, “Dara Hodges?”

Dara bounded from behind the counter. “That’s me.” She accepted two gargantuan cardboard boxes from the guy and slapped a tip into his palm.

“Thanks! Enjoy your pizza.” With a wave he clomped back out into the cold.

Dara plopped the boxes on the table. “Dinner’s served!”

Meg brought plates and utensils from the kitchen and MC wrested a stack of paper napkins from the condiment stand and paused to dribble some cream into her coffee. "We have enough food to feed the entire city."

"Zane, join us," Meg said. "Have some pizza. If someone comes in, you can pop behind the counter quick."

After everyone had a bellyful of pizza and the leftovers were stored in the fridge, Meg and MC watched Dara and Zane wait on a sudden rush of customers.

Meg asked, "How are you doing? Honest answer."

MC checked surreptitiously to make sure Dara wasn't in earshot. "I'm surviving. Most days I arrive at work on time. Some days I can concentrate. Other days not so much."

"We're here for you. Please don't push us away. We've missed you. And we miss her, she was part of us, too." Tears pooled in Meg's eyes.

MC gave her hand a quick squeeze. "I know. Thank you for being patient and persistent with me." She felt devastated by the idea that her friends encouraged her to rely on them to keep her tethered to reality. She needed to learn to stand on her own, except for her ever-present helper, Grey Goose.

The rush finally fizzled, and Dara left Zane to handle the last customer in line to rejoin MC and Meg. "Hey, buddy. Have you considered going to an AA meeting with me?"

Meg cringed.

Dara seemed oblivious to her partner's reaction. In her gruff way she forged ahead. "I think you'd be amazed at how helpful meetings are."

"I don't need an AA meeting." MC stood. "You couldn't let it go for *one* evening. Just one frickin' evening?" She shook her head, rage bubbling to a quick boil and bit her lip to prevent further confrontation, especially with customers scattered around the shop.

Zane's head had swiveled in their direction at the increased volume of the conversation.

Dara said, "I'm sorry. You're right. C'mon, don't leave angry. Stay. Let's talk some more. We have some news to share."

MC's fuse had been lit. She kept her cool. But she needed a stiff nightcap, not more discussion about a damn AA meeting. She wrenched her coat off the chair. "Thanks for dinner. I'm beat and I have an early start in the morning. Think I'll head home."

Meg grasped for MC's hand. "We love you. Please let us know what we can do to help."

"I agree with Meg." Dara said quietly. "We're trying to be supportive. But we really need to talk to you. Please don't be mad at me about—"

"I'm not angry, Dara. Forget it. Thank you both for dinner." She waved at Zane. "Nice to meet you."

"Thanks, nice to meet you, too. Have a good night."

Dara rounded the table and approached her. "C'mon, MC. Don't leave. Sit. Please. We have to talk."

MC absorbed the pleading tone, the serious set of Dara's face, but she couldn't extinguish the anger. Pain overrode her circuits.

With one last quick embrace from Meg, MC bolted and practically jogged the six blocks home to her apartment. Home to the Goose. To reward herself for making it to and surviving dinner with her friends, she added a fresh slice of lime to the clear liquid.

A definite crevice had opened in her life, separating her from friends and coworkers. No one understood the depth of the abyss she'd fallen into. She didn't possess the language to open a dialogue—to let anyone in on the absolute grief, the verifiable guilt.

She drank to fill the chasm.

One drink to quiet her . . . irritation?

A second to numb her.

The third made her question herself. Her life.

A teeny bit of curiosity was piqued by her friends' plea. What had they wanted to talk about? MC was too bleary to care.

Dara clenched a bottle of disinfectant cleaner and a towel. She attacked the tables in the shop.

Meg patted her on the shoulder when she passed by with the broom. "Go easy on those poor tables. They didn't do anything wrong."

Dara leaned both hands on the tabletop and pushed the towel, a limp white terrycloth pile, off to one side. "She makes me so damn mad. MC is drinking significantly more than is good for her. I'm trying to save her from making the same mistake I made years ago. She didn't even give us a chance to tell her about your diagnosis."

"I understand. Truth be told, I think MC does understand. We have to bide our time, until she's ready to face her demons. The onus is on her to quit, to seek help. No one else can make that decision. And if you don't kibosh the AA comments, you're going to push her completely away. Her demons are controlling her."

"What about our demons, *your* demon? We have to tell her what the doc told us." Dara faltered and slid onto a chair.

"All in good time. When the appointment is scheduled for the lumpectomy, we can try again. Be patient and gently persistent. But stop bringing up AA meetings."

Meg's calm tone somewhat eased Dara's anxiety. "I'll try. I know she doesn't have Barb here to kick her ass, like you did me when I thought I had all the answers."

"And who'd guide me over this bump in the road, if not you? We have each other. I'm thankful every day for you and our life. MC will come around. I believe in her. We need to give her some space. Work with her."

Dara sighed. Banging and clanging rang out from the kitchen. She assumed Zane was elbows deep into washing dishes. She moved on to the next table, spritzed the top and scrubbed until the blond wood gleamed. "What are we supposed to do? Leave her to battle the bottle alone?" Not let her know how selfish she's being, Dara thought. Meg might be dying, and she was worried about not pressuring MC? Life sucked.

"Unfortunately, I don't think we have much choice." Meg swept a pile of sandy grit into the dustpan.

"Dammit, Meg, I don't accept that. I can't stand around and wait for her to hit rock bottom." Or to possibly lose you, to know the pain of the worst possible loss, she thought.

"If you push too hard, you may drive a wedge into the friendship you won't ever be able to pull free. Are you ready to cross the bridge of no return? Possibly lose MC forever?"

Dara threw herself into a chair again. "Of course I don't want to lose her forever. What's worse? Standing on the sidelines watching her self-destruct while we fight our battles? Or nudging her toward the faint light at the end of the tunnel?"

"You're not exactly nudging. It's a tough call to make."

"WWBD?"

Meg emptied the dustpan into the garbage. She stood, empty dustpan in one hand, broom in the other, facing Dara. "What on earth are you mumbling?"

"WWBD—what would Barb do?"

"If Barb were still alive, this conversation would be moot. I'm going to check on Zane while you finish with the tables. Don't forget the countertop." Meg shuffled away.

Dara called after her, "I can't let it go. I'm not a true friend if I don't push her to recognize how destructive her behavior is, how she's killing herself. Dammit, cancer might be killing *you!*"

Meg disappeared into the back without another word.

A great gust of wind walloped the front windows, rattling them in their frames. Dara gazed out the front of the shop. A swirl of ice pellets scraped the storefront and skittered into the night.

A sign from Barb? Dara shook her head to clear the cobwebs. "No worries. I won't quit on her. You can count on me."

Meg and Zane came out of the kitchen carrying trays of clean mugs. Meg said, "Count on you for what?"

"Um, nothing. Count on me to clean these tables and dump the trash."

"I like MC," Zane said. "Strong but wounded. I've seen folks like her at my meetings."

Dara said, "Meetings?"

"AA." He repositioned a tray of mugs on the counter.

Dara was impressed with the ease with which he shared this bit of himself. A true dedicated recoveree. "Me, too. More than twenty years sober."

"Impressive. Two and a half for me."

If Dara had her way, MC was going to join their ranks. MC may hate her for a while, but eventually, hopefully, they'd travel this space-time continuum together and be solid for Meg.

Meg needed her self-made family now more than ever. Meg wouldn't impose her problems on MC. That wasn't in her DNA. Still, it was vital MC hear the news, sooner rather than later. Dara knew MC wouldn't forgive herself if something happened to Meg, and she hadn't stepped up. Another layer of guilt would crush MC. The result? A double dose of guilt from which Dara was certain MC would not recover.

The ice pellets had segued to a dry snow falling in great gusts in the wintry night. Dara watched the flakes and hoped MC had made it home safely.

Chapter Five

"Person looked like they were trying to land a humongous fish. Except we weren't on no lake. They seemed pretty nimble. Quick. Yanked the line, netted a tangle of envelopes."

"So you're saying this guy used a device on a string to pull mail from the blue collection box?"

"Exactly, ma'am. You took the words right out of my mouth. He dropped this great big giant lure down in there and took the mail right outta the box."

MC listened to the elderly man on the phone and scribbled notes. She didn't mention that what he saw was actually called mailbox fishing, but obviously he already got it. "Mister Farrington, what time did this happen?"

"Was 'bout six o'clock last Wednesday morning. Not light yet."

"You were trekking alone? In the middle of February?"

"Of course. Inspector, I embark on my daily constitutional the same darn time every day no matter the weather. It's my routine."

"Alone?"

"Yep. Alone. My wife passed some twelve years ago."

Lonely hearts club. Little did he know that she was a member of that club, too.

Focus.

"Can you give me a description of this person?" Fingers crossed the old guy had decent eyesight.

"I was about half a block away, maybe a bit closer. He, or she, was average height."

MC thought about the height of the collection containers. Taking into consideration they were usually bolted onto cement slabs three inches above ground, and the boxes measured forty-nine inches at their highest point, it was a fair estimation that total height was around fifty-two inches, almost four-and-a-half feet.

"Envision the top of the box in comparison to the person. Was the top shoulder height? Chest height?"

"Hmmm, good question. When the person, ah, he, she? I can't say for sure if it was a man or a woman. I should've tried to get a closer look. In any case when he stooped over, his head was level with where you drop the mail in."

"We can go with 'they' for the purposes of the report. So, how about when they stood upright?"

"I want to say it was below their chest. Not sure. Wait! In fact, I saw them lean an elbow on the top easily."

So the person Clancy Farrington saw was pushing six feet tall—or more. A start.

"Good. Now, what about the clothes?

"Dark clothes. Black, maybe dark gray or dark blue. Hard to say for sure. Definitely dark. They had a hood over their head, hair completely covered. Oh, and the hood was from a jacket under the winter jacket. Do you know what I mean?"

"A hoodie? Like a hooded sweatshirt under the outside jacket?"

"Yes. Exactly. Seems to be the style these days . . ."

MC glanced at the clock, watched the secondhand tick-tick-tick while listening to the guy ramble on about today's fashion, or lack thereof.

"Mister Farrington—"

"Please, call me Clancy. Everyone does. No need to be formal."

"Clancy, what else can you tell me? Was the person alone?"

"Appeared to be. I didn't see no one else around. Except for me." He laughed.

A knee-slapper. Not. "What about a vehicle?"

"Nope. This was a quiet neighborhood corner, not on a busy street. Like I said, it was early morning. Not a single car drove past. And the person didn't drive off."

"What happened after you saw them pull the mail from the box?"

"No boots!"

"Wait? What?"

"Sorry. I remembered they weren't wearing boots. Winter boots? It was colder than a witch's—"

"Okay. No boots." She could do without hearing an old geezer say tit. "What type of shoes was the person wearing?"

"Let me think. Dang. I can't remember. Other than I know they weren't boots. I thought to myself, 'their feet must be freezing with no boots on.'"

"So, no boots. And what happened after the mail was snagged?"

"He—she—they jammed the clump of mail into a plastic bag. The kind you get at the grocery or Targets or the gas station?"

"Target, you mean?"

"That's what I said—Targets."

MC shook her head. Maybe it was a generational thing. He wasn't the first person of a certain age who added an 's' to the popular discount store name. "Mail went in the bag. What next?"

"They must've heard the squeak my boots made on the packed snow because they looked smack dab at me and twisted quick to hide the bag. They took off, slipping and sliding along the street away from me."

"Did you see where they went?"

"Headed west on Fifth Street is all I know. I walked south on Twenty-Fourth Avenue, and when I arrived on the corner there was no one around. Not a soul in sight."

MC thought the guy might've ducked into a house or into a getaway car parked on a different street. Could've gone anywhere. She had hoped for a more solid lead. Alas, it wasn't to be.

"Mister Farr—ah, Clancy, is there anything else you remember?"

"I think I told you everything. You're going to find this guy, aren't you?"

MC took a calming breath. "I'll do my best. If you think of anything else that might be helpful, please call me at my direct number." She rattled off the ten digits.

"Will do."

"Thank you. Have a good day."

MC hung up and considered the number of complaints her office was starting to take about mailbox fishing. After several years of occasional incidents, lately the numbers had escalated. Criminals had figured out how to steal checks and other data from the mail deposits, and the fraud could end up in the hundreds of thousands of dollars. Great. Yet another thing she would need to add to her list of topics for post office training sessions, especially for carriers and those doing the mailbox collections.

She flipped a page in her notebook, reviewed the notes. She'd almost failed to reel in Mr. Farrington when he waxed nostalgic about the great mail system from "the old days, back when people didn't think it was okay to take what didn't belong to them." He'd gone on and on, and the challenge of keeping him on track in the interview had resuscitated the low-level thrum inside her skull.

Absolutely not related to the three or four glasses of Goose she'd imbibed last night after dinner at Flannel.

Dara's words about an AA meeting rang in her ears. To add insult to injury, she'd voiced her opinion within earshot of Zane. Great first impression.

Dammit.

What had Dara said? The night was a bit fuzzy. She had a nagging feeling she'd missed something, and maybe she ought to touch base with them, but at the moment she couldn't handle a conversation with Dara.

MC retrieved the always-present bottle of ibuprofen from her desk drawer and chased three capsules with the remnants of her now-cold coffee.

Thusly fortified, and with plenty of time before lunch, she reviewed the report about another customer mail theft incident.

She looked over the notes from the caller. Was this the same blue collection box from which Mr. Farrington had witnessed a mail snatch? A quick cross-check of her notes showed this wasn't the same container. MC accessed Google Maps and determined both sites fell within the boundaries of NE Minneapolis though.

A pattern?

MC checked the caller's name, one Rachel Wu. She dialed the numbers off the report sheet, and someone picked up after three rings. "May I speak to Ms. Wu?"

"That's me."

"I'm US Postal Inspector MC McCall. I'm calling regarding the incident of possible mail theft you reported."

"Yes. Thanks for calling me back."

"Ms. Wu—"

"Please, call me Rachel."

"Rachel, can you explain what happened?"

"Sure. Today's what, Friday? What happened was a week ago Wednesday I dropped some mail in a blue mailbox on Central Avenue, the one by the Organic Foods Co-Op. Normally I'd use the one on Thirteenth Ave and Third Street, by my work."

More details than MC needed. She scribbled down the pertinent ones.

Rachel continued, "When I stopped to buy eggs at the co-op, I remembered some envelopes to mail that I'd left in my backpack. Figured I was lucky 'cuz there was a collection box near the co-op's driveway exit. Yesterday my landlord called, said my rent, which was due on the fifteenth, was late. I know I dropped the envelope in the mailbox on the eleventh. Normally he gets the check two or three days after I mail it. I called the bank. They confirmed the check and another I'd written to Xcel Energy, also dated the eleventh, hadn't cleared yet. That's nearly ten days."

MC said, "I'd recommend initiating stop payments on both checks if they haven't cleared your bank by Monday."

"I already did the stop payments, which cost me a chunk of change in fees. But I didn't want to wait any longer. To avoid late charges, I went to Xcel in person to pay and dropped a check at my landlord's. The mail is reliable, in my experience, so I thought it best to report the situation."

"That's exactly the correct thing to do. To confirm, which collection box did you deposit the mail into?"

"The one on Central Avenue outside the Organic Foods Co-op. I already told you that." A huff of air crackled in MC's ear.

"You did, but I need to verify I have the exact location for my report."

Rachel paused for a few seconds. "Now that I think about it, I put the mail into the box late on the night of February tenth. I'd say around eleven. The co-op closes at eleven and they locked the door behind me when I left."

"I see." MC slashed the eleventh, wrote in the tenth. "In the future, you might want to check the schedule posted on the box. It's best to drop your mail in close to the collection time. Another option, drop your mail inside the local post office."

"That's great advice. But shouldn't we be able to trust our mail is safe inside the blue mailboxes? I mean, I'd think a government agency like the postal service would be able to ensure customers' mail is safe. Due to my hours, I can't drop the mail before the collection time. Sounds like you're placing the burden of responsibility on the customer, which isn't fair. What's the government doing with all our tax dollars?"

MC counted to ten. "Ms. Wu—Rachel—your tax dollars don't have any bearing on the postal service. Sales of stamps and other products are what fund the post office, not taxpayer money. I didn't mean to imply it was your fault the mail was stolen." MC massaged her temple with one hand. Good grief, how much longer before the damned pain reliever kicked in? "All I'm doing is providing guidance—options for you. We'll perform due diligence to investigate the missing mail. And I assure you, we'll do everything in our power to prevent it from recurring."

"I apologize, but it's so frustrating, not to mention inconvenient. Like I said, my schedule doesn't always allow for me to access the post office or arrive at the mailbox before the collection time. Isn't there something else you can do to make sure that mail drop is secure?"

"As I said, we'll conduct a thorough investigation and examine the box as well. The post office is gradually phasing in a new style of container that should prevent this type of theft. Your collection site probably has not received the updated box. Do you recall any other details? Was anyone hanging around when you dropped your mail in the box? Or maybe you noticed a vehicle in the vicinity?"

"Nothing that I remember. It was late, after my shift at The Anchor Fish and Chips. I waitress there four evenings a week."

"You said around eleven p.m., correct?"

"Yes. We're done at nine thirty, then we spend about an hour cleaning and doing prep for the next day. Then I hotfooted it to the grocery before they closed. I can't say a specific time, but around eleven."

"You saw no one else on the street? No one sitting in a parked car?"

"Nope. Kind of spooky quiet, if that makes sense. Central is a busy street normally. I guess late at night in the middle of the week . . ."

MC pictured the woman shrugging.

"If you remember anything else or have any questions, please call me." MC provided her office phone number and spelled her name for the woman. "And I may need to contact you again during the investigation."

"That's fine. I don't suppose I'll be reimbursed for the two thirty-five-dollar stop payment fees my bank charged me?"

"That issue is between you and your bank. The postal service cannot reimburse you for those fees. I'm sorry."

"Figures."

"If there isn't anything else, I'll let you go. Thank you, Ms. Wu."

"Thanks, for nothing."

The line went dead.

She completed an incident case report and had enough time to enter into DigiCase a summary of the phone conversations she'd had.

After lunch, her calendar showed two afternoon appointments at city station post offices. She was scheduled to speak to employees about safety and security on the street. MC made a note to mention the recent collection box issues and to request carriers' vigilance, especially those assigned to routes on which collection boxes were located.

MC tossed her messenger bag onto the passenger seat of the car and dropped behind the wheel. Her eyelids drooped and she stifled a yawn. Her second meeting, which was at Quarry Station, had gone past the hour allotted. Evening rush hour to St. Paul from Northeast Minneapolis promised to be a mess.

She made up her mind to stop for some LeeAnn Chin takeout at a sleepy strip mall, even though it'd probably be cold by the time she made it home. That's what microwaves were for.

MC twisted the key in the ignition at the same time her cell phone buzzed. She grabbed for her phone and damn near dropped it in the process.

"Detective Sharpe?" Her fingers and palms dampened.

"Inspector McCall, hello."

"Is there news?" The words spilled from her mouth and the phone almost slipped again. MC smashed it against her ear.

"No updates. You called earlier in the week. I wanted to touch base because you'd left a message."

More like five messages. She'd called every day. She'd formed a habit, maybe a bad habit, of calling every weekday since that horrendous day in November. Black Friday.

"No new intelligence?" Keep calm. Breathe. "Please, detective, spare me the 'I can't discuss an ongoing investigation' bullshit." MC squeezed the phone tighter. She wasn't afraid of dropping it now as her anger built to full-on volcanic eruption level.

Control. She needed to maintain control.

"I know this is frustrating for you, Inspector. We're . . . I'm . . . exasperated myself. We have no solid leads."

"What about the traffic camera on Ford Parkway? Did you check footage from that day?"

"Rest assured I'm covering all the bases, Inspector McCall."

Great non-answer. MC swore her phone groaned under her grip. "What about city cameras? Anything? Have you found any private security cameras? It's a residential neighborhood, maybe someone has a camera on their house or garage."

“I’m exploring every possible lead, even if it seems like a long shot.”

This guy achieved GOAT status for avoiding direct answers.

“I believe you. It’s—I could help.” She’d blanked on looking for security cameras on neighbors’ homes in all her solo investigating since Barb’s death. Her focus on traffic or city-owned cameras had blinded her to the obvious. Why hadn’t she thought of the idea months ago? She did a mental head slap.

“Please don’t. Remember what I said about putting yourself in danger. I don’t want to have to worry about you. Let’s both do our jobs. Okay?”

Why don’t you do your fucking job, she wanted to scream into the phone, but she kept her voice even. “Thanks for the update, Detective.” Another big fat nothing burger.

“Take care. I’ll be in touch.”

MC slid the phone into the cup holder. She closed her eyes, leaning into the seat’s headrest. She tried to calm herself. Maybe she’d download one of those new mindfulness apps. Help her relax and achieve a better headspace. Or not.

Determined to find some clue she’d missed, she did another perusal of the green notebook. Food forgotten, she reversed from the parking slot with the call of the Goose, and not the winged type, echoing in her ears.

The image of the milky-colored bottle summoned her home.

MC revisited her old neighborhood again.

Around midday on this sunny, albeit cold, Saturday, MC cruised the block around the house she’d shared with Barb. Today was her eight-hundredth recon mission since Barb died, and her singular focus was to scope the area for security cameras on neighbors’ houses and garages.

MC slowly motored along the ice-rutted alley behind the old house. She noticed what looked like a camera tucked under the eaves of a home two houses over and across the alley from where she’d lived.

The yard was surrounded by a six-foot-high treated-wood privacy fence. The structure blocked her view. In a split-second decision, she reversed and parked in Hank’s driveway, then cautiously traversed the icy landscape of the alleyway on foot.

Hope propelled her forward.

She jiggled the latch on the outer gate of the house in question. A booming bark split the morning silence. She flailed backward, regaining her balance a nanosecond before falling on her rear. Heart pounding, she peered through a crack between two slats and saw a dog reminiscent of Cujo pacing in the snow. The animal spotted her and went ballistic. Spittle and foam flew. Great gusts of cloudy vapor rose from its snout.

MC backtracked to her car. She drove to the street-side and knocked on the front door. No one answered.

Who leaves their dog outside in below-freezing weather? And where the hell did it come from? She didn't recall ever seeing or hearing that monster when she and Barb lived nearby.

She gave the door one more thorough pounding. Still no answer other than the giant-ass canine bellowing in the backyard.

MC traipsed into a neighboring snow-covered yard. She spotted a side gate and a glimpse of the house. She eyed a toilet-paper-roll-sized grayish camera mounted next to the security light above and to the right of the back door.

Cujo either heard her or smelled her and was now at that side gate. A cacophony of deafening snarls echoed from behind the fence. She fully expected neighbors to come running to see what the hell was happening, but either folks weren't home or were used to this animal's psychotic performances. Afraid to turn around for fear the Stephen King-esque scenario would continue via an encounter with a wild-eyed rabid cat from *Pet Sematary,* she slowly pivoted. A sigh of relief escaped her lips when the coast remained clear of any supernatural appearances. She retraced her route.

Safe from any canine or feline misadventure, she climbed behind the wheel of her car. With the heat cranked to inferno-level, MC snared her green "Life After Barb" notebook off the passenger seat and a pen from the cup holder. She recorded the address and details about the camera. Perhaps one evening after work she'd stop to chat with the homeowners.

She pondered the possibility that Sharpe knew about the camera. MC opted to keep the intelligence under wraps until after she spoke with the homeowners. Best case scenario, they stored their recordings to the cloud and hadn't deleted any files. Worst case, the people hadn't lived here in November and the previous owners hadn't had a security camera. Either way, she planned to try and find the answer.

No other clues jumped at her. No killer ran to the car, arms flailing while screaming, "I killed her! It was me."

Despite this possible new discovery, she remained a hollow vessel. Helpless. Or as Doc Z had eloquently phrased it—bereft.

For a brief moment she considered hashing over the situation with her friends. The memory of how their dinner together had ended the other night muted her. Best to leave sleeping dogs lie.

Instead, she stopped at the grocery store for food and the liquor store to replenish her vodka supply. She purposely ignored Dara's voice in her head expressing disapproval.

In an effort to solidify her promise to be more focused on the job, MC spent the semi-sober moments of the weekend researching and creating a PowerPoint presentation on mailbox fishing. She'd use the slideshow at meetings with customer service managers from the city stations over the coming week.

Chapter Six

Monday doldrums battered MC's brain. She'd managed to arrive at work on time, barely, with coffee she'd brewed at home, thus avoiding an early morning encounter with Dara. Bonus points. She'd achieved her goal to be at her desk before Crapper arrived.

The first two hours, she tallied four more mailbox fishing incidents. Using a street map, she determined the bulk of the thefts had occurred at collection boxes in NE Minneapolis. One incident across the river into North Minneapolis, another in the middle of the University of Minnesota West Bank campus. Six fishing scams but MC discerned no pattern. Each theft appeared to be a one-off as none of the boxes had been hit more than once.

She jammed the notes into her messenger bag and gathered her laptop and paraphernalia. Two meetings were on her calendar. First, the weekly meeting at the downtown Minneapolis Main Post Office with all the Managers, Customer Service from Minneapolis City Stations. And immediately afterward, she had a meeting at the Bluffside Station in East St. Paul, where the manager had requested she speak to employees and supervisors about safety and security when delivering mail. She fully intended to be on the road before Crapper summoned her to his lair.

MC rolled into the parking ramp next to the block-long downtown Minneapolis Main Post Office. She badged into the building feeling slightly victorious for having escaped the office without any sign of her boss. She'd requested a time slot at the weekly meeting of the managers from the twenty Minneapolis city stations in order to bring awareness about the recent uptick of mailbox fishing crimes.

The murky residue from the weekend clung to her like a fog over a swamp, but she pushed it aside. In the conference room, she plugged in her laptop and dug in an inside pocket of her messenger bag for the thumb drive containing the PowerPoint presentation. Her energy level mirrored a sedated sloth. She was desperate for a strong java infusion but had to settle for a Styrofoam cup of shitty coffee. Budget must be tight if they can't afford better coffee.

MC greeted the three Managers, Customer Service Operations. The hierarchy for the delivery and customer service operations began with the top dog, the Minneapolis Postmaster. Next in line were the MCSOs who were responsible for overseeing a group of six or more city post offices each, followed by the Managers, Customer Service, one at each city station. The workhorse of the management chain, the Supervisor, Customer Service did not attend the manager meetings.

The hands of the clock nudged toward ten as she nodded to a few managers she recognized.

She'd spoken at many of these meetings over the years, so she stood and eased into the routine. "Good morning. For those who don't know me, I'm Inspector MC McCall. I'm here today to talk about recent reports of mail theft in the city. We've had reports from customers who've mailed bills with checks enclosed and those payments never made it to the companies. The assumption is many more items didn't make their destinations but haven't been reported."

MC projected the slide show she'd worked up on a white vinyl screen and faced the audience. "We've got an uptick in the old-fashioned steal-the-mail fishing trick."

Someone raised their hand. "Are you saying we're too focused on electronic phishing? Maybe bad guys figured they'd have an easier time going after the physical mail while our attention was on digital theft?"

"That may have some impact. But not much. Some people, especially the aging population, tend not to trust electronic or online payment processes. They fear their accounts being hacked, their money stolen."

A woman in the back of the room said, "I don't understand why we're making such a production over the sporadic stealing of a few pieces of mail. Cybercrime's a bigger threat to the postal service and customers."

MC had anticipated the possibility of this type of pushback. "Customers drop checks, money orders, gift cards, and more into collection boxes. The bad guys know this. Tens—possibly hundreds—of thousands of dollars are swiped across the country every single day."

She felt affectless and tried to drum up an enthusiastic tone. She surveyed the twenty or so people in the room. Several were engrossed with their phones instead of paying attention. A manager's job was so hyper-focused on the day-to-day operation of their city post office and all the budgetary constraints that she could easily understand their lack of attention to the increase in mail theft. The group required more inspiration, better motivation. These folks needed to be wrangled like calves at a rodeo. Their buy-in was imperative to successful future crime prevention.

"Okay, everyone, listen up. This may seem like small potatoes. It's not. This low-tech method of stealing mail requires hardly any equipment. No computers. Tools of the trade are simple. Now, I'm going to share some video clips from New York and New Jersey that depict the gear inspectors found when they apprehended mailbox fishers."

She clicked the play button and a video streamed on the screen. An inspector held a string attached to an empty clear plastic water bottle and explained that the container was covered in some type of sticky substance, maybe glue.

MC paused the segment. "The fishers drop this goo-covered bottle called 'the bait' into the collection box, swish it around, and pull up whatever sticks. They retrieve their bounty, rinse, and repeat until they've captured all they can carry or they're interrupted. The thieves hotfoot it to a safe space and tear through the haul, hunting for checks, credit cards, and cash. Here's another example."

She hit play to show a second video where the thief used a sticky, rectangular-shaped piece of cardboard attached to twine.

MC took a sip of the now-cold shitty coffee and scanned her audience, most of whom were raptly watching.

The video ended and all eyes turned to MC.

"That second clip showed a basic sticky trap for catching mice. The tool was slightly different, but functionality's the same. You can see why the devices are labeled fishers."

MC watched their heads bobbing affirmatively. Way better than nodding off.

"All of these items can be purchased virtually anywhere, grocery stores, hardware stores, gas stations. The materials are uncomplicated and inexpensive—not to mention easy for the bad guys to get hold of. You can get glue and twine for two bucks at any dollar store and grab a plastic bottle out of any recycling bin."

A murmur filled the room along with some underlying grumbling.

One of the three MCSOs, Leah, raised her hand. Her male compadres sat on either side of her apparently willing to let her guide the ship. "Quiet, folks."

The fidgeting ceased. A lull in sidebar conversations followed.

"What advice does the Inspection Service have for postal employees, especially carriers, to help combat this outbreak?"

God bless Leah. She and MC had always had a great rapport, and Leah wasn't shy about wrangling attendees who attempt to go rogue at these meetings.

"Great question. We need to devise ways to harden our targets until the postal service can afford to retrofit all collection boxes across the country with security enhancements. In the meantime, we must ratchet up security of the mailboxes by asking for carriers' vigilance while out delivering the mail. But—we want to ensure they remain safe in the process. They shouldn't confront anyone seen tampering with a collection box. Note what the person looks like, what they're driving. If they can snap a photo on their phone and grab a license plate number, even better. Then they should call the local police and us ASAP.

MC took a breath, knowing her next statement might trigger some pushback. "Upper management might consider funding the purchase of theft-deterrent collection boxes across the system."

Before anyone could protest, Leah said, "I'm not sure there's any money in the budget this fiscal year. I'll make it a discussion item with the postmaster. Let's table the topic for further review after we obtain cost estimates for the boxes and installation." She nodded at MC as if begging for relief.

"I completely understand the concern regarding expense. Maybe a pilot program to select one or two high-risk areas in the city would verify if the cost is justified. I'm willing to request feedback from my counterparts out East who've already implemented the updated collection boxes and determine if the expenditure's worth it." She surveyed the room. "If no one else has any questions . . . All right then, I'll leave you to the remainder of your meeting. Thank you for your time."

A station manager approached MC and asked her if she'd come to their post office and share her insights on the fishing issue with their employees. MC reviewed her schedule and they settled on a date the following week. That was a win in her book.

The traffic goddess shone on MC, and she arrived at the Bluffside post office on the east side of St. Paul with ten minutes to spare. She conducted a session on street safety and security with the carriers, reminding them to also double-check that their vehicles were secured while on their routes.

When she was done, she snagged a sandwich at a Davanni's restaurant conveniently located on her route back and headed for the office.

At her desk, she'd barely taken a bite of her "Assorted Hot Hoagie on Ciabatta Bread" when her desk phone rang. She dropped the sandwich in the container, eyes glued to the display showing her supervisor's number.

MC swallowed and steeled herself. "McCall."

"McCall, nice of you to grace us with your presence today. My office, now."

"On my way." Obviously, a heart attack hadn't mellowed the angry troll.

She knocked on the door to Roland Chrapkowski's office.

"Come in."

MC swore his bellow made the doorknob vibrate beneath her hand. She sucked in a deep breath and entered Crapper's inner sanctum.

"McCall, have a seat." He shuffled folders on his desk and leaned back, his bulk making the chair squeal in protest. His face was a palette of yellowed eggshell and misty gray. Not a healthy look. His clothes, rumpled and creased, had obviously never come in contact with an iron. In essence, nothing had changed.

Fuck me. She reluctantly sat as ordered.

He clamped his hammy fists and rested them on top of his desk. "I see you've not improved in my absence. You still require a heavy hand in order to toe the line. I'll clue you in on my expectations going forward."

MC clenched her jaw tight to prevent a verbal red-hot poker of anger from spearing him between his beady eyes. Go ahead, tell me how it's going to work. You inept piece of—

"McCall! Are you paying attention?"

She leveled her gaze at the reptile sitting across from her. "Yes, I'm listening."

"Sanchez filled me in on your recent snafu during the drug search warrant last week. Let's set all the other crap aside and focus on that incident. You're going to clean up your act now, or I'll show you the door. If I'd been here, I'd have suspended you. Consider this your free pass."

He leaned forward and MC swore she could smell the rot on his breath.

"I'll be watching you every second of every day. Believe me, there will be no get out of jail free card from me."

Free pass? Get out of jail free? Was he serious? The job wasn't a board game. Jesus. Besides, she hadn't done anything against regs. She'd been a bit careless, but her actions hadn't reached the level of suspension. She guessed a verbal reprimand wasn't out of the realm of possibility.

She swallowed the response he deserved, which was "go to hell," and reminded herself that she planned to file a harassment complaint against him. Sweat drew a chilled trail down her back and she clenched her fists until her nails dug halfmoons in her palms. Her feet were planted firmly on the floor, ready to propel her away from the asshole before she committed a fireable offense.

She thought, remember who you're dealing with, McCall. Eyes on the prize.

"Thank you, sir. I'll be on my best behavior." The words came out literally tasting bitter, like regurgitated coffee. She struggled not to make a face.

"Good. I'm glad you're finally seeing the light of day. Going forward you will report to me daily on your activities. You don't do diddly-squat without checking with me first."

Crapper suddenly looked like he'd rolled through a sauna. Sweat beaded on his forehead. He withdrew a yellowed handkerchief from his suit pocket with a shaky hand and dried his damp forehead.

MC tracked his every movement, letting him know she saw his weakened condition, which had to drive the asswad nuts.

"Are we clear, McCall?" He coughed into the limp cloth before ramming it into his pocket. "Or do I need to draw you a picture?"

"No sir," she tried hard not to sneer, "we're crystal clear."

"Fine. Before you leave today, I want to know what you've done and what your plans are for tomorrow."

"You can review my Outlook Calendar, sir. All my appointments are logged into it. All my case work has been entered in DigiCase."

"What part of my instruction did you not understand?" he thundered, then gasped like a wounded rhino.

What the hell? "We've always used the calendar for tracking appointments and meetings, sir."

"I thought I made it very clear, McCall. You'll call me or speak with me before you leave each day until I'm satisfied you're able to work on your own."

Last time MC checked, inspectors were not micromanaged. In the past, when someone mishandled a situation, they'd never had to deal with a helicopter supervisor. Was she a twelve-year-old needing to ask permission to go somewhere after school? Apparently yes.

Demeaned and dehumanized by this demented lout, she sat, an empty husk occupying the chair. “Fine. We finished?”

His gray eyes, washed of color, matched the rimy ring of hair around his bald head. “You seem to have a hard time taking direct orders. I’m telling you, get yourself in line or you’re done. Go on.” He flapped a ham-shaped hand toward the door. “Women. Worthless.”

Crapper’s mumbled words fueled the fire in her belly. She was definitely going to write a record of this meeting and his disrespectful words and use it in her complaint.

She strode to the door and paused. *Don’t take the bait, MC*, she ordered herself. She heard it in her head like a loud shout. She stalked away almost colliding with Jamie who was waving a fistful of papers. Now what?

She crooked a finger for him to follow her to her office. Crapper didn’t need to hear whatever was coming.

“MC. I tried calling you.” They halted in her doorway. “You okay?”

“Fine.” She didn’t offer an explanation. If she reiterated her conversation with Crapper now, she’d burst into flames and melt in the conflagration.

“We received a boatload of new mailbox incidents this morning.” He thrust the sheaf of papers at her.

“I’m on it.” She thumbed through the documents.

“I think there’s seven or eight,” Jamie said. “Might have a repeat offender. Or maybe a group?”

“Or possibly random hits. I’ll provide a synopsis at the team meeting tomorrow.”

Jamie pushed his glasses up snug on the bridge of his nose. His hazel gaze homed in on her.

MC was momentarily mesmerized by the Ray Bans logo on the side of his black plastic frames. His crewcut blond hair was razor-sharp today. A tidy white dress shirt and designer tie completed the package. Jamie seemed to have it all together, unlike her these days.

“New glasses?” MC asked. The silence made her nervous.

“Yes, and they need adjusting. Tend to slip. I look like Poindexter.”

MC cracked a smile. “Maybe a bit. Thanks for this.” She held up the scroll of pages.

“You bet. Gotta run. Hope things are going okay with Roland’s return. Remember, I’m around if you need me.” He hustled down the hall.

At her desk, MC managed to choke down half of her now-cold sandwich and crammed the remainder into the wastebasket. She created individual file folders for the new reports and stacked them on the corner of her desk. Before she dug into the latest and greatest, one task needed her attention. She opened her “Life after Barb” notebook and recorded the meeting with Crapper for posterity. After ten minutes she’d worked out her fury through pen on paper. And she triple-underlined the words “women” and “worthless.”

At some point, when she had more solid footing, she resolved to go to Crapper and request a transfer to Jamie’s team. If he resisted, she’d lay it out for him. He was harassing her, plain and simple. If he wouldn’t approve the transfer, she’d have no choice but to go over his head and reach out to the Assistant Agent-in-Charge in Denver and let him know the situation.

God, how she longed to rehash the situation with Cam. But he’d made it clear he was done helping her. Did listening to her bitch about Crapper equate to “help”? Probably.

She was on her own. No one to help her on the job. No one to help her find who killed Barb. Radio silence from all corners. Fine. She’d juggle her work and personal struggles solo. Silent service.

Except, she reminded herself, she might be able to wheedle some details about the murder case from a certain SPPD Officer named Kiara Reece. She put a pin in that for later consideration.

Screw ’em. For now, she’d handle everything. With reinforcement from her trusty sidekick, Mister Grey Goose, how could she go wrong?

The walls boxed her in, and her focus was shot to hell. She stowed her files inside the messenger bag and bailed. A change of scenery to clear her head was the best solution for what plagued her. She approached the bubble, the glass-enclosed area where the receptionist, Chelsea, sat before she remembered the directive from Crapper. MC did an about-face and stormed down the hall to tell her supervisor her plans.

Her new normal definitely wasn’t palatable.

The seven new reports Jamie had supplied indicated all the recent thievery occurred in Minneapolis, again mostly in the Northeast area of the city. None matched the previous six locations.

MC had informed Crapper she'd patrol each collection box location listed on the theft reports. Later she might need to take photographs and familiarize herself with the businesses and residences nearby. It was possible that someone saw something but hadn't reported it, so she might have multiple interviews in her future.

The mundane undertaking of locating the twelve boxes would consume the remainder of her workday. She drove her own car, Barb's Subaru, instead of a government car so she could go directly home at the end of her shift.

She plotted a rough course and embarked on her journey, trolling the streets of Minneapolis to pinpoint each box. The one on the corner of Twenty-fourth and Fifth Street, had been hit twice. Her first duplicate site.

The mapped locations coalesced into an oval over Northeast and North Minneapolis, and the box that had been hit twice sat smack dab in the center. Two other sites were outliers, one on the West Bank of the U of MN campus and another at the edge of downtown Minneapolis. Was she looking at multiple offenders? Or was she hunting a serial thief?

MC ended her journey at the Quarry Station post office and examined their collection box setup. Four blue behemoths screwed into concrete slabs resided on the north side of the parking lot. The two end boxes stood on taller slabs to accommodate high profile vehicles like trucks and SUVs. The boxes had been modified with a snorkel-like top and a narrow slot instead of the pulldown door of the older units. Definitely a useful "fish" deterrent.

Her cell phone rang. She snagged it from the cup holder and answered.

"MC, you still in the field?" Jamie asked.

"Yep."

"We've had a report of a suspicious package at Broadway North Station in Minneapolis. We advised management to evacuate everyone in the building. I need you to head over and assist the team."

"I'm about ten minutes away."

"Great. Cam's in charge. Find him when you arrive. I'm monitoring from the office. Oh! I almost forgot another mailbox fishing incident was reported." A rustling sound, perhaps papers, filtered through the phone. "Location was Northeast Minneapolis. Twenty-fourth and Fifth Street."

"Thanks for the update. And ah—"

"Is there a problem?"

"No problem on my end. Let Cr—ah, please let Roland know you've sent me to the call. He, ah, he's given me a directive to let him know my whereabouts and what I'm doing twenty-four/seven."

"Seriously?"

She swallowed a sarcastic response. The eye roll she performed would've given anyone a case of vertigo. "Yep."

Jamie blew out a loud breath. "I'll let him know." Some indecipherable mumbling followed, then he ended the call.

Apparently she wasn't the only one whose life was made difficult by Crapper.

MC arrived at the Broadway North Station and parked behind the gray windowless panel van belonging to the inspectors. She scanned the crowd standing in the waning late afternoon light across the street from the building on Broadway Street. No sign of any inspectors, but plenty of uniformed postal employees mingled with customers and looky-loos.

She approached the building, caught sight of Cam, Inspector Eli Andersen, and a newer inspector just inside the glass front doors. The huddle broke up and she approached Cam.

"Hey, Cam, what do we have?"

"Hey. Package that's buzzing."

"Everyone's out?"

"Building's empty. The manager asked to remain inside. A request I promptly denied, had to practically shove her out the door." Cam brushed a clump of hair from his eyes. "We brought the portable X-ray. About to scan the culprit now."

"What would you like me to do?"

"Find the station manager, Liz Vanderlin, and let her know we've verified the building is clear, and we're going to X-ray the parcel. Once we know what we're dealing with we can talk options."

"Sure. What's she look like?"

"Trust me. You'll know her when you lay eyes on her."

"Ten-Four. Be safe." MC walked outside and crossed the street. She scanned the crowd, noticed a towering, slender, youngish-looking woman dressed in a navy business suit. Her reddish-blonde shoulder-length-hair whipped around the cellphone clamped against her ear. She was talking to someone a mile a minute. Had to be her.

"Liz Vanderlin?"

The woman held up a finger.

MC wasn't familiar with the manager, though she knew several throughout the Twin Cities District. Ms. Vanderlin appeared to be fresh off the collegiate graduation stage. Or maybe everyone looked super young these days as MC crawled ever closer to fifty.

Liz completed her call and said, "I'm Liz. You are?"

"Inspector MC McCall. Inspector White asked me to give you an update. The facility is clear—no one inside—the team is about to X-ray the package. After a determination is made, we'll inform you of how we'll proceed."

Liz thrust her phone in her suit coat pocket and rested fisted hands on her hips. "I don't need one more problem today."

"Hopefully this won't—"

"MC!"

She whipped around at the sound of Cam's voice. He waved a hand for her to join him.

"Liz, hang tight. I'll be back."

A line of cars in both directions kept MC curbside for several seconds. When she saw a break she dashed across the salt-crusted pavement. "What'd you find?"

"You're not going to believe this."

The other two inspectors stood next to a mini X-ray machine. That's a good sign, she thought. A red-haired geeky inspector, said, "Hey, McCall, did you bring any toothpaste with ya?"

"Nope." What was his name? He'd been assigned to the Twin Cities three months earlier. Shit for memory. "What is it?"

Cam pointed at the X-ray screen. "Check it out."

"Am I looking at a cordless toothbrush?"

"You betcha."

MC's cell buzzed. She was surprised when she saw it was from Dara.

Dinner at Flannel 2nite?

Thankful her friend had sent such a succinct text she hesitated, then fired off a reply. *Sorry. Can't tonight. Maybe this wknd? In the middle of a situation. Hugs to you two.*

She shocked herself by her longer than usual response. Hopefully she'd deterred a more drawn-out discussion since she was busy with work.

Toothpaste man opened his trap again. "I laid odds on it being some chick's extra special vibrator, a super-sized Magic Wand or something.

Best guess based on the shape and plain packaging. Tell me you disagree!" He elbowed Inspector Eli Andersen.

MC barely stifled a groan. "Hope you didn't lose any money on that bet, Red." How did this guy make it through Basic Inspector Training? The twelve-week intensive training course wasn't solely about brawn. Trainees at the Career Development Unit in Potomac, Maryland, had to slog through about eighty blocks of instruction. The program covered everything from US Postal Service and Inspection Service policies and procedures to interview/interrogation techniques and firearms training. MC had no doubt this guy had aced the physical components, but the brainwork parts had her wondering.

Her phone buzzed again. She checked it. *Ok talk soon* flashed on the screen.

MC sighed. The guilt tried to swamp her. She really was doing a number on her friends. Dodging them. Barb so wouldn't approve.

Back to business, McCall.

Cam and Eli were veteran inspectors, and the Louis C.K. wannabe she'd called Red was the newest addition to their domicile. He'd joined the IS over a year ago, but clearly he was still working through some middle-school-level immaturity.

MC refocused. "We're clear then? There's a group of frozen folks outside and a manager wearing a path into the sidewalk. I'd like to be able to tell her all's safe."

Cam said, "You handle that and I'll have these guys," he shot a thumb over his shoulder at the other two inspectors, "move the equipment to the van. We can reconvene in the manager's office for an exit meeting."

"Good plan." MC headed toward the front doors.

"Hey, MC?" Cam called.

She stopped, one hand on the door.

"Thanks for the backup. Sorry for the newbie's poor attempt at humor."

"No problem. Glad it all worked out. I'll let Liz know the building's safe."

She'd kept her head in the game. A solid score. As the cold air hit her in the face, Barb's voice chimed in, "One instance of reliability does not equate to a reliable person. Consistency and steadfastness lead to trust, which might earn you a spot back in Cam's good graces."

So much for patting herself on the back.

By the time they'd had the exit meeting with Liz Vanderlin and discussed the situation amongst themselves, it was after five p.m. The station bustled with employees conducting end-of-day tasks, mostly outgoing mail dispatches and waiting on last-minute customers at the window.

Cam said he'd take on the task of entering the field notes into DigiCase. "Anyone have anything else?"

Eli shook his head no.

Newbie piped in, "I could write up that I thought it was a vibrator. That'd probably get a few laughs from someone."

Cam ignored him. "MC?"

MC didn't have any physical notes, which was unusual for her. In fact, the Moleskine notebook had remained in her coat pocket. "Nope."

Cam's eyebrows about shot off his forehead. "What? The chronic note-taker has nothing?"

"Funny. But true. Not a single note." She flipped the notepad open to her last entry. "All I've got is mailbox fishing. I was working on that when Jamie called me."

"Mark this date on the calendar. First time I've witnessed MC McCall work a case and not record it for posterity in her omnipresent fancy notebook."

She smacked him with the pad before stashing it in her jacket. "You taking lessons on humor from the newbie?"

It felt good, parrying with Cam. Maybe their relationship was on the mend.

After the Broadway North Station non-explosive event, MC was buoyed. She'd packed a lot into one workday. The dashboard clock let her know it was nearly six o'clock. Night crept in and the tug of the bottle rode its coattails. How could she ignore it?

She wasn't ready to go home to her empty one-bedroom apartment. Not that she hated the place. She liked it, liked the simplicity. It lacked the coziness she'd had with Barb. No matter where they lived, Barb had a way of making a home warm and inviting. The apartment was merely a roof over her head and a space to battle her demons alone. The demons definitely held the upper hand.

MC detoured, parked on Western Avenue, north and east of her Dale Street and Grand Avenue neighborhood. She sat inside the Subaru, engine running, and contemplated the brick structure across the street.

She lost her nerve for a moment. Almost continued on to one of the hip restaurants on Selby Avenue for some Thai takeout. But the soft glow from the bar beckoned.

The Lavender Tavern.

Could the name be any more obvious? Maybe if they'd named it the Rainbow Room.

She and Barb had often discussed stopping at the establishment for drinks, but never seemed to find the time. They'd socialized mostly with Dara and Meg. Bars weren't on the rotation of hotspots for the foursome, for obvious reasons. Now, though, she didn't have to worry about Dara being tempted or uncomfortable. She was alone. Anonymous. She wasn't exactly hiding.

Maybe she was. A little.

Despite Dara's insistence, MC knew she didn't have a drinking problem. Before she changed her mind, she shouldered her messenger bag and crossed the street to the door.

She'd enjoy a nice drink while she went through some paperwork.

Lavender light bathed the doorstep and reflected off the black metal door. Interesting choice. A touch of darkness? Or a symbol of strength? Maybe a promise of anonymity.

The Lavender Tavern had opened two years earlier. Barb had heard about it from a gay teacher friend.

The bar was nestled on a corner in the Frogtown neighborhood of St. Paul. The dark reddish-brown brick structure was a solid mini-fortress with lilac-hued lights reflecting in the windows. MC had heard the two women who'd bought it were partners, one an award-winning bartender, the other had left a lucrative career in investment banking to embark on the adventure of owning their own establishment.

MC pushed that black door open and strolled inside. Size-wise, the tavern was reminiscent of the old-time hole-in-the-wall bars. Somewhere you'd expect old factory workers would've stopped for a pint or two of beer after their shift ended. Or maybe where old retirees bellied up to the bar in the afternoon to share war stories, ignore the "honey do" lists their wives had been nagging them to finish.

The joint was all aged wood and leaded-glass windows. Shiny. Clean. Those details might be a tad different from the olden days, she guessed. The establishments of yore exuded a noir atmosphere. Sticky wood floors. Sometimes peanut shells on the ground. The ubiquitous fog of cigar and cigarette smoke

No smoking allowed now.

The black and white checkered tile floor was not grimy. Transom-style windows ran across the front. The windows were sealed tight on this chilly night, but she imagined they cranked open in milder weather.

Lavender-colored leather booths with chunky dark wood tables lined the right side of the room. Retro metal-framed chairs boasted cushy violet-hued seats and were placed around square gray and white laminate-topped metal-framed tables. Tables for two intermingled with roomier tables for four. A sight straight out of *Happy Days*. Nineteen-fifties throwbacks.

Maybe fifteen purple-cushioned chrome bar stools lined the length of the mahogany bar. The bartender was a woman with light brown hair secured into a tight ponytail. She wore a white button-down shirt, a black plastic name tag with "Beth" in bold white letters and was chatting with a twosome of women while she mixed cocktails.

The bartender paused her conversation to call to MC, "Welcome! Seat yourself anywhere. When you're ready to order c'mon over."

MC thought Beth's thousand-watt personality was going to trip a breaker in the bar's circuit box. She scrounged a smile, though not nearly as powerful Beth's. "Thanks."

Shelves in front of the mirror behind Beth showcased an array of glass bottles, a veritable rainbow of liquor. MC spied the familiar opaque Grey Goose. Perfect.

A chalkboard advertised light snack options: pizza; various flavors of potato chips; and dill pickles. A gargantuan jar lurked beneath the board along with two pizza toaster ovens.

The best attraction? A popcorn machine crammed into a rear corner with stacks of red and white paper boat-shaped containers to fill and share.

MC lamented her first visit to the dazzling gem of a bar was a solo run. But she sought a break from her world, desperately needed to step outside of the bubble she'd created. So she'd drown her sorrows in relative anonymity. On this Monday evening, she spotted only five other patrons, all women.

This teeny tavern fit the bill nicely.

She completed her self-guided tour, including a quick scan of the rest rooms, and claimed the second-to-the-last booth directly across from the popcorn machine. Beyond her booth was a shallow nook housing the two restrooms—gender-neutral single holes.

MC removed her coat and tucked it into a corner of the booth. She spread out her notebooks and grabbed a pen. She perused the white cardstock menu on the table. The fancy drinks were listed by types of alcohol: gin, whiskey, tequila, and vodka. Wines were listed on the other side along with some local craft beers.

She ambled to the bar and ordered a Grey Goose and tonic with a slice of lime.

Simple.

The drink made her feel less like she needed to find an AA meeting than if she'd ordered a double shot neat.

At her booth with her drink and a boat of popcorn, she poked the lime slice with the skinny plastic stir stick until the citrus was wedged on the bottom of the glass. Bubbles fizzled upward at warp speed, then slowed. The first tangy sip snapped in her mouth. The bite of the alcohol cut through the carbonated tonic. A jolt lit her system. A solid pour.

The place was worth the stop already.

She barely refrained from smacking her lips, and nibbled popcorn while she reviewed her notes on the mail thefts. She perceived a definite circuitous pattern to the drop-boxes that had been hit, except for the one on Twenty-fourth and Fifth Street, which had been fished twice—no make it thrice with the newest incident Jamie mentioned earlier. The location was off the beaten path, in a remote residential area with railroad tracks on the western perimeter.

Was this a clue? If so, what did it mean?

Moving on in her notes, she was interested in a camera mounted above the traffic signal on Broadway and Johnson Street facing east. A blue collection box sat on the edge of a commercial strip adjacent to a gas station at that intersection. Maybe she'd get lucky and the camera caught someone.

She made a note to contact MnDOT—Minnesota Department of Transportation—as traffic cameras were under their purview. She'd remember to cross-check with the City of Minneapolis, too, in case the device in question was one of theirs.

Was there a ring of robbers?

Or a daring duo?

Perhaps a lone wolf?

Possibilities spun around in her head. One box hit multiple times pinged her radar. She jotted a note about decoy mailpieces with tracking chips embedded. Or maybe an iPhone dropped in the box, and they'd be able to track using the phone's GPS. The device might be too heavy to be snagged by the fisher's line though.

Tomorrow at the team meeting she'd seek input from other inspectors, hear their thoughts. Enough work for one day. She packed the stack of work paraphernalia into her bag and focused on the green "Life after Barb" notebook.

Barb's case was more mind-boggling than an all-black three-thousand-piece jigsaw puzzle. If she was going to dip into its dark depths, she'd definitely need another drink.

MC stood at the bar while Beth mixed her another drink while conversing cheerily with her and two other women seated on stools.

"Here ya go! One Goose and tonic." Beth slid the tall glass across the shiny surface.

"Thanks." MC wrapped her hand around it like a drowning person to a life raft.

"Anything else? Chips? Pizza?"

One of the women said, "Oh, you have to try a pizza. They're the *best* frozen pizzas!"

Her . . . date? Partner? Friend? chimed in. "Good grief. They're frozen pizzas." She rolled her eyes. "You're not overselling it much, are you?" To MC she said, "You'd think we own stock in the company. Have to agree, though, they are good. So good, in fact, now I'm hungry for one." She said to the barkeep, "Beth, would you toast us a double pepperoni?"

Despite the five-star almost-Yelp review, MC chose to pass. "I'm good with the popcorn. Enjoy."

In the booth, MC sipped her drink. The mellowing effects of the Goose eased through her until a gust of cold air and raucous laughter harshed her mellow.

A group of five, two guys and three women, approached the bar. The men, obviously together, were discussing which spot was best for their fivesome. One guy said, "Let's push two tables together so we won't be cramped."

Guy number two said, "The booths are roomy. Unless—are you implying I need to lose some weight? Do I look fat?"

"Baby, no I'm not . . . oh, forget it. You're *perfect.*" The first man wrapped an arm around his partner. "We'll let Kia decide."

MC peered around the edge of her booth. Her heart did a double beat when she recognized St. Paul police officer, Kiara Reece. She hadn't set eyes on the woman since her initial meeting a couple months earlier at the Saint Paul Police Department Headquarters when Homicide Detective Sharpe told her he didn't have any news on Barb's murder investigation.

So much for finding a place where nobody knew her name. She definitely preferred the opposite of the *Cheers* effect. Maybe Reece wouldn't see her. Or remember her.

Unfortunately, the group meandered her way. The three women slid tables together while the guys made goo-goo eyes at each other and gushed over wanting whatever drinks made the other happy. They were congregated in her backyard.

She angled away from the group. The sounds of their settling in drifted over while MC dove into reading the scribblings she'd recorded about Barb and her thoughts on who killed her. The sometimes angry, more often painful and guilt-riddled journaling had garnered her more heartache. The words provided no leads on who had murdered her beautiful partner three months earlier.

"Hey! I know you."

At first MC didn't register the words.

Kiara Reece stood next to MC's booth, a frosty mug of beer in hand. "Don't tell me. I'll remember. Starts with . . . ah, friggin'-A . . . why can't I remember?"

MC winced under the focus of the four sets of eyes trained on her and Kiara. "MC McCall." Her voice cracked. What the hell? Was she nervous?

"Right!"

For fuck's sake, of course she's right. She knew her own damn name.

Reece looked much the same. MC remembered the tawny-colored, shorn afro, light brown, smooth-as-silk skin with a smattering of darker brown freckles across her cheeks. Those intense emerald-green eyes. Bet nothing gets by this woman, MC thought.

"Nice to see you, Reece." At least this time she wasn't in tears, practically begging Sharpe to let her in on his investigation. Her first encounter with Kiara Reece had definitely not been one of her better days.

"Reece? Call me Kia. All my friends do. This your first time here? You alone?" Kiara took a pull from her beer, set the mug on MC's table. "Okay if I set this here for a second? Heavy coat's makin' me sweat."

"Sure. No problem." Why couldn't she set the mug on the table by her friends? MC felt like a trapped animal in search of an escape route.

How quickly could she swallow the drink in front of her? Seconds? A minute? Then she'd gather her possessions and bail from the bar.

Kiara slid into the booth across from MC. "How're you doing?"

Make yourself at home. Apparently, Kiara chose to ignore MC's lack of interest in idle conversation. A direct approach was in order.

"Listen, I—"

Kiara took another pull from her beer. "Damn. I'm sorry. I shouldn't assume you want to talk." She motioned to the open note-book. "You must be working, and I'm going on like we're old pals getting re-acquainted. Sometimes I can be obtuse." She knocked a knuckle on the side of her head.

"It's fine. I'm not working. I was working, but this is personal, about, about . . ." Words failed her. She gulped her drink. Fire lit a trail to her belly. She gasped.

Kiara said, "Easy there, cowboy. Take a breath. This about your late partner?"

Did she say, "take a breath?"

MC was impressed Kiara remembered. She supposed it wasn't often she ran into a situation like MC's. And they'd clicked that day. Kiara had offered to help MC. Or maybe MC imagined—or mis-remembered it?

"Hello?" Kiara waved a hand in front of MC's face.

"Sorry. Yes. My partner, Barbara Wheatley." Time to end the interaction. Finish her drink. Go home. MC imagined every eye and ear was glued to her and Kiara. A spotlight shining like they were center stage would complete the picture.

"Small world," Kia said.

MC said, "I'm sorry. What?"

"I happened to be in Homicide last week, and I overheard Sharpe talking to another detective about your—Barbara's—case."

The endless looping mindfuck that had seized MC skidded off track. "What about her case? What did he say?"

"Sharpe must've asked the other detective to research prisoners who'd landed in the federal system thanks to your hard work. Get my meaning?"

Blood thumped hard in her veins. MC finished the last of her drink. "He's developing a theory her murder was an act of retribution. Someone who was pissed they were locked up due to a case I worked. Payback?"

"Sounded like it to me. I heard a guy had been released prior to the date of the murder. Sharpe was going to pay him a visit."

"A plausible track. Did you happen to catch the name of this maybe suspect?"

Kiara took a pull from her half-drained mug. "Nope. That I didn't hear. When Sharpe caught sight of me, he clammed up. I pretended I hadn't heard a word and handed him the file I'd been asked to deliver, which was the reason I was in the squad room."

MC flipped the notebook over and wrote the details of what Reece had shared with her. A newfound energy rippled through her.

Kiara said, "Wow! You sure do write quick."

"Uh huh. No name for this person of interest. Anything else you can remember? A date? Release date, I mean?" She finally made eye contact with Reece.

"Sorry, no. Like I said they kiboshed the convo when they saw me. Wish I had more for you."

"This is helpful. I don't know why I didn't think about checking into this myself. I definitely will."

"You sure you want to travel that road? I mean, I understand. In your shoes, I'd want to know who did what was done. But Sharpe is *really* good at his job. I'm not just saying that. His closing rate in homicide is the highest in the department. He'll find whoever is responsible. You don't want to mess with that."

MC set the pen aside. "You don't understand. I *need* to find who did this. It's not about whether or not Sharpe is good at his job. I'm not sure I agree with your rosy assessment of his case-solving abilities. To me it's about justice. Justice for Barb. I'm the sole voice Barb has, and I won't let it be stifled."

Easy, MC. Barb's voice in her head. *Don't unpack your frustrations on the messenger.*

Barb's voice? Whispering to her? She may need to mention this to Dr. Zaulk at her next therapy appointment. She'd been hearing the voice more frequently.

Reece stood, beer mug in hand. "I didn't mean to upset you. I did offer to help you back when we met at the station. I dunno, maybe think carefully about how you proceed?"

One of the women from Reece's foursome hollered. "Hey, Kia! You gonna join us sometime tonight? Bring your friend along!"

Reece arched an eyebrow at MC. "You heard the woman. Wanna join us?"

MC slid her gaze toward the jovial group. "Maybe another time. Please, let me buy you another beer, a thank you for taking time to talk with me?"

"Sure. I'm game for another. Surly Furious. Thanks."

MC scuttled past the group and heard Reece say, "I'm going to have one more with MC."

With a mug of beer and another vodka tonic in hand, MC returned to the table. "I appreciate you sharing information with me. You certainly didn't have to."

"Happy to help—what little help it may be. I can't imagine such a loss."

MC knocked back half her drink to wash away the stale tide of guilt and sorrow. Off the cuff, she steered the topic to Reece's personal life. "Tell me, you with anyone? Dating?"

Reece remained silent for what seemed like forever to MC.

Shit. MC hoped Reece didn't think she was hitting on her. "Sorry, Kia. Didn't mean to bombard you with personal shit right off the bat."

"No worries. I guess I'm still healing. I went through a pretty horrible breakup last summer. July Fourth weekend to be exact." She glugged beer from her mug. "I've been—still am—single. Recovering from the sting of it all."

"Sounds bad. Sorry for dredging up painful memories. Sometimes my mouth works before my mind has hashed through details."

They chatted about work and being women—and gay—in law enforcement.

When all that remained in MC's glass was a shriveled lime slice and melting ice cubes, she called it a night.

"Time for me to head home. Early day tomorrow."

"I'm off until Wednesday, otherwise I'd be home sound asleep."

"Thanks for the company."

Reece rose to move toward the other table. "You take care, MC. If you need to talk, I'm around. Hey! Let's swap numbers."

"Good idea," MC said. They plugged each other's contact info into their devices.

"Be sure to call me." Reece said, "It'd give me an excuse not to get drunk with those goofs." She inclined her head toward the raucous and rowdy crew.

MC recalled similar scenes with Dara and Meg when Barb was still alive. Bittersweet memories. She tugged her coat on. "You're lucky to have such great friends. Enjoy them. Life goes by in the blink of an eye."

Reece laid a hand on MC's arm. "I can't imagine what you're going through. I don't say this lightly, but I'm a great listener. If you need someone to lend an ear, I'm your gal. And remember what I said about Sharpe. He's an outstanding detective. We good?"

"We are." They were definitely good. Reece had possibly provided her with a viable lead.

MC settled her tab with a generous tip and ordered a car from a rideshare app. No sense in tempting the DUI fates.

The car arrived inside two minutes, and she hustled into the full-on dark night half-wondering if fate had drawn her to this particular place on this night at this time for a reason.

Something she'd contemplate at length over a nightcap at home.

Chapter Seven

Had anyone noticed she'd slipped in twenty minutes after her scheduled start time? Not having to punch a time clock helped, and thankfully she'd arrived before the team meeting began.

Crapper wasn't in the conference room when MC scooted in. Earlier she'd stopped by his office to let him know she planned to spend the morning revisiting the fishing locales. A proactive attempt to ward off flak from the ogre. But his office was dark, and the door locked, so she marched back to her office and zipped off an email and left a voicemail for him. Bases covered.

After the shock of meeting Reece at the Lavender Tavern, she'd run like a scared kid directly home to the bottle. In addition to the three drinks she imbibed at the bar, she remembered drinking at least two more at home. The previous evening's alcohol intake had served up a whopper of a hangover this morning.

Her imprudent decision to fly solo at the local cocktail lounge had resulted in leaving her car parked there. She'd retrieved her vehicle this morning, putting her behind the eight ball, late again. Crapper's threats rumbled in her head.

Speaking of Crapper, he still hadn't made an appearance. No skin off her nose if he wasn't around.

Jamie opened the meeting as inspectors from both teams settled in. MC's turn to give her update came midway through the meeting. Her headache had improved to a dull pulsation in her skull, enabling her to at least put a smattering of thoughts together.

"I've been working mail theft. One case was specific to a residence in Minneapolis. The remainder," she paged through her notebook, "here we go—thirteen—appear to be mailbox fishing."

Jamie said, "Roland has more for you. I handed them off to him late yesterday. Wanted you to know."

She made a note. "Thanks. I looked for him this morning, but he wasn't in." Why the hell hadn't Crapper left her the new reports from Jamie?

Jamie said, “He had a medical appointment this morning. Maybe he forgot to share that with you all.” Crapper definitely hadn’t shared that news with MC.

Typical, she thought. He rides my ass, wants to know my every move and doesn’t have the courtesy to let his team know his schedule. Lead by example? She nudged those thoughts aside for further contemplation later.

“Anyway, mailbox fishing—”

One of her team members said, “What about the residence theft? Is it related to the mailbox fishing?”

“No. Unrelated. I interviewed the person who reported the incidents—two reports for the same home—which ended up being a misunderstanding. The suspect happened to be the nephew of the homeowner who was on vacation. He collected mail for his aunt until she returned. My two cents, a nosy neighbor was miffed about not being in the loop on the other homeowner’s whereabouts.”

Maybe a harsh assertion, but she wasn’t feeling generous this morning. It’d been a rough night. Her mind swirled with the scant details Reece had divulged. Who had a grudge against her? Who harbored so much anger he’d plot a home invasion and murder Barb? Or had it been nothing more than a random burglary?

If memory served, none of her previous case investigations had been painted with such violent strokes. Sure, defendants had been defiant, angry over being caught. But threatening violence against her, against any inspector—she recalled nothing of the sort.

Jamie said, “MC? You okay?”

No, she wasn’t okay. Why’d he ask such a dumb question?

Easy, MC. Damn, was that Barb’s voice in her head? *Take a breath.*

She recalled Reece spouting the same words last night. Unnerved, she choked out, “I’m fine.” She surveyed the room to be sure Barb—or her ghost—hadn’t joined the meeting. “I’ve determined there’s no connection between the residential report and this new outbreak of mailbox fishing. Yesterday I went to the locations of all the collection boxes that were hit and plotted them out on a map. We have an oval-shaped pattern, with the exception of the one box that was fished three times.”

Jamie asked, “The others were all ripped off just once?”

“Correct. The box hit three times sits dead center of the ring of other boxes. I’m not certain if that has any correlation. But it’s worth noting.

I do have one eyewitness who saw a potential fisher in action at the multi-hit container. The description was vague at best. No accomplices or vehicles sighted."

Jamie clicked his pen. "Next steps?"

"I thought about decoy mailpieces with embedded trackers. Or an iPhone planted in a padded envelope."

An inspector said, "I'd go with the iPhone right off the bat. GPS tracking provides quicker results. Why mess around with anything else? Hit 'em hard. Reap the rewards, man." He looked around, an eager puppy begging for a pat on the head. Same guy who'd made the jokes yesterday about the vibrator.

MC did a mental head shake. Kids these days. She said, "I think—"

"Wait! You don't want to go with my suggestion?" He sounded shocked and slightly hurt.

Deep breath. "Thanks for your input. I'm leaning toward mail with embedded tracking devices. Make the culprit think there might be checks or money orders inside. Dangle the carrot in front of the horse."

"What's that mean?"

Was this guy for real?

MC chose not to respond. "Mail with embedded trackers. The iPhone is a great idea." Give the wet-behind-the ears rookie a tip o' the hat. "But it might be too heavy for the line. Based on what my eyewitness saw, the fishing device was made out of a string with an empty plastic bottle attached. An iPhone would be too weighty." She glanced around the group, purposely avoiding eye contact with the jokester. "Besides, the iPhone might be a better option if the thief jimmied the rear of the box and dumped the container versus dropping a line through the top. Anyone else have ideas? I'm seriously open to your input."

The meeting dragged. Antsy didn't begin to describe her state of mind. She itched to get her hands on old cases. Review the files and determine who'd been recently released from prison. Find possible suspects for an unsolved murder. She hoped Reece's words from the previous evening took her on a road to . . . where?

The consensus was to try the fake mail with the trackers. Newbie needed to take a chill pill. Listen. Learn. Not jump the gun.

Other inspectors provided updates on their active cases. Cam continued to work an extensive narcotics case. He said, "I may need assistance with executing search warrants."

"Roland and I discussed your particular case," Jamie said. "We decided all hands on deck for the search warrants. Stay tuned. Everyone be ready to roll when we call. Understood?"

The room rumbled in the affirmative, including MC. She owed Cam. Big time. They still hadn't completely repaired the rift from her last screwup. She wanted any opportunity to prove her dependability.

Still no sign of Crapper. She dropped her work notebook on a corner of her desk, sat down primed to burrow into DigiCase, hoping to catch a scent and follow the trail to Barb's killer.

Ha! If only it were that simple.

MC mined the digital files. Eventually she unearthed two possibilities: Bobby Briscoe and Wade Anthony Perkins. Bobby Briscoe sounded like a criminal's—a murderer's—name. Dastardly. It slid slimy off the tongue.

Armed with the names, she accessed the Bureau of Prisons web page and used the "Find an inmate" tab to reveal their release dates. Briscoe and Perkins had been paroled within weeks of each other the previous year. Briscoe was kicked from the low security Sandstone Federal Correctional Institution where he'd been doing time for stealing mail from a postal vehicle. Perkins had been convicted of identity theft and served time in the medium-security Duluth Federal Prison Camp.

MC blew out a strangled breath, fighting off nervous energy and the vestiges of the hangover. She visited the restroom and splashed cold water on her face. After mopping off the dripping water with a brown paper towel the texture of fine-grain sandpaper, she hit the break room for vending machine coffee and a bag of pretzels. Not the most nutritious lunch, but along with another dose of pain reliever, it'd suffice.

At her desk she crunched a pretzel and dug into the multitude of databases at her fingertips, hunting Bobby Briscoe. He now lived in Austin, Texas. He'd put Minnesota in his rearview the minute he'd been released. MC put a giant red "X" through Briscoe's name, back-burnered him for now. She'd have to focus on Perkins.

The search for Wade Anthony Perkins was where she hit pay dirt. At least she hoped so. According to the DMV, he lived in Forest Lake, Minnesota, in some type of multi-unit structure. He drove a silver 2008 Ford Escape. MC recorded all the details, including his license plate number, in the green notebook.

In the DigiCase files, she drilled into the Perkins investigation. The final note in the case file was from over four years earlier. Perkins had been sentenced to three years in federal prison for using an elderly man's identity to steal approximately twenty-five thousand dollars. The US District Court Judge had imposed a three-year prison sentence followed by one year of supervised release.

Wade had been less than pleased with the sentencing. He'd threatened in court he'd "get even" with those responsible for his incarceration. She guessed the idea he made his own bed hadn't registered.

MC vaguely recalled that at the time, she'd blamed the threats on his detoxing. He'd spent a good portion of the stolen funds on alcohol and drugs. He'd been released a year ago, which meant his year of supervised release was set to expire at the beginning of next month.

Perkins was a free man on the date Barb was murdered.

A free man living in Minnesota.

A voice whispered, "Now what?" Barb—or her ghost—was not going to convince her not to take action. She ignored the question and planned to go sit outside Perkins's house. If he left, she'd follow him. She squashed any pushback from her voice of reason.

Maybe she should confront him face-to-face. Outright ask him where he was on the day after Thanksgiving? She opted for the first choice. Lowest risk for now.

Where had the time gone? Late afternoon already. She wasn't prepared to call it quits, despite the stirrings of her thirsty inner monster.

Not yet. Patience. More to do.

While she was at it, MC sent a request to the Minnesota Department of Transportation asking for images and/or video on vehicles captured by the traffic camera on Ford Parkway and Cretin Avenue on November 28, 2014, between six a.m. and nine a.m. A long shot, sure, but Detective Sharpe wasn't giving her anything. She needed to dip her toe into the water, be proactive.

To add an air of legitimacy to her request, she added a second location. The traffic camera mounted above the signal on Broadway and Johnson in Minneapolis, facing east. One of the fished collection boxes was located on the edge of a commercial strip close to the intersection. Maybe the camera footage contained answers, though probably not. She inserted a date range and thanked the agency for their time and efforts in assisting her.

To fulfill her official duties and to avoid a clash with Crapper—or Jamie—she remembered her decision to deploy decoy mail with embedded tracking devices. She completed the requisition for and obtained six envelopes containing trackers. The collection box with multiple incidents seemed the best option for catching their fisher. Hopefully the miscreant was greedy and would revisit the scene of the crime soon. She half-formed a supposition that the fisher lived in the neighborhood where that box was located. They had no transportation. No job. And when they needed cash, they went on a fishing trip to the blue box in hopes of hauling out a big one.

MC checked Crapper's office. Dark as dead of night. Looked like Crapper had skipped work altogether. Damn. Long doctor appointment. Maybe they were injecting some humanity into the asshole.

Into a lockbox in her brain, she crammed her frustration over not having access to the new reports Jamie'd given Crapper.

MC stopped by Jamie's office. "Hey, Cr—uh, Roland still isn't in." Close call on calling him Crapper to Jamie. "He directed me to let him know my every move. I've left him a voicemail and sent an email. I figured if I tell you that counts extra."

Jamie said, "I'm sorry he's handcuffed you. I'll fill in. What's the plan?"

MC said, "Nothing earth-shattering. I'll drop decoy envelopes into a collection box to try and net a fisher. Probably go home from the site."

"Works for me. Hope you nab the culprit."

"Have a good night. See you in the morning."

And she was out.

MC deployed decoys in the central, multiply-hit blue collection box in Northeast Minneapolis. Her day was done.

Official quitting time.

A strip of fast-food joints appeared on the horizon. She struggled to remember the last time she and Barb had eaten at one of those spots. She drew a blank.

She hung a right, maneuvered the Subaru into the drive-thru of the burger place with those infamous golden arches. She ordered a quarter pound burger with cheese—no onions please—fries and a large coffee. Still chilly, and with a possibly long evening ahead, she needed the warm, caffeinated beverage.

After she received her bag of food and drink, she slotted into an empty parking space and used her phone's map app to find the most direct route to the home of Wade Anthony Perkins.

The tantalizing smell of French fries permeated the car. With the route mapped, MC followed the route given to her by the app's driving direction voice, which she'd dubbed "Marge."

Early evening traffic northbound on Interstate 35 was slow-moving. MC used the opportunity to dig into the fries. She tuned the radio to MPR and listened to the latest news, shivering at the predicted low overnight—five degrees. Damn cold.

Marge accurately did her job and MC arrived at Perkins's address in Forest Lake, a town twenty-seven miles northeast of St. Paul. The modest apartment complex sat amidst a grouping of more grandiose, newer-looking apartment buildings. The street address, 400 Works Way Circle, was a no outlet street with the apartment structure on her right and a Public Works utility building on her left.

Behind the apartments, she caught sight of two sets of four detached garages and a parking lot. She cruised the lot and spotted a silver Ford Escape tucked along the rearmost side of the first set of garages. License plate matched. Bingo. And no outlet on the far side.

She continued through the lot and exited to the right where she landed in a circular turnaround, the apartment lot to her right, the Public Works property to her left. Her headlights revealed a pathway that continued past the end of the road marked by a sign, "No Motorized Vehicles." A silver cyclone fence with barbed wire attached to the top bordered the area behind the Public Works building. MC picked out a water tower in the distance, a half block from her location.

The driveway was the only avenue of egress or ingress to the apartment's lot.

On the Public Works side of the street, she counted three parked vehicles. She completed a U-turn and snugged in between a rusting truck and a Volkswagen Beetle. She left the engine idling but shut off the radio.

MC ate her burger and the straggler fries left in the cardboard container. When she was finished, she stuffed the trash into the paper sack and tossed it onto the passenger-side floor.

The Moleskine notebook felt heavy in her hands. She opened it to record the time, date, and her observations of the area, including a rough sketch of the building. Lights glowed in windows, but the outdoor space was deserted. If anyone were to question her, she'd tell them she was lost and had stopped to remap her route.

Easy peasy.

With all the loose ends she could think of tied together, she commenced to wait. She ran through her next move if Wade didn't show during the evening. No way could she afford to camp out all night, not on a work night. Nine o'clock would be quitting time, which put her home by around ten, plenty of time to cure the tickle in her brain that required Grey Goose before going to bed.

A vehicle exited the parking lot on her left startling her loosey-goosey thoughts. A light-colored . . . silver . . . Holy shit! Perkins.

She slammed the Subaru into drive.

He stopped at the corner, hung a left.

MC hit the gas, rounding the corner as Perkins made another left at the next intersection.

Hot pursuit. More like lukewarm. He was driving normal speed.

Take a breath, MC. Damn Barb's voice. Good advice though, so she followed the suggestion and felt her shoulders drop.

Less than a minute later she saw Perkins's car parked next to a pump at a sleazy gas station. She slowed and angled the car toward the curb. He wasn't in sight. She was weighing the risk of going in when a man exited the store. Perkins's driver's license had him at six-feet and two-hundred-thirty pounds. This guy appeared to fit the bill. He pumped gas he must've prepaid for, then motored across the street to a rickety structure called the Liquor Shack. The name fit. A mobile home park behind the store completed the every-small-town picture.

She considered indulging her nagging need for the spirits within but didn't want to chance being noticed. The store was too public, not the place she wanted to confront Perkins. She'd bide her time.

He exited the liquor store with a case of Michelob Golden. Soap suds. Yuck. Perkins jawed with a guy on the sidewalk for a minute before they parted ways.

Back on the road, she tailed him to the old homestead. Boring guy.

She stayed on the side street this time instead of pulling into the parking lot behind the complex. Her view of the rear of the building was blocked. Had he gone inside? After a solid thirty seconds—she lacked patience—MC drove through the lot.

His car was parked in the same spot. No sign of Perkins.

Back to the street.

Twenty minutes later the car was again on the move. Perkins wasn't alone this time. A woman rode shotgun.

MC fell in behind the pair, tried to stay far enough back not to be made. Perkins signaled left at the first street followed by a right at the next corner. Opposite direction from his earlier outing.

Within five minutes they entered the parking lot of a grocery store.

Damn! MC smacked the steering wheel.

Perkins snugged into an empty slot, climbed out, and waited by the car for his passenger to finish whatever she was doing. MC entered the row and parked directly behind their location.

In her rearview mirror, MC watched the woman pull a baby from the backseat. The happy cherubic family headed for the entrance.

Go inside?

Nah. Best to avoid a commotion inside the store in front of God and who knew how many witnesses, not to mention security cameras.

Tonight wasn't her night.

MC calmed the wave of agitation that knotted her gut.

She wished she could tail this guy during the day, but if she bailed on work Crapper would have her head, not to mention her badge, on a platter.

Best to fly under the radar. She called Detective Sharpe and left a quick voicemail: "MC McCall here. Thought you'd want to know I unearthed a guy you might be interested in. Call me."

Chapter Eight

In the cramped confines of her office, MC slammed the notebook on the desk and dropped into her chair. A battle waged in her head. She'd found Perkins but had no chance to confront him.

Take a breath, MC.

She needed more than a breath. She craved, *needed*, some Grey Goose, but it was too early to contemplate a stiff drink with a full day of work looming.

Would time-off clear her head? Dissipate the waves of gobbledygook churning in her noggin?

Suck it up, McCall, you have a job to do.

But instead of concentrating on her work she dove headfirst into the murky waters of searching for Barb's killer without knowing what was concealed beneath the surface.

Not good.

Not safe.

Was she seeing things where nothing existed? Making a mountain out of a molehill? Was Wade Perkins the easy answer? Too easy?

Take a breath, MC.

She whipped around, checked behind her. The damn voice interjected more and more. Barb—or her ghost—was in the room.

Was she truly and honestly losing her shit? Tomorrow she'd mention it to Dr. Zaulk. Hopefully the good doc would have an explanation to put her mind at ease and not just recommend she be locked up.

MC moved the mouse on her desk to wake her computer and typed in her password and her email populated the screen. A response from MnDOT on the security camera footage requests was the first message she opened.

The Ops Supervisor had provided some interesting facts. The angle of the cameras generally precluded grabbing a readable license plate. The combo of distance, angle, and video compression made that ability virtually impossible.

Then there was the fact that the video was buffered for five days and then overwritten. The cameras weren't made for law enforcement. They were intended for monitoring traffic conditions with the ability to zoom in on specific incidents.

Mister Ops Supervisor went on to recommend she try local law enforcement to see if they had any cameras in the areas she was inquiring about as the police might have different retention periods more to her advantage.

Not happening. No way was she contacting SPPD or Sharpe to ask about cameras.

Another dead end.

With still no sign of Crapper and no new mailbox theft reports, she'd sally forth and drop by two or three stations in Minneapolis and continue meeting with managers or supervisors about the mailbox fishing situation. Afterward, she'd drive past the collection boxes, maybe chat with a carrier or two if she encountered them. The goal was to devise tasks to stay away from the office and Crapper.

Like the obedient officer she was, she informed Jamie she'd be in the field and asked him to let Roland know. MC hit the road as the afternoon cold bled the sky of color. She hated winter. Or maybe she hated life.

The drudgery.

The dreariness.

The lifelessness of it all.

Deep down in her core she heard the titillating call of the Goose. Her one constant. Not quite time.

Things to do.

People she hoped to see before the night's end.

MC wanted to beat northbound rush hour traffic, so around four in the afternoon she hopped onto I-35W from northeast Minneapolis.

She'd grabbed grub via a drive-thru near the on ramp. Same order: cheeseburger, fries, and a mega-sized coffee. Fat. Caffeine. Salt. Perfect fortification for the evening's operation.

What wasn't good were the annoying every-three-minutes fund drive announcements on the local public radio station. She already gave a couple hundred bucks a year. But the month-long plea for funding made her want to tear her hair out.

MC fumed when she hit a clump of stopped traffic. She knew better. Should've left Minneapolis early enough to miss the jam. She took the opportunity to switch to the podcast app on her phone.

Myriad true crime podcasts were available. She randomly chose one and hit play on the first episode. The hosts, a trio of lawyers, were talking about a 1999 case in which they believed the defendant had been wrongly accused of killing his girlfriend.

Her interest piqued, MC listened to the voices weaving the story. Traffic thinned and was soon moving at the posted speed.

Forest Lake traffic was fairly bustling this evening, exuding a Mayberry RFD-feel.

MC rolled up to her destination and parked across the street instead of on the dead-end side street. No sense drawing attention to herself.

Dusk drooped over the trees. Naked branches shivered in the breeze. Endless winter.

She consumed her dinner and sipped her coffee.

Over the next hour, halfway into the second episode of the podcast, five vehicles entered the parking area behind the apartment building and one exited.

None of the vehicles belonged to Perkins.

She ran the car every fifteen minutes to thaw out. Best not to freeze to death while conducting an unsanctioned stakeout. Imagine being discovered frozen in a parked car in a town in which you didn't live and had no connections. Not a great way to go out.

Time ticked, minute-by-minute, toward the eight o'clock mark. Full dark had descended. Still no sign of Perkins or his silver SUV.

Around eight-fifteen she did a pass through the parking lot. The silver SUV was parked in the middle of a row along the rear of the complex.

Perkins and company must be tucked in tight on this cold winter night.

She threw in the towel and drove home.

Inside her apartment, MC stowed boots and coat in the closet and changed into flannel pajama pants and a shabby sweatshirt.

The next order of business, which should've been first, was to half-fill a tumbler with Grey Goose. The drink was not a form of enjoyment or a soothing end to a rough day. No, the forty-proof liquid was a tool to ease ripples of frustration, a way to deaden the pain enough she might attempt sleep.

She sat cross-legged on the couch and journaled the day's events.

Sharpe hadn't returned her call from the day before, but no matter. MC remained undeterred and she'd try again tomorrow night.

The glass drained, MC weighed her options. Watch TV? Another stiff drink? Should she send a quick "check-in" text to her friends? She shook an imaginary Magic 8-Ball and the little triangle floated up to the circular window, "My reply is no." Perfect. She was, after all, avoiding them.

She pushed the notebook aside and hauled her weary bones off the couch. In the kitchen she refilled her glass. The black eye of the giant goose on the bottle seemed to study her intensely. MC made a mental note to stop at the liquor store. Reserves were running low.

In the living room, she punched the remote. Local news lit the screen. Did she want to hear about more death and destruction? She polished off her drink and killed the TV. She washed the glass in hot soapy water, the suds circling the drain much like her life was. If she cleaned the glass, then she might be able to fall asleep without the temptation of another drink . . . or two . . . or three.

The next day, Thursday, she had her weekly appointment with Dr. Zaulk. Time to come clean, tell her about the voice. See if the good doctor had an explanation and advice for how to handle the spirit haunting her.

Chapter Nine

Coffee in hand, MC struggled to badge into the building, thankful the usual bongo drums weren't reverberating in her skull. A warmer sunnier day was forecast with hints of spring, which she hoped was a good sign.

She called a quick greeting to Chelsea, the admin assistant, as she passed the bubble. A murmur of voices drifted from the conference room. She considered popping in, but instead chose to enjoy the steaming coffee before it cooled.

She'd barely sat at her desk before a knock sounded at her door. "Come in."

Jamie entered. "Morning."

"Hey, good morning. How're you?"

Jamie said, "I'm well. You got anything critical on tap?"

"Hmm. Let me check." MC sipped coffee and shimmied her mouse to wake the computer. She perused the screen. "Nothing that can't wait."

"Great. There's a situation. I'd like you to join us in the conference room."

"Right behind you." She retrieved her notebook and a pen, thought about the coffee, and left it behind.

She and Jamie joined Cam and Jim Bob, who were yammering at each other about God knows what.

Jamie said, "Listen up. SPPD called. They're at a death scene at a home." He consulted some notes. "Decedent is a child."

A collective groan sounded from the assemblage.

Jim Bob said, "Why'd they call us?"

"I was getting to that."

MC wanted to slap Jim Bob upside the head, maybe lecture him on the virtue of patience. Probably be wasted energy, though.

Jamie continued. "The detective unearthed a cardboard box—Priority Mail—in the room with the child. Peeled-off backing from some type of patch inside the box along with pills—possibly oxycodone or a variant."

MC said, "Let me guess, the kid swallowed the pills or the patch?"

Jamie said, "I don't have any details. I want you three on scene to investigate the drugs. The detective's name is Sharpe."

MC did a double-take, pen poised over her notepad. "Did you say Sharpe? Detective Victor Sharpe?"

"Yes. Why? Is there a problem?"

"No. No problem. He's assigned to Barb's case."

"Ah, right," Jamie said. "I can assign a different inspector if you need to pass."

Did she? The case may present an opportunity to ask Sharpe why he hadn't returned her calls. Better yet, she'd prove she was professional and do her job without mixing in personal matters.

"MC?" Cam gave her a concerned look. "You okay?"

She steeled herself. "I'm fine. Took me off guard. I'm in."

"Excellent." Jamie consulted a sheet of paper on the table in front of him. "The address is 1420 Flanders Street East."

MC jotted it into her black notepad. "Got it."

Cam said, "I'll snag a set of keys."

"You and Jim Bob go ahead. I'll follow in my car." MC closed her notebook. "I've got an appointment later. I'll need to leave from the scene."

"Sounds good. See you in the lot."

MC rose to leave, then pivoted toward Jamie. "You'll let Roland know I'm on this?"

Jamie said, "He's not in yet but I'll apprise him of the situation."

"Thanks."

In her office, MC entered a notation on her Outlook calendar: "Out of office on scene w/White & O'Malley." And she called Crapper's number and left a voicemail with the same info. Covered her bases, zero ammo for Crapper to claim misconduct or insubordination on her part.

Good God, he was a pain in her butt. She hoped the multiple communications annoyed the hell out of him.

MC parked behind Cam and Jim Bob's black SUV and got out. SPPD squads blocked either end of the street. The scene was at a blue vinyl-sided two-story house mid-block.

The Ramsey County Coroner and a Saint Paul Police Forensic Services white van joined the multitude of vehicles lining the street. An eerie carnival of lights flashed blue and red, reminding MC of a similar scene at her home several months earlier. Suddenly she realized they were in the vicinity of All Saints Catholic, the school where Barb had taught second grade.

She shook free from the Grim Reaper's skeletal claws and took a read on her surroundings. Across the street from the vic's house, on the north side, was an empty field—no, check that, a storm drainage field surrounded by six-foot-high cyclone fencing. A maintained area covered in pristine white snow. MC had direct sightline to the Bluffside post office the next street over.

A behemoth four-door white pickup truck with ladders strapped to both sides sat in the driveway.

Cam stopped alongside her, Jim Bob in his shadow. "You good?"

"Yep. Getting the lay of the land. All Saints isn't far from here."

Jim Bob said, "What's All Saints?"

Take a breath, MC.

She took the voice's advice and sucked in a deep, cleansing breath. "All Saints is the grade school where my partner used to teach."

Jim Bob seemed unfazed by the revelation. "Okay. What do we do now? We go in? What's the plan?"

Patience of a gnat, MC thought. "We check in with Detective Sharpe. It's his scene." What would Sharpe's reaction be when he caught sight of her?

The inspectors approached a patrol officer, clipboard clutched in one hand, posted at the puny front entry of the home. "Everyone's gotta sign in." She handed over the clipboard and they all scratched their names, agency, and the time.

Another patrol officer stood inside the foyer, leaving barely enough space for the three inspectors to squeeze in. The house was a split-level. Directly in front of the entry, a set of seven stairs led up to a living room, dining room and kitchen. A hallway off to the left probably led to bedrooms and a bathroom.

Detective Sharpe climbed the stairs up from the lower level to the left of the threesome. "Inspectors." He hesitated when his gaze met MC's. "Inspector McCall. Who are your associates?"

Before MC could react, Cam responded, "Inspector White and Inspector O'Malley."

Sharpe seemed unruffled by the cornfed younger inspector towering over him. "Detective Victor Sharpe, SPPD. Thanks for getting here so fast. Here's the deal. One deceased. Female child, age seven. In the basement in the father's home office. Parents have been separated for interview purposes. Mom and baby are in the baby's room with a female patrol officer and Dad's in the kitchen. I want to let the Forensic Services Unit finish their photo and video work before we head down. But to give you some idea, the Priority Mail package that precipitated the call to your agency was lying adjacent to the child's body. Box is about the size of one of those old VHS tapes. We tilted it using a pen to look inside, and that's when the pills and other items were discovered."

"Okay," Cam said. "We'll do our own photos. Also, we'll bag the drug-related items for submission to our lab."

"I figured. We'll share with you, and you'll share the results of your work with us?"

While the two men hashed out the administrative details, MC scoped the place. Through the sturdy wrought iron rails lining the edge of the living room to the right, she studied the tidy pocket-sized space. Carpet was worn, but clean. Paint on the walls seemed fairly fresh, no scrapes or gouges. The home appeared to be cared for. Eight-by-ten-inch framed family photos decorated the wall above the sofa on the far side of the room.

Family of four. Now a family of three.

She swallowed the knot that had formed in her throat and turned back to Sharpe. "Fill us in on the family?"

Sharpe consulted his fun-size wire-bound notepad. "The father is Ethan Carson, Senior. He's a roofer. Has his own business. Mother is Jenny Carson, a stay-at-home mom. Daughter Emmy is the seven-year-old vic. They also have a one-year-old boy, Ethan, Junior."

The three inspectors dutifully recorded the specifics. Like a patch of skin that itched for no discernible reason, the name Emmy crawled through her brain. Her synapses chased after a clue. These people were strangers, but a strong sense of familiarity crept over her. Where had she heard the name? She shook it off and checked the time on her cell phone. 9:30.

No sense all of them standing around twiddling their thumbs. "While we wait for FSU to finish," she said, "maybe we can interview the father?"

Sharpe sighed. "Tough when it's a kid involved. How about I'll start the questioning. When the drugs come up, one of you can take over. Agreed?"

No matter what order they took, this would be a rough road for everyone. A kid was dead. She swallowed hard. "Agreed." Cam and Jim Bob murmured their assent.

They trooped up and into the kitchen. Ethan Carson, Senior, sat on a stool, hunched over, elbows on the center island. Dressed in a sweatshirt and faded jeans, his brown hair stuck out in all directions. He stared at, or maybe through, them. His eyes were bloodshot. Tear stains streaked his face. This man was shattered. Maybe beyond repair. MC's heart went out to him. His life was forever changed. She possessed firsthand knowledge of such experience.

A ceramic coffee mug with the words "World's Greatest Dad" emblazoned in bright blue on the white background occupied space in front of Mr. Carson. No doubt a gift from his kids. MC contemplated what a painful reminder that simple mug would be going forward. Something that had been a source of happiness and love now represented grief and guilt. She took a deep breath and let it out slowly. She had a job to do.

The sink held various breakfast items. Bowls. Spoons. Juice glass. Crumbs speckled the counter next to a toaster. Typical family morning. Except this was anything but a normal morning.

Sharpe pulled out a stool and sat on the other side of the center island. "Mister Carson?"

"Yes." Carson's voice was craggy sounding. He cleared his throat.

"I'm Detective Sharpe with Saint Paul homicide. These are Postal Inspectors White, O'Malley, and McCall." He pointed to each of them. "We'd like to talk to you about what's happened."

"Oh, God." He rested his elbows on the top of the island and grasped his forehead with both hands.

MC perched on a stool next to Ethan Carson and placed her notebook on the countertop. She watched him struggle through what she knew were unrelenting waves of grief, sadness, loss . . . all the emotions. God, it pained her to watch him. She forced her gaze away. Focus. Keep the personal separate.

"Mister Carson," Sharpe said, "can you tell us what happened?"

He wiped his face on his shirt sleeve. "I don't know. I thought I'd locked it in my desk. Why didn't I double-check? Triple-check? She doesn't usually go into my office when I'm not there. Why?"

Was he hoping *they'd* have an answer? MC hated to tell him he was the one person able to provide the responses. The rawness of his emotions quelled her—for the moment. She wondered if the "it" mentioned was the box, and if so, the inspectors needed to question him.

Sharpe softened his voice. "Mister Carson. Please. We need you to concentrate. I understand this is hard for you. Can you do that?"

Carson made eye contact with the detective, and then briefly with each of the inspectors. A shaky sigh escaped his lips. "I think . . . yes."

"Good." Sharpe clicked his pen. "Go through your morning. Tell us everything, step-by-step."

"Everything. Okay." He released a shuddering breath, peered toward the ceiling. "Uh, Jenny woke early with the baby, with Ethan, Junior. He was fussy. I got up, too, made coffee while she tried to feed him. He kept pushing the spoon away. Whining. Crying. She gave him a sippy cup with milk. That calmed him. They sat in the dining room near the sliding doors overlooking the deck."

Silence enveloped the room. Carson appeared to be losing himself in the memory. MC didn't want him to lose his moorings and float away in a swirl of devastation, so she asked, "What next, Mister Carson?"

Sharpe's eyes drilled her. A reminder to back off, this was his interview. Too bad. The man deserved some empathy. She'd been in his shoes, having to answer questions about a loved one's death, and it wasn't easy to stay focused while trying to process the overwhelming sadness.

"What next? I . . . ah, coffee!"

"I'm sorry?" she said.

Sharpe gave MC another "back off" glare then asked Carson. "What about coffee?"

Carson said, "I poured us each a cup of coffee." He flipped a hand toward the mug in front of him. "I went to our bedroom and dressed. It was my day to drive—" He choked on the words, then rallied. "It was my day to drive Emmy to school. We, Jenny and me, switch off every other day whenever I don't have an early job. Today was my day. I, uh," he rubbed his face, "I came to the kitchen and noticed Emmy wasn't up yet. Jenny asked me to wake her. She'd soothed Ethan and didn't want to rile him."

Seconds ticked by, slow as molasses.

MC couldn't stand it any longer. "You went to wake your daughter, Emmy. Do you remember what time?"

Cam elbowed her. Sharpe cleared his throat and shot her another blistering look.

Easy, MC. Remember Sharpe said he'd take the first round.

Barb's voice. Damn that voice. But she heeded its advice. To Sharpe she muttered, "Sorry."

Sharpe stared at her hard for a second and then peered at Carson. "As Inspector McCall asked, do you remember what time you went to wake your daughter?"

"I'm not exactly sure. Maybe around seven. I remember being surprised Emmy hadn't woken up. Normally if Ethan was awake, she was too. She loved helping with him. She's a great big sister." A huge sob escaped from deep inside him. "Oh, God. Help me." Carson wrapped his arms around his midriff and rocked back and forth.

"You went to her room?" Sharpe calmly reeled him back.

Carson sniffed. Wiped his face on his sleeve. "Her room is the first one on the left, then ours. Ethan's room is across the hall from ours. Emmy's is across from the bathroom."

At least they got the floorplan from him, MC thought.

"I saw," Ethan stared into space and gave the recitation, "her door was half open. I peeked inside. Her bed was a jumble of blankets, toys, and dolls. I don't know how she can sleep with all the things in the bed, but she insists. She wasn't in the bed, though. It didn't register at first. Her favorite teddy bear was missing. Like I said, she has dolls, stuffed animals, whatever."

He fixated on a spot above Sharpe's head, seeming lost in space and time.

MC looked away, wanting to avoid the grief-stricken look on Carson's face. She felt the sting of tears forming and bent her head over her notepad hoping no one would notice.

Behind her, Cam, or maybe Jim Bob, shuffled their feet. The scraping sound interrupted Carson's reverie.

"Anyway, I checked her closet to see if she was hiding from me. She wasn't there. I went across to the bathroom. She wasn't there either. I called and called her."

Sharpe said, "Did you check your room or the baby's?"

Carson seemed confused. "I'd gotten dressed. I knew she wasn't in our room. Ethan's door was wide open, I stuck my head in and didn't see her in there."

Sharpe said, "What'd you do next?"

"Like I said, I called for her. 'Emmy, time for breakfast.' She didn't answer. I heard Ethan winding up again. I went into the dining room and asked Jenny if she'd seen Emmy sneak past her. Jenny was kinda pissed, focused on Ethan. My yelling had scared him, and he was screaming. She told me she hadn't seen Emmy. She and Ethan were facing the deck and backyard. If Emmy'd passed the kitchen, Jenny wouldn't have seen her."

Carson's pallor leaked color like a sieve. He was becoming whiter by the moment. Soon he'd be translucent, and they'd be able to see the veins and arteries and all the organs that kept him alive. Carson obviously needed a break. MC knew an unconscious or unresponsive witness impeded an investigation. "Mister Carson, may I get you a glass of water? Or more coffee?"

He squinted at her. "No. Thanks. I'm . . . no . . ." He wobbled on the stool. Jim Bob, of all people, hustled around to grab him before he landed on the floor.

Pointedly not looking at Sharpe, MC scooped up Carson's coffee cup, rinsed it and filled it with cold water. "Drink."

He gulped half the liquid and thunked the mug on the countertop. "Thanks."

Satisfied he wasn't about to drop unconscious, she returned to her stool. She cast a quick look at Sharpe. He met her gaze and nodded his head. A silent 'thank you'?

"You okay now, Mister Carson?" Sharpe asked. "Are you able to continue?"

"Sure. Sorry about that. Where was I?"

Sharpe consulted his notebook. "Your wife didn't see Emmy, and the baby was crying."

"Then I checked behind the couch and the chair in the living room, to be sure she wasn't playing a game. Re-checked her room. Our room. Ethan's room. I called her name, told her we didn't have time to play, that she needed to get dressed, have breakfast and pack for school. I was annoyed. We were crunched for time. She usually listens. She's a great kid. Jenny was busy dealing with Ethan. She paced with him. I told her to put on a movie, that usually calms him when he's super fussy."

Sharpe said gently, "Your daughter?"

MC was on pins and needles waiting for the blow she knew was coming. This poor guy.

"I had searched everywhere. Jenny told me to go downstairs, said maybe she's in the family room watching TV or playing. She would've answered me though. She'd hear me yelling for her. I was mad now. Thought she was ignoring me. I went to the basement, ready to scold her. No lights were on. I remember thinking it was odd. I flipped the switch at the bottom of the stairs to turn on the hall lights. The family room TV was off, no lights either, so I checked the bathroom, laundry room, and the furnace room. No Emmy. The final place I looked was my office—you get to it through the family room. The door was shut. I tried to open it. It didn't want to move. I pushed harder. It was like pushing dead weight—"

Tears streamed, and Mr. Carson was reduced to a sobbing mess.

Time suspended while the gathering of officers allowed Ethan Carson to come through the riptide of emotion.

Once the man regained some semblance of control, Sharpe said, "I'm sorry. I know this is difficult, but we need all the facts. Okay?"

Ethan Carson sniffed and again wiped his face on the sleeve of his sweatshirt. He nodded and drank the rest of the water in his mug.

MC braced herself for what she anticipated was coming. She scanned the others in the room. Cam's and Sharpe's eyes were glued on Ethan Carson. Jim Bob had returned to his original position behind Cam and was intent on memorizing the pattern of the woodgrain flooring beneath his feet.

Carson's voice was ragged. "So, I . . . um, used my shoulder to lever the door open enough to squeeze into the room." His gaze focused on his shaking hands clasped loosely on top of the counter. "I. She." More tears. He smeared them aside with his palms. "She was lying on the floor in her pajamas, curled around her bear. I thought she was asleep. I knelt beside her, shook her shoulder, 'Emmy, honey. Wake up. Time for school.' She just laid there. I touched her cheek. It was cool, not ice cold, but cool. The basement is chilly during the winter." His voice trembled. "She wasn't breathing. I put my hand under her nose. Nothing. I rubbed her arms to warm her. I saw—"

MC kept her expression neutral. They waited for Carson to fill in the blank.

Sharpe quietly asked, "Saw what?"

Carson swallowed. "Oh, God. The patch. Stuck to her arm, over her wrist. I saw another one stuck to her teddy bear's paw."

Sharpe said, "What kind of patch, Mister Carson?"

Carson's voice shook. "One of my pain patches. For—"

"Where'd she find it?" Sharpe's voice was soft, kind.

"—my back . . . I . . . the box. It was in the box with . . ."

Mention of the box jolted MC. Time for the inspectors to chime in. While they hadn't discussed which of them would take the lead, she'd already connected with Carson, so she took over the interviewing.

"Mister Carson, I'm sorry to put you through this. So very sorry for your loss. What type of box are you referring to?"

"A box. Mail. Priority Mail. Next to her on the floor. Somehow I knew . . ."

MC asked, "What was in the box, Mister Carson?"

"Meds. Pills mostly. Some patches."

"What kind of pills and patches?"

"Oxycodone pills and fentanyl patches. No prescription." He shook his head. "I'm careful. I secure the medicine, make sure the kids can't get hold of it. Oh, God." He lost it again.

MC scribbled notes, giving him time to compose himself. "I know this isn't easy, Mister Carson. Where'd you obtain the drugs from?"

"The Dark Web." He hung his head, a man beaten so low the fires of hell licked at him. "My doctor stopped renewing my meds a few months ago, but the pain—I still have the pain. I needed to work. I learned how to order online. But I swear, I always, I always locked it. Out of reach."

Until you didn't, MC thought. "Where did you lock it up?"

"A drawer in my desk. I must've forgotten this one time." He hung his head. "I didn't want my wife to know. I didn't want anyone to know."

Disbelief swirled through MC. He put his children's lives at risk to hide his drug addiction from his wife. Something pinged in her brain. Wasn't she doing the same thing? Hiding her addiction from everyone? This wasn't about her, though.

Clanking sounded from the lower level. From her perch, MC saw the ME staff in the foyer, hauling a stretcher with the smallest brown body bag she'd ever seen strapped to it. Emmy Carson, barely started on life before her candle flamed out. The air whooshed from MC's lungs like she'd been gut-punched. Time suspended like a morbid game of Freeze tag.

Ethan Carson nearly fell off the stool and lurched toward the stairs.

Sharpe grasped his arm. "Please, Mister Carson, let the medical folks do their job."

Carson collapsed back onto the kitchen stool, mouth agape, perhaps in silent protest. And then the dam burst, he wailed. Tears, snot, and saliva poured out of him. He bent over the counter and sobbed even harder.

MC stood, a witness to grief and to the solemn procession of medical examiner staff and crime scene techs as they exited. In a quiet voice she said, “I think we need to give Mister Carson some time. I’m done with questions for now. You guys?” She looked at Cam and Jim Bob.

“I don’t have anything right now,” Cam said.

“Me neither,” Jim Bob mumbled.

Sharpe turned toward the inspectors. “You all can go ahead with your evidence collection. I’ll stay with Mister Carson.”

MC followed Cam and Jim Bob as they descended from the main level to the foyer where the front door stood open.

Two uniforms stood outside the open front door. MC heard one say to the other, “I heard the kid’s teacher died in November. What a shitshow for the school.”

“Hey,” she asked, “what school?”

Cam and Jim Bob continued down the stairs to the basement.

The officer said, “All Saints Catholic. About half a mile from here.”

She considered pumping them for details, but the two cops were already turning away. Momentarily stunned, she stood rooted to the spot, contemplating how awful and guilt-ridden her own life had become. She shoved the rawness aside in the face of the service she needed to perform.

Emmy Carson had attended Barb’s school.

Had she been one of Barb’s students?

Then, like a sepia-toned vision, MC remembered the paper she uncovered in Barb’s car the day after her murder. A sheet with a child’s hand-shaped turkey drawing. The name, the student’s name, at the top. Holy shit. Emmy Carson. Emmy *had* been Barb’s student. And she was a year younger than Cindy, MC’s sister, had been when she’d died forty-five years ago. Cindy had been four years older than MC and might have even been a grandmother by now if she’d lived and had children of her own.

MC vowed in that moment to catch the scumbag responsible for Emmy’s death. For Emmy. For Cindy. For all the children taken much too soon.

Six degrees of separation?

A ferocity for her work fired through her.

Cam’s case wasn’t only about cutting off narcotics rings. MC now had a personal connection, a deeper meaning behind the pursuit of the asshats shipping drugs through the US Mail. An innocent had died, a tiny human. She should’ve been shielded from the dark side. Instead, she’d been swallowed by the black hole.

Aloud, MC said, “I’m gonna nail these assholes.”

Another cop entered the foyer. “Amen to that.” He shook his head. “Inexcusable. What parent . . .”

Who was he to place blame? She’d almost fallen into that mindset herself, but the loss the Carsons faced was of epic proportions and she felt crushed for them. MC slid away to find Cam and Jim Bob.

She stayed silent and didn’t let on she had the thinnest of personal connections to this case. She’d carry on in silent service.

The three inspectors located the Priority Mail package on the floor in Carson’s home office. The box contained tiny clear zipper-seal baggies of pills, along with patches of some form of oxycodone or—the newer kid on the block—fentanyl. Lab tests would provide the answers. Cam bagged it and Jim Bob took possession to ensure chain of custody.

She checked the time. Crap. An hour until her appointment. “Hey, guys. Sorry, I have to hit the road. Appointment in an hour and I can’t miss it.”

Cam said, “No worries. Before we leave, I’ll touch base with Sharpe about further questioning and getting a signed statement from Carson.”

She called Crapper to let him know she left the scene to make her scheduled weekly appointment. Lo and behold, he actually answered the phone.

Once she was through reporting her every frigging movement, Crapper said, “Fine. What’s the latest on the mailbox thefts? Where are you at on that investigation?”

MC stifled a snarky response. “More recon. Also, comb for security cameras, city-owned and private. Maybe I’ll get lucky. Have you received any more incident reports?”

She chose not to convey to Crapper that after end of shift she’d use her investigatory skills on stakeout in Forest Lake.

Crapper coughed and wheezed for a solid twenty seconds before he managed, “If I had anything I’d have passed it along.”

Asshole, she thought. “Excellent. So, I’ll end shift from the field.”

Crapper said, “I expect to see updates in DigiCase ASAP.”

“Will do.” She one-finger saluted him and disconnected.

➢⮘

At the appointment, MC dove in and told Dr. Zaulk she'd had dinner with Dara and Meg the previous week.

"Oh?" Dr. Zaulk perched on her usual chair. "How'd it go?"

"Great. Good. Ah, it was okay . . . mostly." MC shifted in her seat and avoided eye contact.

Dr. Zaulk said nothing, and the silence roared in MC's ears. She cleared her throat, met the green eyes focused on her.

"You hit a bump." Dr. Zaulk held MC's gaze. "You started all gangbusters, optimistic, and ended ambiguously. Let's dissect the situation."

MC flinched. Her heart pounded. Suddenly she was awash in an intense heatwave. She uncapped her water bottle and took a deep gulp. "Dinner was great. Pizza. We talked. I met their new barista, Zane, who seems like a great guy. All in all, the evening sailed along swimmingly. Until . . ."

"Until?" To her credit, Dr. Zaulk refrained from the handroll everyone does when they want someone to move the story along.

Get your poop in a group, McCall. She wanted to scream, "Dara couldn't NOT broach the subject of AA, thereby ruining the evening." Instead, she unscrambled her thoughts and gave the blandest of answers. "Dara and I had a disagreement."

"About what?"

MC shrugged. "Can't recall."

Liar! But no way was she going to divulge that Dara constantly harangued her about going to AA. Doc Z didn't need to know about MC's alcohol consumption or the bottle with the image of a one-eyed bird in front of a mountain backdrop. MC had it under control.

"I didn't want to make a scene in front of customers or Zane. In my mind, the best option was to call it a night and go home." Run away pissed off is more like it.

"You can't remember the point of contention between you and Dara? How was Meg?"

"Meg was . . . Meg. She wanted us all to 'get along,' spend time together. She's very much a mothering type. Keeps Dara in line." MC gave a derisive laugh. She'd keep me in line, too, if I'd give her the chance.

Dr. Zaulk apparently had enough of that topic because she changed the subject. "How are things at work? You're interacting with co-workers?"

"Work is busy. I came here from a crime scene. Narcotics investigation. And I've been handling mail theft investigations. My plate's pretty full."

Wouldn't you like to know, Doc Z, that after work the past few evenings I've stalked a person of interest in Barb's murder? But that's classified info. Need-to-know only.

"Where'd you go, MC?"

"Huh? Oh. Sorry, I was thinking about the case from this morning."

Liar, liar, pants on fire.

There was Barb's voice again. Should she mention it? What the hell. She should know if she was losing her mind.

"I've been hearing this, uh, voice, I guess you'd say. I hear it, and then nothing for weeks. But lately. . ."

"Lately what?"

"I'm hearing it daily. Several times some days."

"When you say you're hearing a voice, is it external? A noise in the environment around you? Or is it internal?"

"At first I thought it was outside of my head. I'd glance around the room and no one else was there. Must mean it's inside me, inside my mind. Honestly, the voice sounds like Barb, but I don't believe in ghosts."

"Possibly, you're hyper-focused on your loss. Your mind is searching for a healing salve. A prescription to soothe your soul. I'd bet Barb's voice calmed you, yes?"

"Absolutely. She could talk me off a cliff's edge. She could make everything right."

"I think it's part of your healing process. Are you finding you hear this voice during specific circumstances?"

MC widened her eyes at the fact that the doc didn't want to slap a strait jacket around her, have her committed, a seventy-two-hour hold at the very least. Instead, she implied the voice was natural, equivalent to waking in the morning or going to sleep at night.

Nothing to see here, folks.

Keep moving.

"I guess I've mostly heard it when I'm stressed or making not-so-great decisions." Understatements of the century, McCall.

"Share a specific instance or instances. We can take a deep dive and analyze a pathway to reducing your stress."

"Mostly it's a work-related thing." MC executed a mental slap upside her head. She's the one who broached it so why wasn't she more forthcoming with Dr. Zaulk? Honesty was the best policy. Give the doc a fighting chance at treating her properly.

No, not a good idea. Better to keep her trap shut. Dr. Zaulk would have her yanked from active duty the second she admitted to her self-prescribed nightly vodka binges and the pursuit of vigilante justice.

The job was her lifeline. Plain and simple. So, pull yourself together, McCall.

Doc Z closed her notebook. "Think about it. We'll continue at next week's session. Stick with your journaling. And I know you don't want to hear it, but I believe you'd benefit from joining a grief support group."

The doc and Dara behaved like participants in the Fantasy Football of support and recovery teams, Dr. Zaulk rallying her to attend grief group and Dara urging her toward AA. The constant clash made her head spin. She preferred the solo event—finding Barb's killer.

"The group gig isn't my thing."

"All I'm suggesting is you keep an open mind." Dr. Zaulk stood. "Time's up. Have a good week, and think about the group."

MC stopped at a convenience store and bought a lousy cup of dark roast coffee and a thirty-two-ounce bottle of water. She slurped some water, then forced herself to drink the coffee. The caffeine jolt was necessary.

She made good on her word to Crapper and patrolled the areas where the collection boxes had been burgled. The investigation had stalled, no new witnesses or cameras presented themselves, but she wanted out from under Crapper's fat thumb and figured she'd have better luck on the streets than riding her desk. So far she'd not found any carriers on their routes to interview. MC chomped at the bit to sink her teeth into a meaty lead but driving around the city looking at mailboxes wasn't cutting the mustard. She toyed with the idea of selecting a site and coordinating a stakeout, but such a plan would entail extra bodies. Crapper was sure to nix it, or worse, approve it contingent on her covering the nightshift, and that was not a possibility. Her evening dance card was full doing the do-si-do with a certain person of interest in Forest Lake.

MC rolled through the streets in a grid pattern, searching out exterior cameras on commercial buildings in the three areas where mail had been swiped. A twinkle of hope lit inside her when she found three more unobtrusively placed cameras. In two of the instances, she was unable to access the buildings to speak to anyone. She Googled the businesses and obtained phone numbers. Of course, no one answered her calls. She left voicemails with her details requesting a callback.

At the third site, an industrial area in northeast Minneapolis, she entered a long-haul trucking business. The guy behind the counter imparted bad news. They had a security camera, but it hadn't worked in over six months. No money for a replacement.

MC handed him her business card and asked him to call if they noticed anyone messing with the mailbox on the corner.

She penned notes to enter into DigiCase in the morning, insurance to keep Crapper off her back. A quick glance at her phone showed her it was four o'clock, time for her to clock in on her moonlighting job.

She drove to the Golden Arches. Another fast-food dinner. At least she'd be able to tell Doc Z she was eating.

While she waited for her order, her phone buzzed.

MC answered, "Cam. What's up?"

"Thought I'd fill you in on the Carson situation."

"Hold on, let me find a parking space." She muted him and rolled forward to accept her bag of greasy goodness along with a slightly better cup of coffee than the convenience store swill. She slid the car into a parking spot at the rear of the lot next to the trash and recycling shed and unmuted the call. "Sorry about that. I'm all ears."

"No problem. Basically, Sharpe brought Carson in for official questioning. Jim Bob and I were in an observation room, feeding him some questions. Long story short, he definitely has a drug—an opioid—problem. He's been buying off the Dark Web for months. Carson got careless, failed to secure the box. Said he'd transferred the drugs from the original package to an empty box from an order of office supplies to hide the drugs from his wife. Kid found the box, stuck a fentanyl patch on her arm and one on her teddy bear." He cleared his throat. "Probably, the kid died of an accidental overdose. We'll wait on the autopsy report for official cause and manner of death."

Silence pushed against her eardrums, like the pressure on an airplane during takeoff or landing. MC wondered if the call had dropped, but Cam's voice came through.

"Sorry. This is difficult. Shit, MC. She was a kid. Not much older than my own."

"I know, Cam. Believe me." She debated, then chose to withhold the detail that Emmy Carson had been Barb's student. No sense making waves.

"Sharpe will send a copy of the official signed statement."

Paper rattled in the background. She figured Cam was reviewing his notes, which would be meticulous.

"Macadocious Market is the Dark Web marketplace. The vendor was BlackFarmaRoad. Carson said he'd searched other sites, but they didn't have patches. Someone in cyber'll work to pinpoint the IP address. Might take a while."

"Okay." MC jotted down the particulars Cam shared, then fumbled in her messenger bag to retrieve the green "Life after Barb" notebook. She removed the folded sheet from the pocket inside the back cover and opened it. A child-sized handprint had been made into a colorful Thanksgiving Turkey drawing. Emmy Carson's name was in the top right corner, printed neatly, with a slight downward slant.

She was both gutted and determined. How could this precious child be gone? Would they track the drug supplier responsible? How would Ethan Carson live with himself knowing his addiction led to his young daughter's death? Does a parent recover from such an event?

"MC? You there?"

"I'm here. Taking notes."

"I'll have Jim Bob enter the stuff in DigiCase tomorrow. Give him practice working with the case management system. We logged all the evidence: laptop computer, teddy bear, credit card statements, several Priority Mail boxes, including the one with pills and patches inside. We'll send it to the lab ASAP." He fell quiet for three beats. "Let's call it a day."

"You guys did a bang-up job, sounds like. I'm about to be done myself. Been a long day."

Cam said, "See you in the morning?"

"Yep. Tell Jane and the kids hello from me."

"Will do."

She set the phone on the passenger seat.

Emmy Carson.

Barb.

Both needlessly, senselessly, taken from this world.

Her sister, Cindy. Her parents. All gone.

A fierce determination settled in, and the world moved on around her.

The scent of French fries from the grease-stained paper sack caught her attention. Once she finished eating, she maneuvered the car from the parking area and jumped onto northbound Interstate 35W. Thoughts of Emmy Carson were relegated to the back of her mind. For now, she needed to focus on Perkins.

Night number three. She chose a new spot to park, though she doubted anyone noticed her. The neighborhood was quiet as a tomb.

She hit play on the iPhone for the next episode of a true crime podcast—a new favorite stakeout partner. Time passed quicker when her mind was engaged.

Night cocooned her inside the Subaru. Seven o'clock. She'd give it another hour before calling it quits, one more episode of the podcast. Her gut told her if Wade didn't materialize by eight, then he was probably snug as a bug with the fam for the night.

Her finger poised over the phone screen when it brightened.

Incoming call. Jamie's number.

The battle over whether to answer or not ended when she caught the reflection of headlights coming her way from the apartment parking lot.

MC dropped the phone, unanswered, into the cup holder.

She straightened, averted her face, not wanting the occupants to catch a glimpse.

Hot damn! Perkins and company.

MC fell in behind the car. Perkins hung a left at the first street, then a right at the next corner. Grocery store, again?

Several minutes later they entered the Walmart parking lot. He slid the vehicle into the first spot after the handicap spaces.

No way was she going inside. Same protocol she'd used the other night, hang outside. Not the best circumstances. How was she going to catch Perkins alone? The family of three appeared to be attached at the hip. Her best bet would be to approach them when they returned to the car. Mom would be preoccupied with the child and MC could confront—or rather, chat with—Perkins.

Not able to contain her nervous energy, MC left her car and darted to the entrance. She paced near the doors.

Slow night at Walmart.

After about twenty minutes, she was contemplating popping inside to warm up when the doors opened, and the threesome floated out on a heat-filled gust of air.

Perkins pushed a full-to-the-brim cart loaded with plastic bags of merchandise, including a pack of disposable diapers large enough to cover a dozen babies.

Mom and Dad focused on the babbling baby—cooing, doing shit all parents do to interact with their itty-bitty humans who aren't able to tell them what the hell is up.

She shuffled behind the family hive. The baby burbled among the nonsense emanating from the parents. The infant was doll-sized. How old? Weeks? Months? She had no clue.

Perkins fobbed the vehicle to unlock it. Mom took li'l buckaroo to the rear passenger-side. MC came alongside him from the driver's side as he loaded bags into the rear hatch area. A quick peek around assured her no one else was in the area.

"Hey, remember me?"

He swung his head toward her, bags clutched in both fists. Clearly puzzled.

MC said, "Let me refresh your memory." She kept her voice level. "I was in the courtroom at your sentencing when you tossed out a threat as they hauled you away."

Thankfully the now whimpering baby distracted Mom, who murmured sweet and low, probably attempting to avoid an all-out squall.

Perkins tossed the bags into the hatch and his face reddened at her words. "Take a hike, lady. I don't know you. Got nothin' to say to you."

"Four years ago, you threatened to 'get even' with whoever put you away. Remember? You exhibited a lot of anger that day."

"I told you I'm not saying nothing. I've left that life behind. I'm—"

"Where were you on the day after Thanksgiving? This past Thanksgiving?"

"What the?"

"Answer the question and I'll leave you alone. Where were you on the day after Thanksgiving? Black Friday? Where the hell were you?" She gritted her teeth. Steam built inside her like an old-time locomotive. She fisted her hands to keep them from shaking.

Perkins slammed the hatch closed, headed for a cart corral. "Leave me the fuck alone."

MC ignored him. "Tell me where you were. It's a simple question."

He slammed the cart into the corral and stomped toward her raising his fist.

Shit. Was he going to punch her?

Instead, a finger pointed in her face. "Leave. Me. The. Fuck. Alone!"

The force of his words drove MC back a step. Adrenaline pumped through her veins like someone had cranked a spigot wide open. Then she planted her feet firmly and stood her ground. Everything around them faded to dark. All that existed was this moment. This guy. Possibly the person who'd killed Barb.

"Wade?" The woman stood at the vehicle. "What's going on? Who's she?"

The lighted lot came back into focus. MC kept her eyes on Perkins, but she called out to the woman, "How long have you two been together?"

"What? Who?" She looked at Perkins.

"Don't worry about it, Olivia, get in the car. I'll handle this."

Olivia obeyed without further ado. Good little wifey? Girlfriend?

Perkins pivoted toward the driver's door and paused. He spun around. "You can go to hell. You and whoever you work with. You've done enough to ruin my life." He scraped a hand over his face. "I have a family. A wife. A baby." He swept his arm toward the car.

One question answered—wife, not girlfriend.

He continued, "I'm not *that* guy anymore. If you don't leave me alone, I'll call the cops on you." The finger jabbed the air in her direction again.

Perkins yanked the car door open and climbed inside. He gunned the engine and backed out of the space, leaving MC standing alone in the cold.

Well, that wasn't very productive. Damn voice, always stating the obvious.

MC climbed into the Subaru, thankful no one had witnessed the altercation. She replayed the interaction in her head. Her assessment was that she'd acted unprofessional as hell. No wonder she hadn't gotten anywhere with Perkins. Crap on a cracker. She needed to get a grip and act like the federal law enforcement officer she was, for cripes sake.

MC yanked her cellphone from the cup holder. While the interaction was still fresh in her head, she dialed Detective Sharpe's number. This time, she left a detailed message about Wade Anthony Perkins and his current whereabouts.

She neglected to let him know she'd made contact with the aforementioned Mr. Perkins.

At home, she barely managed to shed her coat before she made a beeline for the kitchen. This evening required vodka. A river of it. She sucked down two ounces, mesmerized by the goose's black eye staring at her from the bottle. Then she dumped three more ounces into the glass and headed for the bedroom.

She knew she needed to slow her roll. Her mind was wound tight—a jack-in-the-box ready to pop.

MC drank a couple swallows of vodka. On one hand, she felt a sense of accomplishment. On the other hand, Wade hadn't answered her questions, which sucked the wind from her sails. She went into the bedroom and plugged the phone into the charger next to the bed. When the screen lit up, she was reminded about the missed call and voicemail from earlier. Glass of vodka in one hand, she reached for the phone, then snatched her hand back. She wasn't drunk but thought it best to not engage with work while under the influence.

Chapter Ten

The cell phone vibrated from its usual resting place—the cup holder in the Subaru. MC saw Reece-SPPD on the screen. She signaled and parked on the side of the road.

"Hey, Reece. How're you?"

"Sorry to bother you. I think we may have a situation."

"What're you talking about? Can you be more clear?"

"Not here. Can you meet me somewhere? For coffee? Quick? I promise I won't keep you."

"This is all very cloak and dagger."

"MC, I'm not purposefully being vague. I'm at the station and don't want to be overheard."

"I can meet you at Flannel. A coffee shop on Grand Avenue. You familiar with it?"

"No, but I'll find it. See you there ASAP."

MC was intrigued, but a worm of worry slithered through her. No good came of clandestine meetings on TV shows, nor in real life.

MC wheeled into a parking spot smack dab in front of Flannel's door. She entered and was instantly transported to happier times. Early morning business bustled. A foursome gathered around a table by the front windows. One person, a student perhaps, sat alone with a laptop open, a stack of books next to her. Zane stood behind the counter.

"Hey, Zane. How've you been?"

"MC! I'm great. You?"

"Fine, thanks. I'll take a super-size dark roast with room, please."

MC craned her neck to see beyond the counter to the kitchen area. "No Dara and Meg this morning?"

"No. I'm on all day. Kate is coming in for the late shift this evening."

"Kate. Wow. I haven't seen her for a long time."

"She hasn't been able to work much this semester. But I have a class tonight so I can't close."

"I see. Where are your bosses?"

"At some appointments, I think. No charge for the coffee. Meg told me to never charge you when you come in. So . . ." He focused on slipping a sleeve around her cup.

Appointments? Plural? What the hell. They told her everything. Neither had mentioned any appointments. Or had they and she'd blown it off? Shit. She wracked her brain for some bit of memory and drew a complete blank.

"Here you go." Zane handed her the beverage. "Anything else? Scone? Cookie?"

"No, thanks. Do you happen to know what type of appointments they have?"

He wiped the already-clean counter. "No idea. Sorry."

What wasn't Zane telling her? The worm from earlier returned with a vengeance.

"Thanks, Zane." She slipped a five-dollar bill into the tip jar. MC wove through the tables to the quieter space in back, a private nest of comfy chairs and a loveseat.

Reece plowed through the door as MC selected a chair. Some minutes later, with coffee in hand, Reece joined MC. She wedged herself into the other overstuffed chair, her duty belt giving her pushback.

MC said, "Tell me what's going on. Why we couldn't talk on the phone."

"The scoop is: I heard Sharpe's on a rampage this morning." Reece blew on her coffee and took a sip. "I steered clear. Has to do with Barb's case. Someone threatened to sue SPPD for harassment."

"What? Who's harassing who?"

Reece took another sip of coffee. "Damn. This is good. How did I not know about this spot? Gonna have to tell my friends."

"I'm glad you like it. The owners are my best friends, and they always have the best coffee in town. Spread the word. But somehow I don't think we're here to discuss the quality of coffee."

"MC, listen. I know I told you I'd help you. I want to. But I don't think you going rogue will help solve Barb's case. I guarantee you, Sharpe's going to contact you ASAP. What did you do?"

"What did I do? I didn't do anything."

Reece set her coffee on the side table and stared at MC. "I'm not aware of anyone else outside of SPPD being interested in your partner's murder."

MC let loose a long sigh. "Fine. I did some research. Unearthed two persons of interest from my old case convictions. One was a definite no-go. The other, a guy named Wade Anthony Perkins, seemed like a possibility. I may have surveilled and approached him to ask a handful of harmless questions. Like where the hell was he on the day after Thanksgiving? Totally harmless."

You keep telling yourself that MC.

Damn voice.

Reece whistled low and shook her head. "Negatory on the whole harmless bit. Guy called Sharpe, demanded to know who the woman was who'd confronted him in a Walmart parking lot—in front of his family."

"If you already knew what went down, why are you asking me?"

Get a grip, she told herself. She was on the verge of being unprofessional, nearly a repeat performance of her encounter with Perkins last night.

"I wanted to hear it from you instead of assuming your involvement. Here's a warning—Sharpe will probably rip you a new asshole over this—and don't doubt he's going to come after you. My source told me he had already looked into this guy. I thought you'd want to be ready with some answers for Sharpe."

"Sorry if I sounded defensive."

"Like I said, I want to help. But let's be smart about this. Can't be working against the grain."

"I appreciate you having my back. Don't put yourself in a position where you'll take any heat. This is my problem."

Reece snagged her coffee. "Time to hit the streets." She stared at the cardboard cup in her hand.

"Something else on your mind?"

"Social media."

"What about social media?"

Reece took a sip of her drink, apparently not in a hurry after all. "Have you considered using social media to crowdsource information?"

MC sat back in the chair. "What? You mean like Tweet at people? I don't use Twitter."

"I was thinking more along the lines of creating a Facebook page."

"I do have a Facebook page." She didn't mention that she thought it was possessed because, somehow, notifications suddenly appeared on Valentine's Day. "I don't remember the last time I posted on the site. Barb was a social media butterfly. She enjoyed reconnecting with old friends and meeting new friends. Wait. Are you suggesting I use her page?"

"No. Probably it'd be more effective to create a new Facebook page separate from either of your personal pages. Either a memorial or tribute page to Barb, maybe a combo memorial and call to action?"

"Interesting concept—rally people to help solve the case. Crowd-solve. I'll give it some consideration."

Reece shifted her utility belt. "I'm around if you want to bounce a game plan off me. Good luck with Sharpe. We good?"

MC stood. "We are. Be safe."

MC barely got her coat off when her desk phone rang.

"McCall." She kicked the chair away from the desk and sat.

"Inspector McCall. Detective Sharpe."

Shit. Shit. Shit.

Take a breath, MC. She seized upon the voice's advice, filled her lungs and breathed out through her nose. The voice belonged to Barb, no doubt in her mind.

"Good morning, Detective."

"What's good? Listen, I'm not going to mince words. I'm pissed. I've asked you—told you—to leave investigating Miz Wheatley's murder to me. Whether you believe it or not, we do know what the hell we're doing."

Damn. He was pissed with a capital P. MC had never heard Sharpe talk like this. He'd always been insistent, but professional. Her patience, if she'd ever had any, had worn thin with the slow train the investigation traveled on. Then again, maybe there was more happening behind the scenes than she knew.

"Do you understand what I'm saying?"

MC said, "Sorry. I missed the last part."

After a string of muffled words, she figured were expletives he came back loud and clear.

"Wade Perkins didn't kill your partner. Stop messing with my goddamn case."

"Why didn't you tell me about Perkins if you knew about him? He threatened revenge in open court. I know he remembered me. Plus, he was released prior to Barb being killed. Everything fit."

"No, McCall. Everything does *not* fit." He expelled a great gusty breath, a windstorm crackling through the phone lines. "The guy has a rock-solid alibi."

"But—"

"No, McCall. You . . ." MC heard papers crinkling or maybe the connection was scratchy. "Okay, listen, I don't want to lose my shit with you, but you're frustrating the hell outta me."

She envisioned him beet red, trying not to blow his top. A war of uncertainty waged inside her. Deep down she knew Sharpe was absolutely right and she'd overstepped, but she also didn't want to sit on her hands and wait for something to happen. Her heart felt like a lead balloon sinking fast. How could she make him understand the need to know? The grief? The guilt she felt?

"And . . . wife . . . hospital."

Wait. What was Sharpe saying?

"Would you repeat that?"

"I said, Perkins was at a hospital with his wife who was busy giving birth to their child. He's accounted for during the time Barb was murdered. His alibi was solid as a brick shithouse."

Shit seemed to be steamrolling downhill.

"I don't need to share this with you. But since you've kicked the hornet's nest and we now have a threat of a lawsuit for harassment, I'm telling you, stop. Do *not* approach Perkins. Or anyone else. You're your own worst enemy. And now you're becoming my worst fear, an out-of-control investigator who thinks she knows more than I do about how to work a murder." More indecipherable mumbling. "Please."

The door to her office burst open. "McCall! My—" Crapper's gray-tinged bulk filled her doorway. He stopped when he saw she was on the phone.

Fan-fucking-tastic. Could this day be any worse?

She pointed at the phone in her hand. Miraculously, he took the hint.

Crapper lowered his voice. "My office when you finish the call." He exited and slammed the door.

Sharpe's voice in her ear. "McCall? You with me?"

"Yes. My boss busted in. He's gone now."

"Don't make me have to call him. I'd rather not go down that road, but I will if you force my hand. And you're teetering on the edge."

You're all about taking the high road, she thought. Maybe a bit unfairly. Sharpe probably was doing everything possible. Maybe she should cut him some slack.

"I hear you, Detective. But if you'd shared what you knew with me, we wouldn't be having this conversation. Think about it, keeping me in the loop would've saved us both a headache."

Another rash of expletives burned through the lines. She held the phone away from her ear until it ended, and he calmed. "I'm serious. This is my case. You need to stay behind the yellow tape on this. I've told you a thousand times, trust me to do my job."

This dance might go round-and-round for hours. Time to acquiesce to Sharpe and shuffle down the hall to learn what had Crapper all atwitter.

"Fine. I'll back off." Not really. But she needed him off the phone.

Maybe Reece had a point. The idea of using social media percolated in MC's head. Time to try a new tactic.

Next agenda item: Crapper.

She rapped a knuckle on his office door.

"Enter!"

"You wanted to see me?"

"Sit, McCall." He jammed a sausage-like pointer finger at a chair in front of his always neat-as-a-pin desk. Crapper boggled her mind. He exuded rudeness, incompetence as a leader, and wore disheveled clothes, yet his desk was immaculate. Pristine.

He'd summoned her, his agenda. MC crossed one leg over the knee of the other and balanced her notebook on her lap. She allowed the silence to grow while he worked his way through a stack of pages in a file folder. She took in the water-stained ceiling and the furry dust on tan plastic vertical blinds covering the two windows behind her supervisor.

"McCall, I've been back since Monday and already you're sitting in my office. Day five. Why do you suppose that is?"

Captain Obvious, you ordered me to your office. MC bit her tongue to keep it from loosing her stream-of-consciousness into the room.

"Nothing to say for yourself?"

"About what?"

"About what? Christ. You take the cake, McCall."

"Roland, I have no idea what you're talking about."

He huffed a gust of fetid air between his blubbery lips. "Fine. We'll play it your way. Jamie told me you didn't answer his call last night. Nor did you respond to his voicemail message. Ring any bells?"

Fuck me.

"I was busy last night. Didn't hear the call come in and I missed the voicemail. My apologies, but I was deep into a personal issue."

"Weren't you present at the team meeting where everyone—last I checked everyone includes you—everyone was instructed to be ready for an 'all hands on deck' call?"

Take the high road.

"Yes. I was present. Yes, I heard Jamie's instruction. Like I said, I was inextricably entangled in a personal situation. So, I didn't hear the call or the message. Truly, I wasn't avoiding work, and I'm sorry."

She couldn't admit that by the time she remembered to check the notifications she was deep into her second drink. Shit. What now?

Roland's voice rose about a hundred decibels. "I've half a mind to issue a suspension for your blatant disregard for duties."

"Blatant?" MC counted to ten. "Roland, honestly, I didn't blatantly disregard anything. I've explained why I didn't take the call. I apologize, truly. Did the team encounter problems with the warrants? Were they short-handed?"

"No, McCall. No thanks to you. That's not the point, is it?"

She counted backwards from ten this time, relief washing through her. "What is the point? I come in. I do my job. I'm always available. And I do a great job despite your unfair treatment." Oh, Lordy. Cat was out of the bag now. No going back. "I don't hear about you tying anyone else's hands like you do mine. Making them report their every move to you. This is beyond ridiculous."

Oh Lord, won't you buy me a Mercedes Benz? Why the hell a Janis Joplin song lyric popped into her head now was beyond comprehension. It broke her stride which probably saved her from spouting words she'd later regret.

"You finished?"

"No." Good grief, MC, pull yourself together. Don't go over the cliff. "You put constraints on me and withhold files. How am I supposed to do my job with you working against me?"

"What the hell are you talking about?"

"The latest mailbox fishing incidents. Jamie told me he gave them to you, but you neglected to give them to me. This leads me to believe you're tampering with my work in order to make me look bad."

"No, McCall. I'm not trying to make you look bad. You're doing a fine job all by yourself. For your information, Sanchez gave me the paperwork after you left on Monday. And I wasn't here Tuesday. Right?"

Grudgingly, she said, “Right.” But it was now Friday. Why hadn’t he passed them on yet?

“Hmmph. Now that we’ve settled that problem let’s move on to the issue at hand.”

Wait. Nothing was settled. He’d glossed over not providing her the paperwork.

“Tell me why I shouldn’t immediately suspend you for last night.” He folded his meaty paws over his mountainous gut and leaned in his chair.

“I’ve explained my actions.”

“Lack of action is more like it.”

“I’ve explained myself and apologized. The rest is up to you.” She refused to dig herself a deeper hole.

“Damn straight it’s up to me. Best you remember that.” He thrust the file folder toward her. “Here’s the material from Sanchez. Conference room now. There’s an update on the op from last night, the one you conveniently missed.”

“So, may I assume I’m not suspended?”

Deep furrows appeared on his forehead ready to swallow the caterpillars over his eyes. “My advice. Never assume. When you assume you make an ass outta you and me. I ain’t no ass.”

Jeezuz, this guy with the cliches. She needed a hefty drink. A frosty thirty-two-ounce Big Gulp of Grey Goose. Hell, forget the glass, give her the bottle.

“Move, McCall. Conference room. I’ll get back to you by end of watch whether or not to report on Monday.”

Ah, hell. She slapped the folder off his desk.

“Can’t wait,” she mumbled.

“What’d you say, McCall?”

“See you in the meeting.” She skedaddled before his purpled face exploded like an overripe eggplant.

Both teams of inspectors gathered in the conference room. Jamie and Cam were already present when MC entered. She slipped into an empty chair four seats to Cam’s left.

Crapper, the grub, waddled and wheezed his way into the room and closed the door, wedging his sickly-looking ampleness into the chair beside the door.

Jamie opened the meeting with a recap of the search warrant execution the previous evening. All went down without a hitch.

Jamie wrapped up and said, "I'll let Cam give some details."

Cam leaned his arms on the conference table. "We took into evidence several packages with narcotics and cash. The postmarks were from different Minnesota towns: Two Harbors, Silver Bay, and Grand Marais. Who knows if that's a ruse? I doubt the sender lives in any of the towns."

MC wrote furiously in her notebook. Best to be fully engaged. The task helped assuage the guilt she had for disappointing Cam. Disappointing everyone. Her goal, to be more reliable, was beginning to sound like a broken record even to her.

Cam continued, "The packages recovered showed a chicken-scratched name—Wooll. Maybe Waall—mostly indecipherable. Unfortunately."

Jamie said, "Who puts their real name on drugs and mails it?"

"Exactly." Cam shifted some files around. "More than likely fake name. The address is unreadable. Probably fake too."

MC recorded the possible names. She stared at the wall behind Cam. A faraway ping sounded in her brain. The reason for the alert eluded her.

Cam continued reporting about the case, then Jamie assigned inspectors to help Cam do the deep dive work, cataloging and sending evidence to the lab. Blah. Blah. Blahbitty-blah.

Suddenly, the answer she sought hit her. Wooler. Might the name be Wooler? She remembered the name from another case. MC blurted out, "Stennard," before she could stop herself.

Everyone's gaze swung toward her.

Jamie said, "MC?"

"Cam, remember the killings in the Stennard case? The Arty Musselman murder, specifically? Wooler was one of the names we heard, wasn't it? I swear . . ." She flipped through the pages of her notebook. "Damn. Those case notes must be in my previous notepad. Is the name Wooler?"

Cam said, "I don't know. The writing's horrific. You can check for yourself in the evidence locker."

Take a breath, MC.

She muttered, "Shut up."

Cam's brows scrunched together. "What?"

"Oh, sorry! No. Not you." Now here was a new progression—responding to the voice in the presence of people. Better get your shit together before Crapper has you committed. "Talking to myself. I'll look in DigiCase." And find that notebook too. "I'm almost positive that name was part of the case."

Crapper said, "If White has doubts, then it probably isn't the name. Maybe don't waste time on it."

Now everyone focused on the floor or anywhere else in the room except her. Fuckin' Crapper. The burn spread across her cheeks like wildfire, but she managed to restrain herself and reeled in the righteous anger.

Jamie gave Crapper a look. "Moving on. Cam and I met earlier to discuss a plan of action. We want to determine if the packages from last night's raid are similar to the ones obtained from yesterday morning's scene in Saint Paul. And I think it's worthwhile to send a person north to investigate on that end."

The newbie, Jim Bob, asked, "How long we talking?"

"Undetermined at this point." Jamie looked at the inspectors seated around the room. "Any volunteers?"

Jim Bob groaned, "Up north? End of February? No thanks."

MC looked over at Cam. He raised his eyebrows, returned her stare.

What? Was he serious?

No one said a word. The HVAC system thrummed to life.

The walls closed in.

Jamie said, "MC?"

Shit. Jamie must've intercepted the eye-to-eye quiz Cam had thrown her way.

"I don't know if it's a great time for me to be gone. Between the mailbox fishing incidents increasing—"

"You dropped some decoys?" Cam asked.

"I did. On Tuesday."

Jamie jumped in. "We can have Jim Bob monitor the progress. Lessen your load. What else?"

MC drew in a deep breath. "I'm knee-deep in personal issues. Seriously, it's a bad time for me to be away." Why was she being grilled in the presence of every inspector?

Crapper said, "McCall, you're not in a position to pick and choose assignments right now." He glared at her.

MC shivered with outrage and disgust. The boss was loathsome.

Jamie said, "Roland, maybe we let everyone else go back to work and we'll discuss next moves?"

Roland colored a shade of reddish-purple reminiscent of Violet Beauregarde in *Willy Wonka & the Chocolate Factory.*

His turn to feel the burn, she thought. Easy there, big guy. MC squinted and hoped the whale wouldn't blow in front of God and everyone.

Crapper gave MC a scowl. "I'll be in my office." He rolled from the room.

Jamie said, "Everyone has their tasks. Make sure new details go through Cam or me. Go forth and conquer. MC. Cam. You mind staying for a minute?"

MC avoided any eye contact as the room quickly emptied.

The threesome remained at the table.

Cam spoke first, "MC, why the pushback?"

MC said, "Why won't you look into this possible link to Arty's case?" Why was she being pissy with Cam? They'd always gelled. Respected each other. The pit in her stomach ground deep. What she couldn't say, the truth, was she had things to do, like solve Barb's murder.

Jamie said, "We need a game plan. Cover all the bases. This case is expanding quickly."

"We need boots on the ground up north." Cam's gaze landed on MC. "Someone reliable and experienced to chat with the employees in those offices."

She held her breath. Stifled the sarcasm ready to rip forth because she realized she was lucky to still have a job after all her blunders. Her track record since December was less than stellar. Cam was right. Of course he was, and she needed to get her head in the game before they relegated her to the bench, or worse. She needed to focus on being more dependable.

Jamie said, "Cam, get to work. I'll handle Roland."

Cam stood. He paused at the door, looked at her, and exited without another word.

Jamie said, "MC, what's going on? It's not like you and Cam to be at odds."

MC said, "Why won't he acknowledge the Wooler connection to Arty's case? Maybe it's nothing, maybe it's relevant."

"You're pissed he didn't take immediate action on one possible piece of the puzzle? A weak thread, at best. On a case you're not actively working?"

"Yes. And I don't appreciate being put on the spot in front of everyone." She sounded whiny but couldn't stop herself.

Think this through. Don't act like a teenager whose prefrontal cortex isn't fully developed.

"I think there's more to it." Jamie sized her up. "You're not at all yourself. Not being available last night, aside. What aren't you telling me? Is it Roland?"

"Jamie, I'm sorry about last night. I know it was 'all hands on deck.' I was in the middle of a personal situation. Believe me, Roland already crawled up my ass for it. I'm waiting to hear if he's going to suspend me or not. After the developments in the meeting, I'm sure my fate's sealed. We finished?" She stood.

"Not quite. Please. Sit."

She slid back into the chair.

"Thank you. What's the reason you don't want to go? Is it really the mail theft cases? Honestly? Or does something else have you handcuffed? What's the real deal, MC?"

"The mail theft cases . . ." She let her statement hang.

"I can easily reassign the work to another inspector. It'd be a perfect assignment for Jim Bob to get his feet wet. I think your skills would be better utilized on the narcotics investigation. What's the issue?"

She sucked in a breath. "I was serious earlier. My head's clanging like a ten-alarm fire alert. Wooler. I'm ninety-nine percent certain Wooler was a name in the Stennard and Musselman cases."

"MC, I know you believe there's a possible connection. Maybe there is, maybe not. All I'm saying is what we have is inconclusive. The best use of your expertise and time will be ferreting out what's going on up north. Find us concrete evidence."

"Concrete."

"You're a team player, despite your recent actions or lack thereof. Be that inspector now. Besides, time apart from Roland can't be a bad thing."

"True, I guess." She propped her elbows on the table, hands over her face. Besides, she reasoned, if she gave in on this, Jamie would probably talk Crapper into reconsidering the suspension. A win-win, not to mention the right thing to do. MC lowered her hands. "Fine. I'll do it."

"That's the spirit. C'mon, we'll continue the discussion in Cam's office."

➣⮘

Jamie said, "Let's devise a strategy."

Cam warily eyed MC. "You're on board?"

"I am." Not exactly the full-blown enthusiasm they were looking for, she was sure. But it was all she was able to muster.

"MC, we need you pounding the pavement in the towns where the packages originated: Two Harbors, Silver Bay, and Grand Marais." Jamie consulted some notes. "Talk to the postmasters. Interview clerks and Postmaster Reliefs. You know the drill."

She wrote the details in her notepad and then looked up. "The assignment sounds like more than one or two nights. A lot of road to cover up there." She gathered her thoughts. Could she handle being away for an indefinite period of time? On second thought, why not? She had no one. Not accurate. She had Dara and Meg, but no Barb. No ties holding her back. A change of scenery and time to recharge her batteries began to sound enticing. "Here's an idea. My—"

"Cabin!" Cam said.

Jamie's face folded, like he was on the outside of an inside joke.

MC caught Cam's eye. "Great minds."

Jamie said, "What?"

MC brought him in from the cold. "I own a cabin—it's a year-round place now—north of Two Harbors. Haven't been there in a while."

Cam bowed his head and said in a reverent tone, "Since Barb?"

"Precisely." MC thought back to a crisp December day. She, Dara, and Meg letting Barb's ashes fly over the Lake Superior waves. And the garden plot on the lakeside of the cabin. With effort, she shook free from the web of memories. "I could work from there. Save the agency money on hotels. If Jim Bob has questions about the mail theft investigation he can call or email me. By the way, I've been meaning to ask—is Jim Bob really his name?"

"Why?" Jamie asked.

MC shrugged. "I don't know. Seems gimmick-y."

"He came onboard while you were on leave. You missed the full intro."

"When you said it in the meeting, I wasn't sure if you called him that because you're a fan of *The Waltons*, or if that's his name. Who on earth wants to be called Jim Bob? Sounds like a farmer, not that there's anything wrong with being a farmer."

"MC," Cam laughed, "you nailed that one. Kid's from Iowa and his dad *is* a farmer."

Jamie said, "I guess he's always gone by Jim Bob. Said he's named after his dad, James Robert O'Malley, and didn't like being called Junior. His dad goes by James, so—"

She held a hand up. "Okay, that's way more than I needed to know. Back to the topic at hand, another plus is I have full connectivity in the cabin. Internet access won't be a problem."

She felt surprised at how eager she suddenly was to jump on the bandwagon. She'd sink her teeth into the meat of the work. This time, she'd honestly prove her reliability. Especially after the miscue last night. Crapper appeared to be the lone person perturbed by her absence at the op. Jamie might be a bit disappointed, but he seemed ready to let her atone for the mishap.

The more she thought about it, the more sense it made for her to blow town. Give Sharpe a chance to cool off. Crapper, too.

The decision was made that MC would head up north on Monday, and Jamie left to lay out the plan for Roland. MC crossed her fingers wishing Crapper forgot about the suspension, which meant she'd back-burner dealing with any fallout.

Cam said, "I'm supposed to be on a conference call. And I'm leaving early. Kids have doctor appointments."

"The kids okay?" A pang of guilt rippled through her. She'd been lax in the friendship department.

An unhappy Barb reprimanded MC for her inability to stay connected. *Do better. Friends are important.*

"They're fine. Vaccination time. We managed to schedule both on the same date. Great parenting decision since we'll have two cranky kids, but you gotta grab the time when it's available."

"I hear cookies cure cranky-kid syndrome."

"Ha! I wish. So, we done?"

"Sure." MC felt good to be even somewhat back in Cam's good graces, but she still fully intended on pursuing the Wooler matter, despite his brush-off.

At her desk, MC dug in a file drawer where she kept her full notebooks. She was elbow deep when a knock sounded at her door.

"Yes?"

The door opened and Chelsea Grey, the admin assistant, popped into the room. "Hey, MC. Some mail addressed to you."

"Oh, thanks, Chels. Can you toss it on my desk? You didn't have to hand deliver it, but I appreciate it."

"You doing okay?" Chelsea placed a slew of envelopes on her desk.

"I'm fine. Why do you ask?"

"It's—I'm worried about all you've gone through and now with Roland back—"

"Roland's rough. I'll figure it out. Thanks for your concern." Understatement of the year, but she had enough sense not to speak her truth out loud.

"Good luck. Stay strong." Chelsea quietly closed the door behind her.

MC continued rummaging through the file drawer. The fourth notebook she extracted was labeled Stennard/Musselman Notes. "Yes!"

She shoved the mail aside and whipped open the black Moleskine. Echoes of Cam's voice teasing her about the fancy notebooks distracted her for a second, and she wished they were back to their easy camaraderie.

Concentrate. She skimmed pages.

Bingo!

Right before Christmas she'd had a phone conversation with FBI Agent Ferndale. He'd given her names of two persons of interest in the Arty Musselman murder: Nick Wooler and Quentin Laird. Wooler and Laird were employed by Len Klein, head of security for the now defunct Stennard Global Enterprises.

The two in question hadn't been actual employees of the business. They'd been paid under the table by Klein. No one had been able to interview either Wooler or Laird during the investigation. In fact, the duo had curiously disappeared off the planet. And to her knowledge they were still disappeared.

Notebook clutched in one fist, MC made a beeline for Cam's office. She knocked once and entered when she heard his voice. "Check this out."

"I need to finish this before I leave. Can it wait?"

"No, I don't think it can. Remember earlier when I said Wooler sounded familiar?"

"C'mon, MC. Please. Can we not do this now? I'm buried here." He rubbed his eyes.

How had she not noticed earlier how fatigued he appeared? "Hear me out." She laid the notebook flat in front of him with her finger on the page. "Read."

"Okay. Great. But the name on the packages may not be Wooler."

"Cam! C'mon."

"Again, doesn't prove anything. It could be a coincidence."

"For the record, I don't believe in coincidences. So, for shits and giggles, consider the fact that no one on Arty's case had been able to locate either Laird or Wooler. We weren't able to question them. Gone. Melted away like snow on a warm sunny spring day."

Cam pushed back from his desk. "You're right. I'll make a note of it."

"Don't ignore this, Cam," she pleaded. "It might be the linchpin."

"This investigation is a mean machine with extensive moving parts. MC, you've been all over the map lately." He raised a hand. "I empathize with what you're going through. I don't know if I'd be able to stand upright, much less function at work, after going through the horror you've encountered. We're friends, but we're also colleagues, and I need to know you'll pull your weight on this."

"Don't worry about me. I'll be fine. And I'll do it. I'll pursue the line of investigation—"

"No. I mean, I guess if you come across something that's great. But please, don't get sidetracked. Don't—"

"What?"

He hesitated. Dragged a hand through his already disheveled hair. "I know you're still after finding out who killed Barb. Please don't go hellbent off the rails on me on this. Okay?"

"This isn't about Barb's case." A twinge of hurt cut through her. "It's a possible lead that might link the drugs case to Arty's case."

"That's a reach, though. Can we agree the spotlight needs to shine on finding drugs?"

"Cam, whoever Arty's phantom kidnapper was, Stennard hired them. Stennard pulled the trigger, but he admitted he'd hired someone else to do the deed. I know the murder isn't our case, but if the players could be the same, don't we have a duty to check it out?"

"I'm sayin' I know your intensity when it comes to nailing the bad guys, whether it be Barb's killers or Arty Musselman's. But Arty's case is under the purview of the FBI, not us. The task force was disbanded."

Why wouldn't he consider the option of nailing the villains in the Musselman case? But his pushback against reviewing the old case notes wasn't the only thorn in her side.

"Maybe at least acknowledge the possible thread? Possibly, the new narcotics cases somehow tangentially connect to these two dudes from the Stennard/Musselman cases." She leaned on Cam a bit. "I know our responsibility is for paperwork and testifying if there's a trial. Do we blow off a possible link? Like it doesn't exist?"

"Other than," he held up his thumb and index finger with the thinnest of spaces between them, "a slight similarity in names, there's no connection between the narcotics investigation and the other. It's a stretch."

MC capitulated with a sigh. "Okay." No sense in pushing him.

"You'll concentrate on what we need while you're in the northland?"

"I said you can count on me. I meant it. The possibility of a connection between this narcotics case and the Stennard/Musselman cases, you're right, it's a reach." MC needed him to know she'd be solid. Mostly.

"The main focus is on what you can uncover. This stuff is killing people. Opioids along with this newer synthetic—fentanyl. This shit must be eradicated. I can't imagine if my kids . . ."

Like Emmy Carson from yesterday, MC thought. Gears shifted. Her mindset switched like a train onto a new track. At this point, the quicker they captured this band of killers, the better.

"I'm with you. Promise. I'll do a bang-up job." She couldn't refrain from one more shot. "How about I leave the notebook with you? In case you want to take a peek?"

"If I want to look at it, I'll get back to you. At the moment I'm swamped."

"You know where to find me if you change your mind. Tell the fam hello."

She ducked out.

In her office she packed her laptop and notebooks, including the one she'd tried to convince Cam to review. She set the bulging messenger bag aside, ready to take when she left for home.

Not knowing how long she might be domiciled at her Northwoods abode, she surveyed her desk to ensure she hadn't missed anything of vital investigative importance.

The envelopes Chelsea left caught her eye. She swept the stack in a pile and shuffled through them, all were the decoy mailpieces she'd dropped in the blue collection box earlier in the week. The bait she'd sent had been processed, but none had been hooked by an errant fisher. MC fastened the bunch with a rubber band. She plastered a yellow Post-it note on top with her findings. In the copy room where each inspector was assigned a cubby for mail and correspondence, she tucked the pile inside Jim Bob's slot.

Back at her desk, she wiggled the mouse to wake her desktop computer. She sent an email to Jim Bob letting him know the test mailpieces had all come back and she'd left them for him. Let him determine how to proceed, she thought. He's a full-fledged inspector.

She reviewed her Outlook calendar. No meetings or tasks were on her docket.

MC opened the case management system and accessed the Carson case. Despite the horror of yesterday's death scene, and the crushing knowledge that time was of the essence in nailing the purveyors of the goods that had killed a child, a wink of optimism sparked in MC. She wasn't convinced there wasn't a link to the pair of missing men in the Stennard/Musselman debacle.

Time would tell.

A bright spot in all this fuckery? A break from Crapper. She heaved a sigh of . . . relief? Definitely worth a bit of a celebration.

"And I know the perfect way to celebrate," she said to the computer screen.

She signed off DigiCase, headed to the ol' homestead.

Another excuse to dive into the bottle, the voice echoed around her.

Dara would agree if she'd been there to hear the whispered admonishment.

Maybe she'd stop by to check on Dara and Meg, ask about the appointments Zane had mentioned. Inquire what they'd wanted to talk about when they were last together. Before Dara brought up AA for the millionth time.

Her blood boiled thinking about it. Did she want another confrontation? Especially after the bloviating from Crapper earlier? Not to mention the shellacking she'd taken from Detective Sharpe.

Nah. Go directly home.

Do not pass go.

Do not collect more angst and anguish from her friend. She'd navigate that tightrope when she had more capacity, after the current investigation was completed.

A glass of Grey Goose sat on the nightstand next to the bed where MC's suitcase, about the size of a steamer trunk, gaped open. She quickly filled it with an array of khaki pants and oxford button-down shirts for work along with jeans, sweatpants, flannel and waffle-weave crewneck shirts for everyday wear. She took a swallow of vodka and nabbed her toiletries kit, intent on gathering all the necessities from the bathroom when her phone buzzed.

Text message from Dara. *Hi. Long time no see. Wanna come have a cup of coffee with us? Maybe help us close? Like old times.*

Shit.

She wanted to avoid a confrontation with Dara about AA. Or about anything for that matter. A part of her wondered about the mysterious appointments. Go? No?

She typed a quick reply. *Sorry not a good time. Busy. Soon tho.*

Dara sent another message. *Pls. We need to talk. An hour?*

MC sighed. *Srsly. I can't. I'm leaving town tonite. Work. Up north. Not sure when I'll be back. Can we make a date later?*

She hadn't planned to leave until morning, a departure change provided the perfect avoidance tactic. And saved her from being labeled a liar.

A sip of vodka failed to soothe MC. Fingers crossed Dara would back off, she sat on the edge of the bed next to the suitcase. Enough time elapsed for another healthy slug from the glass. The phone buzzed.

North? The cabin? Maybe Meg and I could join you on the weekend? Give us a chance to talk?

Too damn many questions. Definitely not the response she hoped for. She gave Dara an "A" for persistence. Be nice, she chided herself.

Maybe another time? Super busy.

MC drained the remainder of the Goose. Ice clinked against the glass.

Another text. *How about one day. Tmrw? Or Sunday?*

This weekend won't work. I'm on duty. She needed some space! Why was Dara so insistent? Again she pondered whether Dara's invitation had anything to do with the appointments Zane had mentioned.

Please.

The lone word glared at MC from the phone screen. Accusatory? Pleading? To add insult to injury, the dreaded three gray dots glimmered.

Shit.

Dara was typing another text.

MC's head pounded in sync with the pulsating dots. She wanted to know about those appointments, but she couldn't muster the energy to deal with it at the moment.

The circles disappeared.

She stared at the phone. Relief flowed through her. Then the damn dots reappeared followed by another text.

Sorry to be a pest. Safe travels.

Way to go, McCall. A mix of sheepishness and relief flooded through her.

A shadow of guilt draped over her as she washed the glass. She held the tumbler, mesmerized by the crystal-clear waterfall. The flow of the liquid gushing—or maybe the rush of self-reproach—woke the demon, the thirst.

No. No more Goose.

She tidied the kitchen. The fridge was empty but for condiments. She'd dumped the trash earlier. All set.

MC finished packing, taking extra special care to cushion the unopened 1.75L bottle of Grey Goose, like the precious baby it was, inside her second suitcase. The food stores she had in the kitchen were slim pickings: a package with three bagels, some butter, and raspberry jam. She tossed the whole shebang into a brown paper grocery sack. At the last second, she included the three packages of instant ramen noodles from the cupboard, a throwback to her college days when she lived on the salty noodle soup. The supplies would tide her over until she had time to visit the grocery store in Two Harbors.

She surveyed the piles and suitcases. Someone might think she was moving out. She huffed and puffed through three trips from her third-floor apartment to the parking lot. Sweat coated her brow despite the freezing temp.

Evening segued to night. She cranked the key in the ignition and glanced at the time on her phone. After six. With one stop in Hinckley for gas and maybe a cinnamon roll from Toby's, she'd arrive at the cabin around nine.

She worried about distancing from Dara and Meg. They'd understand her need for some space. Eventually.

Dara laid the phone on the table and rested her hands over it.

Meg asked, "What'd she say?"

Dara looked at her partner. "Unequivocal no. What the hell's wrong with her? I was polite. Didn't mention AA. I avoided all the triggers. I think I did anyway."

Meg sighed. "What exactly did she say?"

"She's leaving town. Work."

Meg shrugged. "There we go. Work is work. She can't help it if she has to leave."

"Meg, she's going to the cabin. I tried to convince her to give us some time. We could have joined her. Relaxed and had the opportunity to share your news in a setting where she'd be able to absorb it all."

Meg sipped her tea. "She refused?"

"Correct." She gazed around the coffee shop, not certain what she was looking for. Every fiber of her being screamed for a stiff whiskey.

Dara slapped the chair into the table. She pursed her lips to keep her pent-up anger, sadness, and annoyance from spouting like a fire hose. MC was to blame for her sudden urge to drink. More than twenty years since her last drop of alcohol but, in this moment, she could easily slide the slippery slope into the oak-barreled bottle.

Nope. Stop it. She gripped her head and shook some sense into her noggin.

"Dara. Please. Come sit."

"How can you be calm? I'm so flustered I—"

"You don't need that drink you've convinced yourself you need. We both know that. Going to a meeting tonight might help."

Dara snorted. She'd been adamant that MC needed AA, maybe it's what she herself required.

Then the drink lust departed, carried off into the night.

Dara gazed at Meg's pale blue eyes, wordlessly imploring her to be okay. Her silvery-blonde hair fluffed around her head. Dara wondered how long Meg would have her hair. Was shopping for a wig in their future? Or Meg might go with knit caps or scarfs.

The sting of a thousand bees hit her eyes. Tears flowed. Dara slid her butt onto the chair.

Meg engulfed one of her hands. "Don't cry, hon. Please. If you start, I'll join, and we'll be a sobfest for the whole shop to watch. We don't want to scare our customers away."

Dara squeezed Meg's hand and choked back her sorrow. "You're peaceful. Caring. I don't know how you do it. I don't deserve you."

"Oh, stop! Don't talk like that. Stop disparaging yourself."

"Why is MC being like this? We're her family. She's our family. We need each other. Now more than ever."

"We can't know what's in her mind. You did your best. MC knows our door, our hearts, are always open for her. She's on a journey which she needs to navigate on her own. I'm convinced her compass will find her true north and point her to us."

"I'd hoped to tell her about your cancer before your first treatment. She'll be upset when she hears after the fact. Dammit, it'll be her own fault if she's not there. It's not like we haven't tried to clue her in on the situation." Anger bubbled. "This obsession with finding Barb's killer has her frozen in a time warp. Nothing matters. Not us. Seems like not even her job. The murder—a singular focus—it's not healthy. MC's in a destructive state of mind."

She tried to cool her jets. Meg needed her calm, not flying off the handle. But she couldn't help herself. "We have to guide her, Meg. Show her the way. Or I fear the outcome will be catastrophic."

Meg squeezed Dara's hands between her own. "We have a bit of time until my first treatment. Maybe she'll come around. If not, we'll bring her into the fold when she's ready. That's all we can do." She patted Dara's cheek. "I love you."

Dara dammed the tears ready to again let loose. A bit of time? Meg's first radiation appointment was less than three weeks away. "I love you." She leaned over, kissed Meg softly on the lips, not caring one whit about the six or seven customers scattered around the shop. All she thought about was this woman. Her rock. Her safe harbor who needed her to be solid now. They'd battle this demon together. With or without MC.

Chapter Eleven

The late morning sun beat on the dry pavement on Minnesota Highway 61. Bright blue sky opened wide overhead. Not a cloud in sight. MC was southbound from Silver Bay toward Two Harbors. Her day had begun at the butt-crack of six in order to make it to the Grand Marais Post Office, forty miles south of the Canadian border, by half past eight.

The first half of the drive was misty, like a black and white movie in the heart of London. She half expected to see a cloaked Jack the Ripper sweep into sight. Then the sun rose and the fog burned off, revealing forested areas sans Jack the Ripper.

Last day of February and the day hadn't brought a snow squall. Lake effect snow was problematic along the North Shore. She enjoyed the ease of the dry, unencumbered highway with the still snowy outline along the sides of the road.

The postal clerk on duty when MC arrived was less than helpful. Not a negative attitude, but because she was from another town and filling in for the regular person. She had no idea about customers bringing in quantities of Priority Mail boxes or if there was a list of such customers. MC determined there were no lobby cameras. A bust, but good to know.

She left her business card and a note for the postmaster to call her on Monday morning to schedule a time to meet.

MC scrutinized the area outside the office, which was built into a hill like a bunker. There literally was no back to the building on the outside.

She stood in the parking lot. The loading dock was on the left and a glass door where employees entered and exited was about midway along the building. Through the window, MC saw a wall of silver post office boxes. The customer entrance was around the side along Second Avenue.

She faced away from the post office and spied a bank, a hotel, and a gas station across the highway. Beyond the hotel, she saw the steely vista of Lake Superior. The freshwater lake always took her breath away.

MC recalled a segment on Lake Superior shipwrecks Minnesota's Public Radio had broadcast in the fall on the anniversary of the sinking of the *Edmund Fitzgerald*. The host talked about how there'd been about three hundred and fifty shipwrecks on Lake Superior. Folks said Lake

Superior didn't give up her dead. More than ten thousand lives had been taken by the waters of *gichi-gami*, the Ojibwe name for the lake, meaning "great sea." The name was fitting because Superior was the largest freshwater lake in the world.

The idea that thousands of people had lost their lives in the dangerous, yet beautiful, waters boggled the mind. To remind her exactly how powerful it was, the waves and crashing ice echoed. A chilly gust of wind whipped across the expanse. MC hopped into her car and pointed it southward.

Her stop at the Silver Bay Post Office was also disappointing. Ten minutes was enough time for the temp employee to tell her he had no clue about customers and loads of Priority Mail packages. Again, she left a business card and note for the postmaster.

She thought about stopping for a coffee but didn't see any coffee potential in the strip mall where the post office sat tucked next to a True Value Hardware store. And she didn't have time to drive through the sleepy hamlet in search of some java. The Two Harbors Post Office closed at eleven thirty on Saturdays. According to the map app, the drive took thirty-four minutes. She'd barely squeak in before the doors were locked.

At the Two Harbors office, her luck changed. The postmaster was actually on duty. MC waited for a white-haired spitfire to pay for her postage stamps while she praised the postal service for their ongoing dedication to service and affordable stamp prices.

Certain she'd missed the part of the program where the bundled, elfin woman disclosed all the town's weekly secrets, MC found the gal's effervescence uplifting.

The woman said, "Thanks, Pete! You're the best."

The guy grimaced like he had a bad case of gas and shooed the woman out.

The spritely one yanked her knit winter cap over her ears and winked at MC. A multitude of wrinkles around her sapphire eyes indicated a life filled with jubilation. She sped past MC with a little hand waggle. "Have a great day!"

MC said, "Thanks. You too," then she hurried to the counter. "Morning. I'm Postal Inspector MC McCall." She showed him her ID. "You're the postmaster? Might we chat?"

The man behind the counter frowned. He scanned the office behind him before facing MC. "Of course. Sounds serious. Come on through.

And yes, I'm the postmaster. Name's Pete Norgrove. Call me Pete." He unlocked the gate at the end of the counter and hefted the countertop upwards to allow MC to pass through. "You here for some type of unannounced audit?"

"Audit?" She hesitated, worried about his reaction to her inquiries. "No, nothing like that. I'm working a case out of the Twin Cities and need some help."

"That's a bit of a relief." The postmaster stood a hair above MC's five-feet-eight-inches. He sported a shock of bright white hair floating over somber brown eyes. "Been postmaster here for," he gazed at the ceiling, "doggone, I guess it's twenty-nine years. Never had problems with an audit. Before that I was a clerk in Duluth. I do recall a couple of audits there." He shook his head. "Time flies."

MC speculated he'd been eligible for retirement for some time. Like many small-town postmasters, he'd keep the job until he couldn't do it anymore.

Another scowl crept across his face, and he checked his watch. "Go on and take a seat." He pointed to an office not big enough to swing a cat around, with a desk crammed inside and barely room for one visitor chair. "I'll lock the front door and post the closed sign."

MC lowered herself into the dated, though fairly clean, visitor chair in front of his desk.

Pete was back in a flash. "What brings you here from the Cities in the middle of winter?"

"We think narcotics—opioids—are being shipped from here via Priority Mail. Possibly in weekly allotments. Are you aware of any customers who mail loads of Priority Mail items on a weekly basis? Or on any consistent schedule?"

Pete scanned the water-stained ceiling tiles in the office.

MC peeked upward, wondering if there was some magical answer written on the squares. All she discerned were a bunch of rusty-brown spots that could be used for a Rorschach Test.

His gaze came back down to earth. "We do have a few folks who send Priority Mail packages weekly. People who do eBay sales on the Internet and the like. My two clerks haven't mentioned anyone suspicious, though."

"Anyone you don't know? I assume you're familiar with most of the people who come in, especially during the winter when tourists are safely tucked in their homes in the Cities, or maybe in warmer climates south of the frozen tundra that is our great state."

Pete rubbed a finger across his chin. A faint scritching sound accompanied the movement. "Hmmm."

MC tried not to frown. For Pete's sake, no pun intended, can we move this along? Was he being deliberately obtuse?

"Now you mention it, I do recall there's a younger fella. Comes in weekly. I don't know his name. Seems nice enough." He settled his puppy-dog gaze on her.

Nice or rude mattered naught. MC meticulously recorded in her notebook the tidbits Pete provided her.

"Does he come in every week?"

"Yep."

"On a specific day or days?"

"If I remember correctly usually Tuesdays. Late afternoon."

MC curbed her impatience at the plodding pace. Pete was, after all, answering her questions, which was better than having to extract details from him like a dentist digging out a tooth. She took a breath and proceeded. "Does he bring in the same number of packages each time? Any consistencies you can define?"

"If memory serves, he drops off a plastic tub. One of our flat-mail tubs, the deep ones, filled with Priority Envelopes."

A veritable deluge of information.

Patience, MC.

The hairs on MC's neck raised up. The voice had followed her to the northland.

MC said, "Always envelopes?"

"I didn't say that."

"Could you elaborate?"

"I dunno. I guess maybe sometimes there are boxes. Of course no perishables or flammables. That sort of thing. The clerk always asks the pertinent questions of all customers before accepting any packages. We always follow the rules in this office. We believe in good customer service."

"Good customer service is important, but it's not the concern in this instance." Did Pete not comprehend the import of what might be happening in his office? "So, do the packages, er, envelopes have postage affixed or—"

"No. I don't think he uses Click-N-Ship. I believe he pays in cash." He sat in his chair, mouth scrunched sideways in thought. "Yes. Cash. I've mentioned Click-N-Ship to him."

"What'd he think about your suggestion?"

"Didn't seem at all interested. Said if the line was too long, he'd find another office to mail from."

"Didn't that seem like an odd response?" She was seeing red flags flapping in the wintery breeze.

"No. Should it?" A scowl crossed his face. "Unlike Joy, who you met earlier, some folks like to take care of business."

Joy. Of course. The Christmas elf who had danced past her earlier was named Joy. MC consulted her meager notes. Tuesday Drop-off Guy sounded like a person of interest. "The loss of revenue doesn't bother you? I'd think you'd want to bring in all the business possible."

"It's all the same. USPS is an immense organization." He shrugged. "What one office misses another gains."

Pete's take on postal business didn't align with the attitudes of others who worked in post offices across the district. Some of his answers pinged her Spidey senses.

"Listen, Pete, here's what's going to happen. I don't know if your customer is our guy or part of a ring or none of the above. Maybe he's a run-of-the-mill postal patron. But because he mails packages on a fairly consistent basis, I'm going to contact my supervisor and ask him to authorize our technician to install cameras at your front counter."

Pete stared at her. His face had faded to a ghostly white. "Cameras? Is that necessary?" He fiddled with a mess of papers on his desk, not making eye contact. He straightened them and arranged them into a neat stack. "Will they only be at the front? When will that happen? Do I need to tell my clerks? Or the carriers?"

Suddenly good old Pete was full of questions. Were those beads of sweat popping on his forehead? He looked as if he might lose his lunch.

MC kept her voice calm. "The cameras would be in the front. I think it's best we install them before the end of tomorrow night. When you open on Monday, we'll be ready to rock. For now, there's no reason to say anything to the employees. Maybe speak with the clerks about being aware of people with multiple Priority Mail items. Make extra sure they're above board. Review the return addresses, see if anything seems odd. But for now, keep the camera install under wraps. If employees know about the devices, they'll stare at them, drawing unwanted attention." MC grabbed her cell phone. "Give me a minute to start the ball rolling with my boss."

Pete catapulted from his chair. "I'm going to count my drawer and prep the outgoing mail while you take care of your business. Let me know if you need me." He disappeared toward the front of the building.

MC contacted Jamie and explained her plan. He agreed it sounded like a good move. He'd send a tech to meet MC and Pete at the PO Sunday afternoon. The technician would mount the cameras and a separate DVR device and would train them how to view live feed from Pete's desktop computer. All the details set, MC left Pete to his business and exited out the dock door because Pete had secured the front lobby area. She'd taken half a dozen steps away from the building when a booming clatter sounded behind her. She considered returning to see what had made the noise and if Pete was okay, but the door had closed, and no one was on the dock. A postal box truck, or what MC thought of as a semi-truck wannabe, trundled into the parking lot and backed up to the dock. The driver rang the doorbell and Pete opened the door. He was upright, obviously not in need of assistance so MC went about her business.

The sun shone bright in the sky. MC soaked in the rays all the way back to her car, breathing in crisp air that was a refreshing change from the musty building.

Despite Pete's inexplicably odd affect, MC felt confident she'd put the wheels in motion to find the asshats dealing opioids. The thought of little Emmy Carson losing her life so senselessly was the catalyst to flush out those responsible.

The afternoon opened wide before her. She headed toward the supermarket. Time to fill the bare cupboards.

MC spent a solid forty-five minutes at the grocery store and hauled away four bags of nearly everything the place stocked. Next stop was the gas station on the north end of town. She filled the Subaru's tank and ran the car through the car wash.

Prisms of light dazzled her eyes as she drove away in her freshly clean vehicle. The little things in life were worth enjoying.

Next stop, Harbors Pizzeria. She deserved a treat. A pepperoni pizza fit the bill perfectly. The next store over, Lighthouse Liquor, was a beacon calling her name. MC purchased a Paul Bunyan-sized bottle of Grey

Goose Vodka and a six pack of Castle Danger Cream Ale, her favorite from the local brewery and a superb match for pizza.

The inside of the car windows steamed from the warm pizza. MC's mouth watered at the thought of diving into the pie face first.

She tromped on the gas pedal, anxious to be home. Four miles outside of Two Harbors she slammed on the brakes, narrowly avoiding rear ending a junk truck. Her mind had been occupied with a task list, and she'd failed to notice a beat-up truck full of flotsam slowing to a stop in front of her. The back taillight signaled a left into a place called Gunderson's Salvage Yard and Gun Range.

Interesting combo, she thought.

The truck trundled over a frozen, rutted gravel driveway. Its slatted wood sides bowed outward in an effort to contain the load. The vehicle passed a steel pole barn and approached a ten- or twelve-foot-high chain link fence with black privacy slats and a rolling gate. The gate opened, probably in response to a device like she had for the cabin's garage door. A flash of orange and black caught her eye before the truck blocked her view. Stacks of something? In a junkyard, it could be just about anything.

A horn sounded behind her. She tossed an apologetic wave at the driver and set off.

Ten minutes later she drove into her garage and took two trips to unload the car. The winter silence calmed and disoriented her at the same time. She locked the garage door and followed the walkway to the house, a sense of 'belonging' settling over her. She put the groceries away and changed into sweats and a long-sleeved t-shirt. MC left a lamp on in the bedroom and made her way down the hallway toward the small living room. Above her, the loft area, which was her favorite spot, held a small office alcove for her to work and towering windows facing the lake. On the other side of the loft, across from the windows, was a stone fireplace, above which a TV the size of a drive-in theater screen hung. A comfy couch and a couple of recliners completed the room.

Back in the kitchen, MC tore a golden-colored can of beer off the plastic ring and slid several square-cut pieces of pizza from the cardboard box onto a plate. Thusly fortified, she sat at the kitchen table, facing the sliding patio doors and looking out onto the lake to enjoy her repast.

The whisper-voice was silent.

MC surveyed her abode. Her home, her northland home.

Warm.

Quiet.

Peaceful.

But mostly . . . lonely.

She cleared the detritus of her meal and traded the empty beer can for a glass of vodka.

Now would be a good time to work on the Facebook page, before she swirled into the evening's vodka-induced spiral to hell.

At her desk in the cabin's loft, she opened her laptop.

First order of business was to create an anonymous Gmail account. BFK_2014@gmail.com seemed fitting. BFK for BlackFridayKiller and the year. She navigated to Facebook where she completed the specifics for a basic Facebook account. MC sucked in a mouthful of liquid courage and clicked to create a community page she named Catch My Black Friday Killer.

She typed a brief description:

> **Help my family and friends bring my killer(s) to justice. If you have any info—no matter how inconsequential it may seem—please comment or message this page. Peace and love to all.**

For the cover photo on the page, MC pasted a snippet of map showing the area of their old neighborhood. And for the profile pic she used Barb's last year's teacher photo.

The first post read:

> **The day was snowy. Black Friday. I came home from an early morning shopping spree. My yuletide joy was blown to smithereens when I entered my home via the back door. Bags of gifts and holiday decorations in hand, I was shot and fell dead on my kitchen floor. Who were you? Why were you in my house? If you were burglarizing us, why not take what you wanted and leave? What did I do to you? Did I know you? I had a lot of life left to live—WHY? If anyone has any knowledge of who murdered me, please message or comment on this page. My family and friends deserve to see my killer(s) caught and punished.**

Whew . . . that was thirsty work. MC downed the clear liquid, eyes glued to the shimmering screen with the alcohol burning the back of her throat. She set the empty glass aside. Finger poised to click the publish button, she wavered. Was this a good idea?

Progress required forward momentum. She clicked and was now officially enrolled in the world of online sleuthing.

Before she changed her mind, she logged off Facebook and closed the laptop. She texted a message to Kiara Reece: *Did it. FB page. Catch My Black Friday Killer.*

MC silenced her phone, half afraid Reece might reply with recriminations about the social media page. She feared, too, that she'd not receive any response. Which would be worse? These were the types of ponderings that fed her guilt-riddled mind.

Hours of nocturnal loneliness loomed ahead of her. She went down to the kitchen for a refill, the second of *X* number of shots, to wash the desolation away and power her through another night. She refused to outright acknowledge the undiluted clear liquid was an alcoholic's anesthesia.

The Two Harbors Post Office was a beehive of activity. Monday mornings were obviously busy, even way up on the North Shore. Three of the four carriers were chattering with one another about their weekends. The fourth, a twenty-something Ichabod Crane-type, had a set of headphones clamped over his giant mop of curly brown hair and sorted mail into his case at a speed that made MC dizzy.

Pete was knee deep, counting stamp stock, while his window clerk waited on customers, one after another.

The hubbub made MC's insides frenzied. Not able to sit still, she explored the rest of the building. The four carriers' mail sorting cases lined one side of the office. Two restrooms and a break room were squished next to a utility room. In the break room, an apartment-sized refrigerator, microwave, and snack machine left barely enough space for two round tables with four chairs each.

A set of wide, swinging doors was behind the carrier cases. To the left of the doors, four plastic pallets leaned against the concrete wall. An odd spot for pallets, but who knew what logic Pete used to run the show.

She wandered over to the doors and discovered they were locked with steel shafts pushed into the top of the door frame and into the concrete floor. A thick chain looped through holes in the doors was an extra deterrent for thieves.

Following security regs. Check.

MC peered through the safety glass windows and scanned the concrete loading dock. To the left she caught a glimpse of kelly-green. She remembered Saturday seeing six green plastic recycling containers staged on the dock.

In the parking lot, four LLVs—Long Life Vehicles from which deliveries were made—were parked in a row, good soldiers waiting to be filled when duty called.

A voice behind her said, “Need the door unlocked?”

Startled, MC pivoted and had to tilt her head back to see the speaker’s face. Mr. Mophead. His headphones were looped around his neck, and she thought she heard polka music coming from them. Polka music? Really? “No, thanks. I’m Postal Inspector McCall.” She extended her right hand toward him.

Ichabod stared at her hand, one foot tapping to the music. “I’m Graethem Birch. City carrier.” He shook her hand. “Nice to meet you. Can I help you with anything?”

“No. I’m waiting for Pete to finish. Am I hearing polka music?”

Graethem inclined his head. “Yes ma’am.”

“Interesting choice.” Why would a young guy be listening to music her grandparents had probably been into?

“I know it must seem odd for someone my age—I’m twenty-six by the way—to be into polka, but I credit my grandpa. I loved listening to him play his accordion in a three-piece ensemble when I was a kid. I begged my parents to let me take lessons. Now I play alongside my gramps.”

Was this guy for real?

Be nice, MC. Barb’s voice keeping her in line.

“What a great treat for you and your grandfather. A wonderful connection.” She never imagined she’d be having a conversation with a complete stranger about polka music.

“Guess I’ll get back to work. Let me know if you need anything.”

“Thanks. I will.”

Graethem stalked to his case in literally two strides. Damn guy must be seven feet tall.

"Inspector McCall?" Pete's voice interrupted her musing. He stood near the front counter. As she strode toward him, the clerk hustled to wait on a customer. The glass door opened, the bell tinkling, and two more folks entered from the outer lobby. The clang of someone slamming and locking a post office box echoed and the door swung closed.

Busy, busy.

Surreptitiously, she peeked at the ceiling. Two petite bullet cameras, one at either end of the counter were angled downward to capture the most real estate in the transaction area.

MC said, "Okay, Pete. Looks like everything's in order. A minute with you in private, please?"

He slouched into his office with an audible sigh.

MC ignored his impatience and followed. "Are you comfortable with how to view the live feed on your computer?"

"I guess." He stood behind his WWII-era metal desk, eyes glued to the screen. "You understand I won't be able to sit and monitor this," he waved a hand toward the computer, "all day." His tone bordered on that of a petulant child. God help her.

"I don't expect you to spend all day watching the screen, Pete. I recommend keeping it open in the background. You can monitor it a few times during the day. No need to revamp your routine. In fact, I prefer you stick to your normal schedule. We don't want to draw unnecessary attention to the investigation."

Like the big bad wolf, he huffed and puffed. "Fine."

"Good, I'm off to visit other offices." She handed over a business card. "If you need to reach me, call me on my cell. I wrote the number on the back."

Pete, seemingly reluctantly, accepted the card. "What exactly should I look for?"

"What we talked about. Keep an eye on mass quantities of Priority Mail dropped off, especially if you're unfamiliar with the person or if they act in a suspicious manner. Don't be obvious. We don't want to show our hand."

"Uh huh." Pete flipped the card over and examined the inked number.

"Everything okay?"

"Fine." He tucked the card into his trouser pocket. "I'll unlock the back for you, if that's okay. Easier than tangling with the customer line in the front."

MC said, "No problem." He ushered her out the opening and closed it behind her without another word.

What was his issue?

Preoccupied with Pete's odd demeanor, MC climbed into the Subaru. Was he hiding something? Or was he annoyed with her presence and the attention directed on his office? Some people didn't like to have their routine disrupted.

Maybe she should've chatted with the window clerk. A germ of distrust toward Pete gnawed at her.

MC used her phone to check the Facebook app. A glut of users emoted "Sad" faces under the Black Friday Killer post. She counted seven comments, no serious content. One commenter claimed to have witnessed a UFO on the morning in question and wondered if Barb had been abducted by aliens. Good grief, there were some nutters. None of the comments warranted further research.

Maybe the Facebook angle was a bad idea.

No text messages from Dara. No word from Reece. MC was spinning her wheels, wasting time.

She sighed. A fog of breath clouded the interior of the car. She shook off her worries and cranked the engine. A true crime podcast would be the perfect travel companion.

Winter fell away on the calendar, but every Minnesotan knew snowstorms and cold temps lingered into April or May, especially in the north. For the time being there were no storms on the horizon. A bright yellow sunlight-drenched snowscape made the drive along MN-61 North almost pleasant.

Grand Marais, a town on the very north of the North Shore, had a population of approximately thirteen hundred. It was the Cook County seat and its lone municipality.

MC and Barb had driven along the North Shore many times over the years. One of their favorite restaurants was My Sister's Place, located around the bend north of the Grand Marais Post Office. Their Northshore Walleye sandwich was a deep-fried delight. Afterwards, they'd work off the calories by visiting Artist's Point, in the harbor, and scale across the seawall, weather permitting. The rock-strewn shoreline was beautiful, no matter the season.

Late morning sun reflected off the glazed, snow-coated boulevard as MC parked.

Inside the north-facing entrance, MC encountered a line of five customers. Beyond them was a wall of post office boxes. An old man leaned on his cane and held what appeared to be a threadbare canvas shopping bag with one hand and removed a fistful of mail from his box with the other. He deposited the envelopes and magazines into the bag, locked the silver door, and stumped out.

She waited off to the side, perusing assorted mailing paraphernalia while the line of customers dwindled.

After the last customer left, MC approached the counter. A heavyset woman, maybe late fifties, with reddish-blonde hair greeted her. She wore a pale blue polo shirt with a postal emblem sewn on the left chest.

"Good morning, may I help you?"

MC showed the woman her ID. "I'm Inspector McCall. Is the postmaster on site?"

The woman's cheeks paled under the freckles, her light brown eyes darting every which way. MC understood that the appearance of an inspector caused apprehension for whomever was working, whether they'd done anything wrong or not.

"I—I'm—my name is Martha Feldman."

Was the woman going to keel over? MC readied herself to hurdle over the counter to perform CPR.

Martha cleared her throat. "I'm the postmaster. Did we do something wrong?"

The words came out, but MC sensed Martha working to keep her breakfast from spewing like Mt. Vesuvius.

"Not at all." MC was quick to put the woman at ease. "I need to discuss an investigation and how you may be able to help us."

"Really! Whatever I can do." Color reappeared on Martha's cheeks, bringing her back from the brink of faintsville.

"Great. May I enter?"

"Oh! I'm sorry. I'll unlock the door. Meet me over by the PO boxes."

Martha let MC in and guided her to the office. She cleared a hodgepodge of junk from a dilapidated chair and wobbled around her desk to drop heavily into her own chair.

MC gave her the spiel about the narcotics investigation.

Martha listened attentively and took notes. Very different from MC's experience with postmaster Pete.

When MC finished outlining the case, Martha said, "We have customers who ship bunches of Priority Mail packages. Folks who sell on Etsy sites or eBay. Mostly they use Click-N-Ship. The customer pays for the postage online and prints a shipping label, of course you're aware how it works. Listen to me babbling like you're not familiar with postage." She waved a hand. "My point is only a smattering of folks pay at the counter."

"Did anyone attract your attention? Odd behavior? Anxious? Conspicuous?"

"No. Some days we're busier than others, especially during tourist season. But nothing comes to mind. My clerk has never mentioned any concerns. Except . . ."

"Except what?"

"About two weeks ago we had to refuse a customer's mail. Guy brought in fifteen Priority Mail envelopes he wanted to send out. He wasn't at all pleased when we refused."

"Why did you refuse the items?"

"The contents were loose, some seed, nuts and bolts, that type of thing."

Pen poised over her notebook, MC hesitated. "What?"

"I kid you not. There's an old farmer in town. He conjures these harebrained ideas. This time it was defective items he intended to return to the manufacturers. He wrote letters, ranted about how horrible their product was and dumped samples of said products in with the letters. I'm not sure what his goal was, a refund or to spout off at someone."

"How'd you discover what was in the envelopes?"

"I asked. He even opened two of the envelopes to show me. I explained to him trying to send nuts and bolts or loose corn would be ineffective. The packages wouldn't make it through the sorting machines, much less to his intended audience."

"I've heard some strange stories in my time, this is a first. Good job putting a halt to that crap entering the mailstream."

"He wasn't happy. I assured him a searing letter mailed to the Better Business Bureau might work wonders. Food for thought . . . until he forgets and tries to mail a more outlandish item, like a tractor wheel. We keep an eye on him."

"Other than Farmer Nuts-n-Bolts, anyone else stand out?"

"Not that I can recall. I'll ask my clerk when she comes in this afternoon, she's due in at two. Or I guess you can, if you're still here."

MC checked the time on her phone. Noon. Even if she took a lunch break there'd still be more than an hour wait. "How about you speak with her and call me if she has any information?" MC jotted her cell number on the back of a business card and handed it across the desk.

"I'll call you after I finish talking with her, rest assured." Martha set the white card on the desk next to her notepad.

"Thanks." Her growling stomach reminded MC it was time for some fuel intake. A quick lunch at My Sister's Place was just the ticket.

Her belly full of walleye sandwich and salad, MC could've easily taken a nap. Instead, she lowered her window a sliver to allow some fresh, frosty, lake-scented air to keep her alert on her drive southward from Grand Marais to Silver Bay.

MC arrived at the Silver Bay Post Office mid-afternoon. Vehicles occupied approximately half the space in the parking lot of the L-shaped strip mall. A good show of commerce for the lakeside town.

When she entered, the post office was mostly silent, save the sound of a radio playing Seventies music somewhere inside the cramped space. She rang the bell atop the pitted surface of the counter. A twenty-something woman peeked around a tall case set near the back. "Be right with you."

"Thanks." Interesting choice in music genres for her age, MC thought.

A couple minutes passed, then the woman approached. Her brown hair was swirled together atop her head with a pencil harpooning the mass in place. A black plastic name tag pinned above the postal logo on her polo shirt proclaimed her to be "Heather."

"How can I help you?" she asked.

"Hi, Heather." MC withdrew her ID. "Postal Inspector McCall."

The woman's green gaze absorbed the gold shield, then met MC's eyes. "What can I help you with?"

Opposite reaction from Martha's. Perhaps the age difference? Maybe the Millennials or Gen Z or whatever they were now were less flummoxed by authority figures. "Are you the postmaster?"

"Nope. She left early. She'll be in on Wednesday."

"Are you a clerk?"

"I'm the PMR, postmaster replacement. I work when Edna is off."

"Great. Time for a chat?"

"If you don't mind my working while we talk. I'm alone here and have to prepare the outgoing mail for dispatch."

Heather allowed MC access to the crammed space, not much bigger than three ice fishing shacks.

She returned to the case where she'd been working. Next to it was an iron sack rack with four mail sacks attached to the hooks. "Fire away with what you need."

MC eyed a rest-bar, a stool with a sled-like bottom footrest and a rung below the seat. The adjustable seat tilted to allow a carrier to lean on it while sorting mail into their cases. She dragged the rest-bar alongside Heather.

Along a rear wall, flanking the typical double doors leading to a dock area, MC noticed a cage filled less than halfway with Priority Mail items. She launched the interview. "This is for your and Edna's ears only."

"Okay." Heather tossed bundles of mail into different sacks. "I'm listening."

"We're working on a case that involves narcotics being sent via Priority Mail. Evidence indicates the packages are originating from along the North Shore. I notice a lot of Priority Mail." She nodded her head toward the cage. "Are those all from today?"

Heather scrutinized the cage. "Yes. But that's a lot for us. We don't usually have that much."

"Anyone you recall who consistently brings in significant quantities of Priority Mail?"

"No. Most customers usually have one, maybe two parcels, not much more than that. I've worked other offices where people who have some type of home business, like eBay sales, bring in heaps of packages weekly. More during the holidays. Not the case here."

"No stray customers, not necessarily a local, you can think of who may have stopped in over the last several weeks or months and mailed large quantities of packages?"

"Not a single one. If I'd been working, I'd remember. Not like a whole lot goes on around here." She continued to sort mail.

"It's possible, though, on days you don't work that someone may have mailed a considerable number of packages."

"Sure. I think it would've stuck out to Edna and she'd have mentioned it to me when we saw each other. Like I said, we don't get a whole lot." She flicked her hand toward the current haul.

MC withdrew a business card. “Here’s my card. Would you please have Edna give me a call when she’s back in the office?”

Heather set a bundle of mail aside and took the card. “I don’t know what good it’ll do, but I’ll let her know.”

“Please contact me if you think of anything or if someone comes in who fits the bill.” Her gut told her Heather wasn’t being difficult, she was playing straight. She knew the office and the customers. No point wasting time trying to piece together a puzzle where there wasn’t one.

Heather said, “Yep, I can do that. Anything else?”

“No. Thanks for your time.”

“You’re welcome. Here, I’ll let you out.” She hustled toward the front.

MC thanked her and exited the office. Not a single customer had come in during the thirty minutes she’d been inside. She wasn’t ready to completely write off the office, but it definitely had fallen to the bottom of her list.

In the car, she jotted a quick addition to her notes and pondered putting in a call to Detective Sharpe to see if there was anything new in his pursuit of Barb’s killer. Instead, she checked her phone for text messages. A red dot with a number one hovered over her messages app.

Reece: *Checked the FB pg. I’ll share it from my pg. Get some legs on it.*

MC: *Thnx. Any suggestions on next move? Do I post daily?*

Reece: *Not daily. Maybe weekly? Give it a few days. See what happens.*

See what happens. Basically, sit tight. The exact type of situation that drove her to drink. She thumped the cell phone against her knee. The device buzzed with another text.

Dara: *How ya doin?*

MC hesitated, thumbs hovering over the keyboard, cursor blinking in the empty reply field.

She dropped the phone into the cup holder and cranked the engine to life.

Coward. The whisper-voice came from behind her. She checked the rearview mirror—of course, no one was in the backseat. Not Barb. Not an ax-murderer. Not a wisp of a ghost.

The voice . . . Barb . . . was correct. Avoiding Dara, ignoring her, was definitely cowardly. Why couldn’t she face her friends? They were her family.

No. She was better off on her own. No need to make everyone’s life miserable because her own was an unending cycle of wretchedness.

Hyperbolic much? Damn voice.

MC slammed the gearshift into drive and rolled through the strip mall parking lot toward the highway. She was craving a shot—more than a shot—of the Goose. Enough to dampen the drearies. Enough to douse the demons. Was there enough on the planet to accomplish this task? Probably not.

A weight, heavy as the wettest of snowfalls, fell over her. Was she wasting time? Coming at this all wrong?

She'd felt pretty good about things yesterday. This morning Pete gave her the bum's rush. What was his issue?

Martha in Grand Marais was a bright spot in the day. At least she'd wanted to be helpful.

Indifferent Heather's reaction indicated to her that Silver Bay probably wasn't the place she'd find her suspect.

Her brain banged every which way. Resignation was ready to ride roughshod over her. She battled the beast back. At least there was one struggle she'd get the upper hand on. Hopefully. No. Definitely.

Be assertive.

Back to Two Harbors.

She'd hang out near the post office for an hour, until closing time. See what, if anything, happened. Maybe she'd nail a nimrod driving a U-Haul brimming with Priority Mail packages full of opioids.

Dream on.

MC watched the last customer pull out of the parking lot. No U-Haul full of drug-filled packages appeared. Tomorrow might be a different story. No self-respecting drug peddler would do business on a Monday. Slow and steady wins the race, she told herself.

After a quick stop at Subway for a sandwich, she headed home. MPR played low on the radio, a backdrop to the mishmash of thoughts in her head. The investigation was dragging, a replication of the hunt for Barb's killer.

Time stood still. Time plowed on.

Patience, Grasshopper.

She needed to stay focused. Review what she knew and devise a plan. Tomorrow morning she'd deal with emails. She might have time to FaceTime with Dara and Meg. In the afternoon, she'd revisit the post offices.

A glimpse into her rearview mirror revealed a black pickup closing in on her. The idiot was exceeding the speed limit. She herself was a few ticks over. What the hell? They weren't on the Brainerd International

Raceway, for fuck's sake. The vehicle passed her and within five hundred feet, the left blinker flashed.

Now stuck behind the truck, MC was ready to read the driver the riot act, or better yet, his rights. Finally, southbound traffic thinned and the truck, a Ford F-150 with over-sized tires, zoomed into Gunderson's Salvage Yard and Gun Range. Large tires, small . . . Don't go there, don't stoop to that level.

While she chided herself over thinking a certain part of the driver's anatomy was microscopic, MC managed another glimpse of the area on the other side of the fence and got a better visual than she'd had the first time. Stacks of pallets teetered, mimicking the Leaning Tower of Pisa. If those pallets were what she thought they were, Gunderson Salvage was looking at some trouble.

She made a left, rolled into the drive, and saw the black truck go through a gate, probably remote-controlled access, then hit a gravel road that wound toward the rear of the salvage yard. MC punched the gas pedal and popped through the opening. The gate closed behind her.

How're you going to get out? Barb's voice. She was aware of her impulsivity.

The truck continued ahead of her on the rutted road. She stopped her car, left the Subaru idling, and popped open the driver's side door to seek a better view of several stacks of black and orange plastic pallets.

Effing thieves.

MC took in the hundreds, maybe thousands, of pallets, which were the property of the USPS. The pallets were Mail Transportation Equipment, sole property of the USPS used to transport shrink-wrapped loads of various types of mail. Customers were authorized to reuse USPS containers and pallets to move mail, but they were not allowed to retain possession of MTE.

She snapped photos using her phone, thankful the area was lit by bright LED lights spaced every twenty feet or so. Stockpiling USPS property was a crime. MC suspected Gunderson's wasn't stockpiling, more than likely they were selling the pallets for profit.

MC returned to the Subaru and continued on the road the pickup had taken. She aimed to give the driver a piece of her mind for his erratic driving techniques.

The road was more rutted trail than actual road. She bumped along the frozen ground for a quarter mile, her teeth clacking together with each jarring bump. Ahead, the road branched in two directions. One arced to the right, the other continued straight and uphill. The right path wound through a stand of magnificent pine trees, and through their branches, MC barely made out a house set maybe a hundred or hundred-fifty feet back.

The truck was parked next to the cabin . . . home? Shack? A temporary tent-like structure protected two vehicles, the truck and a mid-sized light-colored SUV, from the elements.

The home was lit, though the interior wasn't visible through the windows. A single arc lamp spilled a pallid glow over the yard. The area back here was designed to hide, whereas in the junkyard the light revealed the treasures.

Suddenly the interior of the car was ablaze, blinding her. She opened the door and was greeted by a six-foot-tall Sasquatch.

Disheveled. Hairy.

The man stood next to an all-terrain utility vehicle, which had a moveable spotlight attached to the driver's side front post of the roll cage.

Sasquatch lumbered toward her with a limp. "What do you think you're doing? This is private property."

MC said, "I followed that truck. Need to have a chat with the driver about their dangerous driving—nearly caused an accident on the highway."

"I don't give a good goddamn about no one's driving skill, lady. Why don't you put yourself inside your vee-hicle and get the hell outta here before I call the law!"

Vapors hung in the air in front of MC. Steam from her bubbling anger. "Sir." God bless her parents for instilling politeness in her. "I *am* the law. US Postal Inspector, to be exact." She flashed him her badge.

"Postal what? You ain't no law here."

"I am the law. Mister Gunderson, is it?" Wild guess on her part.

"What of it?"

"Let's discuss that stockpile of plastic pallets near the entrance. How'd you come to possess them?"

"The what?" He shifted nervously, twisting to look behind him.

MC wondered if he'd called for reinforcements. She didn't want to be blindsided. She dug a hand into her pants pocket, revealing her gun holstered at her hip, hoping Gunderson caught the message that she was the real deal.

"Oh, darn. I'd give you my business card, but I don't have any on me." She'd given her last one to Heather. "Tell you what, I'll come by tomorrow and we'll chat about returning those pallets to the postal service."

Gunderson leaned to his right, favoring his left foot. "Whatever."

A loud crack tore through the evening. The echo ricocheted on the icy air.

MC ducked and drew her gun.

"No need to get your panties in a twist. That's comin' from the range over that hill." He jabbed a finger in the air.

"Range?"

"Don't postal police or whatever you claim to be know how to read? This here's a gun range and a salvage business."

Gunderson's Salvage Yard and Gun Range. Jesus. Rather than kicking Gunderson's ass for being a sarcastic dickwad, she reholstered her gun. "You live here? Who drives the truck?"

"None of your business. Like I said, time for you to hop in your crunchy granola-mobile and drive off my property."

"Fine. Like I said, I'll see you tomorrow." She summoned every bit of dignity she possessed not to let loose a stream of invectives at this asshole. "Which way to the highway?" She wanted a moment longer to see if anyone materialized from the cabin. Not a scintilla of movement. Damn.

Gunderson pivoted on his right foot and limped to his ATV. "Dumbass cop. Follow me." Back at the entrance, Gunderson rolled over a strip of hose that initiated the opening of the gate.

Outside the junkyard, MC kept her eyes on her rearview mirror. The gate retracted and sealed the salvage yard and Gunderson from view. On one side of the rolling fence she noticed a sign with an image of a video camera and the words, "under surveillance," which explained how Gunderson had found her so easily. She should have observed that on the way in. Note to self: be more aware of surroundings, especially in strange places.

She'd revisit Gunderson tomorrow, arrange to divest him of the pilfered pallets, and then cuff him and throw him behind bars. To follow up, she'd coordinate with local postmasters to educate community businesses about returning unused postal equipment to post offices.

Even in the middle of a narcotics investigation, MC wasn't about to blow off this infraction. Those pallets were worth twenty bucks apiece. If Gunderson had three thousand, he was sitting on upwards of sixty grand, a chunk of change in recovered assets she wasn't willing to leave by the wayside. Gunderson seemed like a scumbag who probably had his fingers in more than one illegal pie, too.

MC pointed the Subaru toward the cabin. Hunger—and the pervasive craving—waited to be satiated. Maybe she'd find something of interest on the new Facebook page.

Quentin kept his gaze locked on the sixty-inch TV, his thumbs working the game controller to direct a multitude of animated characters racing across the screen in his *Mario Kart 8* game. "Man, c'mon. Stop. No way was it her, Nick. The road has to be at least a hundred feet from here. You can't possibly ID someone, especially in the dark."

Nick paced the room like a caged tiger. "Fuck you. I saw her with my own eyes."

Quentin thought, you saw her with your blitzed out, high-as-a-fricking-kite eyes. "Chill. I totally doubt it was her."

"Fuck you, chickenshit. You're no help at all. Won't carry a fuckin' gun."

"I don't need a gun."

"I don't need a gun." Nick mimicked in a whiny voice.

"Real mature." Quentin wondered for the millionth time why he continued working with Nick. The paranoia and vindictiveness driving Nick were so out of Q's wheelhouse. Why stay? The money. The totality of his commitment was the cash flow. The funds kept his mom's care going, and that was the only reason he stuck around.

Nick had come home fifteen minutes earlier after driving to Two Harbors for pizzas and more beer. They'd barely started to eat at the wobbly card table when Nick leapt up and ran to the front window. He'd seen a flash of light on the road. He'd yanked the cord for the blinds and slid them over the windows. Then he'd peered out from around the side of the blinds.

Next, he'd scooted to the counter where the pill packets were stacked ready to be boxed and sent out in future orders and popped another pill from a bubble-topped foil sheet. "I know what I saw."

Quentin tried to ignore Nick, but his concentration was shot. He hit the accelerator button too soon at the start of the race and spun out causing him to lose, which pissed him off. He tossed the game controller aside and rose to sit at the crappy card table again, phone in hand, to scroll through his Facebook page while he scarfed down a last piece of pepperoni pizza. A new Messenger notification from his friend in St. Paul stated that his mom remained the same. Some good news.

Food gone, he shoved his paper plate into the trash. Time to go back to his favorite game. This time he wasn't going to lose focus.

He sat on the couch, his leg bouncing up and down, and started a new game, but his mind was only half on Mario. He couldn't stop worrying. Nick continued to play fast and loose with Dirk's money and product. Now Nick thought he'd seen the postal cop from the Cities here in the middle of nowhere. In a junkyard two hundred miles north of the Cities. No way could it be the same cop Nick blamed for them losing the easy-money gig when Stennard was arrested last year.

They were screwed if that cop was on their trail.

Quentin needed to quit before Nick blew a gasket—again. He cursed himself for allowing Nick to drag him so far from home. Visions of a six-by-nine-foot concrete prison cell freaked him out.

Nick ranted some more. He stomped to the bunk room, returned with a Glock in hand. He popped the magazine, made sure it was full and rammed it back in place. "Maybe I'll go talk to Alfie. See what happened."

Quentin liked the idea. If Nick went to the salvage office, he and Alfie Gunderson, the owner, would have some beers. Maybe they'd go to the range and shoot. Quentin could game in peace and quiet for a change.

The doorknob on the front door rattled. A ham-fisted pounding ensued, shaking the door on its hinges.

Christ. So much for peace and quiet. Quentin paused the game and stood to answer the door, but Nick beat him to it and let in Dirk Black.

Quentin swore a dark aura swirled around Dirk. He dropped the gamepad on the couch and jammed his hands into the pouch of his hoodie and shuffled to the far side of the sofa, as far from Dirk as he could get.

Nick tucked the Glock into the waistband of his jeans. "Hey, Dirk, uh, Boss." Nick stood midway between the door and the TV wiping sweat from his forehead.

Dirk took in the scene. His black eyes followed Nick's movements, then he noticed the TV screen, and the paused Mario on a motorcycle. He said to Quentin, "What are you, ten? You're a grown-ass man. If you're going to play games, at least attempt to act like an adult. Don't be such a pussy. Play *Grand Theft Auto* or *Halo*."

Quentin kept his mouth shut.

Perhaps convinced that Quentin wouldn't engage in an argument, Dirk, a sinister spirit, glided across the floor to the card table. He sat in a rickety chair, one black-trousered leg neatly crossed over the other, facing the living room and Nick and Quentin. "My accountant tells me the supplier called—last week's payment came up short." He examined his fingernails. "Know anything about that, guys?" He leaned the chair back. His dead-fish gaze slid between Nick and Quentin.

Quentin wondered if Dirk's "accountant" was actually an accountant or a peon with a fancy title. He kept his wonderings to himself. Tried to fade into the woodwork.

Nick bounced on the balls of his feet. "No effing way, man. We don't know about no missing cash. Q will back me."

Quentin said, "Sorry, Dirk. No idea why the payment was off." His guts coiled. His breath stuck, like someone had kicked him in the breadbasket.

Dirk dropped off clean money. They boxed it up, like the drugs. Mailed it to the supplier in Minneapolis for the next shipment.

Dirk wasn't a guy you messed with—or stole from. Quentin understood that, without question.

Nick didn't have the same mindset. "Maybe he miscounted?"

Dirk stood. "I doubt it." In the blink of an eye he was over to the corner of the dining room where a desk held a computer and printer. The adjacent L-shaped kitchen counter was their processing line. The pills and wax packs of powder Dirk delivered weekly were stacked alongside mailing materials.

He ran a finger along the tiered packages of opioids and their newest item—packets of heroin. Dirk whistled softly.

Was that the whistle from the movie, *Kill Bill*? The one where the one-eyed nurse was going in to kill the Bride?

A chill ran down Quentin's spine. His mom used to say when you felt an unexpected chill it meant someone walked over your grave. The point being—he was freaked the fuck out.

For once, Nick kept his yap shut.

The silence was unsettling, even for Quentin, who normally enjoyed it.

Dirk slid out a combat-style knife with a three-inch curved blade and cleaned beneath his fingernails. "Tell you what, guys. You be extra careful. The supply guy will be triple-counting the cash on the other end.

We'll probably do a product inventory sometime this week, to cover all the bases."

Nick gulped audibly before he answered. "Sure, Dirk. Whatever you say. Right, Q?"

Quentin was hypnotized by the black titanium folding knife. "Yep." This encounter gave him anxiety like he'd never known.

Dirk raised his arm, knife in his grip. His hand swung toward Nick. Quentin didn't want to witness Nick's throat being slit. The sound of flesh meeting flesh shocked him. He opened his eyes to see Nick's lip bleeding, presumably from Dirk's fist connecting with him.

Where'd the knife go? Dirk was a fucking magician.

Dirk said, "Listen, dumbass, relative or no relative, do your job. I expect you to perform to my precise expectations. If you can't—or don't—comply, we're going to have a monumental problem. One you will not enjoy the resolution to."

Nick, to his benefit, didn't respond.

Dirk stuck a finger in Nick's face. "You hear me?"

Nick's face was as red as lava spewing from a volcano. He shot a sideways glance over at Quentin.

Was he looking for Quentin to help him? Or maybe he was embarrassed to be tongue-lashed in front of Quentin? Either way, the outcome wasn't good. His mood was bound to be profoundly fucked up after Dirk left, his hard-ass persona in tatters.

The thought train chugged through Quentin's head. He didn't relish the idea of what Nick might do. Especially when he appeared to be extremely pissed and terrified. Running afoul of Dirk Black shaved years off their lives.

"I hear you," Nick said, "loud and clear."

"Good. We understand each other." Dirk eyed Quentin as if daring him to disagree.

Quentin clamped his jaws together to keep his teeth from chattering. Dirk scared the living hell out of him.

"Get your shit together, Nick. No more warnings. New shipment due day after tomorrow. Keep the Internet orders flowing. No funny business. I mean it."

Dirk left, slamming the door behind him.

Quentin ran his hands through his hair, which had grown from the shaved-head look he'd sported in the before-times—before they'd arrived to live this nightmare existence. In fact, Quentin had changed his whole look since they arrived. Along with growing out his blond hair, he dumped his matching ball caps, jackets, and shoes for hoodies, jeans, and a Carhartt winter parka. Timberland boots completed his ensemble. His goal was to blend in, not stand out.

Nick, on the other hand, hadn't changed a thing. His tattered black leather jacket matched his dull, soot-colored eyes. He favored jeans and worn work boots, unless he had a hot date. Then he swapped the busted-up Redwing boots for a pair of pointy-toed cowboy shitkickers.

Nick blew out a gigantic sigh. "Fuck."

Quentin said, "Maybe you oughta lay off the pills. At least until Dirk cools."

"Stop being a pussy. Do the mail drops. Let me worry about Dirk. Living *la vida loca*, baby."

"If you say so."

"What's your problem, man?"

"Nothing."

"Don't tell me 'nothing.' You obviously have something you wanna say. Go ahead." Nick rolled his hand in the age old "bring it on" motion.

"Fine. You're gonna get us killed. I mean, I know Dirk's your cousin, but you're stealing from him, man. Frankly, I'm not comfortable with all this." He waved an arm at the drugs. "The whole setup makes me nervous. Bringing all the packages to the post office. Shit. Someone is going to suspect us, sooner or later. This is not my thing. Someone's gonna catch us, I know it. And now Dirk's on our asses. Shit's going south."

Nick lit a cigarette. He paced, a nicotine stream trailing him. "I ain't taking any more than I'm entitled to, Q." He blew smoke at Quentin. "Mind your own business. Do your job. Keep quiet. Or else." He yanked the Glock from his waistband, slammed it on the table.

Quentin's heartrate hit warp speed. "You threatening me, Nick?"

"Giving you the lay of the land. Go play your damn game. I need to talk to Alfie about that woman."

Quentin was and wasn't afraid of Nick. He'd seen Nick at probably his worst in St. Paul. Nick dug them a hole impossible to climb out from. Now they worked for Dirk, probably the meanest, most sinister person on earth. The gig paid well, but Quentin was losing himself. Nick seemed incapable of understanding their peril, more likely he plain didn't give a shit.

Nick expected Quentin to follow his lead, but Quentin was weary of 'the life.' On the run.

Supplying faceless people with opioids to feed their addictions or kill themselves wasn't how he wanted to make a living. To complicate matters, the feds might be on their trail.

Could life be any worse?

What to do?

He wanted out. Needed out. Like his very life depended on it. And he knew it did.

Chapter Twelve

A hint of snow hung in the air. MC filled her silver travel cup with hot coffee and popped two Ibuprofen. A pack of vodka hounds howled in her head. The quickest way to silence the baying would be a dose of hair of the dog. Not an option with a full day of work on the docket.

The idea of driving to each post office this morning depressed her. Answering piles of emails dragged her lower. She was spinning the proverbial wheels.

Why couldn't she gain some traction?

Perhaps she'd have a change of luck at the salvage yard. She pushed off the mundane tasks she'd planned for the morning. Instead, she hit the road determined to burrow to the bottom of how Gunderson came to possess postal property. It was something she could at least sink her teeth into until something broke on the narcotics case.

MC rolled down the frozen driveway at Gunderson's. The fencing was flush against the right side of the metal pole barn structure. The gate stood sealed. She got out of the car and approached the door. The single-digit temp was a slap in the face. MC tried the door.

Locked.

A faded sign screwed into the metal siding listed the days of the week along with the hours for the business: Tuesdays and Thursdays 10:00 a.m. to 8:00 p.m.

She checked her phone—ten past eight. Roughly two hours until the shop was due to open.

MC scoped out the area. Security cameras were placed on either end of the building and above the light over the door. A stroll toward the gate proved Gunderson was very security conscious. She spied more cameras along the fence line.

At the moment she had no choice but to return later, preferably while there was still daylight.

Inside the car, she blasted the heat to thaw her frozen face. Her cell buzzed.

Dara. *Morning. Chat today?*

Shit.

Avoidance is not healthy. Barb's voice, plying her with unwarranted advice.

Still, she chose to wait to communicate with her friend.

Friends are important, MC. True. She couldn't deal at the moment. The tedious and so far non-productive monitoring of post offices required her attention.

Postmaster Pete was behind the counter when MC arrived at the brick building in Two Harbors. "Morning, Pete."

A loud scraping reverberated from the rear of the building. "Inspector McCall, didn't know you were stopping by this morning What can I do for you?"

"Truck at the dock?"

Pete moved from behind the counter to straighten the racks of postal supplies for purchase. "Yep. He'll be gone soon."

"Anything show on the camera feed yesterday?"

"Not that I saw."

"Mind if I run through the footage?"

He blew a sigh heard round the world.

What's his problem? His resistance was palpable. He's hiding something. But what? "If you'd log onto your computer I'll run through the recordings, and you can go on with whatever you need to do."

"Fine."

She followed him into the office and waited in front of the desk while he logged into the desktop.

"All yours." He flattened himself against the wall, making room for her to pass. "I'll be in the back if you need me."

"Thanks." MC draped her coat over Pete's chair and sat. She moused into the files for the previous day's camera footage. People came and went. Some stayed longer than others to chat. Usually the chatty folks were older and bought a stamp or two, probably for bills or maybe birthday cards to the grandkids.

Which reminded her, March was birthday month for both Cam's kids: son Jameson would be six on March seventeenth and daughter Hailey three on March thirtieth. She set a reminder in her phone to send them cards. Barb would haunt her from the Great Beyond for sure if she missed those birthdays.

She plowed through the remaining recordings. Two people brought in multiple packages, one after the other. MC saw the mail had Click-N-Ship labels, no payment transactions took place. The customers looked like stereotypical Lutheran church lady crafters. Crocheted doilies. Baby blankets. Hats and mittens. Maybe a tree ornament or two thrown in for good measure.

MC worked the mouse and brought the live feed on screen. She was about to double check with Pete, or the clerk working the window, when she noticed a guy hoist two plastic flat tubs onto the counter. The size of a banker's file box, the corrugated tubs were generally used to sort and transport larger envelopes called flats, and also periodicals and magazines. Some customers, such as the man at the window, got hold of the plastic buckets and used them for other purposes.

The customer was youngish, mid-to-late twenties. Blond hair touched the hood of his heavy winter coat. Medium build. Not remotely suspicious, but MC kept her gaze on the screen. She squirmed at a tickle on the back of her neck, like fingers brushing across her skin.

Is this what people meant when they said their hackles raised?

Another customer, a woman with two girls, maybe ages four and six, entered. The trio stood behind the guy. The clerk removed packages from the second container while the guy waited silently. MC strolled toward the front. The only sounds were from the squealing kids chasing each other in the confined space of the lobby on the other side of the counter.

Mom said, "Girls! Behave. Come stand here quietly."

One last high-pitched squeal from the younger one, then her sister dragged her by the hand over to Mom.

Blond guy stood still, hands in his coat pockets, ignoring the melee around him.

Eventually, the clerk picked the final package from the plastic tub. "This one doesn't have a label."

The guy examined the package, a Priority Mail Small Flat Rate box. "I'll take it and fix it. How much do I owe you?"

"We have blank labels if you want to handle it now. Just move to the side and fill one out. When you're finished let me know and I'll take you ahead of any customers waiting."

"Nah. I'm good. How much?" He dug a wad of cash from his jeans pocket.

"If you're sure you don't want to address the one box, the total for the others is one hundred-sixty dollars and fifty-five cents." The clerk shoved the boxes into a canvas sack hanging from a rack behind the counter. The sack was labeled Outgoing Priority.

The man handed the worker several bills, then took the change and receipt. "Mind if I take the plastic buckets for our next shipment?"

"You betcha. Have a nice day." She slid the bins across the counter.

"You, too." He tossed the white box into the top bucket and swerved around the mother-daughter trio.

MC approached the clerk. "Excuse me. Is he a regular?"

"Two times a week he sends Priority Mail, at least when I've helped him."

"He doesn't use Click-N-Ship?"

"No. Always handwritten labels. I talked to him about switching over to Click-N-Ship. It'd be quicker. He didn't seem interested. I didn't want to keep asking."

A high-pitched voice whined from the other side of the counter, "Mommy, I'm hungry."

"If you stand quietly, we'll go for a donut after I'm done."

The clerk said to MC, "Excuse me. I need to wait on the next customer."

"Sure, sorry." MC stepped over to the mail rack and looked inside the sack at the top few packages. The return address on the label: KKW Vendor, 41 N. Hwy 61, Two Harbors, MN 55616. The mailing address on the topmost box was: John Smith, 1801 Evergreen Ave, Blaine, MN 55434. Without a search warrant she wasn't able to have the mail pulled and held, and she definitely couldn't open any of the packages. The packages had passed muster with the clerk with nothing suspicious or obviously dangerous, so for the moment all she could do was look and not touch.

MC wrote the addresses in her notebook. She wandered toward the rear of the building in search of Pete to let him know she was finished with his computer.

The carriers finished sorting their mail, some packing bundles into containers to wheel to their vehicles. MC found Pete on the dock wrestling a pallet onto an existing stack.

MC asked, "Need some help?"

He jumped and the pallet skidded sideways off the pile. "You scared me! What the heck?"

Her Spidey sense tingled again.

"I'm leaving, Pete. I locked your computer. I'll be in touch." She turned toward the exit, then paused. "So, the pallets. You prepping them for transport to the Duluth Processing facility?"

"No. Another office needs some. The rest will be used by one of the local mailers." He looked everywhere but at her. "Don't let me keep you, Inspector."

"Remember to keep your eyes peeled for anything suspicious. Talk soon."

MC descended from the loading dock to the parking lot and strolled around to the front where she'd parked her car on the street.

A silver Kia Sportage SUV drove away from the curb two car lengths in front of her. The blond guy who'd dropped off the packages was behind the wheel. In that split second she elected to follow him. Why not?

Perhaps she'd get lucky, or it might be a giant time suck. She'd never know unless she took the chance.

What about the pallets at Gunderson's? Crap. She still needed to talk to Gunderson, but it wasn't ten yet.

She followed Blondie.

Fucking careless Nick. How the hell did he not label every order? Every batch he managed to miss one or two. Quentin selected Nick's number from his Recents list.

"What?" Nick sounded pissed off. Nothing new.

"You did it again. Last package in the second tub didn't have a mailing label. What the hell? The postal person wanted me to hang around and write the address on a label. Shit, man, I bugged out. I'll take it to another place."

"Don't get your tighty-whities in a knot. I'll check the last order."

Quentin nudged the heater one notch higher. Frozen fucking tundra. What the hell? Did Nick fall asleep or what?

A scraping sound, then Nick said, "You got a pen?"

Quentin pawed a Sharpie from the center console. "Yep."

Nick read the address and Quentin wrote it on the package. "You gotta be more careful man, Dirk already warned us. And we can't risk people remembering all the packages I send."

"Stop whining. Put the damn shit in the mail."

"I'm on it. I'm going to the mall after."

"Whatever. I'm going to do more reconnaissance on the cop. Grill Alfie. I didn't find him last night."

"Why can't you leave it be? We don't need attention."

"Screw you. Bitch done us wrong. I ain't forgetting about it. You hear me?"

"I hear you." Quentin was tempted to point his car south, toward the Cities. Bail on Nick, Dirk, and all this shitty business.

But he needed the money.

"Later." Nick disconnected.

Quentin stared at the phone. Then he stared at the Priority Mail package on the passenger seat. The steel-colored underbelly of the sky pressed down, suffocating him.

Inertia.

He needed to perk up. A drive along the North Shore might clear his head. The box would move whether from Grand Marais or Two Harbors.

Quentin put the car in drive and headed north, invigorated by the thought of spending time alone at his secret spot. Weeks ago, the first time he'd needed time away from Nick, he'd driven to the hamlet of Grand Marais. He discovered the post office off the highway. And he'd driven toward the lake and ended in the parking lot for the US Coast Guard station. Artist's Point was a strip of land that jutted into Lake Superior, creating a natural harbor. A concrete seawall led to the lighthouse, which even in the dead of a Minnesota winter remained a tourist attraction.

The first time he braved the venture, Quentin skated along the icy wall to the halfway point, then lost his nerve and returned to solid land. He'd been mesmerized by the choppy waters mixed with ice sheets crashing into the seawall. Despite the hazard, he discovered a sense of tranquility.

He'd mail the package and recharge his battery at Artist's Point.

MC fell in behind the silver SUV. Traffic northbound was non-existent. She let off the gas and stayed under the speed limit, allowing him to pull ahead of her.

March meant the public radio fund drive had ended. She tuned the radio to NPR's morning news. Cloudy, but no precipitation expected in the region. Another reason to be thankful. The roads remained in passable condition.

At Gunderson's Salvage, MC caught sight of a black pickup retreating in the opposite direction on the highway, the very same pickup she'd tailed into the business the prior evening because he'd driven like an idiot. She backed off from the silver SUV and considered whipping a U-turn to follow the truck. At the very least the asshole needed a safe driver class.

The truck became a fast-fading blip in her rearview. No chance of catching him now. More importantly, a semi loomed in her rearview. She goosed the gas and sped northward. You snooze, you lose.

With her attention refocused on the northern horizon, MC realized the Kia was no longer visible. "Shit on a shingle." A phrase she'd heard her dad utter time after time, spewed forth without her taking a beat to think about it. Is the adage true that the older you get, the more you become like your parents?

For MC that wasn't a bad thing. She'd loved and respected her parents. Robert and Patricia, Bobby and Pat to everyone, had been beacons of light. She missed them every single day since they'd been cruelly ripped from her life over twenty-five years ago. One man's decision to get behind the wheel after drinking himself senseless on a cold January night had irreparably changed her life.

Focus.

On the radio, an NPR commentator spoke about a riot in a private prison in Texas. MC listened to the story and thought about how private prisons were money-makers that fed off the school-to-prison pipeline for people of color in this country. Horrifying.

Where the hell had the silver SUV gone?

Log haulers blew past her going south. The wind drafts rocked the Subaru. MC gripped the wheel to steady the vehicle. She'd passed Gooseberry Falls. Split Rock Lighthouse was ahead. Still no sign of the car driven by Blondie. He could've rolled into Betty's Pies. Maybe he was hungry and wanted breakfast. Perhaps he'd stopped to hike at Gooseberry Falls, which had groomed trails open during winter months.

Crap on a cracker. He could be a million different places. She rolled into Silver Bay and still hadn't come across the car. She stopped at a Java Hut in a scenic turnaround and ordered a twenty-ounce dark roast with cream. She guided the ship around and pointed the bow southward. No sense continuing north, he might've been headed to Canada for all she knew.

Time to head to the cabin and do some computer work. She took a tentative sip of coffee and quickly choked on the mouthful of bitter brownish sludge. Nothing's worse than a crappy cup of coffee. She pawed through the center console and found a plastic container of mints. Two round white disks cleansed her taste buds. She crunched through the remaining candies on the ride home.

Her silver travel cup full of freshly brewed rich French roast, she sat at her desk in the cabin, laptop open in front of her, and gazed at the blinking cursor on the white backdrop of a new email.

A quick check-in to Crapper to keep him off her case had taken all of twelve seconds to throw together and zing off.

The email to Jamie and Cam required a bit more concentration. The cameras at Two Harbors hadn't yielded any clues so far. She typed a list of bullet points regarding her findings from the three post offices in Two Harbors, Silver Bay, and Grand Marais. A mention of the blond guy and Priority Mail packages from this morning completed the itemization. She provided the return address and the mailing address from the one package she'd viewed and asked Cam to research the mailing address and see if there was any reason to monitor and conduct a "knock and talk" with the recipient of the package. She assured them she'd inquire into the return address and pass along any new details.

MC kept to herself her attempt to tail the dude and her encounter at Gunderson's. Until she produced solid intel, she had no reason to share.

For a brief moment she considered sending Jim Bob an email to get a status on the mailbox thefts, but he didn't need a babysitter. Let him learn the ropes. Who knew? Maybe he'd evolve into a super sleuth.

The wind gusted off the lake, rattling the windows. A bold reminder from Mother Nature that she had plenty of winter left to share. MC rubbed her hands together to warm them. She'd notched the thermostat lower earlier and forgot to bump it up. A glint of light off glass caught her eye. She looked to the left and her eyes fell on a framed photo of Barb. She wore cutoffs, her floppy yellow gardening hat, and a kitschy t-shirt picturing a giant woven basket of daisies. The photo was from two summers past. The brilliant azure sky and diamond-tipped ripples of Lake Superior framed her beautifully. MC loved the photo. Barb thought the hat made her look dowdy. MC thought she was beautiful. Happy. Full of love and life.

Now . . . now she was gone forever. All MC had left were memories and photographs.

She called the number she'd memorized months earlier.

"Detective Sharpe."

MC hesitated, considered cutting the call. No. She sucked in a lungful of air. "Detective, MC McCall here. I wanted to check—"

"I spoke with White late yesterday. Sent him an electronic file with the formal interview of Ethan Carson and the mother, Jenny Carson."

Caught off guard, MC remembered they had the Emmy Carson case in common now. "I'll check-in with Cam on that. I was calling to check on the other, on Barb's . . ."

Silence.

MC counted to five. "Detective?"

"I'm still here. I don't have anything new on Miz Wheatley's case. I'm sorry. I know that's not what you want to hear. I'll remind you to not go off on your own again. I'm doing my best."

Wasn't that dandy for him? Her rage level hit the red zone. "Maybe for you it's your best. For me it's a gaping, sucking wound that won't heal."

Take a breath, MC.

Barb always kept her in line, and she was still, even from the great beyond. "Sorry. I don't mean to be bitchy. I hope you understand my persistence."

"I do. But I've told you if we make progress, I'll loop you in, if appropriate."

Same old song and dance. While disappointed, she knew he was right. He couldn't make up something just to keep her off his back. At least today she'd called him early and she wasn't four or six ounces into Grey Goose Land. Which meant she was articulate, though her patience was worn thin as the filaments of a spider's web.

"Thanks for your time, Detective." MC disconnected the call.

Pain like a metal ball with spikes ping-ponged around her insides and shredded her soul.

To take her mind off the never-ending disappointment, she logged on to Facebook and navigated to the Catch My Black Friday Killer page. Lots of comments. A fair number of shares. Good signs. MC clicked on the comments link. One commenter claimed to be a psychic and provided a link to her webpage. More alien-referenced comments. Nothing of any value. She hovered the mouse over the Share link and scanned the list of twenty-four names, one of which was Kiara Reece. She noticed a private message notification she hadn't seen earlier from Reece, letting her know she'd shared the post. At least one person took the page seriously. Although, she shouldn't sit in judgment of the commenters. In their own way, they may think they're being helpful, psychic visions and all.

At the moment, she was stymied on what to do next in the social media world. Add a new post? Reece might have ideas. What was the best plan to help solve this lukewarm, quickly-cooling-toward-cold case?

She stood and shuffled to the windows with a view of the snow-covered yard. Beyond the garden, the icy, roiling waters of Lake Superior stretched to meet the bloated, iron-colored sky. Lake Superior, the most impressive of the Great Lakes, held as much water as the other four Great Lakes combined, plus three additional Lake Eries. Full of dangerous beauty, Lake Superior consumed unapologetically. Local legend said she'd swallowed over three hundred ships, wrecking and battering them before ingesting them and the thousands of souls aboard. The lake was the epitome of beauty and the beast.

A growl from her stomach reminded her she'd not had any breakfast and it was lunchtime. A bowl of soup sounded good on this chilly afternoon.

MC slurped spoonfuls of chicken-flavored ramen. The sodium content was off the charts, and she enjoyed it nonetheless. She slid her phone toward her and reviewed her texts. No more from Dara.

Perhaps she'd invite them to visit on Saturday in an honest effort at being a better friend.

She zipped a quick message to Dara. *Heya. Sry I've been off the grid. Work. How're you 2?*

Three steely-colored dots appeared on the screen. MC killed the screen and quickly finished off her lunch and washed the dishes.

When she was finished, she checked messages again. Two from Dara. Time slowed.

Dara responded. *We understand. No worries. Meg wants to know if you'd entertain the idea of a visit? Maybe Sat?*

Sounded like Dara was on the same wavelength. *Sounds like a plan.*

Not one to allow an opportunity to slip past, Dara's reply was instantaneous. *We'll drive up Sat. Leave Sun.*

MC hit the thumbs up emoji.

That just happened.

She'd need to do some prep, like hide the Goose. If Dara found the booze she'd launch a full-on assault, spout off, no doubt drag her to the closest AA meeting. Engaged in war wasn't how MC wanted to spend her weekend.

One night. All she needed was to go for one night without alcoholic fortification. She tucked the phone in her pocket to avoid the temptation to change her mind.

Time to resolve the pallet issue at Gunderson's.

On the road, slightly off her game after the brief exchange earlier with Detective Sharpe and the looming commitment of hosting Dara and Meg, MC angled into a parking spot outside Gunderson's Salvage Yard and Gun Range. A truck that appeared to be held together by rust was the lone vehicle in the parking lot. All was quiet except for the occasional swoosh of a breeze.

MC approached the metal door. Locked. She checked the time: after two o'clock. She knocked on the door. No answer. She counted to ten and knocked a second time. Another ten count still brought no answer.

She backed away from the door and looked at the security cameras. A worm of unease slithered through her guts. Was she being watched? Hands jammed into her pockets to warm them, she marched over to the gate, which, of course, was secured.

She called the number listed on the sign. Ringing. More ringing . . . after five rings voicemail kicked in. MC chose not to leave a message.

A lack of productivity made for a pissy MC.

In the Subaru with the heater on high to thaw her frozen self, MC contemplated next moves.

Go to the Two Harbors post office?

Drive to Grand Marais, see if Martha had anything to report? A three-hour roundtrip drive this late in the day didn't float her boat. She'd call Martha, save gas and time.

The washed-out, ashen landscape was less than inspiring.

Maybe she'd return to the cabin, change into comfy clothes and light a fire, drain the gray from a bottle of Grey Goose. Watch mindless shows on Netflix on the monster-sized TV in the loft. Humdrum entertainment and vodka, the perfect remedy for what ailed her.

A giant splat of bird crap pelted her windshield. The goo, with specks of she didn't want to know what, created off-white blots across the glass.

Shit.

Literally.

A perfect descriptor for this day.

She twisted the end of the turn signal and washer fluid squirted out. The wipers swished creating a milky film across the glass. Six shots of cleaner later she was able to see through the window with minimal smearage.

Decision made.

Grey Goose and Netflix.

Chapter Thirteen

Brilliant fluorescent light shone in the empty corridor.

No doors.

No end in sight.

"MC, help." Barb's voice, barely a croak.

No choice but to move forward.

Lights out! Darkness now.

Blindly MC fought through a darkness so palpable, she felt as if she'd been sealed up in a coffin. She lost track of Barb.

A scritching sound ahead. Mice? Had the gnarly rodents tunneled into the house? If Barb stumbled upon a mouse she'd freak out. MC had to find it before Barb did. No, that wasn't right. She needed to find Barb. Needed to save Barb.

She faltered. Changed course. Touched a wall searching for the light switch. "Barb?" The name came out muffled.

No response.

What the hell? She moved forward. The solidness of the wall fell away, and her fingers wrapped around fabric. Fabric? She let go. Wiggled her fingers. She no longer heard Barb's voice. Her own hand was not visible in front of her face.

Her feet were cold. She wriggled her toes. Barefoot. Odd she wasn't wearing shoes.

A chattering sound echoed. Her jaw ached. A sharp sting and she tasted blood. The landscape tilted and she slipped sideways.

MC bolted awake, dazed and confused, a coppery coating in her mouth. One foot on the floor and a fistful of covers in her hand.

The nightmare had struck. Once more she'd failed to save Barb. The room was dark and freezing. She hopped from bed, wrapped the comforter around her, and shuffled into the hallway to jack up the thermostat.

The furnace kicked on. MC slid to the floor, curled around the heat register. She touched a finger to her bottom lip. A smear of blood coated her fingertip. The dream was a humdinger.

After what felt like hours, but probably was five minutes, MC dragged herself back to her bed.

A touch of her phone screen showed her it was still the dead of night.

Outside, the wind howled, sharing MC's frustration. The skittering sound wasn't mice after all, but *graupel*, a German word meaning soft hail or snow pellets. A favorite term of Minnesota meteorologists, she'd also heard *graupel* called tapioca snow. When supercooled water droplets collected and froze on falling snowflakes, they formed granular milky-white balls as wide as four or five millimeters, hence the noise she was hearing.

Hopefully, they weren't in for a wicked storm. She drifted off to sleep, wrapped like a mummy in the comforter. Please, dear God, don't let the dream return.

Unfocused. MC fidgeted in the driver's seat. She drove aimlessly, not sure where to go or what to do. Each day another thread in her life unraveled. Soon she'd be mere tatters floating through the air.

This was the worst she'd felt since the day Barb was murdered.

She grasped for anything to anchor herself. Work. Narcotics. Find the Dark Webmasters dispensing poison that killed a young girl.

Emmy Carson. Dead. Hunt the monster responsible.

Choose a focal point.

Not Postmaster Pete. At the moment he annoyed her. A less complicated path: move the rock a notch up the mountain. One notch led to another, kept the momentum going.

She whipped the Subaru into the parking lot of Betty's Pies. Unable to function, she sat in the idling car. This experience, this inability to form cohesive thoughts, was new to her. Her brain misfired in her skull. A fog clouded her vision.

Her heart pounded like a wild stallion in her chest.

Was she having a heart attack? Maybe a panic attack. She'd never experienced either one, so she wasn't certain.

Take a breath, MC.

"Duh," she replied to the voice.

The overnight *graupel* hadn't evolved into a full-blown snowstorm. Dank clouds colored the day gray. The weather was mild compared to the tumult playing inside her.

MC threw the gearshift into drive and scooted onto the highway northbound. Destination Grand Marais. She'd see if Martha had any updates and reward herself with lunch at My Sister's Place. She selected a true crime podcast to pass the time.

Her head cleared while the miles rolled away beneath her wheels. A dam had broken, a plan hatched and grew. She relaxed her grip on the steering wheel. The rhythm of the drive anchored her, and her breathing slowed to a normal rate.

Before she knew it, she was in Grand Marais, the post office to her left, the lake to her right. An agenda fell into order in the file cabinet of her mind.

Compartmentalization grounded her. She envisioned a point, then converted the vision to action.

She accessed her contacts on her phone to search for a phone number for the district Transportation Manager in Minneapolis. MC placed the call and explained the situation at Gunderson's Salvage Yard and Gun Range. The manager agreed to coordinate with someone at the Duluth processing facility to have a postal truck meet her at Gunderson's at three o'clock.

Next, she dialed the number for the Lake County Sheriff's office in Two Harbors. She spoke with a sergeant, requested back up at the salvage business for three that afternoon.

The wheels gained traction. Thank God.

If she kept moving, she'd be okay. If she stopped—better not to think about it.

A chat with Martha, the postmaster, would keep the gears grinding. She had one foot on the ground when another vehicle stopped at the end of the lot closest to the street. A silver Kia SUV.

MC jerked her foot inside and quietly latched her car door. She slid sideways, studying the silver car. A blond-haired guy sat, both hands on the steering wheel. Was he talking to himself? Phone call on speaker?

After many tense moments, he exited the SUV and crossed the highway on a trajectory toward the lake.

MC followed him, keeping enough distance to prevent him from hearing her footsteps on the frozen ground. He passed the Coast Guard station parking area and hoisted himself onto the concrete seawall.

She'd no desire to play slip-n-slide on the barrier. Nope. No way. No how. Instead, she observed him traverse the slick surface. Sure-footed. MC stood her ground, not wanting to lose track of him. She used the time to do a quick check on Facebook. No new comments.

After fifteen minutes, MC called 'uncle' on the waiting game by the lake. Her fingers were just this side of frostbit, so she hoofed it to her car.

The SUV was still parked where the guy had left it. He'd not done a roundabout and snuck past her. She sat, bored out of her skull. Why had she followed him? He'd done nothing illegal. Yet her instinct to stick with him was strong. Used to be her instincts had been spot-on. She *wanted* to trust her intuition now but was no longer sure if she could. A wave of self-doubt engulfed her.

An hour later he reappeared. Shuffled past her. Gloved hands empty. Jacket zipped against the arctic air. Instead of veering to the entrance of the post office, he continued toward the strip mall. MC cranked the Subaru to life and crept through the parking lot.

Traffic was light and she was able to tootle along without causing a traffic jam. She spotted him crossing the mall parking lot, on a steady course to My Sister's Place café.

Her stomach rumbled. Impeccable timing.

MC entered the restaurant. She caught sight of Blondie in a booth, immersed in the offerings of the menu.

At the counter, she ordered a cheeseburger, fries, and coffee to go. Her dietary intake lately skewed toward the danger zone. *Heart attack waiting to happen, MC.* Barb's voice. MC mumbled, "Guess I'm not making great life choices all around lately. What's the point?"

The server set a white paper bag on the counter alongside her coffee. "Excuse me?"

"Talking to myself. Hazards of the job." By the look on the woman's face her joke had sorely missed the mark.

Back at the post office, she scarfed the meal in her car. The silver Kia remained in the parking lot across the street.

Quentin ordered fries and a bowl of chili with shredded cheddar.

The server, Rita, asked, "Anything to drink?"

"I'll have a Coke. Thanks."

She wrote his order on a pocket-sized pad and slid the pen and note-pad into her apron pocket. The door opened, miniature bells tinkling to announce two more customers.

One, an older, maybe sixty-ish woman made a beeline for the booth in front of Quentin. The other woman—forties? fifties? hard to tell because he couldn't see her face—moved to the takeout counter.

Rita set a frosty glass of Coke and a paper-wrapped straw on Quentin's table and continued on to the next booth.

Quentin stuck the straw in the fizzy caramel-colored beverage and swallowed a mouthful of sugary caffeine. He shrugged his jacket off and wedged it in the corner next to him. To pass the time he scrolled through his phone.

Rita leaned a hip on the sixty-something's table. The hushed conversation ebbed and flowed. Quentin's attention piqued when he heard mention of St. Paul and a dead woman.

In an attempt to not be obvious, he leaned forward and pretended to focus on his cell.

"She was murdered in her home?" Rita asked, "How'd you hear about this?"

The sixty-something said, "Jenna, my daughter, she works at a bank in the area. I guess someone posted on Facebook and Jenna saw it. The murder happened near her bank. I'm not solid on the details."

Quentin stopped slurping soda in order to hear better.

A bell dinged in the rear of the café and a man hollered, "Orders up!"

Rita hustled to retrieve the food. Quentin watched her cross the café and set a paper bag and a beverage in front of the woman at the counter. Their voices were indecipherable to him. Within thirty seconds the woman disappeared with her meal.

Rita appeared at Quentin's elbow. "Here we go. One bowl of chili with shredded cheddar and one order of fries. Can I bring you anything else?"

"Um, no. Thanks." Quentin fumbled the round spoon off the plate that held the bowl of chili. Steam warmed his face.

Rita slid into the booth across from the other customer. "Okay, Faye, tell me more. I'm such a true crime junkie."

"You and me both," Faye said. "I don't have my phone with me, or I'd show you."

Rita whipped out her phone. "You said Facebook?"

"Yes. A post about Black Friday."

Quentin inhaled a spoonful of gooey, tangy chili, and a bean lodged in his throat causing him to choke.

Rita stood and leaned around the side of his booth. "You okay?"

Quentin coughed hard. "I'm good. Sorry."

He sipped his Coke to try to push the blockage downward. Choking to death would be the opposite of flying under the radar.

Rita and Faye returned their attention to the phone. Quentin heard some clanging from the kitchen. He hoped the racket would cease so he could hear the women's conversation. He held his breath while he waited. The banging ended and he leaned forward to eavesdrop.

Rita said, "Here we go. *Catch My Black Friday Killer.* Gets people's attention, I bet!"

Faye said, "Read this, it mentions the woman was shot dead on her kitchen floor. How horrible! Can you imagine?"

Quentin's spoon clattered onto the table and clattered to the floor.

Rita popped from her seat. "I'll grab you another one, sir. Hang tight." She snagged the rogue spoon and hustled toward the rear of the café.

Quentin snuck a peak at Faye. She was engrossed with the phone.

"Here you go." Rita plopped another spoon next to his plate.

His hand shook as he grasped the utensil.

"You sure you're okay?" she asked.

Jeezuz. Could he draw any more attention to himself? "Thanks. I'm fine, clumsy is all." He dug into the chili with a feigned fervor.

Rita returned to Faye and their Miss Marple-like convo. "The incident happened soon after Thanksgiving. Check it out. The post reads like the dead woman dictated it. Genius idea. Asking for people to help find her murderer. I swear it's like an episode of *Forty-Eight Hours.*"

Quentin shoved the food aside, gulped most of the Coke. "Excuse me?"

Rita was at his table instantaneously. "What can I get you?"

"Check, please?"

"You barely touched your food. Didn't you like it?"

"It was fine. I just realized I'm late for an appointment." The most over-used excuse in the world, but it worked.

"Should I box the leftovers for you?"

"No, thanks. I'll take the check."

He paid and ditched the murder mystery hour.

Curiosity ate at him, but business first. Afterward he'd look for the Facebook post.

He jogged to where he'd left his car at the PO and grabbed the bucket of mail from the front passenger seat. He mailed the packages inside, no label issues today, thank God.

Quentin kept the empty plastic bin for the next day. On his way out, he held the door for a woman entering, and she thanked him. Was it the same one from the restaurant? Black and gray spiky hair. Dark coat. She looked "official," for lack of a better term, and somehow familiar.

Was this that postal cop? Maybe it was her, maybe not. Did it matter? He was pretty sure it was time to blow this pop-stand anyway.

Now he had time to surf the web. He drove to the Coast Guard Station parking lot, certain he'd be left in peace there.

MC scrutinized the dregs of her coffee and pondered how much longer to wait. Movement in the side mirror caught her attention. She watched Blondie approach the SUV.

He opened the passenger-side door and hefted something off the seat—a white plastic bin of mail. Boxes? Envelopes? Hard to discern from this distance. He hurried toward the post office.

Follow him?

A hive of people exited the building. One held the door open for Blondie.

MC sat, indecisive.

The hell with it. She opted to go inside.

She arrived at the door as the young man exited. They locked gazes. Brown eyes and blond shaggy hair. She pegged him to be mid-to-late twenties. He held the door open and allowed her to pass through.

She said, "Thanks."

The guy inclined his head and brushed past without hesitation.

MC saw Martha sorting items into mail sacks. "Hi, Martha."

The postmaster whipped around. "Inspector McCall! How are you today?" Martha hustled to open the door to allow MC behind the counter.

"I'm well, thanks. Any suspicious customers or mail since our last communication?"

"No. And I've been more vigilant since your visit."

"What about the customer who was in just before I arrived? He a regular?"

"Not a regular per se. Sometimes I see him once, maybe twice a week, but then I won't see him for a couple weeks. No specific pattern. He sends boxes and envelopes, all Priority Mail. Not massive quantities, but usually more than he left today. In fact, today's total was less than half of what I've received from him in the past."

Martha shuffled to the rear of the office with a stack of boxes.

"Are those Priority Mail?"

"Yes. I was going to stack them in the cage. Why? Do you want to take a look?"

"Are they all from the last customer?"

"Let's see." She balanced the load on the ledge of a sorting case.

"Which were the ones from the last guy?"

"Here you go. This stack is from him. Oh, and hey, another guy came in earlier today and dropped off two tubs of Media Mail. I'd forgotten about him. Usually once a week he comes in with two or three containers of Media Mail, not Priority Mail." She pointed to a mound of padded mailers the color of Kraft Cheese Slices.

Martha continued to expound about the Media Mail guy.

MC examined the packages left by Blondie. Nothing suspicious. No leakage or overabundance of packing tape used. Life would be so much easier if she could tear open the parcel and see the contents. Alas, without probable cause and a warrant, her hands were tied.

The return address matched the one on the items shipped from Two Harbors the previous day, which made perfect sense since the same person mailed the packages. The labels were handwritten. All different mailing addresses, some going to St. Paul, and others going to Minneapolis or suburbs. Initials and last names. Probably individuals, not businesses. She memorized the address from one of the packages, J. Green in St. Paul. Another for Cam to "knock and talk" if she established probable cause.

"Thanks, Martha."

Martha asked, "Is anything wrong?"

"No. Continue to be vigilant. Contact me with any questions or suspicions. I'll pop in from time to time. No need to worry."

In her car, MC sent an email to Cam with the name and address from the package destined for St. Paul. She explained that she wasn't sure if there was a connection to the case, but she found it odd that the guy had mailed packages both in Two Harbors and Grand Marais. Maybe a search on the address in St. Paul would lead to intel or an arrest, maybe not. That's how investigations worked. A lot of research and pounding the pavement and not always a lot of results.

That bit of business done, she pointed the Subaru southward. Time to rendezvous with the Lake County Sheriff and postal transportation. No more cat and mouse with Mr. Gunderson.

➣⤙

Quentin searched for the Facebook page the waitress and her friend had been gaga over. More than a hundred people had commented, and the page had been shared forty times. Word was spreading like a forest fire on a red flag day.

The details were thin. No eyewitnesses. The cops must have zilch if someone thought a social media post was the answer. Who'd created the page? The dead woman's family? Friends? The cops? Nah, not the cops. That'd be the equivalent of admitting defeat. Cops didn't utilize social media. Did they?

The main takeaway—someone wanted answers. He felt sorry for her family and friends. Not having answers must totally suck. Kinda like his life totally sucked. The suckage grew worse by the day.

He reversed from the parking spot. The interior vibrated from the rad beats on the radio. He did a quick check of his rearview before he made a left, anticipating the woman from the post office to be following him. No one was there. The street was empty of people and traffic.

Working for Dirk had shot his nerves to hell. Now he imagined people were after him all the time. Nick's neuroses and paranoia had rubbed off on him. He shuddered. Shut off the radio. A peaceful drive to Two Harbors would calm him before the onslaught of Nick's murderous psychosis.

His thoughts reverted to the woman at the post office. Had he seen her somewhere recently? In Two Harbors?

No. Maybe?

Had she checked him out—not in the "I'm a cougar lusting after a twenty-something guy" way—more like in the "what the hell is your story" kind of way?

Suspicion at every turn wasn't how he wanted to live. Quentin needed to make a change before he completely lost his mind. Or before Nick's bad decisions ended with them both dead.

Nick stole opioids and money from Dirk. And he blew off filling the Internet orders. Earlier he'd completed only eight of the more than twenty he'd said were in the queue. He told Quentin he had to go out, they'd finish the rest of the orders later in the afternoon. Quentin confronted him. Told him they needed to be on their game to stay off Dirk's radar. All to no avail. Nick's only concern was his own agenda. He told Quentin to worry about moving the shipments to the post office, and he was gone.

Quentin hoped he'd find Nick hunched over the computer processing orders. They needed to finish the day's work. And he wasn't allowed access to the system. Dirk's orders. So he needed Nick to be on his game. Then he wanted to spend the rest of the evening playing *Mario Kart 8*—or in Dirk-speak, play cartoon video games like a ten-year-old.

MC arrived first at Gunderson's. A marked SUV carrying a Lake County deputy rolled in on her bumper. She parked in the spot next to the locked gate and trudged over to the county vehicle.

The deputy exited from his car. "Inspector McCall?"

"That's me. Deputy . . . ?"

"Deputy Johnson. What's the situation exactly?"

"I've eyeballed stacks of plastic postal pallets in the salvage yard multiple times from the road and once when I followed another vehicle inside. My best guestimate, probably a couple thousand pallets inside."

"Did you speak with Gunderson?"

"Yes. Night before last, he confronted me and uninvited me from his property. I told him I'd be seeing him soon, but I've been unable to gain access since. Not for lack of trying. I've called. Business hours are posted on the door, but no one answered when I knocked. A semi will be here soon from Duluth to load the pallets. We'll take immediate possession as they're postal mail transport equipment—postal property."

On cue, an eighteen-wheeler trundled into the driveway, approximately seventy feet long with postal insignia painted along the sides of the trailer hooked to the front cab. The air brakes squealed and hissed when the driver stopped the rig. He left the engine running.

MC said to Deputy Johnson, "We need Gunderson to let us in. When the gate's open the truck can pull in."

"How we going to load the pallets into the trailer?"

"We'll have to borrow Gunderson's forklift. He must have one. He sure as hell didn't stack all those pallets one-by-one."

Another county squad arrived. "Reinforcements," Deputy Johnson said, "not that I was worried. But three of us make the odds of Gunderson pulling anything way less likely."

"Good call. Shall we?" She waved a hand toward the entrance to the building. "Let's get this show on the road." Every fiber of her being vibrated, ready to vanquish Alfie Gunderson. She needed a mark in the win column.

The trio approached the door. Still locked.

MC took a deep breath and pounded on the metal door. "Gunderson! Law enforcement! Open the door!"

A crash sounded from inside the structure.

Shit.

MC swung around to Johnson. "Is there another door to this place?"

"In the rear. If he left that way, he probably hightailed it to the range. Nowhere else to go."

"I know he has an all-terrain vehicle. He stopped me the other night on the gravel road leading to a cabin and he was in the utility vehicle."

Proving her statement to be true, a motor revved from beyond the building.

Johnson said, "Wait here with the truck. We know another way into the range." He signaled to the other deputy and they ran for their vehicles.

MC yelled, "Wait!"

Johnson paused, one leg into his squad.

She rattled off her cell number. "Call me when you've nabbed him."

The two vehicles shot from the parking lot.

Shit. Why couldn't *one* plan go smoothly? She kicked at the frozen ground.

The truck driver hopped from the cab. "What's the deal?"

"The deputies are attempting to catch the owner. They'll haul his ass back here and we can do our business." Damn if she'd let this collar unravel.

The guy reseated a Twins cap on his bald head. "You're the boss. I'll hang in the truck until you're ready for me."

MC's phone buzzed. She hoped it was the deputies phoning they'd corralled Gunderson. Nope. Cam.

"Hey, Cam."

"Thought I'd keep you apprised of the situation. We're waiting for fingerprint results on the packages in evidence. Those from the initial raid along with from the Carson scene. No word. I've asked for an expedite, but you're aware of how that goes."

"Most times less than expeditiously. Listen, Cam, I'm kinda in the middle of a situation. Can we connect later?"

"Sure. You okay? What's going on?"

"I stumbled upon a shit ton of misappropriated MTE. I enlisted two deputies who're in pursuit of a suspect as we speak."

"What? Is it connected to the narcotics investigation? Never mind. I'll let Jamie and Crapper know."

"I'll call in when I've finished." She loped toward the entrance and the gate started moving.

Hallelujah!

She jogged toward the semi. "Hey! Let's go."

The driver nodded. Airbrakes squealed and gears ground, then the rig shuddered forward.

As the truck rolled, MC glimpsed another vehicle, a silver streak. But she lost it when the semi blocked her view.

At least they were in. She flagged the driver past the pallet stacks.

He lowered the cab window. "This good?" She could literally see how the truck's vibrations shook him.

"I think so. Should have enough room." He shifted into park and shut off the engine.

She checked around the truck, no other vehicle in sight. She'd worry about it later. The two county cars arrived, and one very unhappy looking Gunderson sat in the backseat of the first one.

MC strode to the police cruiser and yanked the door open. "Afternoon, Mister Gunderson. Remember me?"

Gunderson glared at her. "What the hell's going on?"

"I told you I'd be back and we'd settle this issue of illegal possession of postal equipment. Do you remember the conversation?"

"I don't know what you're talking about."

MC hauled him from the vehicle. "This way." She dragged him toward the stacks of plastic pallets.

What the hell? She held Gunderson's upper arm and gazed at the depleted stock. About half the pallets had disappeared.

"Where'd the rest of the pallets go?"

He ignored her.

"Mister Gunderson, when I was here two nights ago, you had twice the quantity of pallets as there are now. What'd you do? Sell them? Recycle them? What?"

He remained mute.

Fine. He wanted to play hardball. She'd oblige. "Mister Gunderson, you're being detained for illegal possession of US Postal Service equipment with intent to sell. Misappropriation of postal equipment violates federal statutes. You'll be detained at the Lake County jail."

She wheeled around to Deputy Johnson. "He's all yours. I'll oversee the load-in then meet you at the jail. I'd like to question Mister Gunderson a bit more in depth."

Johnson said, "C'mon, dipshit," and guided Gunderson to the cruiser to tuck him inside.

Quentin signaled and turned off the highway into the entrance of Gunderson's Salvage. He punched the remote to open the gate.

Why the hell was a semi blocking half the entrance?

He slowed. The gate retracted on the roller system. When he saw the postal logo on the side of the white trailer, a pit grew in his gut. What was Alfie involved in?

To the left of the semi, Quentin caught sight of a lone car parked next to the office building. A figure stood next to it, phone clamped to her ear.

Shit.

Was that the woman he'd seen at the Grand Marais post office? The coat looked the same. The hair. What the hell was happening?

Quentin watched as she lowered the phone and moved toward the semi. He punched the gas and flew past the big rig and down the road to the cabin.

His heart pounded a drumbeat in his chest.

Should he tell Nick?

Was Alfie in trouble?

A humongous postal truck in Alfie's salvage yard rang major alarm bells. Were they dropping off or picking up? Maybe the postal places had junk like anyone else and they needed to offload it. Nobody seemed to have noticed him go by, so he'd go with that line of thought. In which case, Nick didn't need to know.

Mario Kart awaited. Maybe a beer. A beer or two to calm his nerves.

MC rushed back to her cabin for the six-fifteen conference call with Crapper, Jamie, and Cam. She dialed Crapper's office number.

"Team Lead, Chrapkowski."

She didn't have to be in the same room with him for the sound of his phlegmy voice to send spiders scuttling along her spine.

"McCall here."

"McCall, you have issues with following orders. Who the hell instructed you to veer off course and take on this MTE situation? You were sent there specifically to investigate packages containing narcotics. Seemed pretty straightforward to me when we discussed it last week."

MC counted to ten.

"Roland, I'm investigating the drugs case. I've reported daily since I've been onsite. I'm a fully trained veteran inspector. I won't ignore blatant crimes against the postal service. If you want to discipline me, I can't stop you, but—"

"But nothing, McCall. I've been over this with you till the cows come home."

Fuckin' Crapper and his clichés made her want to scream.

"You can't seem to follow orders. That's a problem, for you and for me. The assignment was for you to help White with this drugs case. Instead, what do you do? You go off on some MTE tangent."

Voices in the background wrenched her from the cliff's edge.

Jamie's voice. "Hey, Roland. MC?"

"Yep. I'm here."

Jamie said, "Cam and I are with Roland now."

Crapper's huffing and puffing faded. He must've repositioned his phone on the desk to better pick up the other two.

"Hey, MC," Cam chimed in.

"Hey, guys."

Jamie said, "Roland, you and MC finished?"

MC clenched her fists in her lap. She stared at her cell phone so hard she thought it might explode.

Crapper horked up a big chunk of something like a dog choking on a bone and croaked out, "Yeah, we're done."

Friggin' asshat coward. He wouldn't have the guts to ream her for not following orders while Jamie was in the room. She wondered if Crapper feared Jamie. The more likely explanation was that Jamie was a functional and natural leader. He led without trying, and that triggered a jealous streak in Crapper that bled over everyone, especially MC.

Jamie said, "MC, want to brief us on the situation there?"

"Do you want the narcotics or the MTE first?"

"MTE. Good job, by the way."

Ha! Stuff that in your pipe and smoke it, Crapper. At least someone appreciated her work.

"Bottom line, when I questioned Gunderson at the Lake County Jail, he admitted he'd been stealing pallets for more than a year. He'd observed the dock areas of post offices and mailing businesses here and in northwestern Wisconsin. He sold the pilfered pallets for three bucks apiece, substantially less than their true value of twenty dollars."

Crapper asked, "Was this worth your—*our*—time? Seriously, how many did you recover?"

Behave yourself in front of the others. She threw him a bone. Responded professionally. "The first night, when I discovered the stockpile, I'd say in excess of three thousand. When we arrived today about half had disappeared. Gunderson admitted he'd sold fifteen hundred pallets for three dollars each. A total take of forty-five hundred bucks. He ran out of time to move all the pallets before we came onsite this afternoon. We took possession of the remainder, roughly another fifteen hundred pallets. The actual worth for that remainder is approximately thirty thousand dollars. A good chunk of change recovered. We may also be able to follow the trail to the others he sold and recover them as well."

Crapper said, "Why didn't you bust him the first night? Why waste all this time until today? It's already Wednesday! Now we don't know where the other half of those pallets went."

Jeezuz. This guy. Bust Gunderson by myself? Sure, that would've been safe.

"I attempted to contact him several times after Monday night. Unfortunately, I was unable to gain access to him or the business. This morning I brought in local deputies and coordinated with USPS Network Transportation to dispatch a truck in order to take possession of the MTE stock."

Jamie said, "Good call, MC."

Cam agreed. "I'd probably have done the same."

Grateful for the support, she continued. "Thanks. I wasn't able to convince Gunderson to disclose who he'd sold the pallets to. He claimed to have forgotten. Conveniently, there wasn't an invoice or any type of paperwork involved. We're taking his word on the number of pallets and the dollar amount received. I think it's more than enough, though, to charge him. I called the US Attorney's office in Minneapolis."

Crapper's coarse voice rumbled through the airspace. "You *think* it's enough? McCall you better damn be sure—"

"Roland," Jamie said, "can we dial it back?"

Thank the unicorn gods, MC thought. Someone called Crapper on his shit. Pun intended. "Guys, I'll email the Area Post Office Operations Manager and they can message all the offices that report to them.

Hierarchical messaging will be more effective, I think. I'll fit it in between investigation on the drugs case. Speaking of which, Cam, any luck on the Saint Paul address I sent you?"

Cam said, "To update Roland and Jamie, MC sent me a mailing address in Saint Paul she saw on packages originating from Two Harbors. Correct?"

MC said, "Actually the Saint Paul-bound parcel was from Grand Marais. I witnessed a guy who does frequent drops at Two Harbors. He caught my attention when he didn't want to complete a label for one Priority Mail package. He'd dropped thirty-plus but dipped out for no reason instead of completing a label for the one. Why not take the ninety seconds to address it and be done? I saw him later in Grand Marais. I checked with the postmaster and verified the return address matched the packages mailed through Two Harbors. I saw a recipient's address on a box in Grand Marais and messaged it to Cam."

Cam said, "Tomorrow we'll begin monitoring J. Green and John Smith's homes. The John Smith address was off the package left at Two Harbors, destination Blaine, Minnesota. We'll conduct a 'knock and talk' with these guys when the packages arrive."

MC said, "None of the postmasters or clerks have anyone on their radar as a suspect. They all seem to think that folks who drop lots of packages have an eBay business or an Etsy store or some other online gig. A few of the customers the employees didn't know but thought those persons were new to town, but like I said, no one's set off alarms with the clerks."

Crapper cleared his throat, the sound like crunching glass. "Dig deeper. Make progress. Maybe you need to come back. We'll assign someone who can provide results."

Take a breath, MC.

A breath? She'd like to kick the ever-loving breath from Crapper. Instead, she resorted to her failsafe ten count.

Jamie said, "What's next?"

She waited to see if Crapper added anything, but when he stayed quiet, she took the reins. "I'll stay on the blond guy. He tripped my trigger. Tomorrow I'll finish with Gunderson. Then I'll track Blondie."

Crapper said, "Make sure you do."

Jamie said, "Update us when you're able to. Is there anything we can do on our end to assist you?"

"Nothing I can think of right now."

At least Jamie gave her credit for being able to do her frickin' job.

"Let's call it a night," Jamie said. "Rest. We'll be around tomorrow if you need anything."

They said their goodbyes, and she disconnected the call before Crapper shit all over the good will Jamie had extended to her. Crapper never failed to stomp on her last nerve, and she was ready to blow. She sat in place for a few minutes, taking a breath as her friendly voice kept reminding her to do. Even though she got her anger under control, she still felt out of whack.

Fortifications were required ASAP. The Goose honked from the kitchen. She headed toward the stairs, but before she took two steps, her phone buzzed with an incoming call.

"Jamie? Forget something?"

"No. I wanted to call you separately from the conference call. I chatted with Roland after Cam left. You'll contact me going forward. I reminded him this case was under my team's purview."

"Thanks. I . . . never mind. Appreciate the call."

"You hanging in? I mean, I know you've had a couple misfires over the last few months."

"I'm fine." Now. After a blip earlier. Focused is what she was—focused on the Grey Goose patiently waiting in her kitchen.

"Take care, MC."

"Will do. Bye."

Bye-bye work, hello sustenance. Cooking wasn't on the evening's agenda. MC noshed on a salad and sandwich, the salad to appease her inner dietary critic. She slurped crystal clear vodka to help her digestive juices flow. Liquid fire lit a trail from her belly to her toes.

As she ate, she scrolled through the ever-growing list of comments on the Facebook page. People inquired about a reward. Others simply expressed condolences and stated they'd share the page on their own timelines. Her chest expanded with warmth over strangers willing to help in their own way.

In case she had doubts evil existed, there were comments laying blame on specific ethnic groups. She deleted any such presumptive entries.

A part of her was glad to have an outlet for spreading the word about Barb's murder. But she didn't have much confidence that the effort would bring her any closer to the killer.

She cleaned the kitchen and set the coffeemaker for six in the morning and filled her tumbler with several ounces of Grey Goose. Next, she devised an action plan to disseminate notices to local postmasters for monitoring and securing MTE. The Lake County Sheriff's department had agreed to partner with the inspectors and postal service staff to circle the wagons.

What she needed was a catchy acronym for the project, one that would be impossible to forget. She sipped her beverage and relaxed in her desk chair. The perfect acronym hit like a bolt of lightning. Postal Equipment Retrieval Program—PERP. Easy to remember. The difficult part behind her, she created a document outlining the initiative focusing on how the plan would save the postal service upwards of one hundred million dollars per year in lost equipment costs if adapted nationwide.

She'd speak with Postmaster Pete. Maybe he'd have insight into how the situation had gotten out of hand. After she ensured all the bases were covered, she'd submit the finished proposal to the bosses.

Her glass somehow had gone from full to empty. Evaporation? Did vodka evaporate? The wind whipped off the lake, sounding like the mournful wail of a long-dead soul trapped between this world and whatever came after. More Goose was needed to drown out the eerie moan.

At her desk in the loft, she drank while paging through her "Life after Barb" notebook. The framed photo of Barb drew her gaze again. Her heart seized. A long swallow of fiery liquid produced tears. Was it the alcohol that caused the waterworks? The grief? The loss? The—guilt. Devastation chiseled chunks from her soul each time she thought about the love of her life.

MC guzzled the remaining beverage and opened her laptop. A low-level buzz filled her head, like a swarm of bees inside her skull. The Black Friday Killer Facebook page loomed and pixelated in front of her—Barb's image appearing two-dimensional. The ticker showed fifty shares now. A wall of comments built beneath the post, all the letters like lines of errant ants. She pressed her fingers into her eyes to try to relieve the strain, the sting.

Take a breath, MC.

The voice.

How was it that one moment she was a fully functional human, working and focused, and the next she was a puddle of malleable mush drowning her woes in Grey Goose?

She stumbled away from the computer, in dire need of bolstering of the liquid variety. The night suffocated her despite the warm glow of light in her home. MC poured a half glass of the not-so-golden Goose. She was creeped out by the watchful ebony eye of the giant goose on the bottle and twisted the container so the Mother Goose faced the wall.

The wind moaned. Branches creaked in the yard. She paused at the sliding doors. The gunmetal gray lake filled the horizon and waves roiled and shoved crystal ice sheets onto the rocky shore. Her embattled psyche mirrored the view from her house.

MC trudged up to the loft and contemplated the sleeping computer screen. She nudged the track pad and the login screen leered at her, daring her to jump in. Not one to retreat from a challenge, she wet her whistle and floundered her way back into the Facebook app.

The comments, for the most part, remained mundane and veritably unhelpful. Lots of "RIP," and "sorry for your loss," and "I hope they catch the guy and lock him up for life," etc. Others "shared for awareness." Great sentiments. Not helpful from an investigatory standpoint.

Each comment was a dagger into her soul. Hope leached from each nanoscopic puncture.

The final comment she read made her blink several times. She read it again. The poster's name was Eileen Jenkins, and she wrote: "I remember hearing about this. Devastating. It's near my home. Horrible such an act occurred in our blissful bedroom community. Has anyone spoken with the man walking his dog? Bag of bones wrapped in a thick dark winter coat. Pintsize dog, a yorkie, chihuahua, something like that. I drove past on my way to work that day. Saw him at the opposite end of the block from the house where the woman died."

MC was certain the man referenced was one she'd visited already. He didn't appreciate her questions and mentioned calling Detective Sharpe. MC had turned tail and run before he became any more riled. What was his name? He was a dean at Highland Park High School. Dom? Daniel? Dipshit?

Doug!

Doug Freelander, a.k.a. Mr. Dogwalker. The dog was a scruffy, yippy shih tzu who took an intense dislike to MC.

At least the comment was progress. Input from someone in the area. If enough people viewed the social media post or left comments, maybe a few memories would get triggered.

She closed the laptop. Glass in hand, she made her way to bed. Another long, lonely night loomed ahead of her. She flipped a coin in her mind to guess which way things would go—sleep and an encore of the nightmare; or sleepless and staring at the ceiling.

Chapter Fourteen

The first order of business at the dawning of the new day was to deal with the Gunderson situation. MC sat at her desk in the loft after disconnecting the call with Assistant US Attorney Vince Long in Minneapolis. She was relieved to work with him. He'd been great during the Stennard case.

She'd spent the previous day interviewing Gunderson and conferencing with AUSA Long. They agreed to work with the local prosecutor to file state's charges against Alfie Gunderson for theft. Long brokered a deal for one year probation and restitution to the USPS in the amount of thirty thousand dollars if Gunderson pleaded guilty. The recommended reimbursement matched the value of the equipment Gunderson admitted to selling.

MC preferred to see Gunderson serve some time behind bars, but she understood the process. She wished they'd recovered the items he'd sold. Of course Gunderson experienced a memory lapse when it came to the buyer's identification.

At least they'd recouped over a thousand pallets. Caught with a hand in the cookie jar, Gunderson should consider himself lucky. Maybe he'd follow the straight and narrow in his future business endeavors. One small victory.

Her cell buzzed with an incoming call. Dr. Zaulk. Crap, today was Friday, which meant she'd missed an appointment yesterday.

MC let the call go unanswered.

Within thirty seconds the phone vibrated a second time with a new voicemail.

No doubt Dr. Zaulk left her a stern message about having missed their weekly confab. Eventually she'd have to face the music, pay the piper, whichever cliché applied. A full day of work lay ahead of her. Tomorrow Dara and Meg were on tap. Before the eagle landed, she needed to be sure the Goose took flight. MC had no intention of listening to Dara preach on the pitfalls of alcohol. But first she needed to get through today.

She filled her travel mug with the last drippings from her coffee maker and crammed a dose of Tylenol in her maw. A band of tension wrapped around her head like an embrace from a mighty python, leaving her bruised and breathless. Hangover? Anxiety? A combo of the two? She needed to get her shit together and speak with Postmaster Pete at Two Harbors Post Office.

"I know. Take a breath," MC said aloud as she backed the car from the garage. Late morning sunlight seared her eyeballs on the drive to the post office.

MC knocked on the doorjamb to Pete's office. "Hi, Pete. Got a minute?"

He tore his gaze from the computer screen in front of him and pinned her with a feral look. "Is it true?"

"Is what true?"

Pete craned his neck to check behind her.

She glanced over her shoulder. No one was visible, just a distant murmur of voices.

"I heard Alfie Gunderson was arrested, taken in for questioning. The rumor was a postal officer arrested him. Is it true?"

MC hung her coat on the chair. Ever-present notebook in hand, she sat. "Yes. It's true." She opened to a clean page in her notepad. "What else did you hear?"

Pete ignored her question. "I thought you were here to investigate me. For months now I half expected someone to show up. To ask why pallets were going missing from this post office." He slumped in his seat, face white as Casper the Friendly Ghost's.

"Pete, I wasn't sent here to investigate you for missing equipment. I was sent here on a narcotics investigation. However, let's move the low-hanging fruit out of the way and talk about the MTE issue."

"Postmasters, at least most of us around here, we have a common practice of leaving pallets on the docks. Makes it easier for the transportation drivers to load the mail. And it's more convenient for the direct mail businesses to come by and grab a few when they need empty pallets to ship their mailings. You understand?" He continued without waiting for her to respond. "In a lot of cases, they can't make it before the office closes. They work later into the evenings, so we leave the pallets on the dock for them to retrieve when their schedules permit. For the past six months, maybe more, pallets have been disappearing before business mailers arrive to retrieve them. One time wouldn't be alarming, but it's progressed to two or three times a week, though not every week. When I called around, other offices reported the same issue."

MC said, "Why didn't you report the situation to your boss?"

"None of us wanted to be reprimanded for not following security protocols." He sighed. "It's a poor excuse. I have no idea who'd want plastic pallets. Wood ones folks could burn in bonfires, but plastic? I kept my mouth shut. When you arrived outta the blue I thought for sure my goose was cooked."

Now why did he have to go with the cooked goose cliché? Damn. Now she craved a Goose of a different feather.

Focus.

"You thought I'd been sent to what? Arrest you?"

"No. Not exactly. I don't know!" He fidgeted with a pencil. "Maybe."

"I guess that explains why you've been jittery around me from day one. Pete, I'm not here to arrest you. Like I said earlier, my assignment was to ferret out whomever is sending drugs through the mail. I happened upon the MTE situation when I tailed a truck into Gunderson's Monday night. That's when I set eyes on his considerable stash of postal pallets."

"Now what happens?"

"Gunderson's been charged. What you and your counterparts along the North Shore need to do is revamp your tracking and security processes around MTE. I'll recommend an MTE Recon Team be established at the Duluth facility. The team should collaborate with local law enforcement to monitor businesses, like Gunderson's, and recycling places along the North Shore. We've had reports from other areas in the country where people are bringing postal pallets to plastic recycling places and scoring lots of money."

Pete was writing fast.

"We'll make sure you—the postmasters—receive educational materials to pass along to direct mail business partners to ensure compliance with policies and procedures around use of postal mail transport equipment, including letter trays, tubs, and pallets."

Pete said, "Letter trays and tubs? Did Gunderson have those, too?"

"Not that I saw, but think about this: A person might hit a garage or yard sale most anywhere along the North Shore—or anywhere in the state—and more than likely see one or more of those items being used for private purposes. The misappropriation of postal equipment costs the postal service upwards of one hundred million dollars every fiscal year.

Get the word out: Return unused mail transport equipment to local post offices, prevent misuse, and substantially reduce losses."

Pete moved on to a clean page. "Believe me, I'll do whatever is necessary. I'll do stand-up talks with the employees. Whatever you decide needs to be done, I'm on it."

This was a whole different Pete. Poor guy.

"Good to hear. On our end we'll enforce the statutes. Together we'll be able to recover more renegade MTE and save the postal service considerable financial losses going forward."

Relief spread across Pete's face. He glanced at his computer monitor and then at MC. "Hey. A customer just came in with a couple buckets of Priority Mail."

She came around to his side of the desk. "Same guy I saw earlier this week."

Blondie's fingers danced on the counter while the clerk checked through the packages. She removed them one piece at a time from the plastic container, weighed, and pasted postage on each package.

MC said, "Guy seems jittery."

"I don't know. Maybe he's running late."

MC said, "Perhaps. But he looks worried." In contrast, the window clerk's actions appeared calm and deliberate.

"Hmm . . . Boxes. Envelopes," Pete said. "A substantial—though not necessarily excessive—number of items."

"The guy is practically bouncing in place. Why is he so nervous?"

MC and Pete watched the agonizingly slow, methodical acceptance of the mailpieces. When the transaction was totaled and paid for with cash, the customer snatched both buckets off the counter and disappeared like the Ghost of Christmas Past.

MC made tracks to the front and dug through the packages. In her judgment, the guy's suspicious demeanor justified her actions. The mailpieces showed the same KKW Vendor return address from earlier in the week.

The window clerk, with a plastic nametag that read "Wanda," came up beside MC. "What's wrong?"

"Do you recognize this address?"

"I don't think so. Why?"

"Can you tell me where it might be?"

"Addresses for the highway in Two Harbors begin with one thousand. Maybe it's a typo?"

MC did a Google search on her phone for KKW Vendor. Zilch.

She tipped the phone toward Wanda. “Do you recognize the name KKW Vendor?”

Wanda shrugged. “Doesn’t sound familiar to me.” A slew of customers stampeded into the lobby. “Gotta go.”

MC returned to Pete’s office and showed him the dud Google search. “Does this name ring a bell for you?”

He scrutinized the screen. “Never heard of it. Why?”

“The guy who left all those packages—that’s the return address.” A worm of suspicion inched along inside MC’s head. “Time for me to head out. I’ll email you more about the MTE plans, okay?”

“Sure. Is there—”

“Excuse me.” Wanda stood in the doorway, a cardboard Priority Mail envelope gripped in one fist. “I thought you might want to see this, Pete.”

He waved her in. “What is it?”

She handed over the parcel. “Careful, the bottom corner has a gouge. I was going to patch it with some tape, but when I saw . . .” She trailed off, her face expressing uncertainty.

Pete and MC examined the envelope. A bubble-topped packet containing what appeared to be round white pills peeked from the tear in the packaging.

MC checked the return address. Holy shit. “Thanks. We’ll take it from here. Please segregate the other packages that came in with this one.”

Pete said, “Wanda, you can pile them along the wall behind my desk.” He jabbed his thumb over his shoulder.

Once the suspect mail was in the office, MC closed the door. “Pete, please ensure these packages remain secured. No unauthorized access. Don’t allow anyone to enter your office. If you need to leave, lock the door. Unless your safe’s roomy enough to lock all the items inside?”

He surveyed the packages on the floor. “No, my safe is far too small.”

“I count thirty-one items. Please verify.”

“Same.”

MC said, “I’ll apply for a search warrant to open the torn envelope. No way is that from a legal pharmacy, not being sent that way. We can retain these items for now. I sure hope a warrant comes through, because without it, you’ll have to release the items into the mailstream.” MC plucked a pad of Routing Slips off Pete’s desk. She recorded the time, date, and number of parcels, signed the form, and had Pete sign it, too.

Then she ran a photocopy off on his copier. MC stuck the original inside her notebook and handed the photocopy to Pete. “Keep this for your records. If the warrant comes through, I’ll contact you immediately.”

By the time MC extricated herself from Pete’s office, there was no sign of Mr. Blond Hair. She sent a text to Jamie and Cam—definitely not to Crapper—letting them know of the new development and that she’d apply for the warrant ASAP as soon as she got home to her laptop.

Quentin hit up the McDonald’s drive-thru and ordered a sack of cheeseburgers and fries. He chose a spot in the back corner of the parking lot and chomped on a burger while he surfed Facebook on his phone.

A private message from his friend informed him there was no change with Mom. One less issue to worry about.

He plugged “Black Friday” in the search field and clicked on the Black Friday Killer page. Since overhearing the women at the café in Grand Marais, he’d been intrigued, obsessed even, by the page.

Although he was shocked by some comments, he read on anyway. “When you don’t follow the Lord’s ways, you deserve to die;” and “Who cares about some rich bitch dyin’?” People were sick.

Quentin shoved the last bite of cheeseburger in his mouth and tossed the crumpled wrapper into the sack. He wiped his fingers on his jeans. The black cursor in the comment field pulsed, taunting him. What did he have to say? No sense starting a word war with people he didn’t know on someone else’s social media page. His finger hovered over the screen, itching to tap the letters to say, “I’m sorry for your loss,” or “hope they catch the guy.” Instead, he typed a message to his buddy. Thanked him for keeping the lines of communication going. He hinted he’d been thinking about making his way to the Cities but wasn’t sure yet. He missed his mom.

How’d he let Nick run roughshod over him? He’d sworn to his mom he wouldn’t be a bad apple like his father. But he’d fucked up. The only saving grace was that he wasn’t in prison—yet.

Appetite gone, Quentin threw the remaining food into the trash beside the door. His chest tightened and his breath accelerated as if he’d run ten miles. Time to relax and play video games and give the crap boiling in his brain a rest.

He squeaked his car into a gap between groups of vehicles northbound on the highway, barely making it in front of a red Subaru.

An eye on the rearview, he half-expected a horn honk admonishing him for his move. All clear.

About five hundred feet before the Gunderson's Salvage turn-off, Quentin hit the remote opener for the gate. He had to wait for southbound vehicles to pass. The gate stood open, waiting for one minute before the timer cycled it to close. He punched the gas and popped through, and the chain link fence cycled to the secured position until it clanked shut, sealing him in, for better or worse. One of these days he was going to mis-time the move, and his car would be t-boned.

When he heard someone lay on their horn out on the highway, he braked without thinking. Another long blast split through the sun-bleached, cold afternoon. Quentin clicked the radio off and cracked his window. He considered reopening the gate to see what was going on, but this wasn't his property. Alfie or one of his minions could handle the situation. *Mario Kart* awaited and hopefully Nick would be MIA so he could play in peace.

When she came up behind the vehicle waiting to make a left off the highway into Gunderson's, MC whooped with joy. She recognized the silver SUV, certain it was the same one she'd seen Blondie driving earlier in the week. How lucky. Her heart trip-hammered. She thought for sure she'd have a heart attack on the spot. When a long line of traffic passed by, she followed the SUV, but the gate rolled and latched before she could follow inside. MC laid on the horn. Maybe Blondie would open the gate for her. She was seriously thinking about driving the Subaru through the metal fencing when a guy strolled from the office.

She lowered the window and monitored his approach. He moved like he was on a morning stroll. A few inches shorter than Alfie Gunderson, he was a raw-boned man who'd blend into any middle-American landscape. Maybe sixty-ish with a white buzz cut on a block-shaped head. He wore what looked like Dickies brand work pants and a light brown Carhartt jacket with a hood.

"What's all the ruckus?" Mud-brown eyes under a heavy Neanderthal-esque brow surveyed her. "You trying to wake the dead, lady?"

"Sorry for the commotion. I need access." She pointed at the gate. "Please." MC pasted a thousand-watt smile on her face.

"What for?"

She flashed her shield. "Postal Inspector. I'm working a case, and a vehicle I was trailing just entered."

"What's a Postal Inspector? You're on private property."

Holy Mary, was this guy related to Alfie? "I'm law enforcement, a postal cop. I need inside there."

She crossed her fingers he wouldn't mention the fateful words—search warrant.

"You aren't law enforcement from around here."

She clenched her jaw. "I work in Minneapolis. But we have federal jurisdiction regarding postal crimes. I need to talk to the guy in the silver Kia SUV who drove in ahead of me."

"Federal, huh?"

Good freakin' God. She needed about a gallon of Grey Goose. "Yes. Postal Inspectors are federal law enforcement agents." She showed him the badge again. "I know this must seem odd, but seriously, it's important that I speak with the driver of that SUV. I can't really divulge any more information than that. So, would you please let me through?"

"Okay. I'll buy that. This is still private property, though. You need like a search warrant or whatever. I watch *Criminal Minds*."

Dammit. He'd done it, uttered the dreaded words.

"Ain't I right?"

"Or you simply allow me in. No harm in that, is there?"

"Seems to me you're looking to arrest someone. In my book that would be harmful. To that person anyway." He backed away from the window. "Have a nice afternoon, Inspector."

MC stared at the man's back as he returned to the building and slammed the metal door.

Now what? MC called a number on her phone.

"Hello," a baritone voice answered.

"Deputy Johnson?"

"You got him. Who's this?"

"Inspector McCall."

"What can I do for you, Inspector?"

She rattled off the gist of what she needed. She propped a notepad on the steering wheel and scribbled down the directions he provided her.

He said, "The trail isn't much more than a rutted path cleared by four-wheeler enthusiasts. Your car should make it through if you take it slow. You'll land east of the gun range parking area. Traverse the lot and you'll find the road to the salvage yard. Can't miss it."

"I appreciate the directions. Thanks."

"You bet. Let us know if you need backup."

She got the vehicle turned around and exited the driveway. Within fifteen minutes she'd nudged the Subaru along the wooded trail, praying she wouldn't get stuck in the slushy slop. The car was a trooper though, powering through the muck and the brambles with hopefully most of the paint still intact.

Before long, the path opened into the gun range parking lot. Two trucks occupied the space, neither of which she recognized. No one was in sight. She beat it for the dirt path serving as a road leading toward the house. The closer she got, the house and the surroundings looked familiar from her previous visit.

Nick's truck was gone. The computer was dark and the place eerily silent. Quentin had the cabin to himself.

He lifted a Coke from the fridge and grabbed a game controller, then fired up the console and TV.

Mario filled the sixty-inch screen and Quentin was off to the virtual races. His fingers worked the controller of their own accord. His mind flooded with thoughts of his mom. How much he missed her. A crash on screen drew him from his reverie. He dropped the controller on the couch and chugged half the soda.

He surveyed the rest of the house seeing piles of wax paper packets of powder bindered together in bundles of ten. The blister packs of white pills were ten or twenty to a strip and stacked across the countertop.

The mailing supplies were piled on the floor next to the desk. He stood and strolled through the living room into the prep room. The ink stampers with the black cat image were scattered across a TV tray mingled with blank wax envelopes.

All the accessories of his illegal wranglings. He wanted out.

Maybe he should pack his shit and leave. Now. While Nick was gone.

A pounding on the door made him jump. He set the soda can on the kitchen counter as he passed through. Instead of going to the door, he sidestepped to the window. He had no desire to interact with Dirk alone. No f'n way.

He tipped a slat on the aluminum blinds, checked the doorstep. Oh, shit. Was that the woman from the post office in Grand Marais? The one he'd seen the other day going in when he left?

What the hell?

He watched the woman back away. Was she getting ready to kick the door in? His pulse shifted into high gear. She rested her hands on her hips, her coat gaped open.

Quentin saw a glint. Something shiny in the afternoon sunlight, a gun holstered on her hip. He eyeballed the gold badge hanging from a lanyard around her neck.

Shit.

His insides went cold and wobbly like Jell-O. Was this how it ended? Hauled away in handcuffs?

The knocking resumed, increasing in intensity.

He took one jittery step toward the door. And another. He reached for the knob but froze mere millimeters from the handle. He snatched his hand back as if the doorknob were red hot.

His head pounded in time with his thundering heart. Quentin gripped his head with both hands. He thought about sneaking out the back, but he'd not be able to reach his car without being seen.

The knocking ceased.

Silence pulsed.

He dared to sneak another glimpse through the window.

No one in sight.

A red car was parked on the road. A crossover-type vehicle.

Where'd she go?

As if in answer to his question, someone pounded on the rear door. No need to see who it was. He leaned against the back of the sofa. Please go away. Or maybe not. She might be the answer to his dilemma, be his "out" from under Nick's thumb.

Quentin remained stuck, not moving or breathing, a bizarre one-person game of Statue.

A faint sound of a car engine unlocked his limbs. He lifted the blinds aside and watched the car do a three-point turn and head toward the gun range.

MC climbed into the driver's seat and stared at the cabin. The Kia SUV was parked to the right of the place. No sign of the black truck. No one had answered when she knocked on the door. She'd tried both front and back to no avail. Either Blondie was inside and didn't want to talk to her, or no one was home. He drove the Kia, which was parked under the canopy. Maybe he was hiking the woods?

Now she knew another way in so she could come back later.

She returned to the post office to check in with Pete and found the line of package-bearing customers was six-deep. Pete quickly let her through. "You're back."

"Yes. No search warrant yet. Before I do anything further, I want to go through the packages."

"What are you looking for?" he asked as he unclipped his keys from his belt.

"The usual suspect behavior when mailing prohibited items: the size, shape, weight, excessive tape usage."

Pete handed her his keys. "The office is yours. Let me know if there's anything I can do to help. We can't delay the mail, I mean, if the warrant isn't approved. Or if the packages aren't covered by the warrant. Delivery standards. You understand?"

They'd already gone over that, but Pete was nervous, so she let it go. "I agree."

In the office, MC scrutinized each of the thirty-odd mailpieces. Her level of suspicion ramped up to code orange. The sender had used a lot of clear packing tape on the boxes, but not the cardboard envelopes. Several wraps around the ends of the boxes, more than necessary for such containers. Every package bore hand-written addresses, both addressee and return address.

She set aside the last package and contacted Jamie.

"Talk to me, MC."

"I may have a lead." She ran through what had transpired earlier, including her unsuccessful attempt to speak with Blondie. "I've checked each parcel. With the exception of the one envelope that's torn, none of the others is damaged, so no clue about the contents. All the boxes have an excessive amount of tape. The addresses were handwritten. Can you call the AUSA and see if the search warrant application can be expedited? I'd at least like to check the busted open envelope. I see pills. That should be enough reasonable cause."

She heard a scratching sound. Either Jamie was writing, or they had a weak connection.

Jamie said, "I'll ring the AUSA. Since it's late Friday afternoon and there's no life-or-death situation, I'd guess the earliest we'd expect a warrant would be tomorrow. More likely Monday."

"If what I suspect is true, we're looking at illegal drugs. The longer we wait, the more time for the guy to flee."

"Did he see you?"

"No. I don't think so."

"I don't think we'll be able to get anything sooner. I'll push, see what they say. You should release all but the one package covered on the warrant application. We want to avoid customer complaints about delayed mail."

"I'll ask Pete to lock the one item in his safe. We'll send the others out. Although, truth be told, it ticks me off having to let the bulk of the drop move on. What are the chances one envelope has drugs and the other thirty packages contain CDs or DVDs or candy bars for the grandkids?"

"I hear you. Not ideal, but it'll have to do. I'll brief Cam, put a team on alert. If the AUSA gives us the go-ahead on the warrant and your instincts are on track, we'll want to apply for a search warrant on the residence. Have a chat with your guy and whatever accomplices are on site."

"I'll wait to hear from you on next moves."

"Yep. Good work, MC."

She gave Pete the ten-thousand-foot overview and called it a day. A driving thirst demanded to be quenched posthaste.

A load of laundry swooshed in the washer, and MC blitzed the house clean, top-to-bottom, while she sipped a glass of Goose. Dara and Meg were due to arrive late the next morning.

By seven-thirty she'd finished her chores. The area where Dara and Meg would encamp was dust-free and fresh as a spring daisy, or, in this case, lavender, courtesy of a candle she'd lit earlier to help bring the stale air some semblance of aromatic life.

A stout tumbler of vodka was her nightwatchman, or perhaps jailer, and sat on the desk next to the computer. Laptop opened to Facebook, MC scanned the comments on the Black Friday Killer page. Earlier, Kiara Reece had texted her about a specific comment. A person by the name of Fran Kenzie had shared an insightful story.

MC scrolled until her finger went numb as numerous comments populated the page. She finally came across the one Reece had mentioned. This Fran person's ex-boyfriend was a career burglar. At the time of Barb's death, Fran knew he'd been working the same neighborhood. Fran highly suspected he was the guy they were looking for.

Holy shit. For real?

Boyfriend Burglar drove a white Ford Escape. A white SUV had been seen exiting the alley after Barb was shot.

The screed continued, divulging more damning, although highly circumstantial, evidence. Boyfriend hadn't previously killed anyone—that Fran was aware of. He'd become violent. Knocked her around. She kicked him to the curb. "Dumped his ass" were her exact words.

MC scrabbled through her messenger bag in search of her Barb notebook, but it wasn't there. After a prolonged search, she found it on the floor in the bedroom between the nightstand and the bed. She hurried back to the loft, fearful that what she'd read online had been a figment of her imagination. If it's too good to be true, and all that.

When she skidded into the chair at her desk and keyed the computer screen back to life, the words were still there, black emblazoned on the white screen. She quickly recorded the comment, verbatim, into her journal.

She texted Reece: *Thank you. I read the comment.*

Within seconds Reece responded: *I told Sharpe. Enough there to warrant checking this guy out.*

Damn. She gulped a mouthful of alcohol to calm herself before she went off like a pack of firecrackers on the Fourth of July. *Okay. Keep me in the loop?*

Reece replied: *Will do. Hang tight. Sharpe hinted he might bring the guy in over the next day or two. Fingers crossed. Talk soon. Don't do anything I wouldn't do! Srsly.*

Reece had caught on to her *modus operandi*, though they barely knew each other.

MC itched to be in the Cities scouting the lead. She wanted to take a crack at the suspect in the worst possible way. Frustrated, she finished off her drink and returned to the kitchen for another long pour. The opaque bottle emptied, so she stuffed her feet into her boots and trekked to the garage to deposit the dead Goose in the recycling barrel. She'd need to hit the liquor store on Monday, or maybe she'd be able to sneak away tomorrow afternoon to buy reinforcements and hide the bottle until her friends left on Sunday.

Her mind raced. Hope. Fear. Anger. Impatience. Emotions rolled around like the silver marble inside a pinball machine, and all she could do was toggle the flippers to keep her world from draining into the black hole to nowhere.

Bleary-eyed now, she skimmed more of the comments on the social media site. She was about to call it quits when she saw a private message notification and clicked on it. The message unspooled, wavered. She sipped from her nearly empty glass. The jolt of juice hit her. She bolstered herself, palms planted on either side of the computer.

The letters bobbed and weaved before settling into a semblance of a straight line.

"I know who killed her."

MC blinked hard.

She ground the heels of her palms into her eyes. Opened them. The words glared at her. A dare. A hope?

Koop Koopaling was the sender. When she searched the name on Facebook, she retrieved zilch. Maybe the poster craved anonymity.

Dare she respond?

Sweat greased her palms. Her fingers trembled over the keyboard. She typed two words. "Who? Please."

What more needed to be said? She hit send and exited the app.

Maybe she'd hallucinated the whole thing. She drained the remaining drops of clear liquid and shambled to the bedroom, dreading the dark void ahead.

Chapter Fifteen

Fresh pastries from the best bakery in town glistened on the plate. Flaky, tender bits of shell sifted off the edges. A fresh pot of coffee, the second one she'd brewed, warmed the kitchen with a French-roasted infusion. MC ingested a side of Ibu to calm, if not eradicate, the thumping in her skull.

The scene was set.

A text hit her phone. Dara. *We're here!*

MC opened the rolling garage door allowing them to pull the Jeep in next to the Subaru. The navy-blue Jeep wore a coating of brown and gray muck, a combination of salt and dirty snow that dressed most Minnesota vehicles this time of year.

Hugs all around, then Dara scooped up their overnight bags. Meg tucked her hand in the crook of MC's arm, and they tromped from the detached garage to the house.

Once boots and coats had been tucked away in the cramped entry and overnight bags were deposited on the bed in their cozy corner suite, Dara and Meg met MC at the kitchen table.

"Coffee?" MC asked.

Dara said, "Is it from Flannel?"

"Unless you brought your own stock along, we'll have to suffer with the Peet's brand I bought at the grocery store."

Meg rolled her eyes at MC. "Dara, enjoy whatever brand MC brewed for us."

Dara hugged Meg. "Yes, dear."

They all laughed, the sound so familiar yet achingly foreign. But the ice was broken.

After they devoured pastries and a cuppa, they refilled their mugs and moved to the loft. MC had lit a fire, the glow flickering on the burnished honey-colored wood walls and ceiling.

Meg settled on the sofa next to Dara. "I've always loved this room. Spacious but cozy."

MC sat in a cocoa-brown leather recliner. "Thanks. We, I mean I, enjoy it." Tears pricked behind her eyes. She sipped her coffee.

Dara gently said, "We all miss her." Meg placed a hand on her thigh.

A silence settled over the room. MC took the reins and broke the spell. "I'm sorry I've been a putz. Mega case."

"Let me guess," Dara said, "you can't talk about it."

MC gave Dara a wan smile. "No, I can't." Time to address the elephant in the room. "Dara, you said you two needed to talk to me."

Meg slid her cup onto the coffee table, looked at Dara. "You want to do the honors or should I?"

"You go ahead. It's probably best that it comes from you."

Meg took a deep breath.

A flutter of unease rose in MC.

"I don't know if I'd say I'm the best—"

"For God's sake," MC sat forward in her chair, "someone please tell me what's going on with you two."

"I . . . recently . . . there's . . ." Meg put a shaky hand to her forehead and MC's alarm bells jangled.

Dara anxiously peered at her partner. "Need to rest? Or how about a drink of water?"

Meg shushed her. "I'm fine. Trying to find the words."

MC's gaze ping-ponged between her two best friends. A chasm wide as the Grand Canyon cracked open inside her. "No. Please, no." She took a deep breath. "Please don't tell me one of you is sick."

Dara's dark-brown gaze melted. She inclined her head slightly toward Meg.

For the first time, MC became aware that Dara's hair had gone from mostly silver to completely silver. Isn't that a phenomenon that happens when people go through an extremely shocking experience?

Shit.

She'd been so consumed with her own plight—her loss—she'd failed to see what was happening in front of her eyes.

Meg cleared her throat. "No sense beating around the bush, eh? Cancer. I've been diagnosed with breast cancer, MC."

Now the tears came, and they were all crying.

MC got up from the recliner, rounded the coffee table, and sat on the other side of the couch, next to Meg. She and Dara sandwiched Meg in a tangle of arms.

MC struggled for composure, finally gained control. "Meg. I'm sorry." She kissed her friend's plump, though pale, cheek. Her close-cropped blonde hair was also more silver than MC remembered. Her thoughts segued into wondering if Meg would soon have no hair.

Fear gripped her, a vise-like paralysis.

"Okay gals, give me some breathing room." Meg fanned her face. "Y'all are like a pair of portable heaters. Whew!"

MC scooched over but kept an eye on Meg. "What's the treatment plan? What can I do? How can I help?"

Meg's usually brilliant sapphire eyes shaded to a washed-out, sad blue, a testament that her condition was serious. MC yearned for the old spark.

Meg asked, "Could I have a glass of water, please?"

MC flew through the loft like a circus performer shot from a cannon. She filled a glass and carried it to her friend. "I want to know everything. Tell me. Please."

Meg drank deeply and set the tumbler next to her coffee mug. "The doctor said it's probably Stage One."

"Maybe two." Dara bit her bottom lip. "Either way they caught it early on, which is a good thing, considering."

"After the biopsy, he recommended lumpectomy," Meg said, "followed by radiation treatment."

Dara held tight to Meg's hand.

Words failed MC.

"We tried to tell you. A few times." Dara's voice was tight. "I begged. I pleaded. We wanted you to know. You pushed back."

Heat bloomed across MC's cheeks. She bent her head, gaze glued to the wood floor. She'd utterly failed her friends.

Meg patted MC's hand. "Don't. We're here now. No accusations."

"I didn't mean to sound accusatory," Dara said. "Christ. I wanted you to know we weren't hiding anything from you."

"I'm very sorry I didn't pay attention earlier. I've been selfish." Damn, had she ever. "I've been so entrenched in a couple cases at work, but that's no excuse. I promise to do better from now on." She leaned over and enfolded Meg in her arms, her heart breaking at the thought of the horrible possibilities. Recriminations from Barb for the lack of care and empathy toward their self-chosen family echoed in her head.

MC released her, but Meg held MC's hand with Dara's clamped in her other. "We're all together. Family. We'll weather this storm. That's what families do. No more sad faces or tears. Positive vibes from now on. Agreed?"

"One hundred percent." MC's voice was raspy.

Dara gazed at her intensely. "Agreed."

"Now, if you two don't mind, I think I might nap for a bit." Meg rose from the couch.

MC wasn't used to Meg being low-energy. A pit grew in her stomach as she watched her friend descend to the lower level.

Dara picked up a couple mugs. "I'll be there after I help MC bus the table." She helped MC gather all the detritus from the loft, then they tidied the kitchen.

MC folded the dishtowel over the oven handle. "Next moves?"

"We've got an appointment for a second opinion." Dara sat at the kitchen table. "Her doc is good. I'm sure whoever we see will agree with him."

MC lowered herself into a chair across the table. Sweat greased MC's palms. She wiped her hands on her jeans and gazed out the window, temporarily hypnotized by the muffled crash of ice-sheeted water stacking up like thousands of broken windowpanes along the shoreline behind the cabin. On average, anywhere from forty to ninety-five percent of the lake became covered with ice during the winter, and the ice breaks and the motion of the wind caused the pieces to slide and stack. Some slabs were clear while other, newly formed chunks, bore frost flowers that sparkled in the sunshine, an awe-filled and ethereal phenomenon that only temporarily distracted MC.

All the 'feels' raged inside her, banged around in search of an escape. Her leg bounced up and down. Her demon craved a gallon of vodka.

Silence filled the kitchen. The faint tick of the heat was the solitary sound in the house.

MC broke her trance to find Dara scrutinizing her. Don't, Dara. Not today. Do not lecture me on my drinking. She held Dara's gaze, dared her. For once Dara chose to give MC a pass, to not comment on her obvious jittery state. Goddess bless her, no mention of those two letters MC despised—AA.

MC's phone buzzed, breaking the tension. She withdrew it from her back pocket. Jamie's name lit the screen. "Sorry, Dara. Work. I gotta take this."

"No worries. I'm going to check on Meg and probably have a nap myself." She squeezed MC's shoulder in passing.

MC waited until Dara was out of earshot and answered. "Hi, Jamie."

"Hey. Possibility we'll have the search warrant tomorrow for that one package. If you find what you suspect, I'm ready to zip off the application for the warrant on the residence."

"Tomorrow. Sunday. But not for sure." Her speech sounded stilted in her ears.

"You okay?"

"A lot on my mind. But I'll be ready."

"I'll be in touch."

The afternoon loomed. MC floated unmoored. Maybe a nap? She nixed the idea. Sleep brought the risk of the nightmare.

Phone still in hand, she shot Reece a text: *Any word if Sharpe brought the guy in? I rec'd a private msg from someone named Koop Koopaling – claimed to know who killed Barb. Nothing on FB profile. Prob a dead end.*

She stared at the phone hard, trying to coax a response with her singular focus. Nothing.

Maybe Reece was on shift.

Anxiety made her antsy. The walls squeezed in around her.

What she needed was some fresh air. She left a note on the kitchen table for Dara and Meg and exited through the sliding doors.

The begrimed icy snow crunched beneath her boots as she slogged along the road, her head aswirl. Would Meg survive? How could she have been so cruel to her friends? Would they catch the online drug suppliers? Who the hell was Koop Koopaling—did this person know who killed Barb?

She'd forgotten her gloves. She tucked her hands into her coat pockets and tried to slow the roll in her noggin.

Take a breath.

The voice whipped past her on a glacial gust of wind. Tree branches scratched against each other, all brown and rough in their winter nakedness. Spring couldn't come soon enough. She yearned for the change to bleed color into the world. The dingy gray hues that painted the world depressed her more than she already was.

Should she tell Dara and Meg about the Facebook page? But then again, why add more to their overloaded plate? If the post bore fruit, she'd fill them in.

She checked her phone, surprised to see she'd been gone for almost an hour. Still no response from Reece. The bland, barely visible sun dipped lower on the western horizon. MC retraced the route home—to her friends.

Chapter Sixteen

Dara and Meg left at eleven, after the threesome shared a late breakfast. MC hadn't been able to eat anything. She pushed a slice of toast around a plate while her friends chattered. She drank at least four cups of coffee. Kept herself together while they waved good-bye from the Jeep.

After their car passed from sight, she lost it. Shakes ravaged her and she stumbled inside. She staggered to a chair in the kitchen. The tears came, a waterfall over the dam. Why Meg? The very idea that Meg might be taken was impossible. Life wasn't fair. MC had said as much to Dara and Meg last night before they all went to bed.

Surprisingly, the overnight visit had been a success. MC had made it without any Goose. The two beers with pizza at supper a bridge over her gaping, rushing river of need.

Jamie called after noon. The warrant had come through. The team was waiting in the wings pending news from her.

She washed her face, hoping to alleviate the puffiness. Then she changed into BDUs and layered a navy sweatshirt with the inspection logo embroidered on the front and "U S Postal Inspector – Police" stenciled on the back over a waffle-weave thermal shirt. She shoved her feet into her tac boots and left.

She met the postmaster in front of his post office. "Pete, thank you for taking time from your Sunday to accommodate us."

"I'm happy to help. I'll be happier to have the package elsewhere under someone else's jurisdiction."

Inside, MC donned a pair of nitrile gloves and sliced open one end of the envelope. The pills were round and white with a crease down the center. Easy to use a pill-cutter to take an accurate dose.

Pete stood off to the side, watching intently. "Doesn't look legal."

"Pretty much what I expected."

She called Jamie. "White pills in the envelope. Thirty total, three strips of ten. I don't see any pharmaceutical marking on the packaging. With this and visual of the same guy dropping off multiple packages bearing the same return address and at different post offices, not to mention having tracked him to a house locally, I think we have enough probable cause for a search warrant on that house and to question Blondie."

"KKW Vendor? Were you able to locate the business?"

"Nope. Fake address. Addresses on Highway 61 begin with one thousand."

Jamie said, "Of course. Too easy to think they'd use a valid return address. I'll use all the probable cause you have to request a new search warrant. Chances are, the soonest we'll get it signed and sealed will be tomorrow. I'll ring you when I know." Jamie hung up and MC sealed the envelope and pills in an evidence bag she'd brought in from the kit stowed in her vehicle, then signed and dated it.

Now another waiting game began. She wondered if Dara and Meg had made it home and sent Dara a quick text. MC scrutinized the screen, for once willing the pulsating bubbles to appear to let her know a reply was imminent. Abracadabra. Nothing. She swiped a thumb over the glass to confirm her text had been delivered. Dara usually tripped over herself to respond quicker than the speed of light.

MC thanked Pete again for coming in on his day off, grabbed the evidence bag, and left his cubbyhole. She scanned the empty post office, the carrier cases silent sentinels around the perimeter, before leaving through the front door.

She stowed the evidence in the hatch area of her car in a lock box she kept for such purposes. Then she got behind the wheel to head home. Her cell vibrated and she was disappointed to see it was Cam, not Dara. "Hey, Cam. What's up?"

"Don't sound so excited to hear from me."

"Sorry. I was waiting to hear from someone else is all."

"You okay? Something wrong?"

He was more intuitive than she gave him credit for sometimes. She let her shoulders slump. "I'm trying to deal with some personal news and keep my head on straight on this case."

"What's going on? Is it . . . Barb?"

"Actually, not this time." She grimaced. "It's Meg."

"Meg? What happened?"

"She's having a rough time. I'll fill you in later in person. Right now, there's more than enough to keep us busy with this investigation."

"Don't you dare renege on that."

"I won't. Promise." She'd let Cam down so often lately. She'd make it a point to remember.

Cam said, "Before I forget, I spoke with Sharpe about the Carson case. I still can't wrap my head around a guy leaving drugs where his kid can get at them. But I digress. Sharpe said part of the evidence they'd collected from Carson's home was an old Mickey Spillane paperback. Mrs. Carson discovered another in her husband's nightstand and handed it over."

She felt her phone buzz. Another buzz. And another. Damn. Someone was persistent. Probably Dara, but the present situation required her undivided attention.

"So? He's a Mickey Spillane fan, likes Mike Hammer, the alcoholic gumshoe. Hard-boiled crime fiction. Since when's that a crime? Personally, I think Chandler's Philip Marlowe or Dashiell Hammett's Sam Spade are better, but they're all dark."

Cam laughed. "Damn. I didn't expect a dissertation on the genre. The point is, Mrs. Carson had never seen her husband read a book since she's known him."

Her phone vibrated again, and she resisted the temptation to take a look. Eyes on the prize, MC, she lectured herself.

"Maybe he's trying a new hobby. A lot of guys come to reading later in life."

"You're such an expert on guys and what they do later in life?" He cracked up, took a few breaths and continued. "Anyway, if that's the case, he chose two less-than-ideal books. Both had the centers hollowed out. A square of pages was removed with surgical precision from the middle of both books."

"The drugs were hidden inside the books?"

"Bingo," Cam said.

"Wonder if any of the packages we let go contained any reading materials. Tie a nice big black bow around the case."

"Probably not. But when you find your blond-haired friend, ask if he has a collection of private eye crime fiction novels."

"Will do. Anything else?" She puzzled over the possibility that books were used to mail illegal drugs. Admittedly, it was a good way to get the drugs through.

"That's all I have, MC."

"Okay, I'll be waiting to hear back from Jamie tomorrow on the search warrant. If we get approval, I'll see if there's a stash of paperbacks anywhere."

"Sounds good. Take care."

"You, too. Hi to Jane and the kids." She disconnected and stuffed the phone in her jacket pocket. Having nothing more to do, she aimed the Subaru for home. Her cell did a double buzz, but she was driving so she let it go.

At home she heated leftover pizza in the microwave and cracked a can of Castle Danger Cream Ale. A cold beer on a cold night. Exactly what the doctor ordered. Not really, but the barley beverage sufficed, barely, in the absence of the Goose. Liquor stores in Minnesota were closed on Sundays so she couldn't pick up a fresh bottle.

She took a long pull of the lightly carbonated beer, which quenched her physical thirst, but lacked the kick of her usual juice.

Comfortably settled at the kitchen table with her dinner, she swiped a thumb across the dark screen of her iPhone. Facebook or texts? First, she'd deal with text messages. The notification dot sat like a blob of blood over the top corner of the app. She pressed on the icon. One message from Dara and a flurry from Reece.

Dara first. They'd arrived home safely. Meg was tired, but more at peace knowing they'd had time together. MC's breath caught in her throat, choked with guilt for being so out of touch recently.

She swallowed more beer and moved on to the million messages from Reece. No wonder her phone felt like a rocket launch in progress earlier. Holy shit.

MC scanned the pile of texts. Sharpe had hauled in the guy mentioned in the Facebook comment, someone's ex-boyfriend. A search of his garage and vehicle revealed looted items from several different burglaries in the area where MC and Barb had lived. None, however, had come from MC's home.

Damn. Strike one.

Also, no gun was found in the car or in the house where he lived. When asked, he claimed he'd never owned or even used a gun.

Strike two.

His fingerprints had matched a set taken at a home about a quarter mile from MC's old house. That particular abode had been burglarized the same day—Black Friday. He'd admitted to cruising the area within a six-block radius of the house he'd hit in order to choose his next target.

He conceded it was possible he'd driven past MC's house, either on the street or via the alley. He hadn't mapped anything out, though, having randomly driven the area.

When shown a photo of MC's house he claimed not to recognize it. But he'd hesitated. At least that's what one of the detectives who'd observed the questioning had conveyed to Reece.

Strike three.

Reece's final message: *Sharpe's detained him for the other burglary. He doesn't think the guy's involved in the invasion/murder at your place. Sorry.*

MC guzzled the rest of her beer and retrieved the last can from the fridge. She contemplated the info dump. *Thnx for the info. He still might be the one. Too coincidental. I don't believe in coincidences.*

Her finger hovered over the phone icon. Should she call Sharpe? No, that might shine suspicion onto Reece.

She set the phone down on the table but didn't let go of it. She *could* claim she wanted to chat about the Carson case, see if Sharpe mentioned anything about Barb's case.

He'd probably see through the flimsy ploy in a heartbeat.

Screw it. She called him. Of course, the call went to voicemail. In a leap of faith—or a call for calamity and consternation—she left a message. "Detective Sharpe. MC McCall. I created a social media post, a Facebook post, for Barb. And recently someone commented. Fran Kenzie was the name. She believed her ex-boyfriend was involved. You can read the details of the message online. The Facebook page is Catch My Black Friday Killer. I thought maybe you'd want check into this Boyfriend Burglar? Please call me."

She'd been polite—said 'please.'

Another day gone. Her wheels continued to spin. She needed a break on at least one front.

She drained the second can of beer, cleaned the kitchen. When she was done, she closed her eyes and envisioned Barb walking into the sparkling clean space. No doubt she'd make a crack, "About time you learned to clean up after yourself." MC's smile beamed megawatts of love for her partner.

The pleasant thought faded. She set up the coffee maker for the next morning and called it a night. Fingers crossed the dream stayed at bay.

Chapter Seventeen

Quentin hauled ass out of the salvage yard. The remote popped off his car visor. He left it in the footwell on the passenger-side. Talk about Manic Mondays.

He scanned the rearview, envisioning Nick in hot pursuit. All he saw was the grooved gravel road and the mounds of debris constituting Gunderson's salvage business.

Escape. Freedom. He put the pedal to the metal and hit the highway, the scene fading behind him.

Fucking Nick thought he was king of the mountain and Quentin was his underling. Dirk would no doubt set Nick straight on who was at the top of the shit pile—and it surely wasn't Nick. Quentin did not want to stick around to witness Nick's dethroning.

Why had he become friends with Nick? Nick was trouble. Always. When they worked for Len Klein at Stennard's parties, the money was great, but Nick always had an itchy trigger-finger. Looked for an excuse to pound someone or shoot someone. Not what Quentin signed on for. Now? Now it was worse. Nick was blitzed on the shit they sold. The drugs and his unceasing obsession with finding the postal cop, 'making her pay,' made Nick paranoid. He'd created an untenable situation.

A week earlier, when Nick aimed the Glock at Quentin, on the night he thought the postal cop was outside their house, Quentin had been able to brush it off. Quentin had called bullshit on him. Nick waved the handgun around, trying to be a big man. No actual threat, so Quentin hadn't been rattled.

Today's vibe was different. Quentin told Nick he was too fixated on the officer and not focused enough on the operation. Nick lost his shit. He ranted. Threw Q's video games around the room. Stomped on a game controller—plastic shrapnel shot across the floor. When Quentin told him to chill the fuck out, he did the exact opposite. He crammed more pills into his piehole and stormed to the bunkroom.

Before Quentin had time to think, Nick returned, arm extended, gun in hand. Quentin stared at the mile-long, dark tunnel of the barrel and then at the thousand-yard look in Nick's eyes. If Nick squeezed the trigger, would Q's life flash before his eyes like they said on every TV show? Or maybe he'd be frozen in some macabre game of Statue? The questions dangled unanswered. His brain kicked into gear. The deadly object aimed at his head was the last straw. The threat was real.

Quentin kept his voice calm. Told Nick he was going to take the shit to the post office. He hustled three containers of packages to the SUV. His breath was a diaphanous cloud drifting in the cool morning air.

Nick said, "You fucking haul ass back here ASAP. You hear me, Q?"

Oh, he heard—loud and clear. He had no intention of complying with Nick's command.

"And there's more shit to pack and mail this afternoon. It's Monday. Dirk said he'd stop by with a new supply."

And the shit will hit the proverbial fan if Dirk compares the orders to product on hand and discovers how much Nick has helped himself to in the past week.

Quentin was O-U-T.

The sun shone low on the eastern horizon. The day promised a hint of spring with the temp projected to hit fifty degrees. A time of rebirth. In more ways than one, he thought.

He drove directly to the post office. Mailed the packages. No one was in line and the lady—not the usual one—at the window was quick. Verified labels and tallied his bill. He paid with cash and made for the exit.

What to do? Where to go?

North? A drive along the North Shore to his favorite spot would give him time to plan what to do. How to avoid the postal cop? How to steer clear of Dirk? He was certain Dirk would be looking high and low for him before day's end. It behooved him to ensure he stayed under Dirk's radar. In fact, his life depended on it. He picked a place to turn around and veered back onto the highway, southbound. The best way to hide from Dirk was to leave town.

By mid-morning Monday, MC had made several trips from the desk in the loft where she'd set up her laptop to the coffee pot in the kitchen. Fully caffeinated, she was eager to get the ball rolling for what she hoped would be a fruitful day. For about five seconds she considered making an attempt to contact Blondie at the house by driving in the back way that

Deputy Johnson had told her about, but she didn't want to compromise the search warrant in any way. That was assuming that it would be approved.

How could it not be approved? They'd provided enough probable cause to squelch any modicum of doubt. She desperately wanted to nail those responsible. A child had died. MC's job was to follow the evidence to the perpetrator and ultimately ensure justice was served. She'd do everything in her power to safeguard another child—or anyone for that matter—from succumbing to a similar death.

But then MC floundered on waves of doubt that crashed into her from all directions.

She'd encountered one dead end after another. Always lagging behind. She let loose a scream. The sound bounced around the room and made her ears ring.

Take a breath.

She quashed the voice. She was so far beyond the point of taking advice from a non-existent being. Her shattered mind was just playing tricks and it needed to stop. Now.

MC checked Facebook. No new private messages. She opened the one she'd read on Messenger, stared at the brief statement. "I know who killed her." Five words. No response to her message asking who. She'd said please.

Didn't always pay to be polite.

Could SPPD somehow trace the IP address for the private message? The intricacies of the Internet were a gaping hole in her knowledge base. Sharpe had yet to respond to her voicemail, not that she'd expected him to jump at the opportunity. She took out the Barb notebook and paged through, re-reading all the entries. Nothing new. No answers jumped out at her.

As the time ticked past noon, restlessness overtook her. Still no word from Jamie. She wrestled her jacket on, got in the car, and hit the road to commence sleuthing.

The temp had crept to near fifty degrees. Trees dripped crystalline drops. Black-crusted snowbanks shrank in sun-drenched areas and remained stubbornly high in shaded zones. Minnesota trudged stolidly toward spring.

MC cruised past the Two Harbors Post Office. No silver Kia SUV in sight. She circumnavigated the entire city, drove out to Gunderson's and parked in the lot, hoping she'd what? See Blondie drive in and stop for a chat with her? Of course, no such encounter transpired.

Her stomach rumbled and she motored back toward the city until she reached Betty's Pies. The restaurant was about half full, but she snagged a spot close to the door on a round counter stool and asked for a glass of water and a menu. She kept it simple and ordered a bowl of Baked Potato soup. After she devoured the creamy delicious soup, she splurged and ordered a slice of Raspberry Rhubarb Crunch pie and a cup of coffee. Someone had left a copy of that day's Duluth News Tribune on the counter, so she perused that while she sipped coffee. She checked the time and saw it was already three.

Still no news from Jamie on the search warrant.

The bill paid and a hefty tip left for the server, she got in her car and drove north to Gunderson's again. In the parking lot she did a U-turn. Not a vehicle or a human in sight. Disappointed, she headed south to Two Harbors. Late afternoon light painted shadows along the roadway as she drove aimlessly up and down the city streets. Now that Daylight Saving Time was in effect, the sun wouldn't set until around seven in the evening. Each day would bring a bit more daylight, which tended to improve moods all around. It would also give her more daylight to work with on cases. She rolled past the rear of the post office. She'd accomplished exactly nothing. Frustration built up inside her.

A car ahead of her stopped to make a left at the corner where the post office was located. MC tapped her fingers along the steering wheel, waiting to make a right to pull onto the street in front of the post office. She eased forward, checked both ways . . . and jammed the brake pedal to the floor. The car slammed to a halt. She blinked several times to be sure she wasn't seeing a mirage.

A silver Kia SUV was parked at the curb on the street in front of the post office, maybe fifty or sixty feet from the corner.

Sweet suffering Jesus. Could it be him? Not Jesus, the elusive blond-haired guy.

MC crept forward and slid her vehicle close behind the Kia to block him in. She sucked in the deepest of breaths. Trails of exhaust floated from the rear of the car. Almost certainly her target sat behind the wheel.

MC unhooked the strap over her firearm. Made sure her badge was visible and pocketed her cell phone before she exited the Subaru. She scanned the street—deserted. A few cars sat on either side of the road. The post office had closed at least an hour ago, so the vehicles probably belonged to people associated with other businesses on the block. No telling when someone would show up. And the person inside the SUV hadn't moved. Good sign?

She strode toward the driver's side of the vehicle, right hand loose and ready. Bass vibrations from a hip hop or rap song rattled the frame. Slightly behind the driver's door she knocked a knuckle on the glass. Movement inside. The window lowered to the halfway point. Her muscles tensed, hand on her gun.

Blondie stared up at her. A flicker in his gaze—bewilderment? Recognition? Resignation?

Her eyes scanned the interior of the car and his hands. She didn't see a weapon but kept a grip on hers.

MC pointed at the radio. "Lower the volume."

He leaned over and hit a button with his right hand. Deafening silence. He remained placid, facing forward, phone in his left hand. She peered at the screen. Was that Facebook? The screen faded to black.

At long last, she had him where she wanted him. "Why're you here? Waiting for someone?"

"No. Kind of, I guess. I think I'm waiting on you."

Wait. What? "You're waiting for me?"

"I've seen you around. Here. Grand Marais. Other places."

"What's your name?"

"Quentin."

"Okay, Quentin. Do you know who I am?"

"I think so. I mean . . ." His knee pumped like a pogo stick as he inspected her with a twitchy gaze. "You're a cop?"

"Yes." She showed him her badge.

He read the words aloud. "US Postal Inspector. A postal cop. You're definitely the person I'm waiting for. You need to watch yourself. A guy I work with—let's say he's not a fan of yours." The knee worked double-time. "He might, like, try and hurt you."

Tingles shimmered through her. Goose bumps popped on her arms. "Wait here, Quentin. I need to make a call."

"I'm not going anywhere, don't worry."

She strolled a few feet away and remained facing the car while she called Deputy Johnson.

"Inspector McCall here. I've located him, the blond guy I've been looking for. He's in his car, parked in front of the post office. Would it be possible to send a cruiser to shuttle him to the sheriff's office?"

"I'm three minutes from your location. Is he armed? Do we need backup?"

"I haven't searched him, but I don't think he's armed. We've been chatting. Sort of. Probably better I take it off the street. I'd like to use an interview room at the station."

"That can be arranged."

"Thanks. See you soon."

She surveilled the area. Still, no one around.

She said to Quentin, "Here's what we're going to do. A deputy's on his way. He'll give you a ride to the sheriff's office. I'll meet you there. We can have a nice long talk. You okay with that?"

"Will the deputy, like, handcuff me or anything? Like, I *am* going willingly."

"No cuffs, and it'll be what we call a non-custodial interview. Unless you do something stupid."

Deputy Johnson rolled to a stop in the middle of the street, parallel to the rear panel of Quentin's parked car, and met her at the door. MC faded back and let the deputy get to work.

"Shut off the vehicle and step out." His stern baritone set Quentin into motion. He raised the window and shut off the car. Then he opened the door and exited, hands raised, key ring dangling from a finger.

Deputy Johnson said, "I'm going to search you. Turn—"

"Search me? Why? I didn't do nothing." He darted a panicked look between MC and Johnson.

MC said, "Easy, Quentin. It's standard procedure. Before transporting you, we need to be sure you don't have anything dangerous on you. Keeps everyone safe."

Quentin loosened his stance. "Fine."

Johnson said, "Hand me your keys and place your hands flat against your vehicle. I'm going to do a pat down. Is there anything in your pockets that might cut or poke me?"

"No." Quentin's voice was barely above a whisper.

Johnson did his thing. "All clear." He pocketed Quentin's keys, guided him to the squad car, and cushioned Quentin's skull from the frame as he backed him into the cramped rear seat.

MC leaned in. "I'll meet you at the station. We'll get a conference room. Okay?"

Quentin nodded.

She said to Johnson, "Thanks for doing this."

"See you there."

Johnson and her elusive suspect disappeared down the street. She cupped her hands around her face and peered through the windows of the SUV. Nothing of obvious evidentiary value jumped at her. Crumpled food wrappers and plastic beverage containers were scattered across the seats and spilled onto the floor. No drugs or weapons she could see.

Time to hear Quentin's story.

MC drove the quarter mile to the visually stunning Lake County Law Enforcement Center, which housed one of the three sheriff stations—the main one—for the Lake County Sheriff's department. The 1906 biscuit-colored brick and limestone structure was built in the Queen Anne style. The building was attached to the Court House, MC headed for the entrance.

A deputy escorted her from the lobby through an open-plan, carpeted space containing four desks—all empty at the moment. They moved into a hallway that branched off the main room and past a couple doors to what she assumed were offices. One clearly marked "Sheriff" had frosted glass windows on either side of the door preventing anyone from seeing inside, but MC saw ghostly light pushing against the panes. She checked the time, and saw it was six p.m. already. Probably any administrative staff had left at five and officers on duty were out on patrol which explained why the place was so quiet.

They arrived at a conference room not much bigger than a church confessional with décor a blend of maroons and grays. An overhead light brightened the space. Four cloth-covered chairs of the non-wheeled sort were placed two on either side of a Formica-topped conference table. Definitely an interview room, not an interrogation spot.

The deputy said, "Can I bring you anything? Water? Coffee? Johnson will be here in a sec with your guy. They just cleared the sally-port."

MC said, "Water. Thanks. Could you bring two?"

MC shed her coat, draped it over the second chair on her side of the table, and sat. She could hardly believe she'd finally found Blondie—Quentin, she reminded herself. Or rather, he'd located her. Despite her zealousness, a steely thread of suspicion wove through her veins. MC placed her cell phone and notebook on the table. Patted her coat pockets for her pen and set it alongside the notepad.

The deputy rematerialized, cradling bottles of water. "Here you go. Johnson is behind me."

"Thanks." She rose, and Johnson led Quentin in.

Johnson said, "He's all yours. I'll leave his keys with the jailer."

"Thanks."

"Need anything else?"

"Not at the moment."

"I'm off duty in an hour. If you need anything ask anyone. A sergeant will be at the desk. I'll brief the sheriff before he leaves."

"I appreciate that."

She attempted a pleasant smile for the blond man and gestured toward a chair. "Have a seat. Chances are we'll be here for a while."

Quentin wadded the parka onto the seat of one chair and dropped into the other.

She held out a bottle of water. "Thirsty?"

"Thanks." Quentin took the beverage, the flimsy plastic crinkling in his grasp.

A slow count to five.

Deep breath.

Focus, MC.

She folded her hands over the notebook and leaned forward. Easy. Chummy. "Quentin, I have a hunch you'll have a lot to tell me, and I can't possibly write fast enough to get it all down. Do you mind if I turn on my recorder?"

He shrugged. "Yeah, that's fine."

MC opened the voice memo app on her phone and pressed record. She placed the device between them and opened her notebook. "I'm going to read you your rights—protocol before I can ask you questions."

He opened his mouth, and she expected him to refuse. Instead, he said, "Okay."

That was easy. One more hurdle and she could get to it. "You have the right to remain silent. Anything you say can and will be used against you in a court of law. You have the right to speak to an attorney, and to have an attorney present during any questioning. Do you understand these rights?"

"I understand. But *I* asked to talk to *you*. Why are you reading me my rights?"

"Do you wish to have an attorney present?"

"I told you I wanted to talk to you. *I* looked for you. No, I don't want an attorney. Does this mean I'm under arrest?"

"No. I haven't arrested you. As you said, *you* asked for *me*, but I also need to keep a record of what you tell me. You understand?"

Quentin stared at the tabletop. Seconds ticked by. He raised his head, locked gazes with her. “I understand.”

Thank God. “I’m US Postal Inspector MC McCall. Today’s date is Monday, March 9, 2015. Time is six-fifteen p.m. I’m at the Lake County Law Enforcement Center in Two Harbors, Minnesota, in a conference room with Quentin—what’s your last name, Quentin?”

“La-ird.” His voice cracked. “Laird. Quentin Laird.”

MC straightened. “Spelling?”

“L-A-I-R-D.”

She wrote the name, then took a beat, and studied the shaggy, blond-haired man. Laird? Laird. Quentin Laird?

In each ear lobe fake diamonds—at least she thought the pea-sized studs were fake—glittered. He wore a heather-gray hooded sweatshirt with a dozen silhouetted cartoonish characters on various motorcycles or cars splashed across the front.

Laird? Could this be one of the guys they’d been wanting to talk to about Arty Musselman’s murder? Same name. Holy shit, this might be getting interesting.

She refrained from peppering him with a whole host of questions. Let him tell his story. Should she call Jamie? Or Cam? No. This was her moment. They blew off her earlier attempts to revisit the Musselman case in connection with the current investigation. First, she’d pump Laird for all the details, and then she’d revisit the issue with her colleagues.

“Okay, Quentin.” She reviewed her notes pretending she’d forgotten his last name already, “Laird. Quentin Laird. You told me you were waiting for me. You wanted to speak with me.”

Quentin rested his arms on the tabletop. “Yes. I waited at the post office ’cuz I thought maybe you’d show up.”

“What do you want to talk about?” MC detected the slightest vibration along the table. She scooted her chair backward, glanced under the table, and zeroed in on the source of the movement. Quentin’s left leg jiggled up and down like he was rehearsing for a Riverdance performance.

“It’s kinda like a long story. I’m not sure where to begin.”

“How about starting at the beginning?”

Quentin uncapped his water and tipped the bottle to suck down a slug. “I hooked up with some not-so-great people. I’ve done some bad things. But I want out. I can’t eat. I can’t sleep. I fear for my life. Probably sounds like I’m asking for sympathy, but it’s the truth. I don’t wanna live this way anymore." He slouched lower than he already was. "The worst is . . ." Quentin picked at the label on the water bottle.

MC allowed the silence to grow. She sipped water. Verified the phone was recording. She scrutinized Quentin. Watched. Waited. Gave him the space to formulate his thoughts into a coherent story.

"Before I tell you anything, can you give me immunity? I'm cooperating."

"Immunity from what?"

"Everything. I mean once I give you the details of what happened, you'll be able to arrest the person. Lives will be saved."

"Quentin, you're talking in circles. I need you to be crystal clear. Details. *Specifics.* In regards to immunity, that isn't in my power to grant. I can give my opinion to the prosecutors, but ultimately, it's their decision. Why don't we get the ball rolling? Lay all the cards on the table?"

"I guess." He drank more water. "Nick Wooler. He's your guy."

The coin dropped. Wooler, the other name associated with the Musselman investigation. Dammit. The sneaking suspicion she'd had since the team meeting almost two weeks ago wasn't a crackpot theory after all.

Wooler and Laird were two persons of interest the team had never been able to find to interview. Now one of the duo sat before her and proclaimed they were involved in something bad . . . exactly what, though?

The stagnant air in the conference room made it difficult to breathe. "Quentin, let's take a break here. Use the restroom if you need to. I'll wrangle another round of beverages. What can I get you?"

"Coke. Or another water. Whatever." He stretched.

MC tracked down a jailer to take him to the restroom. In the women's room, she took care of business and an extra minute to splash cold water on her face. A ghost glowered at her in the mirror, water dribbling off the face giving the impression it was sobbing.

This interview was really happening. A tiny segment of her brain again considered calling Jamie and maybe even Sharpe because of the possible Stennard case tie-in. What if she was wrong and they trucked all the way up here only to find her with egg on her face?

She shuffled that thought into a 'to do' file for later. This was hers whether it was helpful or not.

She found a vending area, bought a Coke for Quentin and a coffee for herself. Beverages in hand, she retraced the route to the conference room. Outside, darkness insulated the compound, and she was in a secure place where nothing existed beyond the interaction between her and Quentin.

Again, seated across from each other, MC restarted the recording app on her phone, updated the time, and gave their names. “You ready to continue, Quentin?”

“Let’s do it. The sooner you catch Nick the better for everyone.”

Quentin provided her with a scenario reminiscent of a crime fiction novel. Nick had a cousin who ran a business in Duluth. Nick assured Quentin the cousin had them covered for vehicles, shelter, and jobs.

“This cousin offered you work? Is that why you’re here?”

“More like we had to split from the Cities.”

Long story short, the cousin had taken off their hands the “hot” vehicle they’d arrived in. He provided them with new-to-them rides: Nick the black pickup truck; and Quentin the silver Kia SUV. He arranged for accommodations—the cabin on Gunderson’s property. In return, Nick and Quentin “worked” for the cousin. The work was definitely of the illegal variety. Nick developed an online vendor site on the Dark Web to sell heroin and opioids supplied by the cousin.

“This cousin have a name?”

“I’m not—I can’t remember.” His gaze slid off to the side.

Liar.

“He’s a scary ass mother, though.”

“How do you guys move the drugs?”

“The mail. Nick did all the computer shit ’cuz I don’t know anything about the Dark Web and I don’t want to know. We both packed orders. Wax packets of powder. Heroin. And these bubble strips of pills. We stamped the wax envelopes with a black cat and KKW. All Nick’s idea. I shuttled boxes to the post office.”

KKW. The return address from the packages. “Does KKW stand for anything in particular?”

“Yeah, Nick’s big idea: Krazy Kat Wooler. KKW. Figured it would make him famous or some shit. I dunno.”

“How often were orders filled?”

“Usually every day. Sometimes twice a day if we had backlog. And once a week we’d mail a box of cash, too.”

“Where’d you obtain the drugs and the money?”

"Nick's cousin. Once a week he delivered bundles of cash. And tons of pills, all in blister-topped packets. And bundles of heroin packets. We keep an inventory, but lately our numbers have been off. Nick's helping himself to the stock. Shit. His cousin, man, he's catching on."

"How about you? You help yourself to some? Enjoy some free highs?"

"No! I don't touch that shit. Ever. My mom—she'd kill me if I did. I mean she would've. She's in a coma in a nursing home in the Cities. That's why I needed money. To pay the bills."

The story rang a bell in MC's mind. When the task force searched for Nick and Quentin in relation to the Musselman/Stennard cases, the details they'd had on Quentin were that he'd stopped to see his mom at a nursing home and had paid her facility bills several months ahead. No one had seen or heard from him since before Thanksgiving.

"You guys have this lucrative gig working for No Name Cousin. Why're you suddenly growing a conscience? Seems like good money. Food, shelter, transportation all covered."

Quentin shoved his chair away from the table and stood. He leaned against the wall farthest from MC, hands inside his sweatshirt's pouch. "The money's definitely good. Big bucks. But Nick's losing it. He held me at gunpoint twice in the past week. I don't trust him. Honestly, he scares the fuck outta me. I never wanted this life." He lifted his hands like a preacher to a congregation, a congregation of one. "My goal, my only goal, is to take care of my mom. I've got nobody else. My old man's in prison. He's the reason she's in a coma. Beat her to a pulp. She nearly died. When Nick pitched me on working for Len Klein at Stennard's, I jumped at the chance."

Len Klein. Stennard. Two more pieces of the puzzle. "You two worked for Klein?"

"We did until it all went to hell. When Stennard's went under, Klein had to 'let us go,' as he put it. No more work."

"What kind of work?"

"Off the books security at private events. Parties at Stennard's house. And drugs. Nick had the connection for all the party goodies: weed, ecstasy, oxy—you name it, he handled it. Then it all went to hell 'cuz Stennard was arrested. Klein told us to buzz off. Nick was a loose cannon. He'd devised a brilliant payback scheme, which backfired. Epic backfire. Then we were on the run, and he's been on edge since. He thought he saw you outside the house last week, talking to Gunderson. He was convinced it was you. I didn't believe him, which sent him over the deep end."

"How'd he know me?"

"From Stennard's. You were with a million other cops hauling shit from the business one Saturday. Nick took a pic of you. He . . . "

She waited, holding her breath a few seconds before whispering, "He what, Quentin?"

He slid into his chair, face cherry-red. "He thought you were hot."

Great. An angry stalker. Fucking men.

"Klein canned us. Nick blamed you. When the dumb ass saw you last week, he was ready to go after you, gun blazing. Instead, he came at me. To tell the truth, I think it's a matter of time before his cousin goes after Nick, no matter that they're family. The other night he advised Nick to get his shit together or else. In true Nick form, he blew off the warning and took more drugs, skimmed more money and went on a tear in Duluth. Feels like the end is near."

She'd been so close the night she'd chased the truck inside Gunderson's Salvage. The same night she'd discovered the pallets. All the different irons in the fire were melting together.

Take a breath.

The layers of complexity wove a giant cocoon of fucked-up-ness.

"What do you mean, the end is near?"

"Nick called me earlier today. After I did the daily drop, I hit the bricks to go see my mom and get away from the bad shit. Nick—he ranted again about how he'd seen you in the salvage yard. He's wound tight. High. Said he was gonna track you down, get revenge."

"And you wanted no part in his plot?"

"I couldn't be responsible for—no way. I mean, I didn't shoot. I don't have a gun, never wanted a gun. We carried at Stennard's parties, but I always gave the piece to Nick at the end of those bashes. I hate guns."

MC tried to piece Quentin's words together. "You thought by coming back you'd be able to prevent Nick from killing me?"

"I thought I'd put an end to a long line of bad decisions. Come clean. This kinda shit eats away at your guts, ya know? Can't do it anymore. I figured I'd find you before Nick did. Tell you everything. Maybe you'd help me if I helped you?"

She ignored the offer of a quid pro quo. "Have you spoken to or seen Nick since your return this afternoon? Been to the cabin?"

"No. I drove around Two Harbors, trying to decide if I should go back to the Cities. Instead, I stayed. Parked in front of the post office. I didn't call Nick. Didn't see him. He hasn't called me again. I got no idea where he is or what's happening, other than I guarantee you it's bad."

"Good enough. Tell me about the drug scheme. What all were you selling?"

"Like I said. Powder. Heroin. Pills. Oxy. Opioids."

"Nothing else?"

"Nope."

"You're certain?"

"Positive. Why?"

MC wondered if Ethan Carson had purchased his drugs from these two, though his stash contained pills and patches. She scratched a side note to remind herself to delve deeper later.

"Let's recap. You and Nick worked security for Klein at Stennard's parties?"

"Yeah, security, and we supplied—Nick supplied—a shit ton of drugs he always gave to Klein ahead of the party. Our job was stopping people from going wild. Didn't want neighbors calling the cops."

"Good on you." The bitter dripped off her tongue.

"Huh?"

"Never mind. You two were cut loose when Stennard's business went belly-up due to the fraud investigation. You flee here, dive deeper into the drug trade. Any idea the number of people who've died from these friggin' opioids? From the shit you're selling? Even kids. Kids, Quentin. Children—babies!—die from shit bought over the Internet."

Take a breath.

She'd heard enough, more than enough. MC clicked into mental autopilot. "Okay, based on the facts you've shared, what I'm going to do now is place you under arrest. You'll be booked into jail. I'll contact all the players, other law enforcement agency representatives who will want to have a conversation with you. There are more cases attached to you than an octopus has tentacles. I'll have to confiscate your cell phone."

Quentin slid the device across the laminate tabletop. He slumped in his seat.

"Wait here while I find a deputy."

She didn't see a lock on the door, so she took a calculated risk leaving him alone. After all, they were in the jail facility, and he'd be hard-pressed to escape before someone nabbed his ass.

MC arranged for a deputy to process Quentin. Once he'd been taken away, she returned to the conference room and phoned Jamie.

"Hey, MC. Anything new?"

"Plenty. I've had a helluva day. You and Cam may want to take a road trip. Got a guy in custody at the Lake County Jail. Name's Quentin Laird. I'll call Sharpe at SPPD to let him know as well."

"What'd you find?"

"Laird and his sidekick, Nick Wooler . . ." She let the second name hang in the ether. They'd been quick to blow her off in the team meeting about Wooler. Let him stew for a bit in the vat of "MC was right."

"Wooler?"

"Yes, Wooler. Remember I mentioned him at the last meeting I attended? Both yahoos were hired by Klein for Stennard's personal soirees back in the day. Security. Drugs. All sorts of criminal enterprise. When things went to hell in a handbasket for Stennard, these two fled. I'm unclear on exactly why. Next stop was a cousin of Wooler's. Laird hasn't given a name for this cousin, but he has been forthcoming on the employment opportunity the cousin provided them. Online drug sales. Opioids. Pills. Heroin. Oh, and apparently Wooler blamed me for their loss of income stream with Stennard. I'll request Lake County lasso Wooler ASAP. Tomorrow we'll hit the ground running on interrogations."

Jamie said, "I'll brief Cam. We'll leave early and aim to be in Two Harbors between nine and ten. Good job, MC. Mind me asking how you landed Laird?"

"Oh, I didn't. After chasing my tail for freakin' ever, *he* found me. Had himself a Come-to-Jesus moment and came clean."

She explained the odd circumstances of one man's guilty conscience, and Jamie let out a bark of laughter. "Wow. That's one I've not heard. We'll see you tomorrow."

"I'll call Sharpe next and fill him in. I assume he'll want to be part of this meeting of the minds."

"See you in the morning."

Now all she wanted was to go home and execute a swan dive into a bottomless bottle of Grey Goose. Anesthetize herself to oblivion. She still had one more task.

Still seated in the empty room, she polished off the dregs of cold coffee from the soggy paper cup. Gagged. Swallowed hard and selected

Sharpe's contact. The phone rang to voicemail. Not surprising given the time of evening. "Detective, Inspector McCall. I'm in Two Harbors and have a guy in custody we strongly believe is involved in shipping opioids by mail and may be the drug source from the Carson case. Team Lead Jamie Sanchez and Inspector White will join me tomorrow for interrogations. I thought you might want to participate in the fun. Please contact me on my cell when you hear this message. Sanchez, White, and I will be at the Lake County Law Enforcement Center between nine and ten tomorrow, Tuesday morning."

Whether he'd make an appearance was beyond her control. She hoped he'd show. She'd like to have him in a room and chat about the guy in custody for the burglaries around her old house. Ask if they'd questioned him about Barb's murder.

She left the conference room in search of the deputy who'd taken Quentin. She found him and filled him in on the plans for the next day. He assured her he'd talk to the sergeant, who'd convey the plan to the day sergeant and the sheriff.

The night air bit through her layers of clothing. Stars sparkled in the indigo sky. The crisp air brought tears to her eyes. Time for a close encounter of the clear, soft, winter-wheat-based beverage kind. MC stopped by the liquor store for a bottle of "get me through the night."

Her phone vibrated as she entered the garage. She left the car running and checked the device. "Detective Sharpe."

"Inspector. I received your message. Thanks for looping me in. I'll be there in the morning. See you at the jail?"

"That's the plan. We'll convene between nine and ten."

"See you in the morning."

She bit her lip to stop the diatribe she wanted to let loose at him. "Yep. Bye."

MC crammed the phone into her pocket and hefted the brown-bagged bottle. She'd behaved very professionally. She deserved at least two robust drinks before calling it a night.

Chapter Eighteen

The sheriff's office was overheated and cramped with the sheriff, a sergeant, MC, Jamie, Cam, and Sharpe inside. Since half a dozen people couldn't interview Quentin Laird at once, the group moved to the observation space adjoining the interrogation room.

Jamie suggested Cam and Sharpe take the first round with Laird. The sergeant monitored the computer and ensured all the recording devices worked prior to Laird being brought in.

Cam and Sharpe left for the interrogation room.

The sheriff leaned up against the wall, arms crossed, while MC and Jamie sat at a round table, she with her notebook splayed, ready to record all the pertinent details. "I'm going to use the restroom and grab a coffee."

Cam and Sharpe stood outside the next room.

"Hey, Detective Sharpe." MC said. "A moment, please?"

Cam's eyebrows shot up, but he didn't comment.

Sharpe said, "Sure. I'll meet you inside, White." He joined her on the other side of the hall. "What's up?"

MC leaned against the opposite wall. "I was wondering if by any chance you questioned the Boyfriend Burglar—the man from the Facebook comment—about Barb's murder?"

"I'm not going to discuss Miz Wheatley's case with you."

"You keep telling me that. And I get it. But can't you give me just this one thing?"

Jamie poked his head out of the observation room door. "Everything okay out here?"

Sharpe pivoted away from her. "All good. Inspector McCall had a question that, unfortunately, I was unable to answer. I'll head in and wait with Inspector White." He headed toward the interrogation room.

MC ground her teeth. "Maybe we can continue the discussion when there's a break in the action."

"Or not. I suggest we focus our attention on Laird." He disappeared through the door.

MC sighed. "Jamie, let's go get some coffee."

"You lead the way."

"You bitch!" a male voice behind them shouted.

She spun around. Two deputies herded along a dark-haired man in a raggedy black leather jacket wearing grimy jeans and shit-kicker cowboy boots. The trio swayed in the hallway past the interrogation room.

"I'm talkin' to you! You fucked everything. Bitch."

MC said, "Nick Wooler, I presume."

His eyes were dead as the ashes in the bottom of a charcoal grill. "Fuck off."

The deputy said, "Let's go, loudmouth. We have a nice warm room waiting for you."

MC suppressed a smirk before showing her back to the guy. "Seems like a real charmer."

Jamie said, "His interview should be interesting."

With her coffee and notebook, MC sat at the table in the observation room. Jamie paced behind the table like an expectant father. She wondered if he was nervous about the confrontation between her and Sharpe or anxious about the impending interview.

Through the one-way window, MC scrutinized Cam and Sharpe who sat, backs to the door, on heavy, metal-framed chairs with cracked leather-covered seats on one side of a sturdy metal table. Walls were pale gray. Cameras mounted in the corners behind Cam and Sharpe aimed at the empty chair. A metal loop had been soldered in the middle of the table in case the suspect needed to be cuffed to it. A big, one-way window in the wall to Cam and Sharpe's left rounded out the décor. The layout was similar to SPPD, where the interrogator activated the audio/video recording by hitting a button on the wall outside the room.

Laird was escorted into the room by a burly jailer and pushed in the chair. "Cuffs or no?"

"No cuffs," Cam said.

MC agreed. The best option was to put Laird at ease in hopes he'd open the floodgates and drown them in information.

Cam introduced himself and Sharpe and reminded Laird of his rights. Laird said he understood. He again refused an attorney.

Jamie's attention was focused on the one-way glass window.

Cam and Sharpe questioned, cajoled, and encouraged Laird. They allowed him to roll through his tale.

Laird reiterated the same story he'd told MC the previous evening. Then, "There's one more important thing."

Cam leaned forward. "What important thing?"

Laird glanced at the mirrored window to his right. "I want to talk to the lady cop. The one from last night."

Sharpe said, "Tell us. We're recording this. Inspector McCall will hear it all."

"This is important. I'll tell her. I'll tell Inspector McCall. If she's alone in the room. No one else." He leaned back and crossed his arms.

Cam said, "Again, we're recording everything. If we're not physically in the room we're still hearing and seeing it all."

"Like I said, Inspector McCall or I don't talk."

In the observation room, Jamie said, "Any idea what he's doing, MC?"

"No."

They watched Cam and Sharpe exit interrogation. Two seconds later they entered the observation room.

Cam said, "You heard the man. He'd like to speak to Inspector McCall alone." He rolled his eyes.

Jamie said, "Let's find out his game plan. MC, you're on."

MC gathered her notebook and pen.

Cam followed and stopped her before entering the interrogation room. "You good to go in alone?"

"I'm fine. I spent hours with him last night and he didn't try anything." She returned Cam's gaze. "Odd turn of events. I mean, what else could there possibly be? Why me alone?"

Cam said, "Let's find out."

MC crossed the threshold, ready to hear more details about the online drug scheme. "Morning, Quentin." She used his first name hoping to put him at ease. Enshrine a level of trust.

"Hey, Inspector."

"What is it you refused to tell Inspector White and Detective Sharpe?"

"Maybe—could I show you something? On my phone? I need to access the Internet. It will help you understand."

"I can't give you your phone. It's been taken into evidence."

"Could I use yours?"

"Are you playing games with me?"

"No, I swear. You'll wanna see this. I promise." His body jittered in the chair.

"Fine." She unlocked her cell and slid the device across the table.

His fingers flew across the screen. Taps and swipes. Then he flipped it around to face her.

He'd opened the Facebook app. Five words shimmered on the white background. "I know who killed her."

She swallowed a gasp. Her skin tingled. She flicked her gaze at Laird. "What the hell? You sent this?" Her voice sounded like it came from a tunnel.

He inclined his head in assent.

She stood, fists propped on the table, and leaned forward. "Is this some kind of joke?"

Laird slid his chair back in alarm. "No! I'm not joking." He held his hands up in the air, her phone clenched in one. "Swear to God."

Her back straightened, like a steel rod had been rammed through her spine. MC spun and faced the wall behind her. In the corners the pin-sized red light on the cameras blinked on-off-on-off. A bloody blur.

Was this really happening? Was she in the same room with a person able to divulge the identity of Barb's murderer?

MC, though in the midst of the action, felt outside, cut off, like she was watching from inside a soundproof booth. The others in the observation room were merely an audience to this newsreel. Or maybe the whole encounter was a scene from a silent movie. One in which she played a starring role.

A convergence of multiple investigations in this one human being? Coincidence?

She didn't believe in coincidence.

MC returned to her seat. "One more time. You're telling me you possess verifiable information of who killed Barbara Wheatley? You responded via a private message to the Catch My Black Friday Killer page on Facebook? You're . . ." MC took the phone from his hand to swivel the screen toward her, ". . . Koop Koopaling?"

Laird nodded.

"Quentin, I'm going to need you to verbalize your answer."

"Oh, sure, sorry. Yes, I'm Koop and I know who killed the woman—Barb—on Black Friday."

A knot grew in her belly. "What kind of name is Koop Koopaling?" Really? That's the question she led with? Delaying the inevitable pain? Or a stall tactic to hold Jamie et al at bay for the time being?

"Um," he ducked his head, "a character from *Mario Kart 8*, a video game I play."

For fuck sakes, a video game? Pressure built up in her head like she'd been submerged in deep water. She found it difficult to draw a full breath.

MC, keep it together. Take a breath. No doubt Sharpe and the others were poised to bust in if she fell apart.

"You're able to give us a name? Proof?"

"The proof is I—I witnessed the shit go down. Can we talk immunity?"

"We've covered this. I can't promise immunity. Tell me what you can't tell the others. Why me, not them?"

"You want to hear about Black Friday?"

Yes, damn it! "Sounds like a logical launching point."

Her hand shook a little as she held her pen poised to commit his story to the page in front of her.

"Nick Wooler."

Wooler's name again. Her nerves sizzled. The ground opened, ready to swallow her. "Nick Wooler what?" She held her breath, wrangled her willpower to keep from throwing herself across the table to throttle the shit out of this guy. The voice from her incessant nightmares wormed its way into the here-and-now and its name was Nick Wooler. The antiseptic bright white backdrop from the dreamworld morphed into pitch dark, suffocating realism.

MC dressed her face in her most confident façade.

"He was pissed at—you, I guess. The money from the Stennard job dried up overnight. He went apeshit. His big idea was to tail you, find where you lived, and steal your shit. Payback. For killing our golden goose. But . . ."

But what? She screamed in her head. The world spun like she was on a demented carousel at a hinky county fair. Her gaze locked on Quentin, and she clenched her teeth. Why the hell did he have to mention a goose? MC's fingers itched to open a bottle and douse the fiery conflagration within her.

"I didn't know he'd brought a gun. I thought we'd loot the place, maybe mess shit up and leave. Eye-for-an-eye for us being left high and dry." He polished off the remainder of his water, capped the empty bottle. "Could I have another?" He crinkled the empty plastic in his hands.

"I'll see what I can do, Quentin. In the meantime, carry on with the story." The tale—absolutely riveting and horrifying—cascaded over her.

"The other lady—this Barb I guess—came home. She—she scared the crap outta us. Nick freaked. Pulled his gun and shot her two or three . . . I don't remember for sure the number of shots. But he put her down."

Boom. There it was. Displayed in front of her, a gruesome gift she wished she'd never heard.

Quentin said, "Stuff—holiday ornaments busted and flew all over the damn place. We snatched a bunch of shit and got the hell out. I had to drive since Nick was tweaked to the max. I blasted through the alley like a rocket ship on skis. I remember, I yelled at Nick, 'You fucking idiot! Why'd you shoot her?' He was amped. Geeked out. He pounded the dash, celebrating."

Quentin hung his head.

Was he ashamed?

MC itched to go over the table and strangle Quentin. More so, she craved time alone in a locked room with his pal, Nick Wooler. She dug deep and maintained a mostly calm exterior. "What next, Quentin?"

"Nick said we had to dip out of town ASAP. We grabbed stuff, left what we couldn't carry, and drove north. To here." He waved his arms. "He said his cousin would help us. Hide us. Give us work. I had no idea what kind of work, which leads to the part of the story I told earlier. Can you help me? I mean, I kinda helped you, didn't I?"

Help her? Was he serious right now? He and his pal had paved a path of murder and mayhem for her and countless other people. She'd help him all right. Help him to a set of silver bracelets snapped around his wrists. Help order him a heavy escort to a holding cell.

"Perhaps I need to provide you with a summary."

"A what?"

Christ. "To recap what you said: In retribution for losing your illicit jobs, you and Nick Wooler burglarized my home. You killed my partner when you encountered her unexpectedly. Do I have the story straight? You consider that to be helpful to me? Are you stupid? Or maybe you think I'm stupid."

He squinted at her from across the table. "You got it, mostly. Nick is the one who killed the wo—Barb. Not me. I ain't stupid."

"You were there. You didn't prevent the act. Afterwards you didn't render aid. You fled like the cowards you both are. You left town. Hid from your depraved deeds. On top of which, you dove headfirst into a new set of bad acts. Am I on course?" Sarcasm replaced any goodwill she may have had.

MC, take a breath.

"Not now," she said.

"Not now what?" Quentin blinked rapidly.

Shit. MC gathered the fragments of her wits, reminded herself to refrain from answering the voice only she could hear. "Nothing. Moving on. You and Nick mailed drugs to customers via a site on the Dark Web. And cash to someone, a supplier probably. No-Name Cousin provided product. Nick remained hellbent on taking revenge on me for the Stennard debacle. I appeared on the scene early this week. Nick grew more incensed. He used drugs, threatened you with his gun. All the while Cousin is on his ass because Nick short-changed him on money and drugs." She paged through her notes. "You chose to make like a baby and head out. You grew a conscience when Nick contacted you and said he wanted to shoot me." She paused remembering this was news to the team in the adjoining room but pushed onward. "You returned to the scene of the crime to what? Play knight in shining armor and save me—and ultimately yourself? A sordid form of quid pro quo. Shit, these are all the deets on what you two have done since November, and in return you are convinced that we, the system, should cut you a break."

She needed an oxygen tank after the spiel.

"Um—yeah."

"Quentin, we're done."

She gathered her stuff.

Remain calm. Breathe.

She about tore the door off the hinges exiting the room.

Sharpe was waiting outside the door. He stopped her with a hand on her shoulder. "I'm sorry, McCall. Not the way you should've heard that."

You think? "I'm sure you're relieved I won't be nagging you any longer." She took two steps and stopped, not facing Sharpe. "What kind of gun was used? To kill her?"

"Nine mil."

For once he'd answered her question without a lengthy lecture on investigative protocol. She continued on to the observation room.

Cam met her at the door. Jamie hovered in the background, and the county sergeant busied himself at the computer.

MC said, "Sorry. My fault."

Cam dragged a chair away from the table, guided her to it. "No. Not your fault. You handled that brilliantly. What do you need now?" The skin around his blue eyes creased with worry. "A drink?"

Shit, yes. The most monstrous-sized glass of vodka you can find, she screamed inside her head. The stitches ripped asunder from the tightly knit ball of personal losses. The threads shredding beneath the pressure, her hands shook, and she could barely swallow. "Water, please."

Jamie said, "Stay here, Cam. I'm on it."

MC shook her head in wonder. "That just happened. Can you believe it?"

Cam did not answer her rhetorical question.

Jamie returned with multiple bottles of water, handed them around. "MC—"

"Stop." She raised a hand to ward off the pity or whatever he was about to bestow upon her. After a long draw of water she regrouped, reviewed the pages of notes from the interviews with Laird. "I think they might be the ones Ethan Carson ordered his drugs from. The pills were similar to those at Carson's home." But wait, she thought, there weren't any patches included. Shit. And the packaging was different. Maybe she was wrong. She needed to find out one way or the other.

Jamie said, "MC, you need to take a minute. You've experienced trauma that would knock anyone on their ass. Take a timeout and breathe. Maybe take the rest of the day—or the week—off. We'll take it from here."

Cam slid a chair next to her. "What can we do? Want me to call Dara or Meg?"

MC slapped a hand on the table. "Stop. Please. I want to do my job. What I need to do most is my job. I don't need to be mollycoddled. Can we please move on? Deploy a team to the cabin, bag whatever evidence is there? What about Wooler? Someone needs to interrogate him to within an inch of his life. Find the gun." Squash him like a bug.

"Whoa," Jamie said. "Cam and Sharpe will handle Wooler after Sharpe finishes with Laird."

"What am I supposed to do? Wooler should be *mine* to grill." Her pulse kicked into overdrive. She was heated and ready for battle with whichever enemy was closest.

Jamie said, "I think you know that cannot happen. You can't be in the same room with Wooler. No way."

"A personal connection to a victim doesn't mean I can't be objective." She clenched her jaw, raised her chin. Take it down a notch, she thought. The last thing she needed was to get sent packing and lose out on all the action. Still, it irked her that she couldn't have a round with Wooler.

Jamie shook his head. "You've been through enough. Aside from that, the sight of you aggravates Wooler."

"The feeling's mutual." She bit her tongue because a diatribe would only prove Jamie's case.

He said, "It's best if Cam and Sharpe do the dirty work."

"Dammit, Jamie. I *earned* the right to have a go at Wooler. I. Want. In."

"No. That's my final answer. I *will* allow you to continue with the investigation if you assure me you'll stay on track. I'd like you to oversee the evidence gathering at their residence. But I need assurance you're good with the plan."

Better than being benched. She wrestled the demon into its lockbox. MC looked Jamie straight in the eye. "You have my word."

Jamie's gaze lingered on her face. "We have a team in the conference room; two of our inspectors, a Hazmat Unit; and the sheriff agreed to send a deputy. Rally the troops, tear their place apart."

MC forced her features into what she hoped came across as intense concentration. "I'm on it."

The parade of law enforcement units drove through Gunderson's Salvage Yard to the ramshackle cottage a quarter mile along the winding road. Masked, bulletproof vest under her coat, and with her gun gripped tightly in hand, MC knocked on the front door. "Police! Search warrant."

No response.

She tried the door and found it unlocked. "Let's go." She waved the crew inside. "Police!" They cleared all the rooms, then got to work.

MC tromped through pieces of a busted video game controller scattered across the living room floor. Empty Coke cans were strewn on a side table next to the couch. A ratty blue indoor-outdoor carpet remnant strained to cover the plank flooring. A TV the size of a movie theater screen perched on a wooden chest against the wall facing the door. A Nintendo Wii game console nestled on the floor next to the chest. A battered plaid sofa, someone's butt imprint on one cushion, paid homage to the setup. Lots of dollars invested in entertainment.

To the left of the living room, a card table and two chairs were shoved in a corner under a side-facing window. Crumbs and twisted beer cans littered the top. Next to the table was the "office" area: desktop computer and printer on a cheap desk.

The main attraction, however, covered all the real estate on the kitchen counter. Stacks of blister-pack pills and wax paper packets of what appeared to be powder—probably heroin—rubber-banded into bundles of ten.

Everyone slipped on gloves. The Hazmat unit and inspectors inventoried and bagged all the narcotics. MC searched the bathroom and discovered science experiments in different stages of growth in the shower stall and along the tile floor. The toilet tank yielded rust and corrosion. No bags. No firearms.

What was probably a bedroom across the hall from the bathroom had been converted into a prep space. Cartons of empty wax-paper envelopes hugged the wall under the single window. A folding chair and an old-fashioned metal TV tray were set up like a scene from a sixties living room where people ate in front of their televisions. The wobbly tray on spindly metal legs held a bunch of wax-paper envelopes and several ink stamps. The stamps were of a black cat with the letters KKW underneath. MC moved aside a pile and underneath were stamped, empty envelopes. She lifted one, carried it to the kitchen. "Hey guys," she said to the two inspectors working on inventorying the drugs, "does this match those bundles?"

One inspector held a bundle of wax folds, moved the rubber band upwards with a gloved thumb. "Perfect match."

"Thanks." She returned the empty stamp packet to the room. Along another wall she spotted mailing supplies: Priority Mail Flat Rate boxes and envelopes; shrink-wrapped stock of blank labels; and a half-empty box of black Sharpie permanent markers.

The remaining room, maybe twice the size of the prep room, held two four-drawer dressers and two sets of bunk beds, one on either side of the window. Clothes belched from half-open drawers on one dresser and flopped like beat-up rag dolls over the edge of the top bunk. The bottom bunk was a mess of sleeping bag and blankets. Beneath the threadbare mattress, wrapped in a dirty towel, MC discovered two guns. A thirty-eight and a Glock nine. Sharpe said a nine mil was used to kill Barb. Was she holding the weapon that fired the bullet that took her lover's life?

It was too much. She had to shove that thought safely away or she wouldn't be able to function. She asked someone else to bag and tag the towel and weapons.

The second dresser was tidy. The drawers held socks, underwear, t-shirts, sweatshirts, and jeans, very organized in comparison to the chaos across the room. A blue nylon sleeping bag and two pillows covered the bottom bunk. Two neatly folded blankets had been stacked on the top bunk.

MC deduced Wooler and Laird were the only inhabitants. She was fairly certain Wooler's was the half that looked like a tornado had blown through.

The search and seizure progressed like a well-oiled machine. Evidence was bagged, tagged, and stowed in an Inspection Service SUV for transport to Minneapolis. Samples of the narcotics would be submitted to the Forensic Laboratory Services in Dulles, Virginia, for analysis.

MC called Jamie to report their findings. "Appears this was a base for distribution. No loose powder or scales, so not a mill. Someone provided them with the already-packaged heroin. Same with the pills. No pill presses on site, so pre-packaged and transported here. Like I said back at the station, my money's on they're the shitheads who Ethan Carson bought his pills from, which means those asshats are responsible for a child's death."

Ease up, MC.

Jamie said, "I hear you. But we don't know for sure. We need proof tying them to Carson. Solid proof. This is one cog in the wheel. We'll hit these two hard for names and whereabouts of their supplier. Any idea how much you collected?"

"One computer and printer. Shipping and packaging supplies, Priority Mail materials. Wax paper envelopes and ink stampers. Which is odd because they're not packaging the powder here, but the stamps on the bundles of heroin match the ink stampers. Bagged, my guesstimate is twelve-thousand wax folds of what we assume is heroin. We'll know for sure after the stuff is inventoried and the lab results come back. Estimated worth is about one-hundred-eighty thousand dollars if you figure fifteen bucks a pop. We recouped at least five thousand pills, again that's an estimate. Five milligram doses in strips of ten. Probably worth about twenty-five grand."

"By the time we finish with Wooler and Laird, the list of charges will be longer than a CVS receipt. Good work, MC."

It *was* good work, but what she wanted was to be at the station in a locked room alone with Wooler. *That's* where she belonged. Where she'd make the most difference. She'd exact revenge for all he'd selfishly, stupidly ripped away from her. The bitter taste of retribution filled her mouth.

"MC? You there?"

Shit. How long had she been checked out? She didn't want Jamie to send her packing. Her phone vibrated. "Another call's coming. Talk later?"

"Keep me posted."

MC clicked to accept the incoming call. "McCall."

"Inspector?" A woman's voice.

"Yes. Who's this?"

"Hi, it's Martha, the postmaster in Grand Marais. Sorry to call you so late in the day."

MC had lost track of time. "How late is it?" Why didn't she look at her damn phone? Hell, she was losing it.

"It's sixish."

MC approached the open door of the cabin. Light was quickening toward dusk. They'd been at it all day. The team had already loaded all the evidence. They chatted and packed their equipment. A solid day's work.

"Inspector?"

Shit. She'd zoned out on Martha. "What can I do for you, Martha?"

"There's a situation here that requires your attention."

Maybe more of Wooler and Laird's boxes. The more the merrier.

"What's going on?"

"Remember the gentleman I told you about who ships Media Mail? He finds old paperback books, sells them on the Internet. One of his padded mailers wasn't sealed tight, and frankly, the package was bulkier than I'd expect. I inspected the contents to be sure it qualified for the Media Mail rate. It was a book for sure. But . . ."

For chrissakes say it. MC did a mental eyeroll. "Martha? But what?" Every last nerve was frayed.

"It's what's *inside* the book that's problematic. You see, it appears someone, I assume my customer, although can I assume it was him? I do not have proof. Other than that, he's the one who brought the mail in. I guess it—"

MC tapped her foot on the floor.

Martha droned on. "—has cut away the middle of the book, made space for pills."

"Sorry," MC's voice rose an octave, "did you say pills?"

The deputy shifted toward her, his eyebrows crept up his forehead.

MC waved him off.

"Yes, pills."

"How many packages, Martha?"

"Oh, I opened the one."

"I mean the number of packages he mailed?"

Take a breath, MC.

Friggin' voice always with the unsolicited advice.

"Maybe twenty-five."

"Do me a favor. Look at the return address. Is there any kind of ink stamped image? What do you see?"

"No stamped image. A hand-written return address, 414 Rocky Ridge Road, Grand Marais, MN 55604."

"Is that a valid address?" MC's Spidey senses pinged. Sharpe, or maybe Cam, someone mentioned books taken from the Carson house.

"Now that you ask, I don't think so. I'm not aware of a Rocky Ridge Road. How on earth had I not noticed before now?"

"Don't beat yourself up, Martha. I'm going to ask you to set aside the mail he brought in. Don't dispatch it. I'm busy with a different situation. Tomorrow morning I'll meet you at the office. I'll be there by eight, maybe a bit earlier if I'm not delayed here."

"Scc you tomorrow. Thanks."

"Good night, Martha."

She pressed on Jamie's number, looped him in on the latest development. When it rained, it poured, and the scorched desert of her life definitely needed it.

Chapter Nineteen

MC arrived at Grand Marais Post Office at seven-thirty. Martha had sequestered the Media Mail packages on a worktable. Carriers sorted mail in their sorting cases.

Martha said, "This is the one that wasn't sealed properly. You can see it's misshapen. Bulging. When you look inside it looks like the book's grown a tumor. See the bump in the middle?"

The book smelled musty. Reminiscent of clutter you'd find in your grandparents' basement.

Martha said, "I'll show you what's inside."

"Wait." MC took a pair of nitrile gloves from her pocket. "Let me."

Martha allowed MC to take over.

MC slid the old book from the padded mailer, the plastic bubbles crackling in protest. The book splayed open. The center had indeed been hollowed out. Pages had been removed with surgical precision. Fun-sized Ziploc baggies of pills spilled out from the gouge. Someone had written on the bags, in black marker, the dosages and pill types. Definitely not a legit pharmacy practice.

MC phoned Jamie. "Looks like there's another drug scammer. We need a search warrant. I'm in Grand Marais looking at a Mickey Spillane novel filled with petite plastic bags of pills."

"Same pills from Wooler and Laird's place?"

"Nope. This is a variety pack. The drugs aren't in bubble packs. This guy uses doll-sized Ziploc bags. Writes the dose, type, and quantity on the outside. For example, I see a bag marked 'five mg Oxy, ten each.' There're ten white pills with five mg stamped on them."

"Guess we nailed a twofer, huh?"

"A twofer. Funny. This guy, he's using dusty old books to hide the drugs. Ring a bell?"

"Books?" He paused. "Ethan Carson books?"

We have a winner. Give that guy a blue ribbon. MC said, "Search warrant application?"

"I'm on it. Hang tight. I'm almost certain this'll be expedited."

True to his word, within thirty minutes Jamie called her back. "Warrant approved. I've sent it in an email. All the packages associated with that particular customer can be opened."

MC slit the end of each padded mailer, twenty-five total. Every envelope contained a paperback. Some romance. Some mystery. At least he used a variety of genres. All contained elfin-sized, sealed bags of pills and/or fentanyl patches. The foil-packed patches looked legit. Maybe this guy robbed pharmacies or was a home health care worker who swiped prescription meds from patients.

MC inventoried the packages and sealed them in evidence bags. She scored an empty plastic flat tub to transport the contraband.

Her work completed, she locked the container in her car and went back in to conduct an exit meeting with Martha and caught her in her office. "Got a sec?"

"Sure." Martha closed out something on her computer screen and gave her full attention to MC.

"Let's go over strategy for the next time that customer comes in."

"I don't have a clerk on duty until lunch. I need to open the window in just a minute. Can we talk there?"

"Absolutely." She followed Martha through the post office to the front counter. Carriers were now busy loading carts with sorted mail, not paying attention to anything but their stuffed trays of mail stacked and ready for delivery.

The outside door opened. Chilly air drifted inside.

"Oh! Good morning!" Martha's voice might have squeaked.

MC glanced up from her notebook. The customer might've been imposing if not for the comical wisps of comb-over hair that fluttered around a pair of turquoise faux fur earmuffs. And a mondo schnozzolla. Guy gave Jimmy Durante a run for his money. Sixtyish. He wore a red and black plaid cloth jacket. Definitely not a color-coordinator. He flung a plastic bin onto the counter.

Martha flitted around like a moth. "I didn't expect you back so soon."

MC caught the gist of what was happening when Martha withdrew a cheesy-hued padded mailing envelope from the bucket. Almost identical to the twenty-five she'd just dealt with.

MC came up to the counter beside Martha. "Excuse me. Do you mind if I steal Martha for a second? I need to finish something with her quick."

He shrugged. "I'm not in any hurry."

He may rethink that statement in about a minute, MC thought. She directed Martha away from the counter out of the customer's earshot.

She said, "He's the one?"

"Yes," Martha whispered.

"I'll call for backup. You proceed with the transaction. I'll finish the call and head into the lobby behind him. After he's paid, I'll detain him. Take it slow. Chat with him. A normal customer interaction. Can you do that?"

"I think so. Yes."

"Perfect, go on to the counter." MC hustled into Martha's office and called 9-1-1. The dispatcher said they'd send a Cook County Deputy immediately.

While Martha engaged the guy in banal banter, MC used the door at the far end of the work area leading into the post office box lobby, then went through the door to the regular lobby. She loitered, feigning interest in the items for sale.

When the cash transaction was complete, Martha handed him his change and a receipt and wished him a good day. Durante's nose twin pocketed his money and moved to leave. He came face-to-face with MC. "Pardon me. I wasn't aware anyone was behind me." He edged to his right. MC matched his move. "Sorry, seems like we're doing a dance." He moved to his left. MC mirrored his action. Red blotches bloomed across the man's cheeks.

MC said, "Sir, I'm going to need you to put your hands behind your head and turn to face the counter." A hand went for her handcuffs in the case on her belt.

"What?"

"You heard me. Turn around, hands on your head."

He raised his hands, positioned them behind his head. He pivoted to face the counter, but then did a one-eighty and lunged for the door.

MC launched to tackle him. She got a fist of plaid coat but couldn't hold on as momentum carried him through the outside door. "Shit. Are we really going to do this?" MC burst through the door, scanned the street. Heard a car door slam. She caught sight of a white sedan, but gray slush covered the license plate preventing her from seeing the numbers. The car roared out of the parking lot and onto the street. Had to be him because no one else was around.

She ran to the Subaru and peeled onto the street where she'd last seen her slippery suspect. MC spent ten minutes driving a block-by-block grid in a half-mile radius of the post office to no avail.

Back at the post office, she met a Cook County deputy, a sandy-haired woman named Georgette Jensen, and explained the situation to her. MC provided a description, and Jensen called in a BOLO for the suspect and car.

"Can you hang on while I run inside?" MC asked.

Deputy Jensen said, "You bet."

In the lobby, a few late-arriving carriers congregated, probably dying to know what the hell had happened.

"My goodness, that was exciting." Martha looked like she was trying to convince herself of the excitement factor when her pallor indicated she'd had a good scare.

"Yes, it was." MC scrutinized her face, wondered if she might take a header. "You okay?"

"Sure am. Just not used to that kind of thing. It's usually pretty quiet up here."

"I get it. Do you have any idea the make of vehicle he drives?"

"No! I've never noticed. Sorry."

"No need to apologize. I'm going to have a word with the deputy outside, then I need to get back to Two Harbors. I doubt he'll show up again. If he does, call 9-1-1 immediately. Understand?"

"Yes. But what if he hears me and runs?"

"Let the police worry about that."

Back at the Lake County Law Enforcement Center in Two Harbors, MC filled the team in on the runner. She imagined Crapper berating her for not waiting for backup or for being slow or any of a multitude of miscues. The fact was, he'd be right, and she felt bad about it.

Jamie said, "Sharpe and Cam will finish with Laird and Wooler. We've been unable to pry the cousin's name from either of them. They're more afraid of him than prison."

MC mulled that over. "The cousin probably has connections inside prison. Snitches get stitches."

"Whatever the case may be, we'll keep working them. Sharpe wants them transported to Ramsey County for Barb's case. Between the federal charges and the state murder charges, I doubt either of these guys will see the light of day for some time."

"Is Laird still willing to take a plea?"

"That's the deal. His story hasn't wavered from what he told you. There's enough evidence against Wooler. We'll see what the prosecutor wants to deal Laird for his cooperation. He's asked to talk to you again."

MC's pulse quickened. "I'll do it. Let me talk to Laird again. These guys murdered Barb, Jamie. In. Cold. Blood. On my kitchen floor." A lump formed in her throat. She swallowed hard.

Jamie said, "I get it, believe me. But you need to distance yourself now. Let the wheels of justice turn. Time for you to pack and return to the Cities. Log the evidence you gathered into a locker and go home. Take some time. Breathe. Process. Regroup."

Her instinct was to push back some more, demand to remain in town until they'd finished with Laird and Wooler. Instead of digging her heels in, she chose another tack. "I'd rather stay to work with Cook County on the paperback pusher. He's probably smart enough not to return to the post office, but I'd bet anything he lives in the area. Eventually he'll be out and about for food. Or gas. Something." Her thoughts turned to the idea of leaving town without having arrested the person responsible for Emmy Carson's death, and it sat like a stone in her gut.

Jamie didn't respond right away.

She tried one final time. "What if Cook County finds and arrests Mister Media Mail? Cam has his hands full with Laird and Wooler. You'll need someone to run point on a new interrogation."

"We'll cross that bridge if we come to it. I need you to secure the evidence. And update the investigation in DigiCase."

"What about Cr—ah, I mean, Roland?" The idea of interacting with her supervisor rankled.

"I'll bring him up to date about what's going on and the instructions I've given you. He shouldn't be a problem."

Until he is a problem. "Fine." She felt the energy sap hit like the crash after a sugar high. "I'll stop by my cabin and pack."

MC swore a look of utter relief washed across Jamie's face.

He stood with her. "Excellent. Call if you need anything or think of anything."

"You'll keep me in the loop? On everything?"

"Affirmative."

→←

By two o'clock, MC was on the road. The Subaru was packed to the gills with evidence and her personal paraphernalia. Not sure when she'd return, she'd bagged the perishable items from the fridge and set the trash and recycling bins out for pickup. She'd call her neighbor and ask him to push the containers back against her garage after they were emptied.

She chose a podcast and rolled southward.

True to her word, she hauled the plastic bin of padded mailers inside the Inspection Service office, signed all of it into the evidence room, and secured the envelopes containing the drug-filled books into a locker assigned to her. Key in hand, she signed out and made sure the door was locked.

The hallway was barren. No sign of Crapper. She hustled to her office and perused her notes to transfer all the pertinent information into the case management system. An hour later she did a quick check of her email. Nothing that couldn't wait, so she signed off.

Messenger bag slung over her shoulder, she shut off the office lights and opened the door.

"McCall, when did you stroll in?"

Fuck her life.

"Hi, Roland. I'm on my way out."

"Not quite. I want an update. Follow me." He lumbered to his office.

She followed and slumped in a chair without bothering to remove her coat.

Crapper said, "Do you need a written invitation? Tell me—" A coughing fit overtook him. His face grew purple as an overripe plum, his hands scrabbled through his pockets until he unearthed a withered handkerchief.

MC scooted her chair back, hoping the distance prevented her from being sprayed by the aerosols spewing forth from her supervisor. Good God.

He waved a hand in a rolling motion.

MC peered at him uneasily. "Jamie and Cam are still up north with Laird and Wooler. Sharpe from SPPD is there, too. They're finishing interrogations. Jamie sent me back with the evidence I obtained in Grand Marais. We've enlisted the Cook County Sheriff's office to assist to locate and detain a suspect in a separate drug mailing scheme."

His coughing sputtered, then ceased. "I hear you let him escape."

Don't take the bait, MC. "I logged and secured the evidence. Entered the field notes into DigiCase. Uploaded the voice files. I'm on my way home now."

"I heard you left a mess for others to clean up."

"Listen, Roland. I didn't leave any mess. I did a thorough a job. If it weren't for me, we probably wouldn't have Laird and Wooler in custody and definitely wouldn't have the intel we got from Laird."

"It remains to be seen exactly how helpful you've been." A rumble of throat clearing quickly progressed to another coughing fit.

MC took advantage of the diversion. "If we're finished, I'd like to go." She stood.

Crapper waved at the door.

The hoarse rasping bark ushered her through the portal. She considered calling the EMTs, certain Crapper would expel a lung or two, but nixed the idea. One could hope.

MC made it to her stale, lonely apartment. Home sweet home. She unpacked and transferred the food into her fridge. The bottle of Goose she'd left behind had no more than a shot's worth. She changed clothes and ran to the liquor store for not one, but two bottles.

On the way home she took a slight detour and stopped at Flannel. Meg was nowhere in sight, but Dara worked the counter with Zane.

"Look what the cat drug in!" Dara's voice rattled the glass in the windows. Some things never changed.

Three customers in line rotated in unison and gave MC a once over. Their attention switched to beverage choices, no doubt deciding she wasn't anything special.

Then it was her turn to order.

"Hi!" Zane said, "haven't seen you in a while. Coffee?"

Dara grabbed and filled a large cardboard cup from a giant urn of fresh-brewed coffee. "I'll handle her, Zane. Would you please restock the napkins and check the creamer?" She nodded at the condiment counter.

"Thanks anyway, Zane." MC grinned. "Nice to see you."

Dara handed MC her coffee. "Time to sit?"

"Sure." They chose a table for two. MC enjoyed the aromatic caffeine infusion. "God. Nothing beats Flannel's coffee." She closed her eyes for a moment savoring the blend.

"You're such a flatterer. That Peet's from the grocery store not up to snuff after all?"

"Exactly." MC set the cup on the table.

"You back for the duration?"

"Got home this afternoon. Lots still happening I can't talk about. But I'll tell you this, we arrested the guys responsible for Barb's—" A softball-sized lump clogged her windpipe. Where the hell had that come from? She'd not intended to tell Dara, the most reactionary person on the planet. Tears trickled from the corners of her eyes. She swiped them away. Dammit. Do. Not. Melt. Down.

Dara hollered, "What?"

MC leaned toward Dara. "Shhh, don't tell the whole freakin' world!" She'd not planned on telling her friends about the arrest. It slipped out, and now she couldn't stuff it back where it belonged. "I'm so sorry, I can't tell you anything more. Yet."

What the hell was she doing? She needed to leave. Absent herself from people . . . from Dara. Posthaste.

"Why don't you go to the house? Meg's there resting. I'll call her. I know she'll want to help and be with you." Dara dragged a hand through her hair. "You shouldn't be alone."

"I'm fine." Deep breath. "I need to be by myself. I promised you last weekend I'd do better about staying in touch. Here's me, making good on that promise. The reason I stopped by was to see how Meg's doing. Please understand I can't—I don't—have the energy to talk. Not right now." She used a napkin to wipe her nose and sipped the coffee, wishing with her whole being it was twenty ounces of vodka.

Surprisingly, Dara didn't push. "We're a phone call or text message away. Day or night."

"Thanks." She laid her hand over Dara's. "How's Meg? What can I do?"

Dara said, "Meg's hanging in. Next week's radiation."

"What about the shop?"

"Zane'll cover for all the appointments. The other days, depending on how Meg tolerates treatment, she'll try to be here. Otherwise, she'll be home and I'll be here."

"I'll be in town. Let me know if I can help. Sit with Meg, help you at the café, whatever."

"Thanks, pal."

"I should go. Unpacking . . . laundry . . ." Liar! She wrapped her arms around Dara, grabbed her coffee and left with a quick wave to Zane.

She tossed the half-drunk cup into a trash container out on the sidewalk, the caffeine no match for her real craving.

At home she changed into sweats and switched on the TV. She thought about supper. Instead, she tipped a good six ounces of Grey Goose into a glass. Her heart cartwheeled inside her chest. Her mind spun like a drunken Tilt-A-Whirl.

The Barb notebook stared at her from the couch cushion. Answers she'd sought for four months had finally been revealed. She knew who took the love of her life away.

Fucking Nick Wooler. Fucking Quentin Laird.

She gripped the glass, brought it to her mouth. Liquid sloshed over the rim and dribbled onto her sweatpants. She steadied her hand enough to ingest a powerful slug of Mother Goose.

Beautiful burn. Another mouthful stoked the fire. Her hand shook. She set the drink on the side table, mindful to use a coaster.

The six o'clock evening news anchor shared all the world's woes, which MC barely tracked. All she could think about was Barb's killer. In custody. She wanted him dead. No, that's wrong. She didn't believe in the death penalty. Her mind wheeled, flipped, and ripped loose from its moorings. She heard the muffled buzz of her cell phone. Where the hell was it?

She muted the TV. Silence. Shit. The hum restarted. She lifted the notebook. Nothing. When she stood the tone changed. MC dipped a hand between the couch cushions. Score.

"McCall."

"MC, it's Cam. You're not going to believe this, but we caught another break. Cook County took the Grand Marais guy into custody an hour ago. Jamie asked me to update you. Cyber dug deep and unearthed the site Carson used on the Dark Web. BlackFarmaRoad. Long story short, this guy and a pharmacist buddy in northwestern Wisconsin have been running a massive drug diversion scam. The pharmacist provided authentic prescription pills and fentanyl patches. We're pretty sure the patches will be a match for what killed Emmy Carson. Sharpe agrees. Wisconsin law enforcement is in the process of serving a warrant on the pharmacist. We got them!"

"Holy shit!" She paced a circle around her living room.

"At first the guy tried to tell me he didn't know drugs were inside the books."

They magically appeared, she thought. How dumb did he think they were?

"When we informed him we'd be seeking murder charges and illegal distribution, he closed up like a clam. Asked for a lawyer."

Typical. Deny. Don't cooperate. Lawyer up. Shitheads were all the same whether they were on the street or hidden away in rural America running drug scams on the Dark Web.

Cam plowed on. "I took a shot—told him the murder victim was a seven-year-old child. I thought he was going to lose his lunch on the table. Shit was intense. He folded like a cheap lawn chair. Supplied the name and address for his pal in Wisconsin. AUSA approved a warrant, a judge signed off. Bam. They nailed the rogue pharmacist, too."

Cam sounded like a kid in a candy store. She couldn't fault his enthusiasm. They'd put the kibosh on two Internet narcotics schemes. And solved two murders: Barb's and Emmy Carson's. A crippling pain gripped her. Barb's killer. The tears flowed and she bit her bottom lip to keep the choking sob from escaping.

"And you'll love this—the guy is a retired English Lit teacher. He and his pharmacist pal devised this scam to supplement retirement. He enjoyed telling the story. Waxed on about how he scoured yard sales, garage sales, secondhand bookstores, and eBay looking for paperback books. Even weighed the books before and made sure the renovated tome matched the original weight."

MC cleared her throat. "Sounds like a stickler for detail."

"We still don't have the specifics on how they initiated the vendor site, BlackFarmaRoad, on the Dark Web marketplace. Cyber will work it."

"No doubt. That's great, Cam. When will you guys be back?"

"We'll leave tomorrow, after we arrange transport and housing for all these guys."

"Good job, partner."

"Teamwork. You were great. Gonna be lots of work ahead for all of us. We'll need the cases to be airtight. Can't allow anyone to slither through the cracks. They all need to go away for a long time."

"Agreed." She stood in the middle of the living room. Light reflected off the glass of crystal-clear, mind-fuck juice perched on the table next to the couch. In juxtaposition, a rainbow of colors splashed across the TV screen as *Wheel of Fortune* came on.

"Listen, Cam, you go finish. Thanks for looping me in."

"You betcha. See you tomorrow at the office?"

"For sure. Bye."

She retrieved the glass of vodka. Several long swallows later, the vessel was empty. Her thoughts went from ordered to a jumbled mess.

Time for another drink. She trudged to the kitchen, not bothering with the light, and refreshed her beverage. She carried the bottle with her back to the couch.

Full glass.

Empty life.

She extinguished the lights, left the TV on, and slouched on the sofa, fleece blanket wrapped around her. Drinking steadily, she watched one show after another flicker on the screen.

The low drone of voices, laugh tracks, and dark eerie music were background noise to her battered thoughts.

At some point she passed out, splayed on the couch. She woke to applause on a late-night talk show. Her phone had fallen to the floor. She woke the screen. One in the morning. A headache kicked in—a steady thump pulsed behind her eyeballs.

She struggled free of the blanket and reached down for the Goose. Only half a glass this time. Quaffed the stuff like water and very shortly, her brain went back to a pleasant fuzz. She squinched her eyes, concentrated on reaching for the bottle to pour another pick-me-up . . . or maybe a knock-me-out. The floor tilted. Her hand swiped at the glass container, catching air instead of its neck. Wring the Goose's neck. She laughed hysterically for a moment and blinked hard. The floor righted itself and the fog dissipated. Her hand landed on its mark.

"Juss li'l more won't hurt." Slurring the words out loud made them true.

Take a breath, MC.

She whipped around wildly searching the living room. Nothing. No Barb. Hot tears rolled down her cheeks. "Baby." Her voice was thick. "Come back." Anger, frustration, heartbreak overflowed. A deep sob escaped her throat. "Need you." Gasp. "Home." MC gritted her teeth, struggling mightily for control. "With me."

The words opened a dam of emotion. She hurled the glass at the wall. It shattered in tandem with a howl of loss wrung from the depths of her soul.

Chapter Twenty

"MC, help." Barb. Loud and crystal clear.

Where were they? Not their house. Someone else's home? A hotel? A light blazed at the end of a long dark hallway. MC ran her fingers along the wall. No light switch.

"MC!"

"Coming. Keep talking. I'll follow your voice."

"I need you. Help me. Please." Barb's words segued into a teary plea. "Please. No."

MC's heart thundered like a herd of rhinos. "Hang on." She traversed the hallway, bounced off one wall into the other, like a drunken seaman on the foundering Titanic. The light retreated.

"Help me!"

"Shut up, bitch!" A male voice. Angry. "Better hurry or it'll be curtains for her, copper."

The voice struck a chord. Terror flooded through her. MC quickened the pace. She unsnapped the holster, drew her gun. Barrel pointed at the floor, she negotiated the never-ending hall. A door slammed in the distance. She whipped around. Behind her, a wall where there had been none. What the hell? Were they in some bizarre freakshow maze?

"Barb?" MC screamed. "Talk to me!"

A muffled scream. Ahead? Behind?

She plunged forward.

"Better hurry, bitch. Time's running out."

"I'm coming. Don't hurt her!"

"Don't tell me what to do, motherfucker. It's all your fault. This is on you."

"What's my fault? I don't know what you're talking about." The light grew brighter. She raced forward. "Wanna tell me what's going on? I'm listening."

"Fuck. You." Anger-laced words.

MC's heart leapt to her throat. Her pulse pounded. The gun wavered.

"MC!" Barb's voice was so panicked. "I need you. Please. Help me. He's—"

A heavy thud.

"Barb?"

The sound of crying dragged her along like a lifeline hauling a drowning swimmer.

"I'm coming!"

"I warned you, bitch."

Bam. Bam. The echo of gunshots rocked her. "No!"

She tripped over her own feet. The floor lurched to meet her at a dizzying speed.

MC screamed. Cried. Swore. She sat herself up. Blinked. The latest episode of the nightmare was different from all the previous versions. This time she was able to put a face to the killer's voice. Flat gray eyes. The embodiment of evil in the rough-edged voice. No compunction over taking a life.

Her apartment materialized around her. She'd fallen from the couch to the floor, the blanket twisted around her legs. The TV was airing the early morning national news.

Her head was a ticking bomb. Her stomach heaved and folded in on itself. She scrambled up, dashed to the bathroom, retched, then retched some more. Spitting and gasping, she clung to the porcelain as if it were a buoy keeping her from floating away in a sea of grief.

After several minutes of dry heaves, she stood, albeit shakily.

She brushed her teeth, turned the shower on. Dropped her clothes in a heap and crawled into the shower. The hot water massaged the knots from her neck, shoulders, and back. She washed her battered and bruised body, shampooed her hair. Clenched her teeth against the drumbeat thumping her temples and swallowed hard to keep the bile from rushing up her throat.

The bathroom steamed and the water ran cold before she emerged from the shower and toweled dry.

She swallowed three Ibu with a mouthful of water and felt it all surge upward, only managing to keep it down at the last second. In the medicine cabinet, she found a dust-covered bottle of Tums antacids with about six tablets left. She crunched three and pocketed the others for later. She dressed, gathered her phone, notebooks, and messenger bag and skedaddled.

The moon was setting, and shades of pink announced the sun coming up. If she hurried, she'd make it to work by eight. Her breath drifted in tiny puffs of fog, and the cold air made her eyes water. She slid behind the wheel of the Subaru, in dire need of coffee, and chose to stop at a chain shop instead of Flannel. Best not to let Dara see her hungover self.

She tucked a large coffee, black today, in the cup holder and took tentative sips while driving to the office. When she entered the parking lot, she noticed Crapper's car parked in the first row. She took a deep breath and let herself into the building.

"You're here early, McCall." A coughing spasm shook Crapper's bulk. He braced one hand on the wall, his now ever-present handkerchief clamped to his mouth with the other.

MC thought he looked much as she felt this morning—like death.

"Thought I'd dig in before Jamie and Cam return." Her noggin throbbed. She felt like a boxer was using her brain for speed bag practice. She chanced a few wobbly steps and her stomach lurched. Oh, shit. "Excuse me."

She made a mad dash for the restroom, slapping a hand over her mouth. Luckily the space was empty, and she charged into the first stall, barely securing the door before a violent stream of liquid burst from her mouth. MC ripped a strip of toilet tissue off the roll, wiped her clammy forehead. A second, less spectacular eruption followed. She leaned her head against the cold metal wall.

A ten count. Several deep breaths. Her legs shook. MC flushed the vile mess. A metaphor for her life?

After another slow count to ten, she crept from the metal cubicle to the sink, washed her hands, soaping and re-soaping to ensure she removed any trace of sickness. She ran cold water and rinsed her mouth then scrubbed her face with the hand soap.

MC slunk from the restroom.

"You okay, McCall?" Crapper stood behind her. He'd waited for her outside the restroom.

MC jumped, hand over her heart. "Jesus." Did he hear her being sick? Shit! "Maybe a flu bug."

"Go home."

"I'll be okay. I don't need to go home."

"What we don't need is you infecting every person in this office. You're sick. Go home." He pointed to the door. "I mean it. Get the hell out of here before you infect everyone, and we all end up puking."

"I'll call later. Get the updates."

In his high-and-mighty voice, he said, "You'll go home and not worry about cases until you're recovered."

Earth to MC. You have entered another dimension—and a weird one at that. He almost sounded concerned.

She didn't have the energy or the will to argue further. "Okay, I'll go." A shiver wracked her body from head to toe. "Maybe I do have a fever."

Before Crapper responded she bolted.

MC dropped her bag and coat in a mound as soon as she entered her apartment. Her world was still crashing around her despite having the murderer in custody. And Meg had cancer. What the hell? Nothing was right.

She dragged her body to the bedroom, changed into fresh sweats and a thick pair of hiking socks. MC collapsed on the bed and promptly fell sound asleep.

A siren woke her. The day had clouded over. She slowly rose, then when she was sure she felt stable enough to remain upright, she retrieved her cell phone from her coat and checked the weather. The snow icon appeared for both the day and night. The forecasters predicted between six and eight inches of snow, possibly a bit of rain on the front end before the temps plummeted. Great. Black ice, here we come.

Her mood darkened to match the bulging belly of the sky. She'd hunker down for the rest of the day, recuperate. Plenty of food in the fridge. A bottle and a half of Goose should see her through the tempest.

She'd missed three calls. Two were Cam. Jamie once. The screen flickered and went black. Shit! MC dug the charger from her messenger bag and plugged it into the phone.

What now? Maybe she'd eat. Toast? Her stomach somersaulted at the thought. For a moment she considered calling Meg or Dara but didn't have the energy. Another nap might recharge her engine. With the TV on, she cocooned herself on the couch and drifted off.

Sometime later, MC awoke. Snow had begun to fall. Fat white flakes drifted lazily past the windows. The news was on, and the anchor warned about a slow, treacherous rush hour. She checked her phone, ten minutes past five o'clock. She'd slept most of the day and felt almost human.

After surveying the scene outside, she guessed several inches of snow were on the ground. Her stomach gurgled—in a good way. She padded to the kitchen, stuck two slices of bread into the toaster, applied butter, and ate over the sink. She scarfed both slices and then a third. With a bit of food in her belly she grabbed the booze.

One hand on the cupboard door, the other clasped around the neck of the bottle, she chastised herself. She'd barely recovered from last night's exploits. What was wrong with her?

She watched herself snag a clean glass as the obsidian eye of the Goose on the bottle scrutinized her. Was it judging her or encouraging her? Who cared? She sloshed two ounces of vodka into the glass. Just two shots. Enough to take the edge off. At some point she was going to have to clean up the sink and the counter. MC stared at the liquor, then sipped, tentatively. Would her stomach rebel? After a test drive, she shifted into second gear and tossed the entire contents back in one motion. She blinked at the bottom of the empty glass. How'd that happen?

Another tip. Two shots' worth again. She'd lost control of what her hands were doing. In a somewhat more civilized manner, MC sat at the kitchen table, downing the alcohol in thirds and watching the snowstorm swirl in the growing dark. Each flake joined the others, weaving one giant blanket.

The memory of another snowstorm whisked her away on an eddy of frosty air.

Black Friday.

The day she lost Barb. The day her life irretrievably altered, shattered into a million pointy pieces.

All-consuming pain left her breathless.

Gasping.

Sobbing.

She gave up on using the glass and grabbed the bottle and bolted down more Goose in some far-fetched hope the alcohol would patch her battered body and soul. But the notion was ill-conceived. The vodka created more fractures in her, both mentally and physically.

Would she ever be whole again? Might the bombastic skies lighten? Return color and life into her embattled world? The fucking winter—the long-ass fucking winter—would it ever end?

Perhaps her fate was to be relegated to a gray nothingness, trying and failing to put one foot in front of the other. All she deserved was an existence built on waves of Grey Goose.

Thundering silence pounded her eardrums. She took a hefty pull from the bottle. How might she escape the menace, the grayness? "Drink it away, McCall." She raised the container to her lips, sucked down a mouthful. Her body was numbed to the burn.

No one was present to judge her. Not Dara. Not Cam. Not Barb.

MC choked back a violent onslaught of anguish. The wreckage piled up and she hurled herself at it, full speed. A catastrophe in the making. No way to swerve around the crash and burn. No angel winged its way to save her.

She stared at the empty booze bottle and contemplated her lonely, messy existence. A festering wound laid bare for all to see—and be repulsed by.

MC opened a new bottle and dragged her ragged self to the living room. Searched for the green notebook. Paged through the story of loss, guilt, and grief.

She said aloud, "I thought life'd be different. I'd eradicate the grief and guilt. But knowing who killed you . . . It didn't give me closure. No satisfaction. No sense of relief."

She swiped her sleeve across her tear-soaked face.

MC drank one gulp, then another, let the bottle slip down. Booze glugged onto the carpeted floor. The TV remained background noise. Snow fell in curtains of white.

Eventually she rose, slid her feet into slippers, weaved to the closet. After three tries, she managed to thread her arms into her coat sleeves.

A drive would soothe her embattled soul. Clear the ghosts and demons from her head.

One more drink first. She picked up the half-empty container and guzzled from it. On her way to the door, she snatched her cell phone from the side table. The charger cord grew taut and fought her. One fierce tug freed the device. MC lurched through the door.

The snowstorm raged around her while she stood on the sidewalk in front of her building. Why was she outside? What was she doing?

Drive.

She was going for a drive. Hands patted her coat pockets. Empty. No keys. Where'd her damn keys go? Someone take them? Her head buzzed with a thousand hornets.

She'd walk. Where to?

She tipped and her slippered feet sank in slushy snow. One step. Stuck. She'd barely made it past the end of her building. Darkness pushed in. Snow sucked at her feet—cemented her in place. This must be what it felt like when the mob gave their victims cement boots before tossing them in a raging river.

Her fingers worked the phone screen. She jabbed at the rideshare app and got it on the third try.

What seemed like no time and all of time brought MC to a house she vaguely recognized, a place she and Barb had visited. Kids. Work. Nice people. Friends.

The driver said, "You okay, lady? Need some help? The house looks dark. Want me to wait in case no one's home?"

She mumbled, "I'mma be fine."

"Suit yourself."

She got out. The tires spewed a rooster tail of muck, and the car fishtailed down the street.

The black and white of it all.

MC stood on the sidewalk in ankle-deep snow. Where was she? Maybe someone in the house would tell her what was happening.

She stumbled to the front door. Pounded on it. She couldn't feel her hands and feet. Tears formed into a glazed crust over her face. A monster, dark and spiky, uncoiled inside her. A prehistoric creature she needed to expel before it unspooled, its jagged thorny tentacles shredding her insides to raw ribbons of sinew and bloody organs.

MC leaned to the side, threw up on snow-covered bushes. An outside light flashed on, blinding her as she retched.

The door opened.

A man wearing a long-sleeved Green Bay Packers t-shirt and plaid flannel pajama pants stood on the doorstep. He said, "MC? My God. What happened?"

"Can't . . . Too much." She slipped down and scraped her cheek against the doorframe. "Is that you, Cam?"

"Did you drive? I don't see your car."

"Nope, er . . ." She planted her hands on the snow-covered stoop and tried to hoist herself vertical. Fucking failure.

The snowstorm was a whisper in the background of the cacophony of collapse inside her.

"Come in." He hauled her inside by the arm.

Warmth. Silence. The quiet grew. Hovered overhead.

The inevitable loomed.

Gray to black.

Life to death.

Silence.

Cam said, “Are you okay? Are you going to be sick again?”

She waved a hand in the air and shook her head, then tripped over her own feet.

“No? Let’s get you seated then.” He guided her through a narrow hallway, flicked a light switch, revealed a kitchen twice the size of hers.

Why was she never able to find the light switch? Because she was a failure. Nothing but a loser.

MC’s life pooled into a half-frozen, charcoal-colored, slushy wet mess around her feet. She was powerless to move against the slurry sucking her under.

“Why Barb? Not me?”

How was it possible Barb was pre-ordained to die and she to live?

“Jesus, you’re wearing slippers. What were you thinking, going out in this storm in slippers?” He left the room, returned with a giant fluffy towel. “I’m going to take them off and wrap this around your feet. I’ll see if Jane has some socks for you.” Cam stripped off the sodden slippers and socks, enfolded her beet-red feet in the towel. “Stay put. I’ll be back.”

Cam returned with a half-awake Jane in tow.

Jane plopped down on her knees next to the chair and gathered her in a warm hug. “Oh, MC.”

“S’okay.” Unable to lift her leaden arms, she sat in Jane’s embrace.

Cam handed her a pair of dry socks. “Can you put these on?”

Jane grabbed them. “I’ll help her. Why don’t you put on hot water for tea? See if we have some honey.” Cam did as she asked as Jane took MC’s feet, one at a time, and slipped on the warm wool socks.

MC rocked on the chair. The room slipped sideways. Darkness beckoned from outside the window above the sink. Naked tree branches gestured to her. We all die out here. Come be with us.

Jane helped MC shuck her wet coat. She sat on a chair beside her, draped an arm around her shoulders.

What was happening?

History consisted of episodes where humanity clashed, and survivors clung to any bit of flotsam that might carry them through the bloody waves to shore. On solid ground, people attempted to rebuild, tried to continue living.

MC focused on Jane, then Cam. “Please, help. The Goose. Doesn’t work. Anymore.” Tears dripped off her chin.

Jane's voice. So close, yet so far away. "Cam, do you think it's alcohol poisoning? How much have you had, MC? Can you tell us?"

Cam squatted on the other side of her chair. "MC. Do you remember how much you drank?"

"Bottle." She lifted her hands and held them apart. Then she peered at Cam. "You have more?"

Cam said, "No more."

Jane said, "You hurt your face." She dabbed MC's cheek with the towel.

MC mumbled, "Dunno." She wheeled her arms in the air, listing to the left.

Jane steadied her and raised her eyebrows at Cam.

"I think she slipped and hit the doorframe before I got her inside."

MC slumped and her arms fell to her lap. "'S okay. Goose not hep—helping. Nothin' . . ." She covered her face with her hands. Sobs took over, shaking her.

Take a breath, MC. The voice . . . Barb's voice.

Barb's voice wasn't the ghost. She, MC, was the specter. Her existence was nothing but memories attempting to tie her to earth. To life.

Everyone moved on. She was left tied to one place and time, unable to stop the world from passing her by. Not able to keep pace.

Fucked up. Guilt-ridden.

MC mumbled, "Didn't make it better."

Cam said, "Didn't make what better?"

"Knowing . . . Barb's . . . killer."

She surveyed the wreckage of her life, processed how wrong she'd been. The answer, the *knowing* hadn't soothed her heart, her soul.

She floated. Lost in nothingness. No way forward.

"MC," Cam asked, his tone gentle, "what do you need?"

"Help." The word fell, barely a whisper, from her lips.

"Stay here tonight. Sleep on the couch. In the morning I'll drive you to whatever inpatient program you prefer. Jane and I will help you, steer you toward the road to recovery. You're my partner, MC. I'm not going anywhere."

No longer capable of words she nodded . . . in silent service to the end.

About The Author

Judy M. Kerr writes the MC McCall mystery/suspense series. *Silent Service* is the second book in that series. The third installment is percolating as the current book rolls off the press. She has also published crime fiction short stories in three anthologies. Judy resides with her extended family in Minneapolis, Minnesota. She retired from the US Postal Service in 2017 after thirty-eight years of federal service. Her website is at www.JudyMKerr.com.

Published by:
Launch Point Press
Portland, Oregon
www.LaunchPointPress.com

Acknowledgments

Long known as the "silent service" and viewed simply as guardians of the US Mail, it's high time that the hard work and dedication of the oldest federal law enforcement agency in the US be recognized. I hope I've done so in my books. The USPIS protects the postal service and postal employees and enforces 200 federal statutes related to crimes that involve the postal system, employees, and customers. Postal inspectors investigate crimes from mail fraud and identity theft to cybercrime and child exploitation. Much of their behind-the-scenes procedures must remain confidential, but people should know and appreciate the great work the USPIS does worldwide every day.

Research about USPIS is challenging. In order for my books to pass the "smell test," I was lucky enough to have the assistance of a retired postal inspector. He shared background and basic investigatory information with me and answered a slew of questions. I am forever grateful for his time and patience to ensure I provide my readers with a plausible story. Keeping in mind that this is a work of fiction, all credibility in details is thanks to my resource and any mistakes are my own.

I'd like to thank my family for their continued love and support. Writing is a time-consuming and sometimes lonely endeavor, and my family has been and continues to be understanding when I spend endless hours in front of the computer creating stories.

My Minnesota Minions: Jessie and MB, two amazing and talented authors, without you there would be no book. Thank you for reading and editing and giving me honest feedback. And mostly thank you for your love and friendship.

And readers, thanks for choosing my books. I hope you enjoy reading them as much as I enjoy writing them!

Last, but not least, thank you Lori L. Lake, my editor and publisher. I'm appreciative of your continued faith in me and my writing.

Judy M. Kerr
Minneapolis, Minnesota
February 2022

CPSIA information can be obtained
at www.ICGtesting.com
Printed in the USA
BVHW032354251022
650210BV00007B/95

Advance Praise for *Silent Service*

"With skill and purpose, author Judy Kerr provides a truly satisfying read in *Silent Service*, the second installment of her MC McCall series. The novel is filled with creative language that dances off the page, storytelling that draws you into the lives and environs of its characters and shares an immensely empathetic understanding of the ravages of loss and heartbreak."

~Cheryl A. Head, award-winning author of the Charlie Mack Motown Mystery Series

"In Judy Kerr's stellar sophomore release, *Silent Service*, Kerr thrusts her beautifully flawed, all-too-human protagonist, US Postal Inspector MC McCall, into the middle of a dangerous narcotics investigation stretching from the gritty streets of St. Paul to Minnesota's snowy, windswept North Shore. MC—reeling after the murder of her beloved partner Barb just months prior—must balance her desperate obsession to find Barb's killer with maintaining a decorated, successful career she's on the cusp of losing as she attempts to bust wide open an opioid distribution ring. In turns suspense-filled, heartbreaking, and hopeful, Kerr takes the reader on a journey they'll never forget. I absolutely loved it!"

~Jessie Chandler, award-winning author of the Shay O'Hanlon Caper Series

"Judy Kerr is a writer's writer. Her vivid depictions of characters and settings and her sparse and straightforward style are a joy to read. *Silent Service* is a tight, impeccably told story that grips the reader and sticks with them over time. MC McCall is a strong character who transcends the pages of the book and makes the reader anxious for more. Absolutely recommend everyone to pick up this series!"

~MB Panichi, author of multiple novels

"MC McCall is one of the best protagonists I've read in many years. She's complex, with as many flaws as positive aspects to her personality. This makes her interesting to read, because it's not possible to know with any certainty which she might do next."

~EJ Kindred, author of the Annie Velasquez crime fiction series